EL

EL

Thaddeus Ó Buachalla

Translated from the Irish

MERCIER PRESS
Cork
www.mercierpress.ie

First published in Irish in Ireland in 2022 by
Coiscéim, Baile Átha Cliath
Irish Language Novel of the Year at the An Post Irish Book Awards

This English translation first published by Mercier Press, 2025

ISBN: 978-1-78117-953-6
e-Book: 978-1-80690-012-1

Cover art by Matt Needle

All characters and events in this book, except for those who are identifiably real and recognisable in the public domain, are entirely fictional. Any resemblance to any person living or dead which may occur inadvertently is completely unintentional.

Author and Translator's note

Thaddeus Ó Buachalla is an Irish language author, poet, and musician from Cork City. His debut novel EL won an Oireachtas Literary Award and Irish Language Book of the Year. His work combines fantasy with satirical commentary, bringing metropolitan vitality to modern Irish literature. He is currently completing his second novel, Arrazalius, nó Cathú Antaine.

EL is a novel written in the Irish language. The contemporary chapters of the book are set in present-day Cork City where English is commonly spoken. While the main characters speak Irish amongst themselves, they will speak English with others they encounter, and these sections of text are placed in italics in the original novel. This system has been continued in this translation and, as such, sections of dialogue in italics should be taken as having been in English in the original. The term 'Firíní', meaning little men, is used throughout the book as a proper noun and has been left untranslated, with a footnote when it first occurs.

Act One

Scene One

We'll start so.

It was late afternoon on an autumn day, yet I could still feel the warm air of summer around me like a blanket. There was a house with a palm tree in the front garden. I remember noticing something in the light that evening which gave me an odd sensation. I wouldn't call it *déjà vu* exactly, but it was a recognition of something intangible in some lost corner of my mind, a memory that I couldn't remember. Maybe it was something I saw when I was very young, or some sliver of a dream, a lost moment of which nothing remains now but its shadow. The slanting sunlight struck the gable end of the house with the palm tree in front and, for a couple of seconds, I felt this recognition. I was almost able to lay my hand on it like some lost truth, and then it was gone.

I was walking through Ballyphehane in Cork City and imagining the lamp posts and the wires strung between them as if they were vines in some dark jungle of the tropics, the trees filled with snakes, insects and creatures with big eyes. I felt the electricity of late summer in the air with children on bikes in the street shouting at one another, each shout an affirmation that the summer wasn't over yet, that we were all still alive. The crows stood on the roofs of houses and on the electric cables like Greek gods looking down at us. The little birds were darting about, the air filled with their songs. I felt the first taste of night on the air, and this gave a stir to the slow, syrupy remains of the day.

Ballyphehane or *Baile Féitheáin*. The name that remains even when nothing that relates to it does. Where is that *féitheán* now? A word synonymous with *féitheog* – a vein, a sinew, or even a climbing plant. Does the name relate to the bog stream that's lost now beneath the concrete of the streets? Was that winding tributary the vein in question, the vein that carried water like blood through this land? If so, it runs beneath us now. There's always underground water in Ballyphehane. It was once a bog, and the houses are still slipping gradually back down into its mire today. Or maybe the name came from the vines that used to hang from every tree in this boggy jungle long ago, winding tightly around them and slowly choking them. You could imagine it like a humid primeval forest in the Jurassic period. I was raised in this area but even I don't know whether it was named for a stream now lost in concrete and tarmac, or vines lost in history and dead for centuries. The truth is underground with the waters of the stream.

But that's Ballyphehane. If you close your eyes at the right moment, you can see the vines hanging like curtains from the trees, the smell of honeysuckle blowing on the breeze that follows the bog stream. The otter eating the frog, rabbits and foxes, devilish crows that look at everything. The dead and the living and some slow electricity weaving through it all.

Myself and Peadar walked towards the house, both lost in our own thoughts. We went past the grotto of the Virgin Mary in the park, down the hill and through the traffic lights. He looked directly ahead, like someone deep in his own world. He was tall and thin and walked with a long stride. There was a quiet, contemplative appearance about him always and he spoke softly. The bell rang in the church and its sound filled everything: the cracks in the concrete, the spaces under the windowsills, the wandering thoughts of people. We turned right at the corner and went past a school called Morning Star. I've always felt that this is a strange name for a school.

We were approaching the house. It wasn't our house, but we had rooms rented in it. It was a house that provided student accommodation, and we were both at university at the time. It was fairly rough, but we got by. We didn't know each other when we moved in the year before, but we always got on well enough. I was originally from Ballyphehane myself, even though none of my family lived here now. Still I was happy to come to my own neighbourhood when I moved back to Cork. I was happy as well when I found out that Peadar spoke Irish. There was another student there as well the year before, but he didn't come back after the summer. That was the landlord's business anyway. I didn't care.

'Did you read that book I gave you, Seán?' Peadar asked as we walked along Connolly Road.

'I'm halfway through it,' I said. 'I'm reading another book as well.'

'What's the other book?'

'A story about someone wandering about in the street.'

'Interesting,' he said with not the slightest bit of irony in his voice.

I'm wandering myself now. I have a story to tell you, but I know you won't believe it. The device of this book will serve the purposes of telling it, but I have to let you know from the outset that this is not a novel. These things happened. However absurd a story it may be, I can only affirm to you that it's true. They happened to me personally, and I found out later about other things, historical events, that had a huge bearing on my own tale. As I tell you this story, I'd recommend that you also do your own research on the historical parts of it. You don't have to, of course. You can read this book like a normal novel, and I hope you enjoy it. But if you want, then go on the internet and look at the lives of the people mentioned in the historical parts of this book and the connections between them. You will see strange coincidences there in black and white, and I'll leave it to you to make up your own mind about it. This generation is different from any other generation that came before. We can put our hands into our pockets and take the knowledge of the world out on our phones. That's never happened before. It is a totally new thing in human history, something revolutionary. More revolutionary perhaps than the invention of the printing press.

I'll stop this wandering now. I have to bring you to the house. That's the place where the incident happened, the event that started every subsequent event. After that, the story spread out in every direction like a spider's web. I saw that its threads were tied to every branch in the woods, the woods of today and those of long ago, and I don't know yet how far those threads extend.

We reached the house and went inside. The kitchen and living room were together at the back of the house, and the dishes were waiting for us in the sink. We let them wait where they were and sat down. Peadar took up his laptop and threw himself down on the sofa. I took up the book about the person wandering in the streets and sat in the armchair.

It was strange, but I had just read a line that referred to 'the flies that stick to the great wheels of the world' when I noticed that there actually was a fly in the room. The buzz began to irritate me as it droned from corner to corner, back and forth, making misshapen rectangles in the air. I don't like killing things unnecessarily, but this was driving me crazy. I grabbed a newspaper and stood up. I failed at first, of course, and then again the second time, becoming a bit ill-tempered, I have to say. I saw Peadar looking at me, but he said nothing. I focused my attention on the job, and then the fly's luck failed when it stayed too long in one place. I struck it suddenly and left it flattened into a black and red smudge on the wall.

But I did something then, and it was the root of everything else in this story. There was a microscope standing on the table in the living room. It belonged to Peadar, but he let me look through it from time to time. I looked at the flattened fly and saw that its head was still intact. I took the head on the corner of a piece of paper and put it on a slide. Then I put a drop of water on it and a piece of transparent plastic over that, as Peadar had shown me. I put it under the microscope and looked carefully through the lens. We are now swiftly approaching the point in this story that I said you wouldn't believe. It is a strange story, I accept that, but I promise you that it did happen.

Two men. I saw two tiny men through the lens of the microscope. Apparently, they were inside the head of the fly, but now they were in a drop of water on the slide, stuck under the plastic cover. They wore one-piece jumpsuits of pale blue, and I saw their faces as they drowned before my eyes in a drop of water. I saw their limbs swinging and beating on the plastic barrier above them. I can even see them now as I'm writing. I can remember that in a way, they weren't unlike the characters of some science fiction TV show from the 1980s.

'Peadar!' I shouted loudly, my eye still on the lens. 'Come here quickly!'

He jumped up and I moved to one side to let him come to the microscope. He looked through the lens, and then raised his head suddenly and looked at me, a look of horror on his face. I remember this moment very well. You would imagine in this situation that we would have gone berserk and shouted, but it was too strange, too surreal, to do anything. It was as if we were under some kind of spell. 'What … what are they?' he said, like someone in a trance. He lowered his head and looked again through the lens. 'Little men …' he said. 'How are there little men there?'

'I don't know.'

'This can't be true!' he said, raising his head, and we looked at one another. 'How…?' he began again, but wasn't able to say any more than that.

I looked through the lens again to make sure that the two men were still there. They were, but they were lifeless now. Maybe we should have saved them at the start, but it was too late for them now anyway. I looked up and, in a second, the light changed in the room. Suddenly, we were standing in an abyss with darkness all around. There were flies everywhere. They were on the walls, on the furniture, on the ceiling, even on the ground. Millions of them around us, silent and motionless. The sunlight barely squeezed through their mass which was like a thick shade on the glass of the window, and left a strange dim light in the room.

We stood frozen like stakes stuck into the floor. I didn't have the power to even move my finger. But the flies didn't move either. It was a terrifying stillness. We all know what flies are. They are creatures that are always flying and alighting, rubbing their legs, constantly moving. But it wasn't like this now. It was as still as the grave. I remember the silence as well. There was no sound at all: nothing. I was in a black living cell, like I had been swallowed by an enormous giant and was still alive in its stomach. It was absurd and grotesque. I felt as if I had walked directly onto one of the pages of *Alice in Wonderland* with the Red Queen about to burst in on us and order us to be decapitated on the spot.

We had seen something that we shouldn't have seen; we had turned a page in a book that we didn't understand, and we were on the other side now. We were in a different world. Peadar had the complexion of death on his face in that weak light. There was fear in his eyes, but he looked towards the door and started walking slowly like a person in a trance. I noticed that I was following him. We were under a spell, frozen with fear, but yet something was working automatically within us. Then we were at the living room door and I saw Peadar open it. The flies were in the hall as well. The cold eerie light told us that. But we carried on slowly through it, down through a glen of shadow to the front door. We opened it and the bright sunlight fell on our faces. We slid out onto the path and then into the street.

Our normal understanding of the world around us is dependent on a certain regularity. We understand that the events of our lives follow understandable routines. The sun rises, the sun sets. It is important to us that there is continuity. People live through a system of communication and recognition. We recognise what a person is, what a dog, a house or a car is. These things don't change from day to day. We understand what a fly is. But what would you do if that were all turned upside down?

Peadar looked at me and I saw a lost expression in his eyes. He always had a sensible way about him, but I remembered then that he was a bit younger than me. He was like a lost little boy at that moment. 'What happened, Seán?' he asked me.

I didn't have an answer. I just shook my head like some sort of grotesque automaton, something you would find in a funfair long ago, left in a box to tell fortunes to giddy-eyed yobs. That was me. But I didn't have any fortunes to tell. As if the past was now like particles floating in the air, their connection with dry land lost forever. Where would that leave the future? Who knew?

But my voice did come in the end, squeezing out hoarsely through my lips. 'Little men!' I exclaimed with a gasp. 'How could there be little men in the head of a fly? I put the head in the microscope. That's all, Peadar! And they were there in the water. And how did the other flies get into the room?'

'Let's get out of here anyway,' he said, some authority coming back into his voice.

We walked down the road, speed in our steps now. Peadar looked over his shoulder at the house as if some answer might be found in the shape of the building. I didn't want to do that for fear that I may be turned into a pillar of salt. The world had a surreal appearance. It was about six o'clock, but there was energy still in the air. I felt that I was after walking onto a film set. I looked at the people around me, at the old women, the young boys. They all had the appearance of being actors – or maybe extras. I was waiting for someone to shout '*Cut!*' loudly in English. That was the only explanation there could be: that I was an actor in a film but I didn't realise it. Would that really be stranger than any other explanation for what had happened? It's an odd feeling when you look at the world around you as an artificial creation, like an artwork, something that someone once imagined and now it was there before you.

We saw Noel Murphy's pub in Ballyphehane Square and went in for sanctuary from the uncertainty. The bar was half-full. Two men were standing at the counter who seemed to be half-drunk. There was a group of three men and two women in another corner and one of the women was laughing. Three men were sitting quietly at another table near the door. We went to the bar and ordered two pints from a woman who appeared to be in a bad mood, or so I thought anyway. I remember imagining that her dour expression was caused by her wanting a more substantial role in this film.

There were flies going around in the air, making shapes under the lampshade. We both looked at them, and at each other. A cold shudder ran through me being back in their presence again. We went down to the back and sat with our drinks under the mural of nuns drinking pints in a pub, some sitting at a table and another nun behind the counter. I always liked this mural, imagining that there may be a pub like this hidden in every convent in Ireland. There was something cosy about the image of the two pints of stout on our own table as well, something traditional that took us from the strange world we were in. We both took a sup and laid the glasses down again on the table. Peadar inhaled deeply and seemed as if he was preparing to speak, even though he didn't in the end.

He always had a scientific disposition and looked at the world as something explicable. He believed that there was an answer to every question, and even if it wasn't easily available, it was still there. But his disposition failed him in this case because there was no explanation for what we'd seen. How could there be? I looked at him and I knew that his mind was doing its best to make sense of it all.

'Jesus Christ, Peadar!' I said. 'What the fuck is happening?'

'Are we mad?' he asked. 'Can the same madness affect two different lunatics in the same way at the same time? But that's not how it works, as far as I know anyway. Did we both see the same thing? Explain to me what you saw.'

'I put the head of the fly that I killed on the slide. I put a drop of water on it and plastic on top. I looked through the lens and there were two tiny men there.'

'What type of clothes were they wearing?'

'They both had blue one-piece suits on, I think.'

'That's how I saw them as well. But then what did you see? I'll tell you first what I saw. I saw that there were flies, millions of them on everything, on every surface of the house.'

'That's what I saw too. If we're mad, it's strange that we had the exact same hallucination.'

'Okay so,' he said hoarsely. 'We saw what we saw. But how can such beings exist in this world? I'm a student of science. I believe in the truth of science. But this is science fiction. I don't believe in science fiction.' I heard a tension in Peadar's voice now that

I'd never heard before and I understood that this was hurting him deeply. He believed in the logic of science as if it was part of his identity. His view of the world was based on objective truths and what we'd seen attacked the very ground under his feet. Of course, I felt this as well but, for some reason, I imagined it to be a greater loss to him.

'Maybe it's just me that's mad,' he said. 'Maybe I'm just imagining the whole thing.'

'I could say the same thing. Maybe we should both head up to the mental asylum.'

'This isn't the real world,' he said, his voice getting weak. 'I'm not a character in some tawdry fantasy story.'

'Me neither. But even if the real world isn't a fantasy story, we still have to turn the next page. We are left with a question: what can we do about it?' I spoke here in a sensible voice like a reasonable person, but in my mind I felt like I was sitting inside my head looking out through cloudy eyes at a world whose very existence was uncertain.

'If we accept that we aren't mad,' he said.

'Alright,' I relied, maintaining the same sensible voice.

'And if we accept from this that those *firíní** were actually there, maybe we'll be able to create a plan and put some reason back into our lives. If we don't do that, I promise you that we'll be in the lunatic asylum sooner or later anyway.'

He was right, of course. It was said to me when I was young that the longest building in Europe was the Red Brick. That was the Cork mental asylum that's been closed now for years. An old Victorian building in which the echoes of misery and despair are still ringing from the walls. If there are ghosts in this world, it's there you'll see them.

---

* Firíní – little men

'But what sort of plan do you have in mind?' I asked.

'The bodies of the two men we saw through the microscope!' he said with a new enthusiasm in his voice, 'can't we just show them to the world? It would be the discovery of the age!'

'It's possible, certainly, but you saw the amount of flies that were in the room. Were there two others in every one of them? It's clear that we're dealing with sentient beings. I doubt that the bodies will still be there when we go back.'

It was clear that this took the wind out of his sails. Every scientist wants to find the discovery of the age. 'Maybe you're right,' he said. 'And we could try to capture two others but should we kill them to do it? They are sentient beings, as you said. If we could catch two others who are alive, how do we keep them in confinement?'

At that moment, I imagined those two other firíní in a microscopic prison with the bars made of flea hairs and us putting them on exhibition before the scientific community like little King Kongs. 'There's no chance that we'd catch two others anyway. They'd be ready for us now,' I said.

'Without hard evidence, we'd be on our own. We'd be put in a mental asylum if we disclosed the story,' Peadar said with disappointment. 'So what are they: aliens from outer space or beings native to this planet?'

'But they had human form. How did that happen? Whether they're native to this world or not, there's no sense to it.'

'There's not,' he said cheerlessly, taking a sup from his pint. I saw that he glanced up at the flies that were circling like vultures. 'They're more evolved, more developed than us. We have to be careful. A fly can carry any sort of poison. They could put something in our food. They could kill us, if they wanted to.'

At that moment, one of the flies came down and landed on the top of my pint. It startled me and we both stared at the black mass on the white head of the pint before it flew back into the air again. I closed my eyes. A black despair came over me and I covered my face with my hands. They would kill us. Of course they would, in order to keep their secret. It would be very easy for them. Was that to be the day of my death? Was that all there was at the end? I looked at Peadar and thought it strange that he had a smile on his face.

'I never thought that I'd say this,' he said, 'but isn't it a terrible thing that they can understand Irish?' He picked up my pint from the table with a determined look in his eyes. 'I won't live in fear,' he said. 'If they want to kill us, we can't stop them.' And with that he threw back a huge gulp of it.

I was impressed with his courage, but there was a cold pragmatism with it as well.

There was no chance that we could stop the flies if they decided to kill us. We would have to eat and drink things and we could never be careful enough. We could live on food and drink from closed plastic, but even that wouldn't stop them. 'You're right,' I said. I took a big slug from the same pint, the boldness of doing so giving me courage. We sat there quietly for a while under the image of the nuns on the wall, imitating their quiet life in that convent pub.

'Sooner or later, we'll have to be brave and go back to the house,' Peadar said.

I knew that he was right but I didn't want to think about it. 'But what will we do if they're still there? Can we call the exterminator?'

'It's not the worst of ideas.'

So we finished our pints slowly and left, standing out on the street for a little while first. We walked towards the house like condemned men, and I felt a horrible turn in my stomach. I thought at first that it was the flies' poison working on me, but in the end, it was only nerves.

We reached the gate of the house and walked slowly up to the front door. I opened it carefully and, with a huge sigh of relief, saw that the hall was free of flies. There were no flies in the living room either. As I had thought, the fly's head was gone from the microscope slide. When we looked through the lens, it was as clean as crystal. Even the body of the fly on the wall had vanished. For a moment, I thought that it had all been a bad dream, before Peadar spoke out again.

'We have to do some research and find out if this has ever happened before. It can't be that we're the first people ever to have seen these little men. This must have happened already to someone else. It's been more than four hundred years since Galileo made the first proper optical microscope. If anyone else has seen them, there's a chance that there's a record of it. It's a plan anyway.'

Scene Two

We walked to the university three days later. The sultry weather had dispersed in the meantime, and I felt the cold breath of autumn around me now. But it was the beginning of the academic year and there was a new energy in the college. I looked up at the curve of the old astronomical observatory, the neat lump of cut limestone that hadn't opened its eye in years. It was like a sleeping cyclops, put under a spell and turned to stone. But the same stars were still there, and it waited patiently for the chance to open that eye again. The students gathered beneath its stony feet like restless pups, free for the first time in their lives. In they came from the country to the City of Hills with the balmy smell of freedom filling their lungs.

We went into the Boole library and directly up to the first floor where the books on entomology were. Peadar had done some research on the subject and, unlike me, he understood the scientific approach very well. I followed him to the correct place so I could begin the search. 'It's not entomology itself that we're looking for, but the history that relates to it,' he told me as he handed me a list of potentially suitable books.

So we started to explore, although I found it difficult going through those books with their illustrations of these little creatures and the people who spent their lives trying to understand them. There were pictures of faces with huge eyes and horns on their skulls like people from another planet. I stayed there for a half an hour, but felt that I was wasting my time. I also felt that my impatience was disturbing Peadar.

'Maybe you'll have a better chance if you look in the history section,' he said. 'It will relate more to your own studies anyway.

I don't know whether we're wasting our time here or not. I understand that it won't be clearly written in a book that someone saw two tiny men in a fly's head, but we'll have to follow our instincts.'

'I'll do that,' I said, getting up from the table.

The humanities were on the third floor and I started to wander around aimlessly there. I looked at books by Seán Ó Ríordáin and Pádraic Ó Conaire, by Rabelais and many writers besides. I thought of Máirtín Ó Cadhain and that line of his: 'the flies that stick to the great wheels of the world.' Did he know about what we'd seen? He didn't. How could he?

I was strolling around and walked past shelves of books on the subject of English literature. I loved the Boole library, and was feeling quite relaxed until I saw a big fly hovering around me. This put my nerves on edge but, for some reason, I decided to follow it. It occurred to me that I was like one of the Three Wise Men following a star, but what kind of manger would this black lump find for me? It flew around for a while, and then landed on a shelf and remained motionless. This was directly above one particular book: *Paradise Lost* by John Milton, the story of Adam and Eve and the war between God and the Devil.

A horrible fear overcame me. Was this what was actually happening to us? Were we in contact with the Devil? I was never a religious person, but I was raised Catholic and you can never escape from the seeds that company leaves under your skin. Wasn't Beelzebub 'Lord of the Flies'? I became nauseous and felt as if I might throw up. The fly was standing on the shelf before me. Was that the Devil himself, or one of his agents? That ugly concept came to me: losing your soul, eternal damnation, the pains of Hell. The thought descended on my shoulders like a great weight.

But a logical streak remained in me as well. It was clear that I was dealing with a substantial intellect here, but was it a devilish intellect? Wouldn't they know that a nod in the direction of this religious notion could terrify us, and that this could be enough to scare us off? Was it right that I let them scare me as easily as that? The Middle Ages were over.

I took down *Paradise Lost* and opened it, coming immediately upon a phrase that the Devil says when he first arrives in Hell:

> *A mind not to be changed by place or time.*
> *The mind is its own place, and in itself*
> *Can make a Heav'n of Hell, a Hell of Heav'n.*

I decided then that I wouldn't yield to them just like that, whatever they were. I took the book with me and sat at a table to read it.

I already knew what it was about. I understood that it related to the story of Genesis: Adam and Eve and the loss of Paradise. But when I started reading, I soon came to the part in which the Devil and his henchmen have just arrived in Hell after losing their rebellion in Heaven. We find them wallowing in a lake of fire in horrible torment for nine days before Satan recovers his wits and stirs up the demonic host again. He speaks first with his second in command, Beelzebub. They appear here more like soldiers who have lost a battle than demons in Hell. Satan tells us that he brought an innumerable army of spirits with him who liked the reign of God no more than he himself. They were a broken army now, but we still hear the mettle of the revolutionary in his voice when he proclaims that he would not submit to the king and would never yield to him. I thought to myself at the time that one could imagine this conversation as being between Pádraig Pearse and James Connolly after the failure of the Rising in 1916. It's certainly a political conversation between the two of them anyway.

Then Satan incites the crowd. He calls their names and they assemble in their thousands. He gives them an inspirational speech beyond anything that even Michael Collins himself would have said. In the end, they raise their flaming swords. The revolution was broken but the spirit of the revolutionaries themselves was still alive. They would never yield to the authority of the king. They come together then to build a palace in Hell, with elegant columns and grand halls, and they call it Pandemonium. They gather at this place and establish a parliament to plan a course of action, and to affirm their objective to continue with the fight and win their freedom.

I closed the book at this point. It was difficult for me to understand why I was reading it. Were the little men trying to tell me something, or just distract me? I knew that Beelzebub was called 'Lord of the Flies' and there he was in the story itself. I took *Paradise Lost* and a couple of other books that related to it, and headed back to Peadar. He was still in the same place where I had left him, his eyes sunk into an old book and an intense look on his face. I told him about what had happened with the fly and the book, and he looked at me sceptically.

'Are you certain that the fly was directing you to that shelf? And if that's true, maybe it was an attempt to send you astray. Weren't there other books on the shelf? Why did you pick that one?'

They were all good questions, but I thought it better to stand my ground. 'I haven't found anything else anyway,' I said. 'I'll head home. I was never able to study here amongst the crowd. I don't know, maybe I am going astray, but I'll try it anyway.'

'Grand so,' he said. 'I'll see you later.'

On my way downstairs, I wondered whether or not the fly had directed me to the book. I was no longer certain of anything.

When I went outside, it was dark. I hadn't noticed that it had gotton so late and that the place was now covered with a blanket of fog. It was an eerie landscape, and I almost turned around and went back to the safety of the library. I carried on, but with every step I took, this creeping sensation grew in me. There were cars driving slowly on the street and their headlights glared before them in shining lines like wandering lost spirits. Ghostly forms appeared before me as well, but as soon as they came, they disappeared again into the dark sea.

I remember thinking that I could commit a murder here and that no one would know it was me. But then it occurred to me that the Firíní could easily put an end to me here as well. A cold fear gripped me, and I imagined Peadar the following day when the Guards came to the door to tell him that my body had been found. He would know, of course, that it was *they*, the men in the flies, who had killed me.

But I had to put a stop to this rambling. It was fog, that was all, and it had no relation to the Firíní. The air was full of sounds and voices, but they came to me now like noise from a radio that isn't properly in tune. I walked on like a person in a dream, but then I turned a corner and saw a sanctuary before me: a bus, and the right one for me as well. I ran for it, and nearly killed myself on the footpath in doing so, but I got on board and sat down. The bus didn't move for a while, however, and this disturbed me a little. But I didn't mind really, seeing as there was a light illuminating this space which was a great relief compared to the strange obscure world outside.

I closed my eyes to escape the place for a moment, but then felt someone sit down beside me, someone big. I opened them again and saw out of the corner of my eye that there was a great bulk beside me on the seat. At last, the bus moved off, swimming through the thick vegetable soup around us, and I looked out of the window at the ashen world, shifting from a grey to an orange hue as we passed the street lights. I didn't understand how the driver was able to manoeuvre through it, but somehow he was.

I felt a dark dread again, but just then the person beside me turned and spoke: '*Better to reign in Hell, than serve in Heaven*,' he proclaimed in a light-hearted voice.

I turned my head towards him. He certainly was a huge man anyway. He wore a great black coat, as black as his thick head of hair and the beard that burst across his broad face. He looked at me curiously, and his face widened even more into a broad, playful smile. He had a gold tooth glistening in his mouth and blue eyes that were just as bright as it.

'It's a line from the first book, I think,' he said.

'What book?' I asked.

'The first book of *Paradise Lost*.'

I looked down and saw I was still holding Milton's book. 'Oh, it is!' I said awkwardly. 'Have you read it?'

'I certainly have! It's a great book, isn't it?'

'Well, I've only read a little bit of it yet.' It was a relief to me now that I understood what he was on about.

'You have a pleasure before you so. Milton was a proper republican. Did you know that?'

I admitted that I didn't.

'He was a big supporter of Oliver Cromwell and very happy that King Charles the first lost his head. He preferred the people of the country to be in charge without the tyranny of the King or his heirs.'

He had a roguish, cheerful look in his eyes as he spoke to me. He laid his hand on the rail before him, a hand like a huge slab of meat. He wasn't at all overweight but rather a great, dark mass in a black coat with his black hair and wild beard. He was like an enormous crow sitting beside me on the bus. There was a moment when I became bewildered as to how he was there at all. But however dark this great crow was, his gold tooth and his eyes were still shining brightly. I was awestruck by him as he spoke about the life of this old republican.

'I think Milton put his republicanism in that book. But, as well as that, there are other things there that are difficult to resolve,' he said.

'Like what?'

'Read it and you'll see. I don't want to ruin the ending for you,' he said with a smile.

At that moment, I saw a light that I recognised through the window. It was a shop not far from my house. I jumped up quickly. 'It was nice talking to you,' I said, heading for the door. The bus stopped, and within a couple of seconds, I was in the fog again. I walked like a blind man along a familiar route, my hand on a wall beside me, but I knew that the house wasn't far.

When I was almost there, practically outside the gate, a ghostly face came at me through the fog. It gave me an awful fright, especially when this face spoke to me. '*How are ya, Seán! By God, isn't it gone very foggy*?' he asked me. It was my neighbour.

'*It is, isn't it*?' I answered and the face disappeared into the fog again. A strange feeling overcame me as I took out my key to open the door. I turned on the light which was an enormous relief after the fog.

Then it struck me. I had been speaking in Irish with the big man on the bus. But how did he know that I spoke Irish? I looked at the books in my hand, *Paradise Lost* and other books in English that related to it. There was no way he could know that I spoke Irish – but he did. How? This was another awkward, uncomfortable twist in the story and it disturbed me, I have to say. I went into the living room and put on the television. I really needed the normal world now.

Maybe you were thinking, readers, that I was taking this whole thing rather easily, that I was even relaxed about it. Well, that's not true. Perhaps it was the shock, but I felt a certain pragmatic attitude come over me when I saw that these beings existed. I think that Peadar felt this as well, but that's not to say that the horrible seriousness of the situation wasn't just lurking there still. I sat on the sofa waiting for something on the television to tell me that the whole thing was a trick. That didn't happen, but before long I felt my eyelids become heavy and I fell into a deep sleep.

I had a dream. I was standing on the bank of a little lake looking at the long grass on the other side as it swayed slowly and hypnotically in the summer breeze. But suddenly, everything stopped and the view before me became still and silent. I saw that there was a woman with long, black hair and a long, black dress on the other side standing like a statue amongst the rushes. She was staring at me, motionless. A cold terror ran through me.

I noticed then that there was a boy sitting on a big chair a little distance away from me. 'Who is that woman?' I asked him.

'There is no woman,' he answered coldly.

I turned around and saw her still standing there like a cold, black statue, a blight amongst the rushes. 'Don't you see her!' I said, an icy panic sliding up my spine.

'No,' he said coldly again.

I turned around and walked back from the water and up a dusty earthen path. It was clear to me then that I wasn't in Ireland but in a dry country. Yellow earth stretched out on both sides of the path, with rocks scattered here and there. There were green hills in the distance, but only the odd strangled bush near me here in this burnt soil. I didn't see them, but I knew that there were snakes dreaming between those rocks. I felt that it was early in the morning and saw stars still in the sky, one of them shining brightly above the others. The sky was a turquoise blue, the kind of sky that miracles come from – in dreams anyway. There were big birds – vultures I thought – hovering high up in the sky on broad, motionless wings.

I imagined the cold psychopathic eyes they would have and the beaks like scimitars with which they'd taste my flesh. A soft breeze ran through my legs like a playful dog. I sensed then that there was someone nearby, even though I couldn't see him. His presence terrified me and I woke up again on the sofa.

Peadar was standing in the room. 'Did you see that fog?' he said. 'Isn't it strange?

I mumbled something in agreement. I was still half-dreaming, and I thought that he had a devilish appearance with the hat pulled down over his ears, and a strange look in his eyes. His check coat was tightened up to his neck, and he was wearing black gloves like someone about to commit a terrible crime.

'I'm sorry that I was questioning you in the library about what you found,' he said. 'I didn't find much myself: one or two things maybe.' With that, he went to his room and I was left on my own on the sofa again.

I looked around me at the room as if I'd never seen it before and it struck me that my life would never again be as it had been. What I had seen in the microscope undermined every foundation of the world that had been built around me. It brutally pulled up its roots. It was a simple fact that the Firíní were there, and that tarnished all other facts. What is human society if you factor in this new presence? I felt that the fog was creeping in to me under the door and through the glass of the window.

Scene Three

'Welcome to the world of Post-truth!' she said with glee. 'I find it a strange term: post-truth. Are people suggesting that everything was true up to now? What truth was there ever in the world of politics? Were the "white man's burden" or the "divine right of kings" ever true? They were not indeed! But the internet is bringing to light the fact that you can say whatever you like and certain people will believe you because it suits them to do so. What's interesting to us now, however, is the system that's in place to spread this misinformation.'

She had short red hair that stuck out in every direction, and her jaw jutted out a bit as well. She spoke in a thick County Louth accent with the same mad enthusiasm she always had. She was a remarkable person really, with a forceful look in her eyes that always had you halfway between a keen interest and a terrible fear, sometimes stopping midway in a sentence to look at you as if you were guilty of some horrendous crime. I saw a sharp intensity in her eyes now as she spoke, and I squeezed the cup tighter in my hand. This was a social visit.

But I liked Kate a lot, I have to say. She had called into me at eleven that morning and I made her a coffee. She was clever and honest and would tell you bluntly whatever was on her mind. She was a good laugh as well and could be funny enough when she wanted to be.

We were in the same class for one subject in our first year and used to meet on campus from time to time after that, even though we weren't doing the same subjects then. I carried on with Irish and she did Political Science. By the way, Kate doesn't speak Irish, so this is a translation I made of our conversation so that there wouldn't be long extracts of English in this book.

'It's a good system,' she said, carrying on. 'Choose issues that are controversial and will incite the public. Stick with them even – or especially – if they're shown to be irrelevant or false. Never admit that you're wrong, even in the face of incontrovertible evidence. It's incredible the amount of people who won't listen to evidence anyway, but rather to the person with the most righteous-sounding voice. Tell them that not only is what you're doing righteous but it's the most righteous thing in the history of the world. Always remember that your audience was raised looking at epic films and has an enormous desire to be in the midst of a great historical event.'

I took a huge gulp of the coffee and tried to remember if there was any paracetamol in the house. I had spent three days studying *Paradise Lost*, and then, in frustration, drank three-quarters of a bottle of vodka. That was the night before, and for a while I forgot that the world had gone mad. There was a film on television. I remember that I was able to understand the individual scenes on their own, yet still couldn't put them together into a single coherent story. Now that Kate was sitting before me, I had that same feeling again.

'Accuse your opposition of the things that you yourself are guilty of, so that when they rebuke you for it, it will appear that they're just copying you and don't have proper arguments of their own. If they put 'facts' before you, it doesn't matter. Let the public believe that these facts were created only to have an undue influence over them.'

Even though I liked Kate, I still wasn't ready for this level of energy at eleven o'clock in the morning, given my terrible hangover. She had started a postgraduate degree recently and was examining the populism that was spreading around the world. It was a very interesting subject, and I would have been delighted to discuss it with her if she'd called in the night before when I was drinking vodka.

'It's a different world now. Everyone is on the internet throwing their own two cents into the pot. The conspiracy theory is a fantastic thing for the populist as well. You can always take advantage of these keyboard warriors. Let them believe that the whole world is under the control of a secret society and that you're the only person telling it like it is. I love this phrase: 'tell it like it is'. It lets people believe that you're telling the truth, even though, of course, you're not.'

Different truths being clinically created by devious conspirators to take advantage of the gullibility of the public. Was it true or just some notion? I felt it like ants on my skin.

Maybe I was naive myself, safe and sound in the student world studying the literature of the Irish language. I thought of the two men in the fly, and a shiver ran down my spine. Kate's voice was booming in my ears now.

'In the nineties, politicians started using marketing consultants – spin doctors as they were called – and this worked very well for a while. But people are used to this trick now and any politician who appears too polished seems untrustworthy. So you must create the impression that you are unsophisticated and coarse. Speak bluntly about everything as if it's all off the top of your head, and some people will believe everything you say because *they* believe, for some reason, that blunt people always speak their minds.' She started to laugh at this.

'It's probably a good thing to be able to see what these people are doing from an objective perspective,' I said, hoping that the word 'objective' would decrease her fervour a little.

'Definitely,' she said enthusiastically. 'There are people who believe that *The Prince* by Machiavelli was a satirical work to teach us the tricks of the nobility.'

'But excuse me now, Kate … it's just that you yourself seem kinda taken with these tricks,' I said awkwardly. Maybe I shouldn't have said this but it did seem to be true.

'Well, I'm not. But I see how it could be attractive,' she said with a smile on her face. 'There's a great deal of lecturing going on in this world right now too and some people are tired of it. You know the sort: vegans on locally produced bicycles saving the fucking planet!'

'Well, maybe there's a reason for that sort of argument,' I said carefully.

'Oh there is certainly! There's no doubt about it. I'm talking about the level of self-righteous posturing that goes with it. Even if people are sympathetic to the cause at first, in the end they're so sick of the grandiose righteousness and of walking on their tip-toes around the political correctness of other people that they turn their backs on the whole thing. And that creates a division, the same division that populists exploit. I'm not saying that it's a good thing, but it happens. But I'm only speaking theoretically here, Seán.'

She finished this with the same mad smile. I would never say that Kate was right-wing, but she always hated anyone that she thought was too righteous about some subject just to draw attention to their own virtues. I often heard her argue fiercely with another girl in our class, even though she agreed with her on the matter in hand.

'I understand, of course, Kate. But if I hear that you're standing in the next election, I'll tell the tabloids that this was your plan from the very start.'

She burst out with her wild laugh at this, almost spilling her coffee. 'There are ways of dealing with people like you as well,' she said.

'Oh! I'll be sleeping with the fishes, is it?'

'Oh not at all, Seán,' she said gently now. 'I'll give you a good job in the government.'

'Oh grand so! How about the Minister for Arts, Heritage and the Gaeltacht?' I said with enthusiasm.

'It's a deal,' she said triumphantly and shook my hand.

I was starting to enjoy her company now that the lecture was over.

'How are your own studies going, anyway?' she said, changing the subject. This was a great relief, but I didn't have much to say about it just then.

'I was doing well enough for a while, but then something came up that's hindered it all a bit.'

'Sure, you'll get back to it,' she said. 'You have to take a break from time to time as well.'

'Maybe. Do you know much about Milton's *Paradise Lost*?'

'I don't,' she said with some confusion. 'I thought that you were doing your thesis in Irish!'

'I am but … it's something else.'

'Well, I don't know anything about the poem anyway, but I know that Neil did his master's thesis on it. Do you remember Neil?'

I remembered Neil very well. He was a mature student who was at college as well when I was doing my degree. He was a man in his sixties, from Belfast originally, and I was very friendly with him at the time, even though I hadn't seen much of him for a while. I did English as well for my degree and he was in a few classes with me. He was an intelligent man, and it encouraged me to think that he might give me another perspective on *Paradise Lost*.

Kate left in the end and I found the paracetamol in the press. After a shower and something to eat, I felt much better and called Neil. He welcomed me up to his house to discuss the matter, and within two hours, I was at his neat terraced house, listening to the pleasant music of the doorbell for a moment before he opened the door.

'Seán, it's good to see you! Come on in,' he said heartily in his Northern accent.

Again, I have to let you know here that Neil didn't speak Irish, so this is a translation of our conversation.

He directed me in through a well-kept hall, designed in a style reminiscent of the nineteen twenties, and straight into the sitting room on the left.

'Sit down there, Seán, and I'll get us some coffee,' he said, heading off to the kitchen.

I sat on the sofa and inhaled an aroma of old books and furniture polish.

It wasn't long before he came back with a coffee pot and two cups on a tray. 'Now,' he said sitting before me, 'how are things with ya? I haven't seen ya in a while. How's the studying going?'

'Grand,' I replied as honestly as I could. 'And how about yourself?'

'Not too bad now. I've no complaints.'

I always thought that he was a very interesting man and I knew some of his own personal story. Originally from Belfast, he was a Protestant raised in the Unionist tradition, but he fell in love with a Catholic girl from Cork and married her. This was in the seventies in the middle of the 'Troubles', and it must have been difficult for them at the time. They moved to Cork then and he lived here since. When his wife died, he decided to enrol in the college and that's when I met him.

'But what's this you said to me about *Paradise Lost*?' he asked. 'Are you still studying English literature? I thought your postgraduate degree was in Irish?'

'It is, but there's … a connection between the two, and I'm stuck with it. You did your thesis on *Paradise Lost*, didn't you?'

'I did.'

'There's something peculiar about that book, isn't there? I understand that it's a religious story, but do you think that certain elements of the story are almost inappropriate in the way in which the characters are depicted, their traits and relationships to one another: do you think that it's suitable for a religious story like this?'

Neil settled himself into the chair. He always loved a discussion about literature. 'Well, you're right,' he began. 'It's a religious text, a text that relates very much to Christianity and Judaism. But, as well as that, it's a text that uses the epic style, a style in which a great hero fights against obstacles and hardship. Milton is very clear about this from the start. In using this genre, he places his work in the same realm as the Iliad and the Aeneid, heroic literature. One often finds in this genre of tragedy that the hero has a fatal flaw – perhaps his own pride – and this brings about his ill-fated demise. So who is the hero in *Paradise Lost*? God is a distant character who applies his laws forcefully. Christ is there, but he doesn't have a big role in the story. There's Adam, but it would be difficult to give him the title of 'hero'. He is an ineffectual person who is largely restrained by his destiny. Eve is shown as a naive girl who is easily led astray. There's only one person who has a strong and well-developed character, someone whose actions direct the story, who has a voice and an intellect, who feels that he suffers injustice and fights against it. But he is also a character who suffers in the end because of his own pride and hubris. That's Satan – the Devil.

'Critics like William Blake and Percy Shelley looked at Satan as the hero of the story.

Milton said that he was writing under the influence of his 'heavenly muse' who gave him knowledge that was unknown to humanity, having fallen from a state of grace. In the story itself, moral virtue is not attributed to God any more than it is to Satan. God is a very remote and impersonal character, and the logical argument that Satan puts against his authority is quite appealing. So much so that Blake thought Milton to be an unwitting satanist.

'As well as that, the *coup d'état* in Heaven happened directly because God wanted to give his son authority above that of the angels. That's a hereditary monarchy for you! God created the hereditary title of monarchy in the Heavens, something that Milton was completely against in his own country. Satan's argument is based on republican principles, and that's something interwoven with the historical events in the life of the author: the English Civil War. Milton was a republican who despised the rule of the King and supported Oliver Cromwell. But then he writes a book in which the Devil instigates a rising in Heaven with the same spirit of republicanism. Was Milton an unwitting satanist, or did he allow his Satan to beguile the reader in the same way that he beguiled Adam and Eve, in order to properly show us that great error. It's difficult to say, but this is one of the complexities from which this wonderful work is made.

'I have my own views on the poem as well. In *Paradise Lost*, I believe Satan stands for the human race. Adam is nothing but a device to discuss certain ideas: he stands for our frailties and is a naive person. There's no one but Satan who has the complexity to illustrate the human spirit. He rises up against God – as Milton rose up against the King – and he is sent to Hell as a punishment, but the narrator of the story does not blame him for this uprising. He keeps his strength of character, his voice and his will, and I believe that we must see this as a sympathetic representation. As an epic character, he fails in the end because of his pride – not because he rose against God but because of his attack on the human race – and he does this to make a god of himself. When he comes back to Hell after the treacherous deed he carried out with Eve, and he speaks to the other fallen angels, he says: '*What remains, ye Gods, But up and enter now into full bliss*'. It's clear here that he wanted to be a god himself, but these are the last words he utters before he is turned into a mute serpent. His vengeance was so strong that he used the human race as a pawn in his war with God. The sin he committed was that he turned his back on inabsolute humanity in order to make an absolute being of himself, and it is then that he loses his greatest power: his voice, the voice that allows him to show his reason and to assert the greatest of his qualities – his humanity.'

A wry smile came across Neil's face then. 'Or maybe Milton actually was a proper satanist. He supported Cromwell, and there wasn't much difference between them really. Anyway, you're right: it's a strange tale,' he said in conclusion.

I felt that he'd given me enormous help when he finished speaking. I still didn't know whether or not this text had any relation to the problem of the little men, but, if it did, I felt I had a better understanding of it now.

We spoke of literary matters and much more besides for another two hours until it was time for me to leave. He walked me to the door but spent a few seconds then thinking before he spoke: 'As regards Milton and *Paradise Lost*,' he said, 'sometimes people are telling two stories at the same time.'

With that, I thanked him and left. I thought of the two friends from college I had met that day, and that I had fallen now into the world of politics between populism and a heavenly *coup d'état*.

The truths that exist in the world of politics are as complicated as anything else. They are like religion to people sometimes, truths that are interwoven in their hearts. Religion and politics often walk hand in hand and it is rare that a religious conflict exists without it being a political one as well. I smiled when I wondered whether or not populism was involved in political matters in Heaven. Maybe we would have to read Kate's thesis then as a religious text.

Scene Four

I knew that Peadar had been working all this time to try and find some insight into what we had seen. He would go to the library every day, or else he'd be at home on the internet for hours on end. To tell the truth, I was becoming doubtful that we would ever find anything from combing through these obscure texts, this searching for the slightest hint that this had ever happened to anyone else. But there was a surprise waiting for me. I remember that I didn't stay in the house one night and the battery in my phone had died. When I got it going the next day, I saw that there were messages from Peadar saying that he had found something. I gave him a call and I could hear in his voice that he was excited.

'It's incredible, Seán. I can't explain it to you on the phone. Come back as soon as you can.'

I went directly home and Peadar was in the living room with a thin little book in his hand. 'Look at this!' he said, giving me the book.

It appeared to be very old indeed and written in a language that I didn't understand. It was in the old German font as well and I found it difficult to make out the letters. It appeared to be a poetry book, but that was all I could decipher. It was open on one page and I saw that there were a couple of lines written on the top. This appeared to be as ancient as the book itself. I looked back to the title page and saw the date 1756.

'I told you that my mother was from the Netherlands and that I speak Dutch,' he said. 'I was born there and didn't come to Ireland until I was eight. My mother collects old books like this and so I got used to reading this old font when I was young.'

'Did you get this from your mother?'

'No. I got it in the library. I was looking for information about entomologists who lived years ago and I saw a book that related to the subject. It was a large book, and this poetry book was in between the pages. I don't know how long it had been there. It's possible that no one has seen it in years. Anyway, look at the page that's open. Do you see that there's something written on top of the page? You can see as well that the same hand has scribbled through the first two lines of the poem itself, as if this person was trying to put those lines at the top of the page in their place. It says *Ik vond manieren in een vlieg / Dat was ongewoon*, which means: 'I found manners in a fly / An uncommon thing'. The lines that are written in pen at the top of the page are very similar to this, but very different as well. They say *Ik vond mannen in een vlieg / 't Waaren er twee.* This means: 'I found men in a fly / There were two of them'. Which is exactly what *we* saw.

I was dumbstruck. I looked down at the page and, now that it had been explained to me, I was able to make out the letters well enough. It was incredible that Peadar would find something like this. 'This is fantastic! But who wrote it?' I asked.

'I don't know, but I'd say it was written a long time ago, given the style of handwriting. But it gets better, Seán! Look, there's something else written on it. It says *Swammerdam Bybel der Natuure, lijn 1.* That's to say, 'Swammerdam Bible of Nature, line one'. The large book in which I found this book is about scientists who lived during the Age of Enlightenment. I found it in a part of the book in which there was a description of the life of someone called Jan Swammerdam. He was an entomologist from the Netherlands in the seventeenth century. He was one of the first entomologists to use a microscope and make proper drawings of insects. He wrote a book called *Bybel der Natuure*. I got the full text of it online and this is its first line.'

With that, he put a piece of paper into my hand with two extracts written on it, one in Dutch, and an Irish translation of it.

> Den aard ende het maaksel van de alderminste Schepselen, tegen die van de aldergrootste, omsigtig overweegende; soo ist dat ik gedwongen werde, niet alleen in gelijken graat ofte trap van waardigheid haar te plaatsen; maar ook als boven deselve haar te stellen.

> The nature and the creation of the smallest creatures, as opposed to those of the largest, are carefully considered; so it is that I was forced not only to place them in equal degree or degree of dignity; but also to set them as above.

'It's a book about insects. Swammerdam was in innovator in the field of entomology. It wasn't clear to me at first what connection there would be between this first line and the poem in the little book, and then a thought struck me. They didn't have copyright at the time, and so they often put anagrams in their texts so that they could prove that the things they wrote were their own. If there was a controversy about whose book it was, the real author could show the anagram to the world.'

'And you found an anagram in it?'

'I did! It's incredible, Seán. Look again at the poem. If you put the lines that are written on the top of the page in place of the lines that are printed there, you get this poem.'

With that, he gave me another piece of paper with a poem written on it. I was able to make out the letters much easier now in Peadar's own neat hand:

Ik vond mannen in een vlieg
't Waaren er twee
Sprack met de heeren aldaar
Engelen des tijds

Ik ontsnapte totdat de koorts toesloeg; 'n hel
'n Eed van de Heer van de wrede gele pest gaat mis
Verweer tegen God, boosaardigheid, smaad
Grof als vileine haat
Taai als alle gal

Then he gave me another piece of paper on which there was a translation of the poem written in Irish:

I found men in a fly
There were two of them there
I spoke to the men
Angels of time

I escaped 'til fever struck; a hell
Oath of the lord of the cruel yellow plague goes awry
The act a revolt against God, wickedness, mockery
As loathsome as ugly hate
As quarrelsome as all spite

A strange poem, I thought, but when I looked at Peadar, there was a smile on his face.

'You won't believe this,' he said, 'but that poem is an exact anagram of the first line of Swammerdam's book. I went through it letter by letter. It must be Swammerdam himself who wrote it.'

'That's amazing. But is the poem attributed to Swammerdam in the book?'

'It isn't. The book is a collection of poems by different poets, and this one is attributed to Catharina Questiers. She was a well-known Dutch poet, and I'm almost certain that she knew Swammerdam. They would have been in the same social circles in Amsterdam. I don't know how it happened that an anagram from his book was included here with her name on it, but it tells us something very important. Jan Swammerdam saw the same thing that we did.'

'This is incredible, Peadar. It's amazing.' I said, and I began reading through the poem again.

'It's a peculiar poem,' he said. 'It shows him to be a person who was suffering a lot.'

'Do you have any idea what he meant by "angels of time" or "oath of the Lord of the cruel yellow plague"? And what's this about a "fever"?'

'Swammerdam died of malaria in 1680. I'd say that the fever relates to that. As regards angels of time and lord of the cruel yellow plague, maybe they were the Firíní themselves. If that's true, he says here that he spoke to them, that there was some communication between them. I read as well that people with malaria often get jaundice.'

'How do you get malaria? From mosquitoes, isn't it?'

'Yeah,'

'In other words, flies.'

'Yeah.'

'And don't you get malaria in the tropics. How do you get it in the Netherlands?'

'It was a more common disease in Europe at the time, I think. But still, it's easy to imagine that it was *they* who gave it to him.'

I thought again of the terror I felt when a fly landed on the head of my pint in the pub. Would they give some similar sickness to us? A cold, uncomfortable sensation came over me with this knowledge of how Swammerdam had died. Yet what else could we do but carry on? We couldn't just forget what we had seen that day. 'We should focus our energy so on researching Jan Swammerdam. I didn't find much about *Paradise Lost* anyway.'

'I don't know. Maybe there'll be some connection yet. Did you find anything?'

I told him about my own study on the matter and my conversation with Neil. I have to admit that I was embarrassed at how little I had, compared to his own discovery.

Peadar was more understanding of my work though. 'Well, it's clear that there was cross-fertilisation going on between science and literature at the time,' he said. 'Academia wasn't as divided then as it is today. When was Milton alive?'

'He died in 1674. That's contemporary with Swammerdam, isn't it?'

'Yeah, that's great! Swammerdam lived between 1637 and 1680. The English and the Dutch were often fighting at the time, but it's possible that there was some contact between them. I'm going to the library now to bring the books back and get some others. But I'll keep the little poetry book. That doesn't belong to the library anyway. It was left there by accident or on purpose, but it's ours now. I'll try to find out as well if there was any connection between Swammerdam and Milton.' With that, he left.

When he was gone, I began thinking about Jan Swammerdam. What kind of person was he? Had he seen the Firíní in the same way that we had? I didn't have answers to these questions then, but a lot of evidence came to light afterwards, about him and about certain events in his life. I'd like to tell you his story now in my own way. I'll tell you how we came by this information later on, when we reach the appropriate point in my own contemporary account. I'll write it here as a story, but I'd like to impress upon you that this isn't a fabrication. All these events are true, and I promise you that I'll do my absolute best to stick to the plain facts as I learned them. Maybe I'll add some literary colour to the story, but that's all. And you don't need to take my word for it. I'd recommend that you read history books or go on the internet and you'll find a lot of information that supports everything that I've written. This is not a work of fiction.

I'll start so, in the Netherlands, more than three hundred and fifty years ago.

Scene Five

Leiden, the Netherlands.
3rd September 1663

Jan Swammerdam was ready now to leave the house. He gathered all his instruments into the leather satchel that hung over his shoulder, and closed the door of his lodgings in Pieterskerkhof. He had a room rented for some time now in the house of the printer Mattheys Severijn. He liked Leiden, and he particularly liked living in this district. The town cemetery used to be here, but they moved all the coffins away to somewhere else. Where the dead used to lie, now the living resided. The youth of the country, the youth of Europe even, were here now. It was a sunny day, and he wore a light, black doublet with a white, linen shirt beneath it. His black hair stretched down to his collar, and his good humour that morning could be seen in his dark eyes. The bright sun was suitable for the work he had set before him that day, and he walked the short distance at his ease to the house of his friend Nicolaus Steno.

Jan was a learned young man in his mid-twenties, but he had been engrossed in studies of the natural world since he was a child. His father was an apothecary and had a collection of 'interesting things', as he called them. Amongst them, were coins from distant lands, as well as minerals, fossils and insects. It was a magical collection to his young son, and even though Jan liked everything in it, it was the insects that particularly caught his attention, and he spent long days in his youth examining them carefully. As a young child, he had heard the old stories of giants and monsters, stories that filled him with wonder, but it appeared to him that those little creatures in his father's collection were just like those in the fables. He grew up with this wonder in his heart, but he felt that the greatest joy of his life was that moment when he first looked through the microscope and saw that it was all true, that this other world was there all the time. This world of insects, monsters more horrible and grotesque than anything in the stories of his youth, misshapen creatures, absurd even, yet still beautiful. He saw that this wondrous world was right beside our own, existing in exactly the same space, and he wanted to peer into this secret place so as to read God's creation like a book. Nature was a bible to him now, written by God's own hand, and the world was a church, stronger than any building made of stone and the rules of man.

Steno was living nearby, and it wasn't long before Jan got to his front door. He was a student at the university as well, and they had been good friends for some time. Steno had a garden at the back of the house, and they had planned that day to use the new microscope there, illuminated by the rays of the sun. They used to meet often to conduct experiments or discuss some argument. Jan didn't bother knocking on the door but went directly around to the garden. Steno was there already, sitting on a low armchair.

It was a beautiful garden, coloured with flowers and bushes scattered all around. Ivy was growing thickly on a high wall at the back and birds darted here and there. A silver birch in the centre of the garden stood out beautifully at this time of year, its yellow leaves and white bark shining brightly in the sunlight. Steno had heard once that this tree was the symbol of a new beginning. He didn't understand quite what this meant, but the idea appealed to him anyway.

He was originally from Denmark and Niels Steensen was his proper name. He used Steno, the Latin form of his surname, in academic circles, even though his friends still called him Niels in conversation. He was always level-headed and devoted to his studies, but some change had come over him since coming to the Netherlands. He understood this, but wasn't sure if he liked the change. He'd been a quiet boy when he was young, but now he was a part of the busy social world of academic society here in Leiden. He was a private person with a normally calm disposition, but people close to him sometimes felt that there were strong currents beneath that still exterior. Life in the Netherlands was strange to him. In Denmark, there was only one religion and the world was simpler like that, but here people had more freedom to practise their beliefs. There were even people here of whom he doubted whether or not they believed in the Creator at all. It was difficult to say these things out loud, of course, but the freedom of this country allowed people to circulate those suggestions, and Steno felt this to be a terrible and dangerous thing.

Before Jan walked into the garden, Steno was thinking of the conversation he'd had with Spinoza the Jew (or ex-Jew, he should say) when he had called to his house in Rijnsburg a few days before. It was hard for Steno to say what kind of belief Spinoza had at all, but from what he said, it appeared to him that he was almost like an atheist. Spinoza spoke slowly in a deep voice, his long face and big lazy eyes giving him a relaxed appearance. 'But what is God?' he asked. 'We are scientists, and so we look to understand the rules of science. We see that metal is made from one matter and wood from another. Water and air are not the same. The bodies of plants and those of animals are not the same. Every substance has different aspects and traits, and we work to understand the rules that relate to these substances. But that which is God is the entirety of all natural and physical rules in the universe. God is the substance of the universe, which is limitless in its aspects. And so, the aspects which any other substance has, it must be that God has them too and whatever is in the universe, it is a part of God.'

'But how can you say that God is a 'substance'?' Steno asked him irritably. 'He is a father. He is a being. He is spirit, creator, eternal intellect: that is what we believe! But a substance? That's like atheism. Are you an atheist, Baruch?'

'I have a great belief in God. But perhaps it's a different understanding of him than that which you have yourself. I remember the God who was proclaimed to me in the synagogue when I was young. He was an angry God, a judge who would impose a hard punishment on those who would not do his will. I no longer believe in that God.'

'We don't have a choice of which type of God exists. He exists, that is all! The Alpha and the Omega,' said Steno indignantly.

'I agree with you entirely,' Spinoza said in his gentle voice, and he stopped for a little while before speaking again. 'Forgive me, my friend. I have disturbed you.' He put his hand in his pocket and took out a little parcel, a tiny leather pouch. 'This is a new lens that I have created. It's one of the best lenses that I have yet made. It is yours now. May you discover the truths of the world with it.'

Steno thanked him and left, but the conversation stayed in his mind. It still disturbed him even now, a few days later. He promised himself that he would never tell anyone of their exchange.

With that, Jan walked into the garden with his bag over his shoulder. 'Well, isn't it a fine life you have, stretched out in your lovely garden?' he said cheerfully.

Steno didn't stand up when he saw him but he tried to sweep any trace of uneasiness from his face. 'We'll have a fine day for the work anyway' he said with a smile, and stretched his arm out to give Jan the little leather parcel. 'This is something Spinoza gave me the other day. It's a new lens. He said it's very good.'

Jan took the little pouch and opened it. He placed the small piece of glass in the palm of his hand, and it sat there like a jewel shining in the bright sunlight. He picked it up then and looked through it with one eye. 'He's an artist,' he said. 'I got a new microscope from Johannes Hudde as well. They'll fit together very well.'

He opened his bag and took out a wooden box with the new microscope, a strange instrument that was to them like a key to the mysteries of creation. Jan set it on the table that Steno had prepared. He carefully inserted the new lens and looked into the viewfinder to check if the sunlight was shining through it. Then he laid out the other items: the glass slides, the little books and notes, and a small box with specimens for study. There was a spider's leg and the wing of a butterfly, the internal organs of a maggot, and a small bag containing some tiny lizards. He laid everything out neatly on the table, and they both got to work immediately. They looked at the butterfly's wing first and saw the orange and red colours like the most beautiful silk. Jan made a drawing of the veins that ran across the wing like a river on a map. They were excited peering in on this invisible land and felt like adventurers in a new world. And it was true! This was a new world for humanity.

Steno began dissecting one of the lizards. He was a master at this art and did it with complete care and patience. He took out the lizard's liver and laid it down on a little marble slab. Then he cut a sliver of it and put it on one of the glass slides. In the microscope, they scrutinised the blood and lymphatic vessels, and Jan jotted down notes and made drawings quickly but neatly into a book. There was a different language between them when they were engaged in this work, the language of learned men, and they both spoke it fluently.

But then they heard a sound behind them, and when they turned around, Reinier de Graaf was standing there. He broke the magic spell they had been under and awoke them from the dream in that other world. 'I'm sorry, gentlemen,' he said. 'I knocked at the front door but when I didn't get a reply, I thought that you might be working out here.'

'It's no problem, Reinier,' said Steno. 'You're very welcome. Would you like to join us in the study?'

'Unfortunately I can't, Niels. I'm actually here to take you from your work. Professor Van Horne asked me to summon you. He has received some correspondence for you. It was sent to the university for some reason and he felt that it would be important. He wants you to come immediately.'

'Immediately? But we're working,' Steno began with frustration, but then suddenly stopped. He had great respect for Johannes Van Horne and knew that he wouldn't summon him like this for no reason. 'Though maybe it's important. Very well, I'll come along with you now,' he said. 'I'm sorry, Jan. Stay here and I'll be back as soon as I can.'

The two of them left Jan on his own and he turned back to the lizard's liver. He read through his notes for a while, but his concentration was broken.

But then something happened, something that would have huge consequences on Jan's life from that day on. A big black fly landed on the page before him. He brushed it away, but it came back buzzing around his head. It landed then on the table and, without thinking about it, he struck it with the book and left it smeared across the wood. He looked at the destroyed body stuck there, and a thought occurred to him. Quickly, he took up the head of the fly, still intact, put it on a glass slide and then into the microscope. Excited, he lowered his eye to the viewfinder.

His mind froze when he saw them. There was no objective reason he could use to explain that which was before him. Two men. Two men drowning in water. They wore one-piece blue suits. He saw their faces and their distressed expressions. He looked at them as they drowned and it was difficult later for him to say exactly how long this had taken. He couldn't understand either why he hadn't saved them from the water. The shock of it, perhaps. When he raised his head from the microscope, a feeling came upon him as if he had been dissected out from the real world.

And then he saw the next horror. The tree in the centre of the garden had changed. It had been a silver birch, but it wasn't silver any more. It was black. More like some charred thing from Hell than a living tree. He walked slowly towards it and saw that there was movement in the blackness, a captivating shimmer that drew the eye to it. He didn't understand what had happened to the tree until he was standing directly before it: flies. Thousands of them on every piece of bark, on every leaf, every twig. They moved their wings and that movement ran like waves across the surface, creating ripples. It was horrible.

Jan peered at the flies, his impulse as a scientist trying to get the better of his natural fear before such a fiendish sight. He wanted to place his hand upon the surface, to rub it with his fingers, but a terror ran through him at this thought. The two men in the other fly had drowned. He had killed them, or at least, he had watched them as they were drowning. There could be two more of them in every one of these flies. Now it was he that was the specimen beneath the glare of the microscope.

He kept his eyes on the tree and on the flies that were dripping from every leaf like living oil, but then he felt a new darkness coming from every direction. He looked around him and saw the reason. They were everywhere now, on every flower, every plant and bush in the garden, on the walls and on the furniture. There was even a covering of flies spread across the surface of the lawn. He stared at this terrible sight as if he were in a dream, and felt a tremor on his face, on his lips and on his hands. There was a cold tension in the air that stretched almost to breaking point. Then the tension burst like a soap bubble. Jan whimpered, and at that same moment the flies exploded into a horrible swarm, millions of them filling the air with their deafening drone. They were everywhere, in his ears, in his mouth and in his hair. He felt their little legs on his skin. He stumbled over something and felt a pain in his knee. When he got up, he saw the garden wall and ran towards it. In a second, he was there and trying to climb it, his fingers looking for a grip on the hard bricks. He let out an agonised scream as he climbed and pulled at the firm surface. Somehow, he succeeded in getting over the wall, and fell like a lump down from the top and into another world.

It was a lovely day on the other side. There was a pleasant garden, full of the colours of nature shining in the sunlight. He saw flowering plants and butterflies hovering from one to the next. It was a vision of peace, and this change from Hell to Heaven disconcerted him greatly. There was a gate open at the back of the garden, and he ran towards it now. Out on the lane, there was just a short distance between the gate and the street and he reached it quickly.

He began to walk down the street now like a soldier, his mind frozen with fear. He had never experienced anything in his life that could explain what had happened in that garden. At the canal, he sat down, looked into the calm water and felt the soft breeze around him. The questions came rushing then like a flood into his mind. What happened? What were they? Little men in the head of a fly! But how could beings like that exist in this world? Didn't God create us alone in his own image? Did he create them in the same form, or was something else happening? Wasn't Beelzebub Lord of the Flies? Is there another species living with us in this world, or was it the Devil himself that he had seen?

It was a long time before he had the courage to leave the canal. He didn't know what would await him if he were to go back to the garden, and it terrified him now that the flies would all still be there waiting for him. But he couldn't just leave the devilment he had released into Steno's garden there either. It was his duty to go back so that Steno would not walk into that horror without warning.

So he walked back, and it wasn't long before he was in front of the house again. He walked down through the dark lane and imagined that he was creeping around the back of the Devil's house. But the flies were gone. Steno was sitting on the armchair with a look of deep thought on his face, exactly as he had been when Jan had arrived earlier that day. Jan let out a great sigh of relief and laid his hand on the wall to support himself. He must have looked a terrible sight, with the knee of his britches torn and blood on his stockings, and Steno jumped up when he saw him. 'Jan, what's wrong? When I came back, you were gone and everything was on the ground. What happened to you?'

Jan didn't know how to tell this story. What happened? Wasn't that the very question that was going through his own mind? He walked past Steno to the silver birch in the centre of the garden, laying his hand on its bright bark and rubbing it. It was clean and white now after the ugly, black weight it had carried earlier. He sat at its base, his back lying against its trunk, and inhaled deeply. 'I don't know, Niels. I saw… something …

people. I don't know what they were. Maybe it was the devil. I don't know.' He told him the story as best he could.

Steno didn't speak but listened carefully until the end. Jan wanted to be objective about what he had seen and speak in the voice of a learned man, but this was difficult when he knew that he had left the world of learning and entered some other world, an obscure world that he didn't recognise. He knew as the words came from his mouth that it was an unbelievable story, and that many would regard him as a lunatic. Of course, there were indeed stories such as this in the Bible. Didn't God's terrible curse fall upon the Egyptians in the form of a swarm of flies during the time of Moses? This story was accepted readily, but it happened a long time ago and it was easy for people to accept something when its truth is part of the fabric of life. Jan and his peers wanted to weave a new fabric, a fabric in which the warp threads were made of God's miracles but the interwoven ones would be spun from reason and logic. But now the magic of the olden days was inserting itself into this new world. The mystical threads were sliding in like a snake into the garden of reason.

'Do you believe me, or do you think me deranged?' he asked in the end.

'I believe you, Jan. You're not at all deranged. You are a clever and sensible man. If you tell me that this is what happened, then that's what I believe. We don't really know what's in this world. We are only just beginning and we understand nothing. Is there another race of little men, or is the Devil awaiting us through the doors of knowledge? We don't know. When I was young, I was very sick. They didn't understand what was wrong with me, and even though I improved after a while, they kept me separated from the other children. I would have grown up lonely if it wasn't for my studies and the wonder they instilled in me for the world around us. My father was a goldsmith and

I used to look at him as he worked neatly and precisely with his hands. He died when I was six years old, but my mother married again: another goldsmith as it happened. Two hundred and forty students in my school died of the plague when I was sixteen years old. I remember what my stepfather said to me at the time: 'we cannot understand everything, son. Sometimes we can only live humbly with the ignorance.' Maybe that's not a thing we want to accept as learned men, but it's still true. I went to the university just now when Professor Van Horne called me. There was a correspondence from my mother. My stepfather has died. He was a nice man. They sent for me to return as soon as possible to Copenhagen.'

'I'm very sorry for your loss, my friend.'

'It comes to us all in the end, unfortunately,' Steno said philosophically.

'But what about the university? What about your graduation?'

'They can give me my degree *in absentia*, or not at all,' he answered abruptly, but then he stopped and thought before speaking again. 'You know that you cannot tell anyone what you saw without evidence, without proof. You can't even explain it properly to yourself. How could you explain it to the church? They will see the work of the Devil in it, and it's you that will suffer for that. Guard yourself. Put your trust in God's grace. Write to me in Copenhagen and I'll give you all the help I can.'

Jan thanked him and left. Steno went back to Denmark ten days later, leaving just a little while before Jan's own graduation from university. In the end, they did actually allow Steno to graduate *in absentia*, something that was uncommon at the time.

Scene Six

The city centre was like a clockwork toy. The traffic light's brain worked like an electronic god to stop cars, trucks and buses and to set them moving again. The drone of the engines hung constantly in the air but no one noticed it. The people scattered like insects in and out of buildings, collecting important items for their lives, some of them thrusting buggies through the crowd containing sullen toddlers who looked inattentively at the world. A big truck stopped outside the English Market on the Grand Parade and men in white coats carried half-pigs in on their shoulders. There was a group of teenagers hanging around outside the park, their own specific style designed to distinguish them from other people. An old woman with a stick walked past them, bent and covered in a coat one would imagine as being from another age, and she stared out of alien eyes like a tourist from her own time.

I walked past the gates of the park myself and stopped at the traffic lights at Singer's corner beneath the elaborate mural that stands out boldly amongst the other buildings, its intricate yellow leaves bending in on each other on a black background. I stayed there waiting until the green man would come and allow me to cross. I looked at the people on the other side of this mechanical river, all of us waiting for the same green man. Young girls dressed loudly, a middle-aged man in a worn suit, two women in mid-conversation, everyone waiting for the green man, symbol of a new Ireland. We stood there in the certainty that he would release us. We were right.

On the other side, I wove my body through the crowd until I came to the bend in the road and saw a man coming in my direction, a man I recognised immediately. His face was tanned by a foreign sun now and his dark, straight hair stretched down to his shoulders. He wore a khaki jacket from some army surplus shop and a short rough beard covered half his face. I felt the dark, dangerous presence that was always around him, something intangible yet real, something you would be suspicious of if you didn't know the man himself. He saw me before I saw him, as usual. I looked into the same sharp eyes that I recognised from my youth and saw a roguish smile on his face. It was my cousin Aogán.

'How's it goin' boy,' he said warmly and shook my hand. He was twelve years older than me but we had always been very close.

'Aogán! How are ya? How long are ya back?' I exclaimed cheerfully. He had been abroad for some time, and I have to say that I was very happy to see him.

'I've only been in Cork for three days. I went to Morocco after I left France.'

'And will you be staying around for long?'

'I have no plans, anyway,' he said casually. 'It's great now that I've met you. I didn't have your number, and wasn't sure if you were even still in Cork.'

'I am. I'm up in the college.'

'Sure, you were always the brains of the family,' he said with a smile. 'What are you up to now? Do you have time for a pint?'

'I do indeed, and maybe one or two after that as well!' I replied enthusiastically. 'Great! We'll head up to the Sin É so. Maybe there'll be a trad session there later.'

We went at our ease up the broad curve of Patrick Street, with him telling me all the while of the fine life in Morocco. We always spoke easily with one another and I loved hearing now of the long, sunny days with the Gnawa music beating around him like a machine. I knew I had a strange story of my own as well, and I wanted to tell him, but I was afraid that he'd think I was after losing my mind. That's what I'd think if someone told me a story like that.

'And life is good with you anyway? Studying hard I'd say.'

'Yeah, it's grand. I always liked the college life,' I replied half-heartedly.

If he'd asked me that question a couple of weeks before, I would have been full of news for him. It wasn't right either when he said that I'd always had the brains in the family. He left secondary school early himself, but he was a very clever man and had Irish from the cradle. He could always surprise me with the level of information he had on a broad range of subjects, particularly on Irish history. I could see that he recognised that there was something up with me, but he said nothing. We were outside the Sin É by now anyway.

There was a dark, comfortable atmosphere in the pub when we walked in. It was still too early for the music, but it wouldn't be long. There were people there I knew, or knew to see, but it was still early in the evening and the bar was quiet enough yet. People were scattered here and there around the place, sitting at the counter or over in one corner or another. It was always strange to me that Aogán knew people wherever he went. On the way up through town, he had told me that he'd met a friend of his from Knocknaheeny in a bar in Marrakesh, and I'd believe it! Here in the Sin É, the odd scoundrel came up to him now with a friendly welcome.

When he'd finished his banter, the two of us sat at the counter and turned back to Irish again. He got it from his father and spoke it in the house when he was growing up, which was uncommon enough in the city at the time. Our fathers were brothers but I didn't learn much Irish from my own father when I was young, though I learned it myself afterwards. I remember this cousin when he was a wild teenager, but even then, he was always friendly and natural with me. I think life wasn't easy for him when he was young, and he got into trouble from time to time. I didn't see him then for a long while, but I met him one day and he was very surprised and happy that I spoke to him in Irish. From that day on, we only ever spoke Irish together and I always loved the kind of language he had. It was an Irish full of the city accent, with no attempt to force a Gaeltacht affectation upon it. But it was still Munster Irish, like a good Corkman.

'Well done anyway, boy!' he said, clinking glasses with me. 'It's good to see that you're doing well.'

'I'm doing well enough, I suppose,' I replied casually, in an attempt to change the subject. 'But tell me, are you coming back to Cork now for the winter after being in Morocco?'

'Ah sure, the winters are grand here. If you'd see it in Poland. I spent one winter in Poznan and it'd freeze the bollox off ya if you stayed out in it. I still had great craic though, I have to say.'

I went out to the toilet then and there was a double whiskey waiting for me on the counter when I came back.

'Throw that back there, and tell me what's really going on with you,' he said with a smile. He could see that something was bothering me and that was his way of letting me know, without any pressure, of course. I threw back the whiskey and we were soon ready for two more pints. We carried on like that for another hour or two, him talking about the world and its mother. We'd burst out laughing easily in each other's company, as we always had before, and I forgot for a little while that little men were flying around in flies in this world.

The characters of the bar were coming and going from us at the counter and the crowd was growing all the time. There was a lively atmosphere at about half past six and Aogán got up to go to the toilet. I sat at the counter on my own for a while and could hear that the session was about to start up in the corner down the back. A piper started a tune called 'The Rolling Wave' and a fiddle and guitar followed him. I liked this tune and got the name from one of the lads in the session. The drink was having an effect on me and I was in good company with nothing to disturb me at that moment. That's what I thought anyway, until I saw something out of the corner of my eye.

A big, tall man with a wild, black beard and a long, black coat: the same man I'd met on the bus. I remember that I felt disconcerted by how he had spoken Irish to me without knowing that I spoke it myself. How could he know? It occurred to me suddenly that perhaps he and the Firíní might be working together. That would explain how he'd known that I spoke Irish. The Firíní had told him. And now he was here doing their business for them, spying on me. It didn't occur to me at the time that little men in flies hovering above my head would be far better able to spy on me than a great bulky man in the corner of the pub but, to tell the truth, I was a bit mixed up, with everything that was going on.

But his presence here dragged me out of the comfortable space I'd been in, and now I was directly back in the world of the Firíní. I had to question why he was in the pub. I had never seen this man before, but I'd run into him twice now since I'd seen the Firíní. I met him on the bus and he spoke Irish to me without knowing that I spoke it myself. He spoke about *Paradise Lost*, something that might guide me to the Firíní, as I thought, and that story related to the Devil and Beelzebub: Lord of the Flies. A cold, unreasonable fear descended on me at that moment and I began to imagine that the snares of the devil were tightening around my throat. I was raised Catholic, but it was never part of my make-up to believe in a supreme being. I was an agnostic, but when something comes to your doorstep which assaults your philosophy, what do you do? For example, if you see that there are little men going around in flies and then a big man in a long, black coat starts following you, that sort of stuff tends to undermine the foundations of your world view. Suddenly, you remember your Catholic education and you fall back into the Middle Ages. Had I walked into a snare of the Lord of the Flies? Was it that easy?

I thought of the madness in the Middle Ages in Europe: the Inquisition, the all-powerful Church, the ugly, blunt-witted fear that kept everyone jumping if even the name of the Devil was mentioned. I knew in my heart that something like this couldn't be true, but the thought of it kept going around in my mind as I looked at this huge, bearded man in the corner. Was he the Lord of the Flies in the flesh?

Maybe I had been staring at him, but he looked me directly in the eyes, nodded with a smile, and raised his glass to me. I did the same and, after he said something to his friend, he began to walk over in my direction. I felt as if things around me were happening automatically and that I had no control over them whatsoever. He was like a giant in the pub: Gargantua or his son. His enormous meaty fist was around his glass as if it were a cup from a child's tea set. Then, he was next to me at the counter. 'How's Milton getting on, Seán?' he asked in a friendly voice, but there was no question in my mind now except how it was that he knew my name.

'He's struggling with the world,' I said suddenly. 'He thinks that the truth is always beyond his reach, hovering in the air like a flying insect of some sort.'

'He's right. The annoying thing is that the truth is often going around in circles and squares in the air like flies do, without ever landing definitively anywhere. Maybe Milton was just trying to put whatever knowledge he had together in a way that he himself could understand. Perhaps we're all doing the same thing.' He looked at me and a broad smile spread on his face, his gold tooth glistening in the light of the candle on the counter. 'But it's difficult to be objective when you're in the pit of absurdity. Everything runs through your mind,' he said, winking a blue eye at me as if he understood the consternation that was going around in my head before he had come over. I felt that there was an understanding of some sort between us. 'Salvadóir is my name, Seán. It's good to meet you,' he said, and shook my hand, his own hand like a great, meaty shovel. 'The world must be after turning upside down on you. When did ye see them ... the little men?'

It was strange for me to be talking about it openly in the pub like this. The session was still going on and people were around us in general conversation. We stood there like two people within a glass bubble, separated from the crowd, a great giant and myself at the counter of the bar. For a moment, I felt like the whole thing was a dream.

'A couple of weeks ago,' I said. 'Around the same time that I met you on the bus. It happened by accident. I killed a fly that was annoying me with its drone and I put its head under a microscope out of curiosity. But when I looked through the lens, I saw them. There were two tiny men drowning in the water. They must have been inside the head of the fly. I shouted to my friend Peadar, and he saw them as well. Tiny little men! How can beings like that exist in this world? They drowned in the water. I feel guilty about that, but I wasn't able to do anything at the time. It just gave me an awful shock.'

'I'm sure it did,' he said. 'But it's a good thing that you both saw them. Maybe there are people who see them on their own and they think that they're losing their mind.'

'And then … something horrible happened,' I said. 'The room was filled with flies, thousands of them.'

'I think they do that to frighten you,' he said, 'and it works very well, to give them their due. But I always thought that people would be much more likely to believe that they were suffering from some mental aberration if they didn't put on that big drama every time.'

'Every time?' I asked him. 'So what else can you tell me about them?'

'I found out about their existence when I was young, about ten years of age,' he said. 'I remember the day when they filled our house. My mother had died before that, and there was just myself and my father. I was looking at the *Pink Panther* on the television and my father was at the table with a microscope. One minute, everything was grand, but the next minute I heard my father shout out. I remember the look of horror on his face. And then the darkness descended on everything. Every inch of the room was covered with them. You understand what that is. Anyway, my father grabbed me, threw me over his shoulder and ran out the front door with me.'

It was difficult to picture that image, someone as big as him being thrown bodily over anyone's shoulder, and Salvadóir saw this on my face.

'Well, my father was a big man too, and I was very young at the time,' he said. 'We stayed outside for some time, after which he went in again on his own. I went back when he was certain that it was safe. It was a horrible thing to see as a child.'

'But you didn't see the little men yourself?'

'I didn't, and I've never seen them, but I was with my father until he died, trying to find information on them. He tried to communicate with them as well, but they refused.'

'And what about the *Pink Panther*? Did you ever get to see the end of that cartoon afterwards?' said Aogán. He had been standing behind Salvadóir the whole time and I hadn't seen him, so great was the big man's bulk.

Salvadóir turned around to him. 'I didn't,' he answered. 'I never saw that episode again and maybe I never will, but I'm always hoping. Maybe someday.'

'That's a very sad story,' said Aogán, and he turned then towards me. 'Sorry now, I'm not eavesdropping on your conversation, but I came back from the jacks and ye were talking about little men in flies. What's that anyway: a film, is it?'

Maybe it was the drink or that I wanted Aogán's help with this horror show that had appeared in my life, but I decided at that moment to say it to him. 'It's not a film, Aogán. I saw them. I saw tiny, microscopic men. It's true.'

Aogán stopped then and a disturbed look came across his face. He didn't speak at first but looked at me for a while, trying to find some sign that I was joking. 'Jesus Christ, Seán!' he said in the end. 'I could see that there was something up when I met you, but I hadn't imagined that you'd lost your mind. Are you kidding me? Tell me you don't believe this shite!'

'If I hadn't seen it with my own eyes, Aogán, I wouldn't believe it either. I understand that it's a mad story, but I saw them and I wasn't on my own. There's a friend sharing the house with me and he saw them as well. I'm sorry about this. I didn't want to drag you into this business, and I understand you're worried that I've lost my mind, but I don't think I have. I think that what I saw that day was the truth, and not some mental defect.'

'Stop, Seán,' he said in frustration. 'It's not true. It couldn't be true.'

'I can only say that I saw them with my own eyes.'

'That's bollox, Seán. People see things all the time, moving statues and the sun dancing in the sky. There's no lunacy in this world, however big, without someone who swears that he saw it with his own eyes.'

'It's me that's talking here, Aogán. You know I'm not like that.'

'I used to know anyway. Are you trying to play a trick on me?'

'I'm not. I promise it's no trick.'

'It's not a trick, and you haven't lost your mind. That just leaves tiny men flying around in insects as if they're fuckin' flying machines! You can't think that I'd believe that. Do you think I was born yesterday?'

'Don't be too hard on him,' said Salvadóir, and he laid his big hand on Aogán's shoulder. 'It's a big mouthful to swallow, right enough, but I have experience of this in my own life and—'

'Don't go laying your hand on my shoulder, big man, or I'll teach you something new in your life,' said Aogán abruptly, and I saw a cold look in his eyes. Salvadóir saw it as well and slowly took his hand back. 'I don't know what's going on with you, Seán, but I'm not happy with this. I'll go now and I'll talk to you about this on your own later,' he said. With that, he threw back his pint and walked out the front door.

When he was gone, Salvadóir turned to me with a look of regret. 'I'm very sorry, Seán. I had planned to come to your house and speak about this privately, but when I saw you here tonight, I decided to talk to you straight away. It was a mistake, and I'm sorry about that. I'll go now as well, and I'll call to your house tomorrow afternoon so we can discuss everything properly. I'll see you then.' He threw back his own pint as if it was like an eggcup in his hand and walked towards the door.

'Grand so,' I said distractedly as he was leaving.

I was left on my own at the counter and felt a dreamlike atmosphere around me as I looked at the other people in the pub. There was a middle-aged woman hugging another woman and her make-up smudged in the energy of her affection. A young man started singing and everyone seemed to be talking with their hands. I had to leave. I finished my own pint and went out onto the street, but there was no sign of Salvadóir now. I went home.

Scene Seven

Paris, France
21st September 1664

The coach pressed through the streets of Saint-Germain like a huge, lazy bull. There was a great load of baggage on its back, along with the poor who made the journey at a reduced fare as long as they could keep a grip on the railing. The driver sat on top as well, and you would think from looking at him that his wrinkled face and tough, gnarled hands were made from the same leather as the horse tack. Those horses lifted their legs slowly now. It was six o'clock in the evening and they were tired after the long day travelling up from the south towards the city. This wasn't the biggest thing disturbing them though, nor the great coach they had to drag through the streets, but the horrible stench that assaulted their nostrils when they inhaled deeply under the heavy weight. There were eight people inside the coach who suffered the same stench, and even though they made every attempt to keep the smell out, it crept in through the cracks in the windows and the doors.

Most of the streets of Paris were unpaved, and the people of the city walked every day through a sulphurous mixture of muck, excrement, urine and blood. Human waste was thrown from windows down onto the paths below, and blood ran in the streets from the slaughter-houses every Thursday and Friday. People's feet churned this mixture into a thick black oil that stuck to everything and everyone it touched. It was impossible to clean, and its specific odour stayed on your clothes and in your nostrils.

The people of Paris lived continually in this environment, walking past the carcasses of dead animals lying in the pathways.

They drank that air with each breath and carried hunger, sickness and hardship on their faces every day. They were ragged creatures, fighting continuously against a hopeless poverty that would beat them in the end. They spent their days rummaging, looking for some way to escape a hunger that was forever on their heels. Jan looked out of the carriage window from time to time. It had been a tough journey from beginning to end. He had boarded the coach three days before in Orléans after having then been travelling for ten days. He had spent some time in Paris almost a year before when he was travelling south from Amsterdam, but he was going in the opposite direction now. He didn't stay long on that occasion but carried on to Saumur, where he spent most of the year staying with Tanneguy Le Fèvre, a learned gentleman and professor of philology at the Protestant university there. Le Fèvre was the finest of classical scholars, but also a sincere and honest person, someone who looked at the world in a new way. Jan loved the time he had spent with him, and was very impressed with how he gave a complete education to his young daughter. Anne was thirteen years old but it was clear she had a keen understanding of the classics. Jan spent long days walking the banks of the Loire and studying the animals and insects. In the evening, he would return home to a glass of wine and some discussion on a multitude of subjects: classical or contemporary literature, science, history or religion. Tanneguy could hold a comprehensive discussion on any subject, and Jan liked his easy, open manner very much.

But he was far from the fresh breezes of the Loire now. He was thrust into the narrow box of the carriage, himself and the other sweaty passengers, and steeped in this acidic air. But, in some strange way, he liked this crazy world too, the people everywhere wallowing and rolling in the muck, living vigorously and energetically in a world filled with a great multitude of stories that collided at every moment. He imagined the place as a nest of insects living in the filth: life and death in an eternal struggle each day. There was an attractive simplicity to it all. And of course, there were flies here as well. More of them than there were people … a lot more.

It was difficult for him after the event in Steno's garden because he felt that they were always nearby, looking at him. A horrible paranoia gripped him and he saw them everywhere. There was no escape from them. He would go under the bedclothes so they couldn't see him, or he filled the room with smoke to drive them out. He felt this more after Steno had left for Copenhagen, because he was alone with the knowledge that these beings existed. He would speak to nobody about it for fear that they would see him as a madman, but he didn't himself feel like one. In his mind, he was the same as he had always been; he felt no difference at all. But if it was true that those two little men were in the microscope that day and that the flies came in their thousands after that, what would it mean for the world, for the human race?

In Saumur then some normality returned. The event retreated from view as if it had been a dream, even though he knew that it wasn't. He didn't take a microscope with him on his journey but he would look at insects as his father had done before him. He received correspondence from Steno which didn't mention the horror story at all. Jan had decided to go to Paris to make contact with the learned gentlemen of the city, and then he received a letter from Steno to say that he would also be there at that time. He was happy to read that, but it awoke an awareness in him that he would have to deal with what he'd seen in the microscope sooner or later. Maybe he would do it in Paris.

The wheel of the carriage struck a rock on the street and shook all those inside. There was a young woman sitting opposite Jan with a posy of lilies in her hand. Their fragrant smell filled the carriage, but it created a strange mixture with the sharp odour that crept in from outside. Jan looked out of the window and saw frozen moments in the life of the street. Two old women arguing with each other, one with her face frozen in a hard, angry snarl, her fierce eyes directed like sharp knives at the other woman. There were people selling their wares, and others foraging through great bundles or carrying them on their backs. He saw dogs, sheep, horses, animals of every type in one mad jumble. The smell of food would enter the carriage from time to time and it was almost as bad as the other smells.

In the end, they reached the carriage stop on the quay near Pont Neuf. All the passengers disembarked here and entered the clamour. Jan felt like someone who had been thrown into the tide. The crowd pressed him from every direction. He needed a *fiacre* badly now: this was the name that Parisians gave to little horse-drawn carriages that were hired out for short journeys. Jan liked the idea very much, and hoped that Amsterdam would have this type of carriage someday. He found one easily on the bridge and it wasn't long before he was travelling through the streets of Paris again, only faster now.

He didn't have far to go this time. The fiacre went to the north side of the Seine and turned right. He was going to Rue de la Tannerie in the Marais district. When he was in Saumur, he had received an invitation from Melchisédech Thévenot to return to Paris and take part in one of the academies of learning that were being held there. Thévenot was a noble and renowned gentleman and had twice been made French ambassador, first to Geneva in 1647 and then to Rome in 1652. Two years later, he took part in the conclave of cardinals which elected Pope Alexander VII. Back in France now, he was at the centre of a world of science and learning, and he established an academy to bring together learned men from different fields. Throughout Europe, these academies were being founded in order to create a new understanding of the world and everything in it. Knowledge does not grow in a vacuum but it lives through contact with other knowledge, and Jan knew that he would grow as a scientist from this contact. It was a great honour for him, but he was nervous about meeting this important person as he darted through the streets of Paris.

The fiacre stopped suddenly and Jan looked out at the elegant houses of Rue de la Tannerie. Much of the nobility lived in this district now, and he felt that even the air was cleaner here – though in the centre of Paris that city smell was never too far away. He gave money to the driver, and alighted from the carriage with a spring in his step. When he was in Saumur, he had been steeped in Tanneguy Le Fèvre's world of classical learning. Now he was in the world of science again, and he liked this new energy very much.

When the heavy door opened, a servant with an indifferent expression stood before him. He gave him his card and asked if the master was at home. The servant looked at the card and his expression changed. 'Mr Swammerdam! The master is expecting you. Please come in,' flicking his fingers so that the driver would bring in the bags. The servant took him through elegant halls adorned with statues and beautiful paintings. The classical style was everywhere, Greek myths displayed in bright colours and gaudy, golden frames. They went upstairs and stopped before a big door on which the servant knocked. On hearing a voice from inside, he opened it and directed him in. 'Mr Swammerdam, sir, whose arrival had been expected,' he said in a grand accent.

Thévenot had been sitting on a long chair reading, but he jumped up when he saw Jan coming in. 'Mr Swammerdam,' he said warmly. 'I'm very happy to meet you at last.' Latin was the common language among the learned gentlemen of Europe, but Thévenot spoke to him here in Dutch. He hadn't heard his native tongue often since leaving the Netherlands the year before, and it was strange to hear it in an elegant Parisian house now. Melchisédech Thévenot had a remarkable appearance. He was a tall and athletic man, perhaps in his mid-forties. He didn't wear a wig, but his own black hair came down over his shoulders. Even though his clothes were expensive, they weren't as ostentatious as the Parisian upper class generally tended to wear. He had a relaxed manner, but there was a certain reticence as well. He had a remarkable face, with dark, inquisitive eyes: an intelligent face, Jan thought. He spoke in the measured voice of the nobility, but there was no self-importance or condescension to be heard in it. 'Please, sit down. I hope your journey wasn't too taxing,' he said.

'It wasn't, Mr Thévenot,' Jan said, lying, 'and I'm happy to be back in Paris. I'm not used to the big city crowds after spending such a long time in Saumur.'

'You were lucky to spend the summer there. It's a hard life here in Paris when the heat comes. The smell rises to an intolerable level, but even worse than that, I believe that sickness grows amongst the people. I'm only a fortnight back in the city myself. I spent the summer at my house at Issy. It's a pleasant spot. I'll bring you there on the next visit. It's not far.'

The servant came in to them with two glasses of brandy on a silver tray.

'But you must be hungry after your journey,' Thévenot said, turning to the servant. 'Jean, prepare a meal for our guest.'

'Thank you very much, Mr Thévenot,' Jan said humbly.

'I'm extremely happy that you're able to attend our academy, Mr Swammerdam. I know your work, and I believe that you will add a great deal to our gatherings.'

'I'm very much looking forward to the next meeting of the academy,' Jan answered. 'You have done a great deed in establishing it.'

'I've done nothing,' said Thévenot. 'It's the spirit of the modern age. Throughout Europe, people are co-operating with one another, sharing knowledge and encouraging one another. It's like an awakening. We are going to understand our place in the world better than ever before. In astronomy, physics, philosophy, medicine and anatomy, an intellectual age is growing up around us and it's wonderful to be alive to see it. You will enjoy the intellectual groups that come together here. I do my best to help with these gatherings, but, in truth, they have their own energy. I'm very happy that you're here to share your knowledge with us, and know that you are welcome to stay under my roof for as long as you want.'

Jan thanked him for his generosity. He felt as well that the hope in his host's voice was having an effect on him and awakening his own optimism in this new world.

'There are meetings in this house often and also in the house of a friend of mine, Mr Pierre Bourdelot. I'll introduce him to you tomorrow, perhaps, if you've rested sufficiently after the stress of your journey.'

So the following day Jan and Thévenot travelled south through the streets of Paris to Rue Neuve-Saint-Lambert in the Luxembourg district. Jan was excited amongst these renowned people. Bourdelot was an important man at the centre of French scientific society. He founded an academy which held regular meetings of scientists, learned people, philosophers and the general aristocracy who were interested in such studies.

The house was an extensive and elegant residence, part of a huge collection of buildings called the Hôtel de Condé. Pierre Bourdelot was the doctor to Prince Henri II de Condé and houses were bestowed on him because of this. A servant brought them through the halls of the house, again steeped in the classical style, and showed them in to the man himself, Pierre Michon Bourdelot. He was seated at a grand table down at the end of the room, the remains of a large meal before him and a glass of wine in his hand.

When he saw them, he jumped up with an energy that one wouldn't have expected and his face brightened with a broad, joyous smile. 'Melchisédech, my friend!' he exclaimed heartily. 'And this must be Mr Swammerdam. You're very welcome. Come in! Excuse my manners. I've eaten already, but please have something yourselves.'

'You're very generous, Pierre, but there's no need to prepare anything for us. Your company is nourishing enough,' said Thévenot with a smile.

Bourdelot was a big man. He had the appearance of being tall and thin in his youth, but now in his fifties there was a great deal of bulk to be seen in his face and body. He wore an enormous periwig that came down to his chest, a waistcoat of the most expensive fabric, and a white shirt, open at the neck. He had a broad, cheerful face, and it was clear that he was half-drunk at eleven o'clock in the morning. He was doctor to the Prince now, and to a good many of the grandees of Paris, but he had travelled in his life, taking care of the nobility of Europe. He went to Rome in his youth as doctor to Count François de Noailles, the French ambassador at the time. He had also been the doctor of Kristina, Queen of Sweden, and he was friendly with her even after she abdicated and gave up the crown. It was even said at the time that his advice had a great effect on the Queen's decision in that regard. He received the title of Abbé de Massey from Cardinal Mazarin, despite it being known of him that he was a complete atheist without an ounce of religion in his body. He was a libertine, free-thinker and follower of Epicurus to the core.

'And I hope, Mr Swammerdam, that your journey wasn't too distressing for you. Did you come directly down from the Netherlands?' he asked.

'No, Mr Bourdelot. I spent the summer in Saumur in the company of Tanneguy Le Fèvre, and I came up to Paris yesterday.'

'Ah! Le Fèvre is a good man,' said Bourdelot. 'I should spend some time soon outside Paris. I love it, of course, my city! And I call it 'my city', even though I wasn't born here but in Senlis, north of Paris. But, still, we have the urge at times for the bright clean air of the country and the clean water of the rivers that flow there. This poor Seine is as foul as a soldiers' cesspit. It's diarrhoea that runs through our beautiful city, unfortunately.' He began to laugh at this, and grabbed at the glass of brandy which had appeared without him noticing. He took a gulp from it and declared heartily: 'We have no choice in this life but to drink fine brandy, made from the bright waters of sweet Charente. To you my friends,' and he raised his glass. 'Let us drink a health to foul Paris, the wisdom of savants and the sweetness of fine brandy!'

'And let us not forget the generosity of he who bestows it upon us,' said Thévenot. 'I'll accept the title of bestower of brandy, my friend,' said Bourdelot, laughing. 'And my involvement, for what it's worth, in the wisdom of savants, but I do not accept responsibility in any way for the scour that flows through this city – outside of the unfortunate event that happened the other night after eating a fine meal of cassoulet. And I don't blame the cook in any way but the lowly broad beans from the New World that upset my poor innards. But that's another story!'

'So you have scientific gatherings often, sir?' Jan asked, trying to change the conversation.

'I do,' he answered. 'And I very much hope that you'll be involved in our next one. I've heard wonderful stories about your expertise in anatomy, Mr Swammerdam. I'm certain that there'll be great excitement among the company at any exhibition of your skill.'

'It will be a great honour, Mr Bourdelot, to be a part in any way in your esteemed company.'

'Marvellous, marvellous!' said Bourdelot. 'And there'll be others as well from the northern countries. Do you know Mr Nicolaus Steno from Denmark? Didn't he spend a time in your own country too?'

'He did, and I know him well!' Jan said enthusiastically. 'He's a good friend of mine. We were in correspondence lately and I'm very much looking forward to seeing him again.'

'Excellent! I'm excited now to think of the great gatherings of learning that lay before us. We are opening doors to a new world for humanity, my friends,' said Bourdelot.

'Well, let's drink to humanity,' said Thévenot cheerfully.

'To the human race,' exclaimed Bourdelot. 'And when Mr Steno reaches Paris, we'll all have dinner here together – without the broad beans, I promise you.'

'It's a deal,' said Thévenot.

When Steno's name was mentioned, Jan remembered a bright summer's day in Leiden when he looked at two tiny men drowning in a drop of water, and a phrase leapt into his mind like a dark cloud in a blue sky: Oh murderer most welcome.

Scene Eight

I felt a strange energy that night after meeting Salvadóir in the pub. I knew that it would be better not to drink anything else, so as to deal with this new twist in the tale with a clear mind. Seeing that Salvadóir and Aogán had both gone, I headed off through the city centre and the revelry that was in full flow there. Feeling animated by the alcohol, I kept my head down and marched directly through the crowd. I had enough money for a taxi, but I needed the walk to clear my head. The journey to Ballyphehane takes about a half an hour, and that's what I wanted.

So there were other people who had seen the Firíní. It was a relief to think that we weren't on our own, but it created a lot of other questions. How many of them were there? And who was that man Salvadóir? Was he telling me the truth? How did he know that we knew about the Firíní? Maybe I was actually dealing with Beelzebub after all. But I knew as well that I couldn't let that sort of superstition get a hold of me.

I marched directly out through Friar's Walk and into Ballyphehane, but when I reached the house, Peadar was out and everything was quiet and dark. I threw myself down on the sofa and looked around me. The microscope was still standing on the table like a commemorative statue to the lunacy in which I was now living. I was very disappointed that Peadar wasn't there so I could share the news with him, but I decided against phoning him. The following day would do, but I would have to find something to occupy myself in the meantime.

I took *Paradise Lost* down from the shelf and opened it. I looked at the white pages and at the characters who lived in the black ink that was speckled across them: the Devil and Beelzebub; Adam and Eve; God and Christ (even though he is never mentioned by name).

The blame is often put on the women in these stories, and that's how it is with poor Eve in Milton's poem as well. She's a very silly woman in this book and she destroys the world with her naivety. However weak Adam is as a person, he abides by God's law for the most part, but when this stupid woman goes through Paradise on her own without the guiding hand of her man, everything falls apart. It's the same story with Pandora in Greek mythology. She's the first woman in the world as well, and she's at the centre of the transition from an idyllic world to a world of hardship and death, something that happens as a punishment for her sin against God's law. What happens is that Zeus gives her a sealed jar and warns her not to use it, not even to open it. Just like Eve, she cannot resist the temptation, and every horror and tribulation comes out when she lifts the lid. It's the same story, and I've always imagined that it was the Greeks who came up with it first and the Jews and Christians made their own version later – something that created a doctrinal prejudice against women for the next two or three thousand years.

In *Paradise Lost*, Adam is like a puppy at God's feet, and he's the same when he's in conversation with the Archangel Raphael, but there's one moment in the book where he shows his nobility. He knows well that it was a mistake to eat the fruit and that Eve will be damned for it, but he does not want her to suffer her fate alone. So he chooses to follow her, and eats it as well. He chooses the love of his woman above his love of God. He chooses the human race above God and he accepts the consequences, however bad they are. This isn't in the Bible, of course, but then that's an utterly misanthropic book which portrays the human race as flawed beings from beginning to end. We will never know what damage has been done to the world through the belief that we are a tarnished species. We see this in the present day, even in the opinions of people who aren't religious. But it brightened my heart when I read this passage from *Paradise Lost*:

However I with thee have fixt my Lot,
Certain to undergoe like doom, if Death
Consort with thee, Death is to mee as Life;
So forcible within my heart I feel
The Bond of Nature draw me to my owne,
My own in thee, for what thou art is mine;
Our State cannot be severd, we are one,
One Flesh; to loose thee were to loose my self.

It gave me courage: I stood up from the sofa, raised my hand, and gave the finger to every corner of the room and to any of the Firíní that were there. 'Get to fuck, ye little bolloxes!' I said out loud. 'I am a member of the human race, and don't ye ever fuckin' forget it!' Remember now, readers, that I was still fairly drunk from being out all day with Aogán. But however drunk I was, that speech came from the heart and I felt much better afterwards.

Then I sat down again and began turning through the pages of *Paradise Lost*. Maybe it was Peadar's anagram that put it in my head, but it occurred to me that there could be a similar code in this text as well. Would Milton have put something like that in his book? Absolutely! He was from that generation who would often do it. I looked at the first line and started to make word after word from those letters, but after a while I gave up. Peadar had a clue when he made his own anagram, but all I had was drunken, pointless fishing. I felt that the Firíní were staring at me from the corners of the room, mocking me. I understood then that even if they did exist, and I wasn't mad to begin with, that there was every chance that I might be in the end. I put down the book and closed my eyes. I felt the space inside my head, a clean white space. Whatever else was there, that space existed. I opened my eyes. The last line: I would look at the last line, and then I'd go to bed.

It was short enough anyway. God had kicked out the unfortunate couple and they left Paradise on their own:

Through Eden took thir solitarie way

Were the Firíní like gods to us? I felt them staring at me in the way they say that God sees everything. You would lose your mind if you thought on that too much. Maybe the human race lost its mind because of it. I thought of the Inquisition and the thousands of horror stories that occurred around that religion: the Abrahamic belief that God stares at you, stares at your flaws ... forever staring!

I saw the first word then from that staring. I saw *stare* from inside *solitarie*. Then I found *they* and *at*, and I had *they stare at*, but there was no *me* or *you* or *them* to be seen. I remembered then that this was old English, and I found *thee*: *they stare at thee*. I spent an hour afterwards trying to make more of it but I failed and fell asleep on the sofa.

When I awoke, it was about ten o'clock in the morning and Peadar was standing over me. 'Peadar,' I said hoarsely, 'I have news for you. Put on the kettle.'

I think he sensed the seriousness in my voice and went out to the kitchen quickly. I looked down at the pieces of paper with their lists of words scattered around me, like hieroglyphics from some lost civilisation. But I think the drunkenness of the night before is often like a lost civilisation to us when we think back on it. Anyway, I opted to compose myself a bit. I folded up the papers and put them under the cushions of the sofa.

Peadar came back with two cups of coffee and laid them on the table. 'Ok, what's going on?' he said.

I told him about what had happened in the pub and everything that Salvadóir had said to me. I told him as well that my cousin Aogán had overheard us talking.

'Well, he'll probably forget about it, I suppose,' he said.

'I don't know about that, but leave it to me anyway. I'll tell him something.'

'And this man Salvadóir didn't say how he knew about *us*?'

'He didn't. I was thinking about that myself last night.'

'Did he say at least when he'd be in touch with us?'

'Today: that's what he told me last night anyway. He knows where the house is.'

'Let's just wait so.'

I thought again of the anagram that I'd made from the last line of *Paradise Lost* the night before, or half an anagram, I should say. I was reluctant to mention it to him, and I was almost certain that I was going astray with it, but seeing as we had nothing else to do but wait, I pulled the papers out from the corner of the sofa. 'I was trying to make something out of this last night. I'm ninety-nine percent certain that it's nothing but waffle, but maybe you'll be able to see something in it,' I said, handing them to him.

'What is it?'

'It's an anagram of the last line of *Paradise Lost*, or part of an anagram anyway. I wasn't able to get any further than that.'

He took the bundle from me without complaint, even though I could sense that he didn't quite believe that the book had any bearing on the issue. He looked through it for a while before giving the pages back to me. 'I'm sorry, but I can't see anything in it,' he said with disappointment. 'I had a clue with that book by Jan Swammerdam, but I'm not sure about that line. We could waste our lives with anagrams anyway. Let's wait until we find out what this fella Salvadóir has to say.'

'You're probably right,' I said.

So we waited there patiently and in a half an hour we heard the doorbell and looked at each other nervously.

'Maybe that's him now,' I said.

We went out to the front door together. The big man was very friendly to me the night before and I felt comfortable in his company, but too many questions had occurred to me in the meantime and now I felt uneasy again. We opened the door and there he was like a great, hairy whale on the doorstep with a broad gold-toothed smile on his face. 'How are ya, Seán!' he said cheerfully. 'I'm here to continue our conversation, as I promised.' Framed by the door like that, I thought him even bigger than I'd remembered him the night before. 'And you must be Peadar,' he said and stretched a huge hand out to him. 'Did Seán tell you that he met me last night, and about the subject of our conversation?'

'He did. We were expecting you. Come in, please,' Peadar replied.

The three of us then walked through the narrow hallway, with Salvadóir almost filling the space, and sat down in the living room. He took the sofa himself and we sat on other chairs opposite him. We looked at each other for a moment, uncertain how we would start, but it was he who broke the silence.

'Again Seán, I'm very sorry that your friend heard us talking last night. I'm always very careful with this subject, but, for some reason, I didn't notice that he was there listening to us.'

'That was my cousin Aogán. I'll speak to him later and I'll tell him ... I don't know ... something. Don't worry about it anyway, Salvadóir. He's a good man.'

'What can you tell us about—' began Peadar.

'The little men?' said Salvadóir, smiling. 'Well, I'll tell you everything that I know about them. You saw something frightful, something that shocked you. I told you last night, Seán, about the way in which I myself found out about their existence. My father saw them when he did the same thing that you did. I don't know how it happens or why. Thousands of people must look every day through a microscope at the head of a fly and they see nothing. But from time to time, people see them and their world turns upside down. I've never seen these little men myself, but I witnessed how they filled the room when my father saw them. He told me about what he had seen, and I followed him as he tried to make sense of it all. As far as I know, they don't consent to any direct communication with the human race, and so we need to do some detective work in order to get any information. I can't say what they are exactly, but I do know that they have been amongst us for a very long time and that other people have seen them over the years. If we can get the information which those people collected, we'll be closer to the day when we can make sense of all this.'

'I think it's a good plan, Salvadóir, and as it happens, we've already started on it ourselves,' Peadar said in his pragmatic voice. 'But perhaps we're just running ahead a bit too fast. Forgive me now, but there are questions other than those relating to the Firíní. How did you know that we'd seen them? I must say it seems very odd that people with knowledge of things like this might just bump into each other on the bus, or in the pub.'

A broad smile spread across Salvadóir's face and his gold tooth sparkled. 'You're right, Peadar, and I'm sorry about that. I've spent years now without being in the company of anyone else who's actually seen them. I'm excited that I can talk to people about this now, and I'm running ahead too quickly, as you said. I wanted to tell you everything last night, Seán, but I see now that it's suspicious that I come here to you out of the blue. I've been searching for these little men for most of my life, but I'm also looking for other people who've found out about them too. This is easier now than it used to be, because we have technology today that puts us in contact with one another. You put the English words *little men in flies* into an internet search recently, didn't you?'

'I did,' said Peadar. 'I thought it a good place to start, what with the amount of information that's there.'

'You were right, even though there's nothing there about them at all,' said Salvadóir. 'But before my father died, he knew someone who worked in a certain company: a search engine on the internet. This person did my father a favour, even though it was against the law, and now if anyone looks for little men in flies on the internet, I get an email about it. I often get emails that don't relate to the matter at all, but there are times when it definitely does.'

'And have you ever found these people?' I asked.

'No. It's very difficult. I can't get their address, just the general geographical location and some of the other things that were searched for from the same computer. I failed every time, unfortunately. This is the first time that it's worked. It surprised me when I saw that other people in Cork had seen them. I think that this is a special place for them somehow, but that's a different matter. I saw that you were looking at the university library website for information about entomologists. I went in with the plan that I'd just hang around those shelves and then – miracle of miracles – it worked. I heard you talking, and I heard you, Seán, when you said that you were going home. So, I followed you. I spoke to you on the bus and jumped off directly after you, though you didn't see me in the fog. I'm sorry, but I didn't want to say anything openly to you in the library. I understand how that's strange now after I approached you so easily in the pub.'

Myself and Peadar looked at each other for a while before speaking. I thought myself that the story was plausible enough, even though I didn't like how easily the internet company was able to find us. I saw in Peadar's eyes that he agreed with me about Salvadóir's story, or at least that he was willing to discuss the matter with him. 'It's credible, I suppose,' I said. 'But you must be able to tell us something about the Firíní themselves, something you've found out about them over the years.'

'I can't say anything for sure, but there are some good theories. My father spent the last part of his life trying to answer that question and he failed. At first, he thought they were aliens from outer space, but after a while he changed his mind about that and came to believe that they were a native species to this planet.'

'But how is it that they have human form?' I asked.

'I don't know, but it's possible for two species who are not related to be very similar. In the Jurassic Period, millions of years before butterflies appeared on the planet, there existed lace wings or *Kalligrammatidae*. They were exactly the same as present-day butterflies, but without any evolutionary link between them.'

'But if they are a native species, how is it that the human race doesn't have more information on them, that we don't even know they exist?' Peadar asked.

'I believe that they're more evolved and perhaps more intelligent than us. The simplest answer to that question is that they just don't want us to know.'

'Is there no information about them so?' I asked.

'There is information, but it's difficult to come by, and difficult to put together. My father met a man called Casper Vogel, or Birdy, as everyone called him. He knew about them as well, from his own historical and literary studies, and he and my father became good friends. They shared whatever knowledge they were able to gather, and it's from Birdy that I got most of the information I have. He's dead now as well – he died six months after my father – but he called me a week beforehand to say that he'd found some new discovery – something major, he said. He promised to show it to me as soon as he got his hands on it, but he died before he got the chance.'

'Was his death under suspicious circumstances?' Peadar asked.

'Well, I certainly thought it was anyway. The autopsy said that it was a heart attack, but there were unexplained bruises on his body. There was something else as well. On the day he died, he sent me a text from his mobile phone. I told this to the Guards, but they thought that it was just a mistake because he was an old man who couldn't use his phone properly.'

'What did the text say?' I asked.

'It was very strange. It said *comix bag*. That was all. I've spent years of my life thinking about those two damned words, but I can make no sense of them whatsoever. Neither myself nor Birdy had comics. As well as that, he was a professor and always very precise in his writing. He wouldn't write *comix* instead of *comics* unless he had a reason to. On top of that, someone broke into my house a week afterwards but nothing was stolen. It was all very strange and I was never able to figure it out.'

'So there's a chance that the Firíní killed Birdy. Are we ourselves in danger?' I asked nervously.

'Unfortunately, I can't say that you're not, but I'm forty years old and they've never tried to kill me. Even if it's true that they were behind Birdy's death, how could microscopic men burgle or ransack a house. I think myself it was a normal person who did that.'

'But if it's true that they're more evolved than us, how is it that we saw them at all?' Peadar asked.

'Maybe it happens by accident,' Salvadóir said, shrugging his shoulders, 'but it doesn't happen often. Birdy believed that people saw them years ago, around the time when the microscope was first created, and that this invention took them by surprise. People saw them, and told others about what they'd seen. Birdy only ever had second-hand information, but he was able to collect these stories until he could put them together like a jigsaw puzzle. But the evidence stopped around the end of the seventeenth century. Nobody saw them again for hundreds of years, but then about seventy years ago, people began to see them again. I don't know why.'

'The first time that we have evidence of them so is the seventeenth century?' asked Peadar.

'Yes – definitive evidence anyway. But my father believed they'd had connections with human civilisation for thousands of years. Before he died, he was looking at the history of the Sumerians, but there was nothing definite in his notes. Birdy had gathered a great deal of information himself, but, unfortunately, I can no longer lay my hands on it. His wife took everything when he died and she won't allow me to have access to it.'

'And who were the people who saw them in the seventeenth century?' Peadar asked.

'The scientists during the Age of Enlightenment. Birdy believed that Galileo knew and that he spread the story among other people on the Continent. He thought as well that it had some bearing on his trouble with the Church, but maybe he was only guessing there.'

'Who were the people on the Continent? Have you heard of the name Jan Swammerdam?' said Peadar.

'I have,' replied Salvadóir, scratching his beard. 'I did my own research on Swammerdam later because I knew that Birdy believed that he was involved in some way. He was from the

Netherlands, but he was in contact with people in France and England as well.'

'Do you speak Dutch?'

'I do indeed.'

'Maybe you recognise this,' Peadar said, handing him a piece of paper.

'Yes! That's the beginning of *Bybel der Natuure*, the first line, isn't it? I read it but I didn't find any clues in it.'

'And what about this?' said Peadar, handing him the poetry book.

Salvadóir was stunned when he read the poem and the lines written on top of the page, but that was nothing compared to his surprise when Peadar told him that it was an exact anagram of the line from *Bybel der Natuure*. We could see the joy on his face as he studied the two texts. He raised his head from time to time with a look of elation. 'It's incredible!' he exclaimed. 'It's fantastic. Well done. This is a huge achievement.'

'It was Peadar who figured it out,' I admitted.

'I had a clue, as you see on top of the page,' said Peadar.

'I see that,' said Salvadóir. '*Swammerdam Bybel der Natuure, lijn 1.* It shows that connection between the two texts very well. Very old penmanship as well, apparently. But where did you find this little book?'

'It was in between the pages of another book that I found in the university library. Somebody left it there for some reason,' Peadar said.

Salvadóir stopped then for a little while and I saw that he was thinking deeply about something. 'Maybe Birdy left it there,' he said. 'Anyway, well done! Excellent work. It's a message from times past, someone speaking out plainly about the existence of the little men, and it's Swammerdam! I can see the religion in this poem as well, and he became more religious when he came under the influence of Antoinette Bourignon. She was a woman who founded her own religious cult. Swammerdam wrote a great deal of religious verse in his own book before he died, but the poems were cut out when it was edited after his death. He was very ill in life and it's believed that he had malaria, but this is exactly what we see here: 'I escaped 'til fever struck, a hell'. But the next line is incredible: 'Oath of the lord of the cruel yellow plague went awry!' Is that saying that he was actually in contact with them? He says that he 'spoke to the men' – *met de heeren* – and he calls them 'angels of time'… *Engelen van des tijd.* This is amazing! It appears that they accepted a promise from him.But what promise? A promise that he wouldn't spread the story of their existence if they let him live?'

'Isn't it interesting that it says *'t Waaren er twee*, that there would be two of them in the flies even then, three hundred and fifty years ago,' said Peadar.

'Very interesting indeed! But how did you do all this? You must speak Dutch very well.'

'I do. My mother is from the Netherlands.'

'Birdy taught it to me,' said Salvadóir, and I saw a sentimental smile dart across his face. 'Maybe it wasn't him who left the poetry book in the library. I would have heard about it before now. But who else?'

'If this poem was written by Swammerdam, how did it come to be published in this book and attributed to Catharina Questiers?' Peadar asked.

'I don't know, but it's very interesting. It was published in the year 1756, but Questiers and Swammerdam were long dead by then. It's a collection of different poets. Maybe it was the publisher's mistake. I know Questiers' work well, but I've never seen this poem. I don't think it goes well with her other work either. The reason for that, of course, is that she didn't write it at all. But, somehow, this poem was found amongst her personal papers and was accepted as being part of her work. Maybe it was later recognised as not being hers and that's the reason it wasn't circulated later. She and Swammerdam knew each other anyway because they were in the same circles in Leiden and Amsterdam. Those academic circles in the Netherlands were wonderful back then. The Dutch published far more books than anyone else at the time, and of course, they often used the anagram as a sort of copyright.'

Just then, I saw a cloud come across Salvadóir's face. He stopped speaking and looked down at his hands. When he looked up at us again, I saw an understanding mixed with a sort of shame in his eyes.

'One moment, lads,' he said and he took a pen and a notebook from his pocket. He spent a little while jotting down something and then laid his great palm across his brow.

'Jesus Christ!' he exclaimed. 'I'm a fool! Excuse me now, but I have to go. I'll come back to you in a while.' He was halfway out through the door before we had the chance to say anything. He stopped then, wrote something on a page of his notebook and gave it to me. 'This is my phone number. I'll be back tomorrow with news of some sort. Maybe it'll be important news. Goodbye for now.' He let himself out through the front door and was gone.

Scene Nine

Thévenot's house, Paris.
22nd December 1664

For the sake of decorum, a piece of white linen was first placed over the man's face and kept in position with pins. Many of them wouldn't care, of course, but there were some who might be squeamish, or even conscientious about such a thing. They all gathered around him tightly so they could see everything. The implements were laid out neatly on the table: a collection of sharp knives, a saw, pinchers, and other small things whose function was not yet clear to everyone in the group. They were excited now to be here for this special occasion.

Steno had removed his coat and rolled his sleeves up beyond his elbows. He took a firm grip on the crown of the head and cut through the skin directly above the bridge of the nose with a sharp knife. It wasn't long before his fingertips were reddened with the work. He cut a careful line around the skull until he was back to the point at which he had started. Then he took the saw and followed the same line, as careful again as one could be. The group listened to the sound of saw on skull, that rough grating of metal on a human body. It was an ugly sound, and a painful grimace came over one or two of the faces around the table. He made his way slowly and precisely around the head, and the eyes of the assembled men followed the work patiently until it was done. He laid down the saw and raised his own head to look at the group. With one hand under the chin and another on top of the head, he raised the cap to show them all the jewel inside.

In that place where the vile head of a criminal had been, they now looked upon the prize. It was like a pearl from an oyster: the human brain. Steno took it up from its cradle like a new-born baby made of fine porcelain. He thought to himself that it was like Athena, born from the head of Zeus, but it occurred to him then that it would be strange for a Greek goddess to be born from the head of a criminal, hung in Place de Grève the day before. But he was finished with this ugly head now anyway. The piece of linen had fallen from its face while he was working and he saw the misshapen grimace on its features. He could see broken teeth, and the tongue that would never again speak, hanging from that twisted mouth, squeezed out by the rope, one would imagine. The eyes were still open, but clouded now in death, with the complexion of watered milk. Steno imagined this man when he was just three years old, a lovely little boy playing through the streets of Paris, the apple of his mother's eye. He felt a sorrowful stab in his heart when he thought of it, and of the destiny of his species.

He placed the pearl on a marble slab that had been prepared for it in advance, and then took the head itself, the rubbish that was left behind, and put it back in the rough sackcloth bag from which it had come. Then he cleaned the table and washed his hands. The order of academia had come back to the place which a minute before seemed like a slaughter-house.

Steno was ready to begin.

He cleared his throat, straightened his back and spoke directly to the men who were gathered around him: 'Gentlemen, instead of promising to satisfy your curiosity in what concerns the anatomy of the brain, I do confess here, sincerely and publicly, that I know nothing of the matter. I should wish with all my heart to be the only one forced to speak thus, for I could then take advantage, over time, of the knowledge of others. And it would be very fortunate for humanity if this organ of the body, the most delicate of all, and prone often to dangerous diseases, was as well-known as many philosophers and anatomists imagine it to be. Few of them follow the direction of Mr Sylvius, who now speaks of this matter with uncertainty, although he has worked on it more than anyone else. The majority are undoubtedly those who take great pains to do absolutely nothing in relation to our understanding of this organ, yet it is they who are also so prompt to assert a great multitude in its regard. They will give you the description of the brain and the arrangement of its parts with the same self-confidence as if they had been present when this marvellous machine was built and had understood all the plans of the Great Architect.'

It had been a great subject of debate amongst the public for some time. What connection was there between the mind and the body? At what exact point did that connection happen? Was the soul in the brain? Descartes wrote of these questions, of course, and his opinions on them were often in the conversations of learned gentlemen. He had a hypothesis which accepted the common belief of a psychic breath, or animal spirits as they were called, in the body. These were imagined as light wandering forces that circulated through the body and carried feelings between the muscles and the brain. Descartes' hypothesis was that the pineal gland was the point at which this connection was made. It appeared to him that this was the seat of the soul in the body and the place in which every thought was created. Steno had great respect for Descartes. He had created a system that put a structure to learning in such a way that one could begin with the knowledge that was certain and extend out from this through the function of reason. It was a scientific system that worked for every type of experimentation, and his own precise methodical mind liked it very much.

But could one say with certainty that this was the point at which the link between the brain and the body was made? Where was the evidence? Certainly, the pineal gland was exactly in the centre of the brain and at the point at which the spine meets the brain, but what evidence was that? It was only a hypothesis, but still if you say something, you should do your very best to prove it. Unfortunately, that good man was now dead, but he had a great many supporters who weren't. There were the Cartesians, who adhered dogmatically to their patriarch even though the Pope had put his works on the List of Prohibited Books the year before. There were some of them in the room now.

Steno would begin with that which was certain: the brain itself. It was like a lump of marble as it lay there before him. The wet, wrinkled mass shone in the wintry sunshine that crept in through the window. A few weeks before, he had seen the sarcophagus of Bishop Simon Matiffas de Buci in Notre Dame Cathedral. A marble statue of the bishop lay on top with a little lion at his feet. Steno thought of that lion's mane, carved in hard waves of grey stone, when he took up the knife from the table. He spoke clearly as he illustrated the parts of the brain, the way in which it was divided perfectly into two halves, the lumpy surface which was like a ball of white maggots, and he cut into it with a sharp knife.

The first thing that was clear to the assembled group was his great dexterity, something he may have inherited from his father and stepfather, who were both goldsmiths. Everyone there was impressed by his exactness and patience. He took great care to make sure they could all see everything, and his steady voice illustrated and explained the process from beginning to end. He himself listened to that voice as both speaker and listener, being within it and yet outside of it at the same time, living in two places at once: in the room and in the brain. Was that his own brain, or the brain on the table? It was a difficult question because they were both the same at that moment.

He walked through the cathedral of the brain like a visitor, searching every porch and corner, every secret nook, thinking of it as a city. Were there little men living there? Were they there now looking up at him as he performed an exhibition before the Paris intelligentsia? Maybe they were responsible for whatever offence this criminal had committed. But if there were little men in the head of a fly, that's not to say they were in every head of God's creation. He gave us freedom and would not leave us to the snares of the Devil or the captivity of those little creatures, whatever they were. Jan told him that the creatures he saw that day were in human form, and so in God's image, but they certainly weren't human. Yet, no one could say either that they were angels or devils.

Steno was happy that Jan was in the city before him when he reached Paris. He was a good friend and Steno looked at him always as a sensible and intelligent man. If someone else had told him such a story, he wouldn't have believed it, but Jan was a different sort of person. He wasn't a liar, or a lunatic. However terrible the story was, Steno believed that he had seen that horror exactly as he said. But where did that leave them? One would think that scientists could create some sort of plan, but this was beyond the realms of reason. Jan wanted to talk about it when they met in Paris, and Steno would have liked to provide him with some explanation, but there was no explanation to be found. He could give no help whatsoever except a warning not to speak of it in public. He knew in his heart that information like that could be dangerous to anyone who would circulate it.

But, as well as that, there was more involved here than fear of church and state. As learned men, could they put forward a thesis without an understanding, or even the beginning of an understanding, of the truth of the case? Steno understood that there are two things you can do when you don't know the truth. You can say whatever you want, safe in the knowledge that nobody will call you a liar. Nobody can call a blind man a liar, for example, if he tells you that your shirt is blue. But, on the other hand, you can keep your mouth shut until you have something to say. The first choice is the way of the charlatan; the second is the way of the true scientist.

He directed the point of his scalpel at something like a nut in the centre of the brain: the pineal gland. 'And so, gentlemen,' he said, 'we can all see here exactly where the pineal gland is situated. It is not situated in the middle of the ventricles at all. As well as that, we do not see arteries around it, but veins. We must therefore make the deduction that Mr Descartes was not correct in this respect. As such, we can see no evidence that the pineal gland is the seat of the soul in the brain.'

Someone from the audience then spoke out boldly, his voice intrusive after the solemnity of the demonstration. It was Nicolas Boileau-Despréaux, a poet and learned gentleman who was normally referred to just as Boileau. 'But Mr Descartes says more than that,' he proclaimed loudly. 'He shows us that this gland is the only thing in the brain which is not doubled. As we see one thing with two eyes, as we hear one thing with two ears, we think only one thought at any one time and, of course, we have only one soul. Now, since it is the only solid part of the brain that is single, it must be the seat of thought, and therefore the seat of the soul. There is no other explanation but to say that the soul is not connected to a solid part of the body at all but only to the animal spirits that flow through everything like breezes in the air and, of course, one must believe that this would be altogether too absurd.'

'I understand your argument, Mr Boileau-Despréaux, but I believe that there are so many errors in this theory of Descartes that we cannot accept it. He thought that the pineal gland was situated in the middle of the ventricles, but Galen knew 1,500 years ago that this was not true. He thought that the animal spirits entered the pineal gland through the carotid artery, but again Galen knew well that there were no arteries around it but veins. Descartes looked at these animal spirits as a sort of wind or lively flame, and said that they filled the ventricles in the same way as the wind fills the sails of a ship. But one hundred years ago Andreas Massa showed the world that the ventricles are filled with a fluid, as opposed to any kind of air or flame. And then you say that the pineal gland is the only place in the brain which is single and solid. But what does that matter? What rule is there that says that the soul must be in any one place in the body? Or that this place must be a solid part? As I said at the beginning of this demonstration, we have no knowledge of the brain. Posidonius de Byzantium said imagination was to the fore of the brain, reason in the centre and memory at the back. How did he know this? I will tell you: supposition. Qusta ibn Luqa had another theory, and Mondino dei Luzzi yet another, but the plain truth is that we do not know how the brain works or what connection it has to the soul. This is the greatest danger: supposition. Let us leave that as it is, and accept our ignorance with humility.'

Boileau lowered his head and nodded to accept Steno's reasoning. The demonstration came to an end and everyone praised him for his dexterity and eloquence. There was a good group of learned gentlemen there and many of them wanted to speak to him now. Hands were shaken and the new progress in anatomy was praised. Even Boileau himself was gracious enough and he lost much the pomp he had when he'd spoken earlier.

The group moved into a different and more comfortable room and Steno saw Ole Borch coming towards him through the crowd. Borch was his old teacher in the Vor Frue Skole in Copenhagen. He was fond of the old man, and was happy when he came to Paris and found that Borch had arrived before him. He had been travelling now for four years with his three wards, the sons of his patron, Joachim Gersdorff. It was a tragic story. Gersdorff had died three years earlier in suspicious circumstances, or that's what was said at the time anyway, and his ex-wife was charged with poisoning him. She herself was put to death a fortnight later and her head and body parts placed up on wheels and stakes in the town. That was the mother of these three sons who followed Borch around the room now like frightened lambs. The four of them were on a tour around Europe, and they had visited Steno in the Netherlands before they went to England. They had been in Paris now for a year. 'My boy, my boy. Excellent!' Borch said enthusiastically to him now. 'You were and will always be the gem of our school. The skill of your hand and the eloquence of your voice would overcome anyone I've yet seen. May I say to you, tears almost fell from my eyes when I beheld your precision.'

'Thank you very much, Mr Borch. Whatever skill I have, it is from your wonderful instruction that I received it,' Steno said generously.

'It's kind of you to say so, Niels, but the truth is that you were always talented. But tell me, do you remember the three sons of Mr Gersdorff – Christian, Frederik and Casper,' he said, pointing to the three young men behind him.

'I remember them well,' said Steno. 'Thank you very much for coming today to my humble demonstration, gentlemen.'

'We liked it a great deal,' said Frederik, the most outspoken of the lambs.

'Mr Steensen, may I ask you a question?' asked Casper, usually the quietest son.

'Of course,' he answered politely.

'If the soul is situated in the brain, what do we know of the escape of the soul after death when the body is... decapitated... as in the case of this man here?'

Steno thought of the head of Casper's mother being put up on a stake, a woman who had not yet reached the age of forty. Her name was Øllegaard, if he remembered correctly. He had met her only once, but he remembered well just how beautiful she was, with warm bright eyes that grabbed your attention. She was a lot younger than her husband Joachim, and it was a great scandal when she fell in love with the notorious rake Kai Lykke. The marriage ended in divorce then, maybe seven or eight years before Joachim died – before they both died. He didn't know whether or not there was any basis for the allegations against her. Maybe she was guilty.

Casper had a sickly pale complexion now, a fragile creature with fair curly hair whose lips trembled as he spoke.

'That's a very good question, Casper,' Steno said, 'but I'm sorry to say that I don't have an answer, because there is no answer to it in this world, as yet anyway.'

'Thank you very much, Mr Steensen. It is probably then in the world to come that we shall get answers to ... that sort of question.'

'We will indeed, Casper,' he answered, as kindly as he could.

Steno saw Jean Chapelain coming towards him. He was a poet, literary critic and a good friend of Thévenot, and they had met a few times before at different occasions. He often had an irate expression on his face, but was friendly enough when you spoke to him. 'Very interesting indeed, Mr Steno. I was very impressed with your skill and knowledge,' he said, and he shook hands with him warmly. He knew Ole Borch and the three Gersdorff sons already, and he greeted them politely. 'I have to say,' said Chapelain more quietly, 'that you pleased me greatly with your clever answer to the Cartesians in the room. That's not to say that I am completely against Descartes, our illustrious countryman, but at the end of the day, nobody should be as dogmatic as that.' He winked at Steno conspiratorially and, with a wry smile, glanced in Boileau's direction. Steno understood that there was some animosity between the two men, but he didn't know why.

'Well, we'll have to be going now,' said Borch. 'We will take with us the insight that you gave us today. Farewell for now, Niels. May the blessings of God be on you and upon your important work.' They left with a humble bow from the sons of Gersdorff.

Steno saw now that Thévenot and Jan were coming towards him. 'Congratulations, Niels,' said Thévenot. 'That was excellent! You are right as well in your warning against supposition. People often make the leap between theory and belief too early because it is so enticing for them to believe that they understand something, that they have answers. We are all guilty of it, even a man like Descartes. It takes bravery and humility to say that we don't know.'

'That's what I said to him,' said Chapelain, 'but, of course, I said it much better than that.'

'Well, I'm sorry, Jean, but naturally, I could never compete with you, the finest of poets.'

'Sir, I accept your apology with humility.'

'You are almost as humble as Boileau now,' said Thévenot with a smile.

'May that witless dolt be afflicted by every diarrhoetic spasm there is! And don't you be trying your antics with me now, Melchisédech! Donkey piss to that minnow!' said Chapelain, half-laughing. 'But he's still a very nice man, even though he couldn't write a line of poetry if he were to spend his life at it.'

'I'm certain that you're right, Jean. He is a very nice man. But anyway,' said Thévenot, turning back now to Steno, 'Bourdelot sent us a note. He asked your forgiveness for not being present today, but he invited us to his house.'

'Now?'

'Well, there are still some people here who would like to talk to you about your demonstration. That's the problem that comes when you do good work. But we could go in a while.'

'Let's go so!' said Steno enthusiastically.

'Wonderful! Will you come with us, Jean?' Thévenot asked Chapelain.

'Unfortunately, I cannot, my friends, but enjoy your night. You deserve a celebration, Mr Steno.'

They stayed for another hour discussing the workings of the brain with the learned gentlemen of France, and then Steno, Jan and Thévenot went across the city to Bourdelot's house. The streets were almost empty on this cold, wintry night. There was a covering of snow on everything in the city and a silvery full moon appeared now after a few days of cloudy skies. Jan felt an energy in the air that he couldn't explain. Perhaps it was the great crowd in Thévenot's house, or the beauty of this white night.

Bourdelot was before them at the top of the stairs when they came in. He wore a doublet of rich red velvet and a thick periwig. 'I'm terribly sorry, my friends … and you, Mr Steno. I was called to practise my humble doctoring, and was compelled to answer. A duchess who thought she was dying. It was just gas in the end. Isn't it awful when the farts of the nobility come between you and the wonders of science. Come up and tell me everything,' he said exuberantly.

They went up to the dining room, and before long servants entered with a generous meal and laid everything out on the table. They all sat down without ceremony and began to eat. After a long feast, they went to the study with their glasses of brandy and Bourdelot continued his stories on the way. When they got there, he threw himself into a big, comfortable chair, laughing to himself. His periwig was slightly askew at this point, and locks of his own black and grey hair fell out to one side. There were tears in his eyes which gave them a sparkling appearance in the firelight, and he threw one leg up on a footrest beside him.

'There was uproar, of course,' he said, 'and even though they'd hoped that their petulance wouldn't intrude on their manners, that's exactly what happened in the end. He was a wheedling fop from the beginning, this fellow Magnus. Magnus Gabriel de la Gardie was his name, and he was appointed Marshal of the Realm as well as Lord High Treasurer. He slid his way in there like an oiled maggot through cracks in a dead tree. Queen Kristina was very taken with him when she was young. He was a learned person, which was very important to her, and he was able to organise the pomp and extravagance of the court for her as well. She was happy with that, as of course, was the court. But I don't believe that the poor girl was ever happy being a queen. She was a wonderful scholar and had all the poems of *Ars Amatoria* learned off by heart. She was a driven person as regards learning, and as we know, poor Descartes fell afoul of this academic enthusiasm of hers. She gave him orders to rise very early each morning in that perishing Swedish cold. That was the end of him, and he was only fifty-three at the time.

'I came up two years later because the Queen's own health had failed. She followed that regime of study with severe controls on herself, and by the time I reached Stockholm she was practically exhausted. Her eyesight was failing, she had neck pain, and her blood pressure was flowing like the waters of the Seine. Ultimately, her nerves had failed. Those bunglers around her, who called themselves doctors, were unable to do anything except blood-letting – that insane barbarity! Anyway, I said to her: 'Of course, your eyes are failing and you have a pain in your neck. Isn't your face stuck in a book sixteen hours a day? Throw all those books out of your room,' – and she did it! I gave her orders to get some sleep at night and to lie in a bathtub: in other words, to take it easy. I started to tell her funny stories and she laughed. That's all I did, to be honest, but her health improved wondrously. It was a miracle! Would you believe it?

'But for some reason, the other crowd didn't like that, especially this fellow Magnus Anus, as I called him, and the mother of the Queen herself, Maria Eleonora von Brandenburg. They said that I was trying to lead her astray, and to be honest, maybe I was – but I did it to improve her life. I gave her a book of poetry that I'd hidden in my bag, a collection of poems by Pietro Aretino. It's an obscene, erotic work for the most part. Aretino loved the pleasures of the flesh, but it was never said of him that he was altogether taken with the company of women – if you understand me. I gave her this book, along with stories of the man himself, and she liked it very much. Between you and me, Kristina wasn't terribly taken with the company of men either, and she completely refused them when they pressed the idea of marriage on her at court. She was very fond of her close companion Ebba Sparre, however.

'To bring my story to an end, I returned to France with my pockets full after turning a queen into a devotee of Epicurus. That lout Magnus lost the Queen's affections sometime afterwards, and she got rid of him. But when she gave up the crown a year later, Karl Gustav took it, and wasn't that buffoon Magnus married to his sister, so the oiled maggot slid back into his place again.'

Bourdelot raised his glass in the air and proclaimed: 'To Kristina, a lovely girl and the Queen of Sweden too. She had both those honours. May we live in a world where more respect is given to the former than to the latter. *Bibo Ergo Sum*!'

They all raised their glasses in honour of the storyteller as Bourdelot emptied his own. Even though Thévenot had heard the story many times before, he never grew tired of the spirit of the speaker. Jan had a light heart in this company of wise and learned men. His head was light enough as well after the wine and brandy he had drunk. He liked this life in Paris. It was a lively and energetic city, with beautiful architecture that stood out like gaudy flowers growing in a pile of cow dung. You needed to look at the city through a lens of grime that stuck to everything, but it was still charming.

Of course, Jan very much liked the scientific academies in Paris. That wasn't to say that there weren't scientific circles in the Netherlands. In truth, far more works on the subject of science and the natural world were published in his own country then in Paris. But he liked this group of people. They were driven and enthusiastic about the study of science, and yet also filled with a spirit of wildness. Maybe the Catholicism of the country was behind it with the pomp and drama of that religion taking effect on them.

Jan liked Thévenot's company a great deal. He was an intelligent and generous person, and showed his generosity to Steno by offering him rooms in his house. Jan and Steno were thus both staying under the one roof in Rue de la Tannerie. Not only was Thévenot a patron of the sciences, but he himself was also a scientist, and the three of them often conducted experiments together in the house. One day, he showed Jan an invention of his own, something simple but very clever. He called it a spirit level: a vial of liquid with a bubble in it, stuck to a straight piece of wood. When something was perfectly level, the bubble would be in line with marks on the vial.

But Jan had greater issues now than academies of learning and the company of the nobility. He had seen two men drowning in a drop of water and could not wash that image from his mind. He had hoped that there would be some information to be found in France on what had happened that day, but he was afraid now to bring up the subject with these people. He wanted to speak to Steno about it when he arrived in Paris, but it was clear that his friend believed that he should just forget the whole thing. Jan thought that he looked on it as something outside of science, something dangerous to which the scientific system could not be applied. Steno told him that they should not believe without any evidence that those little men were devils, yet Jan still saw the fear in his eyes when he mentioned them.

The roots of the religion went deep in Steno. Unlike the religious freedom of the Netherlands and the diverse life that sprung from that, Denmark stuck to one religion, the Folkekirken, or Lutheran church of the people. Its mark was obvious on Steno, and Jan could easily see that he disliked the plurality of religion. Maybe that simplicity was the reason why he liked science so much. In science, every theory is either correct or incorrect, and when a theory is proven, it becomes a fact. Steno liked pure facts, and science was full of them. It was the job of the learned man to find these new pure facts. But it appeared to him as well that Steno was extremely taken with Catholicism in France. The Lutheran Church was greatly connected with the public and with a personal connection to God. There were a great many variables in question with that system of belief, but there was a noble simplicity to Catholicism, or that was the effect that the Church wanted to impress upon people, at any rate.

He listened now to the conversation of his three friends in Bourdelot's study: Bourdelot, the Abbé de Massey himself, who wrote *Catéchisme de l'Athée* or the Catechism of the Atheist, in which he suggested that heaven was empty and that there was not an enlightened man in Italy or France who believed in God. The conversation turned to Descartes and his theories when this libertine proclaimed his *Bibo Ergo Sum*. 'What's at the heart of *Cogito Ergo Sum*,' said Bourdelot, 'is that we cannot be absolutely certain about anything in this world except the fact that we ourselves exist. And when I say that, I'm referring to our thoughts. We can't be certain that anything else exists. This table, that wall: maybe this world is nothing but a dream. But still, your mind must exist, or else you could not make that statement: I think, therefore I am. Maybe I am nothing but a dream to you, Nicolaus!'

'I understand the theory,' Steno answered abruptly, 'and I understand that he was trying to find a practical approach to science, to find out which things in this world we can be absolutely certain of, and depend upon in scientific study. But I have to say that I am uncomfortable with it as a theory.'

'And why?' the libertine asked him. 'Is it that you are afraid that if you cannot be certain of anything in this world except your own mind, then your certainty about God's existence is also in danger?'

'I do not like this type of talk. That's not what Descartes had in mind. Not at all. He was no atheist, and it's well you know it. He said that our own awareness of God was proof that—'

'I understand what he said,' said Bourdelot, cutting across him, 'but maybe he was so enthusiastic to drag God into the matter because he was able to see that the theory itself, the *cogito ergo sum*, was able to abolish him, or at least to abolish absolute belief in him. It is a doorway to atheism, and he knew very well that it was.'

'You have your belief on the matter. Well done. Allow me my own, please.'

'Gentlemen, let us be at ease,' Thévenot said calmly. 'Let us accept that we will not solve the great questions of philosophy tonight.'

'You are right, my friend,' said Bourdelot, yielding with a half-drunken smile. 'And I am very sorry, Nicolaus. Forgive me my bad manners. I am a poor host.'

'Don't mention it, Pierre,' said Steno. 'You are a wonderful host. It's just a difference of opinion between us, and is that not a good thing between learned men. I am truly grateful to you for both your generosity and your lively conversation.'

'Well done, Nicolaus! Where would the human race be without differences of opinion! We would be in an abyss of hopelessness if everyone was of the same mind,' said Bourdelot, and he raised his glass with a broad smile on his face.

But then, something happened. A big fly landed on the table. Jan saw it, and he noticed that Thévenot saw it as well. He felt like a person about to plunge himself into icy water. He steadied himself for the question. 'Isn't it a wonderful thing, the body of a fly!' he said, like someone starting a lecture. 'Isn't it a perfect flying machine!'

An inquisitive glint suddenly came into Thévenot's eyes. 'Of course, Jan, you're the expert on the matter,' he said to him.

'But isn't that how God created them?' Steno said abruptly. Jan saw that the blood had drained from his face, which left it with a pallid complexion.

'Yes, of course,' said Jan, 'but let us imagine for a moment, gentlemen, that they actually are flying machines for little men. Men so small that you could not see them at all except through the lens of a microscope. But little men who are looking at us as we sit in this room now.'

A rigidity came into Steno's body and he tightened his grip around his glass. Bourdelot's face lost its merriness as well, leaving a solemn look in its place. The atmosphere changed in the room as if none of them had taken a drop of drink that night. Thévenot looked carefully at Jan first and then at the other two.

'That's ... that's absurd, Jan!' Steno said sharply, his hand shaking a little as he spoke.

Bourdelot put his glass on the table. There was silence in the room outside of the drone of the fly. Thévenot stared at Steno for a few seconds as if he was trying to distil information from his voice and face. Then he turned back to Jan. 'It is indeed absurd, Jan. But that's not to say that it isn't true,' he said calmly. He turned to Bourdelot then and there was some communication in the look between them.

Bourdelot did not speak at all but looked into Thévenot's eyes before glancing up at the fly that was circling under the lamp and casting its bulky shadow on the ceiling. It was as if its drone was getting louder now, and it filled the room in the absence of any other noise. Steno sat like a marble statue in his chair, his eyes fixed on his glass.

Thévenot stared directly at Jan now. 'How long have you both known of this?' he asked.

'Since last year. I saw them, and told Niels immediately afterwards.'

'You saw them with your own eyes?'

'Yes.'

'That's incredible! And they had a proper human form?'

'They had. They died in the water of the microscope. Then they descended on me. A great...' and he stopped here, thinking of the day.

'A great multitude of flies descended on you in their thousands,' said Thévenot, finishing his sentence.

'But how do you know? Have you seen them as well?' Jan asked.

'No, I haven't. But there are people who know of this and I found out about it through contact with them. Galileo saw them and wanted to spread the story, but the Church wouldn't let him. He was locked away, as you know, but he had aides that helped him. Between these people and others who visited him, the story got out. But it's dangerous.'

'That's what I said!' said Steno, getting his voice back at last.

'It's not only from the Church that danger could come,' said Thévenot. 'We don't know what power these little men have. There are people who know but they don't want to say anything. Yet we are learned men at the end of the day. Can we remain quiet forever? I was the ambassador to Geneva and to Rome in the forties and fifties. There was a good friend of mine there who had been an aid to Galileo – Vincenzo Viviani was his name, and it was he who told me of how such beings exist in the world. It was difficult for me to believe at first, but after a while the job of ambassador itself taught me that he was right. There is so much intrigue and conspiracy in this story that it became clear to me that there was much more than just Viviani's imagination involved.'

'Myself also,' said Bourdelot, finding his voice now as well. 'I went to Rome in 1634. I was a doctor to Count François de Noailles, who also had the position of ambassador there, and he had been a student of Galileo years before. The Count did his best to help his old teacher who was under house arrest in Arcetri at the time, but nothing came of it in the end. However, he did get permission to meet him in Poggibonsi, and I went with him then. I was only twenty-four at the time, but I remember the day very well. Galileo was an old man, over seventy years of age, and almost blind, but I never heard anyone speak so precisely and clearly. It was obvious that his intellect was as strong as it had always been, but then he told us this story. I didn't believe it at first, of course, but it was a surprise to me just how much of an effect it had upon the Count. Maybe he had already heard things, like Melchisédech here when he had the same job years later. At any rate, the old man gave the Count a book, *Discorsi e dimostrazioni sopra due nuove scienze*, and I believe that it contained extra pages which related to the little men. From then on, I've been searching for more information on them all the time. It's one of the reasons why I started my academy, to tell you the truth.'

'We can but work together to try and find some understanding of them,' said Thévenot. 'I knew that you were studying insects and I hoped that you would have some knowledge on these beings. It's wonderful to meet someone else who has actually seen them.'

'But is there anyone other than myself and Galileo who has seen them?' Jan asked. A cautious, thoughtful expression came across Thévenot's face and he didn't immediately answer. 'Robert Hooke in England has also seen them,' he said eventually.

'I've heard reference to his work. So he's seen them as well?

'It's very important, however, that we are careful to whom we tell this story,' said Bourdelot. 'It wouldn't be good if we spread it to the wrong people.'

'There are people we can trust,' said Thévenot. 'But still we should be careful.'

Jan looked up at the fly that was still circling the room. 'But isn't everything that we say already known to them anyway?'

'It is, I believe,' Thévenot replied, 'but there's no way out of that. Maybe we only live with their consent. Perhaps there would be a price to pay if we spread their story to the public. The truth is that we just don't know.'

With that, a knock came at the door and a servant entered, a young housemaid of about twenty years of age. 'My apologies, Mr Bourdelot, but there is something in the sky which may be of great interest to you. A comet, if I am not mistaken.'

'Gentlemen!' said Bourdelot. 'This is Jeanette, a clever young woman who is in service in this house. She has learned of the stars and gives me great insight on their movements. Are you certain, Jeanette?'

'Yes. It could be nothing else.'

'Let's go up to the roof, gentlemen,' Bourdelot said. 'This is a special night.'

Jeanette led them with a candle through a little door at the top of the house. Out on the roof, there was a clean, white carpet of snow shining in the light of a full moon. It was a bright, calm night, and the five of them walked out across that white, unploughed field.

'There it is,' proclaimed Jeanette, pointing.

They all looked up and remained silent for a long time. There was the comet, frozen in the air with its tail spread out behind it. It was like a spiritual moment for them, and they felt no cold.

'This is an important night, gentlemen,' said Thévenot. 'We will remember it.'

Act Two

Scene One

While I was writing that last piece, it occurred to me that they weren't unlike the Three Wise Men at Christmas time as they looked up at a miraculous star, a sign of the new age to come. There were people at the time, however, who saw the comet in the sky in 1664 as a bad omen, and many believed afterwards that they were proven correct in this opinion by subsequent events. The history books tell us that many people suffered badly in the years that followed. History is the greatest novel ever written and it is important because it is based on the truth. Throughout this book, I recommend that you look at this history.

But, of course, there are many events in this book that were never written in any history book. For example, the fact that they gathered together in Bourdelot's house that evening, the conversation between them, the servant Jeanette coming in to tell them of the comet in the sky. But I promise you that they are based on the same truth found in stories that we recognise as history. Forgive me if I do not tell you at this point where I came by this information, but I promise that all will become clear in a little while. It's just that I want to tell the story in the correct order.

I accept, of course, that it's an unbelievable story. I am trying to be as objective and as exact as I can, but I know that it's a story that undermines the foundations of our civilisation. But hasn't civilisation itself always been built on weak foundations? The divine right of kings, for example. How many people have been put to death because of that one principle? There are fundamental truths around us all the time and it's easy to accept them, but when our descendants look back on us in a few hundred years, how many of those truths will be utterly absurd to them?

We can only deal with each truth as it comes to us and then pass it around from person to person. That's my business here, readers. But of course, each writer puts their own colour on a story through the act of writing, and I understand that readers have experience of certain standards of storytelling: well-developed characters, descriptive passages and so on. I'm doing my best in this regard, and I'm enjoying it as well, I have to say. Maybe I'll write a novel someday myself. This book isn't a novel, of course.

Perhaps you've noticed as well that I've broken up this text into acts and scenes. I don't know why I like this, but I do. Maybe it's the way that it brings you out of the normal form of prose, with its chapters and such, so that it's made clear to you that this isn't normal fiction but rather something else entirely. But as well as that, I think I like it because it's good to lay the book out as a sort of drama. Isn't the history of the human race in its entirety a drama, with its great characters and flamboyant sets. This story of mine tells of events that were going on all the time behind the curtain, but that's not to say that it isn't as true as that which was portrayed by the main actors: the kings and tyrants.

I can't give you scientific proof that the story is true at this point. That's why I'm writing this book. But, as I've already said, do your own external reading on the subject as well. Take the phone out of your pocket, go on the internet, and find information on these people: Jan, Steno, Thévenot, Bourdelot, Spinoza, Questiers, Galileo, even Ole Borch and the three sons of Gersdorff. You will see the connections between their lives. The book that Jan wrote is on the internet: it's called *Bybel der Natuure*. You'll see that I gave you the first line correctly and that it's a proper anagram of the poem. I'm not asking you to accept this like some conspiracy theory, but I suggest that it's worth being just a little open to the possibilities at this point. There'll be more information coming soon.

I remember that I was on my own in the house two days after Salvadóir's visit. I was sitting on the sofa with a cup of coffee, listening to music. There was a picture hanging on the wall, one that I'm particularly fond of: *La Terre Labourée* by Joan Miró – 'The Ploughed Land'. I saw someone there alright in the corner ploughing with a bull, but there was another world going on as well with strange animals scattered around. A piebald mare was suckling a dog; another dog with spikes like a hedgehog looked directly at you; a sort of stoat in a peaked hat like a dunce's cap spoke to a snail; there were chickens and rabbits, a tree with branches like ribbons and a long-legged spider. There was a house in the centre of the picture, and so everyone was at the back of this house – in that place where *Tír na nÓg* is, the beautiful mixed-up land, as the poet said. I remember thinking then that I was now living in a world like this, a crazy upside-down world that was hidden from normal life. A world at the back of the house that's not seen by people out on the road as they drive past.

The doorbell rang and I went to answer it. It was Aogán. 'How's it goin', boy!' he said with a smile that did a bad job at hiding the seriousness in his eyes.

'Aogán! You went so quickly the other night that I didn't even have a chance to give you my number. How did you find out where I was living?'

'Don't ya know that I'm in Interpol. Can I come in?'

'Of course,' I said, and I directed him to the living room. I put on the kettle and he sat down.

It didn't take him long to come right out with what was bothering him. 'Seán, I was worried about you the other night when I heard the shite you were saying to that big fella. It was all just crazy, and I could tell that you weren't joking either. I wasn't eavesdropping, but your man was so massive and your conversation with him was so intense that you didn't even see me. In the name of God, Seán! I never heard such crap in all my life. What's going on with ya?'

I regretted at that moment that I'd been so impulsive as to say anything to him at all, but I knew that he was too clever to believe now that I was only joking. 'Aogán, I'm sorry that you heard me talking the other night. It was never my intention to drag you into this crazy story, but now that you know, I'll tell it to you in its entirety, for what that's worth. I don't think that you'll believe it, but I can only promise you that it happened. The world turned upside down a couple of weeks ago and I don't really understand it myself, but if you can keep an open mind about it, I'd be grateful to you.'

'I'll do my best anyway,' he said firmly.

I told him then about the day Peadar and I had seen the Firíní through the lens of the microscope and the multitude of flies that appeared in the room afterwards. I told him about the detective work we'd done to try and make sense of it. I told him about Salvadóir, his own story and the way he'd found out about us. I told him the whole story up to that point, and then I stopped.

He didn't speak for a while but just looked at me with disbelief in his eyes. 'Jesus Christ, Seán!' he said. 'Are you out of your mind? Don't you see that something like this cannot be true. It's some sort of mental derangement. I don't know: schizophrenia or something like that. I'm appealing to you now to tell this story to a doctor. There are tablets for stories like this. You're my cousin, Seán, and it hurts me to hear this shite coming out of your mouth.'

'I know that you'd never give me bad advice, Aogán, but I saw these things with my own eyes. I understand that it's more absurd than anything that you've ever seen, but I saw these little men. They were there! If Peadar wasn't with me that day and if he hadn't seen them too, then certainly, I'd be going with you now to the psychiatrist but—'

Then, as if it were a scene in a drama, I heard the key in the door and Peadar walked in. He saw the sombre look on our faces and knew straight away that something was up.

'Peadar, this is my cousin, Aogán. Aogán, this is the Peadar we were just talking about.'

'Is this the Aogán who was in the pub with you the other night?'

'The very man.'

'And are you the scientist that proved how many angels can dance on the head of a pin?' said Aogán sarcastically. 'Or perhaps, should I say how many flutter around in the head of a fly.'

Peadar sat on the armchair in front of the sofa. He had a calm look on his face, as was usual for him, and he looked directly into Aogán's eyes. 'The answer to the second question is two,' he said bluntly. 'I have no knowledge at all relating to the first.'

'The same story so, is it? This tale that you saw little men in the microscope and that the room filled with flies. Are you listening to yourself, boy?'

'It's an absurd and ridiculous story, Aogán, the type of story you'd hear from people suffering from psychiatric illnesses,' Peadar said.

'We agree about one thing, anyway!'

'But however little sense it makes as a story… unfortunately, it's true. I've always thought of myself as a reasonable person. I like science because it makes sense as a subject. You believe in some theory because you know that people arrived at it through the process of reason. You trust that process. Every scientific fact is a brick and the world is built from these bricks, one after another, until it's firm and strong. That's what science is to me. You will understand so, how much of a shock it was when I looked through the lens of the microscope that day and saw those two little men.'

'You're both as mad as a box of frogs,' Aogán said.

At that moment, the doorbell rang again.

'I'll go,' said Peadar, and out he went.

'I can only believe that it's true, Aogán,' I said to him now. 'How could the same mental aberration affect us both at the same time without any warning in our lives beforehand?'

'This isn't right, Seán,' he said, shaking his head with disbelief.

I heard voices in the hall, and then the door opened and Salvadóir walked in like a giant from a children's story.

'Ah, in the name of God! Is there any sense at all left in this feckin' story?' said Aogán.

'It's the bold man himself! How are things now, fella?' Salvadóir exclaimed heartily to him.

'Terrible altogether! And yourself?'

'I'm not too bad now.'

'Oh, I'd believe that. But tell me, are you another member of the Ballyphehane Society for the Bewildered?' he said coldly.

'I'm an honorary member, even though I'm not from Ballyphehane myself.'

'Well, if you see little men in flies, I'd say they'd make an exception to the rules and just let you in anyway. They're very liberal like that.'

'Oh, absolutely! But I've never seen little men in flies, even though I know they exist. I'm sure of it, just as sure as I'm standing here talking to you. I saw a room with a million flies. For me, this is an inescapable fact. Am I mad because I believe that? I believe the evidence of my own eyes and my father's account of what he saw through the microscope. Is that so strange?'

'It is, now that you mention it!'

'People believe in stranger things than that. Look at all the beliefs in this world, some of them so absurd that you'd think they were conceived of in a mental asylum. Belief is a herd animal. A person can believe anything if he sees that enough other people believe it too, but—'

'Absolutely! Jesus walked on water, and the Americans faked the moon landing. But in the name of God, little men in flies? I wasn't born yesterday!'

'We're not trying to trick you, Aogán,' I said, 'and we're not even asking you to believe it. But now that you know about it, I'd ask that you'd be a little bit open to the evidence we have.'

'I'd ask nothing of you, Aogán, except that you'd keep it to yourself,' Peadar said.

'I'll keep quiet about it, because I don't know how I'd even begin to tell this crazy shit to anyone. And I'll be open to it as well, because I'm curious about the next piece of lunacy that comes out of your mouths. But I won't believe it … and I never will.'

'Do you have news for us?' Peadar asked Salvadóir now.

'I do! I have something big to tell you.' But I saw a hesitancy in his eyes and he looked at Aogán.

'Aogán knows the story already, Salvadóir,' I said firmly, 'and I trust him completely.'

Maybe it was bold of me to just thrust Aogán into Salvadóir's confidence like this, but it gave me an ease of mind to think that he'd be part of this company with me. I still saw the hesitancy in his eyes though, and thought perhaps that I'd gone too far, but then Aogán spoke out again:

'Whatever you have to say, big man, it's clear that Seán is with you in this conspiracy, and I'd prefer if I could keep an eye on him. On that account, if you say your piece before me, I promise you that I'll keep your secret as long as I feel that you're not putting him in danger. I'll promise that, but I'll promise no more.'

'Grand so,' yielded Salvadóir with a smile. 'It is what it is, I suppose. Can you all listen carefully to me now. We don't have much time.' With that, he sat on the sofa. 'I told you the other day about Birdy. He was a friend of my father's and a very clever man, with a particular understanding of the Firíní. He told me a little while before he died that he'd made a major discovery. Then he died under suspicious circumstances, but he sent me a text message just before his death.'

'That was the *comix bag* that you spoke of the other day,' said Peadar.

'Exactly! But I'm a proper fool. My father was clever, and Birdy was clever: they were able to tie the strings of history together to find lost things, concealed things. But me? I've failed them. You're clever, and it's a great thing that I'm in contact with you now. It never dawned on me until the other day when you were speaking about the anagram that Jan Swammerdam put in his book, that this text message could be an anagram as well! Birdy must have understood that he was in danger, and he wanted to send me information without sharing it with the person who was threatening him. Maybe he knew that he wouldn't have the chance to erase the text from the phone memory afterwards. Anyway, he sent me *comix bag*. That's an anagram of *magic box*. He had a cabinet, an ancient antique that he got somewhere, and it had a secret compartment. I remember that he called it the '*magic box*' when I was young. It was like a secret between us. That was the message he sent me, and I failed to understand it. He died trying to protect a new discovery. Someone killed him, and now I have to do my duty and find it.

'Where is the cabinet now?' asked Peadar.

'Birdy was married to a woman called Nuala. They were separated for years but they were still legally married when he died, and she got all his personal possessions. He wasn't a wealthy man and all he had were books and some pieces of furniture. She had no interest in the books, and she always hated his search for the truth as regards the Firíní. I went to her after the funeral and asked if I could go through his books and papers in order to find this new discovery, but she refused. She'd known my father too and was well aware of what I wanted. '*My husband's dead. Won't you let his madness die with him!*' she said. There was nothing else I could do. Birdy had letters, written in the seventeenth and eighteenth centuries, in which the Firíní were mentioned. He established a collection of research, more than anyone else, as far as I know, and now it was off limits.

'But the other day, when I finally understood the last message that Birdy sent me, I knew that I'd have to go back to her and implore Nuala to let me look at the cabinet. Birdy died fifteen years ago, but she's still alive. She's an old woman now, as cantankerous as ever, and with no great welcome for me. '*He left me nothing when he died but crumpled bits of paper, torn books and battered old bits of furniture. A colleague of his approached me some time afterwards and asked if he could buy the whole lot from me. A Mr Kane it was, a respectable gentleman from the college. He even took the old bits of furniture and gave me a very reasonable price. It was the least that I deserved after all I had to put up with.*' This talk about Birdy disgusted me and I left her without another word. But she had given me important information, unbeknownst to herself.

'Kane was a colleague of Birdy's and they had written a book together once on the Borgia papacy. Birdy was very friendly with him, but my father had no respect for him at all. I remember him from when I was young. He was a pompous and arrogant man. It struck me then that he might have had a part in Birdy's death, and even that it was he who broke into my house afterwards. I know where his house is now and I went there directly. I knocked on the door, but got no answer. I looked through the letterbox, and saw six or seven letters on the floor. I think he's out of town now, and the house is empty. Then I looked through the window, and what did I see but Birdy's cabinet standing there in the living room. It was only four metres from me. I wanted to break the door down right there and then, but it was strong. I could have done it, of course, but it would have taken time and that would have made a lot of noise. The Guards would have been down on me before I'd have a chance to find anything.'

'But what about the window?' I asked him.

'That's why I'm here looking for your help. I'm too big myself to go through the window.'

'You want us to help you break into his house?' Peadar said, cautiously.

'Who else could I ask but you who understands the story? If there's anything in that *magic box*, it belongs to me. Birdy wanted me to have it. If I'm right, Kane broke into my house first anyway, so I'm only repaying the favour.'

'We'll do it,' I exclaimed.

'Wait a minute now, Seán,' Aogán said abruptly. 'Are you completely out of your mind? You want to break into the house of someone who is possibly a murderer? I don't believe I'm hearing this.'

'We saw what we saw and we have to get answers.'

'Have you ever broken into a house in your life?'

'No, but—'

'But nothing. You're not doing it.'

'You needn't … you shouldn't be part of this, Aogán,' I said.

'You're my cousin, Seán. When our fathers died, I promised that I'd take care of you if I could, and I'll do it now. You're not going.'

'It's my own decision, Aogán. Thanks for your help to me always, but I have to do this.'

'Ok, so. I'm coming with you,' he said firmly.

'You don't have to do that.'

'I'm coming, and if there's any trouble, I'll throw these two idiots under the bus and get you out of there. Don't argue with me. Where's the house?'

'It's in Glanmire. I've the van outside. We can go there now,' said Salvadóir. 'Ok! Let's go so!' said Aogán, jumping up from his chair.

So we all headed out. It was a big van with enough space for Salvadóir to drive it, and the three of us sitting compactly on a seat designed for two. Within two minutes, we were darting east at high speed on the South Ring Road.

Scene Two

London, England
9th June 1665

Jan walked down the gangway and stepped onto the quay between London Bridge and the Tower. This was his first time in England and he felt light-hearted with the excitement of being in a new country. The ship had taken some time winding its way up the meandering Thames, and he felt the lethargic heat that lay heavily on the city now after the fresh sea breeze he'd left at the coast. He felt something else as well – a strange atmosphere that he'd never experienced before, but he told himself that it was just his imagination. He stopped now and observed this new place around him. There were rancid smells hanging in the air of the docks, and he saw ragged people looking suspiciously at him from darkened alcoves.

He felt like an enemy in this country and he knew well that this wasn't his imagination. He was Dutch, and England and the Netherlands were now at war. That wasn't to say that there wasn't a large Dutch community living in the city, but still he would have to be careful. Only a week before, a great sea battle had taken place just a short distance up the coast from London, a battle in which the Dutch forces had lost badly. But Jan had come on a boat from France, speaking French with those on board the whole time. He had left Paris a week before and taken a coach to Calais, where he had to wait three days for the next ship to England. Now at last he had reached his destination.

The stevedores rushed to the ship's cargo then, and tax officials came to collect their dues. A sailor carried his trunk from the ship and laid it down on the quay. Jan gave him some money and he went back on board, thanking him in English. He understood this language well enough, even though his French was far better now after having spent almost two years in France. But he'd spoken some English even when he was in Saumur, with a young man called William from London who was on his own journey through Europe. This young man's mother was from the Netherlands and he said his father was an admiral in the British Navy. He tried to remember his surname now, but couldn't.

A man approached him, speaking in a thick English accent. It was a hackney driver, asking if he required transport.

'I do. I want to go to Bishop's Gate,' Jan answered quickly. 'Gresham House. Is it far from here?'

'No, sir,' replied the driver in his clipped accent. 'About a half-mile, that's all. We won't be long.'

He showed him his carriage of rough wood and the two sickly horses that would pull it. Jan climbed in, and the driver put his trunk on the back. It was clear that there was nothing in the way of comfort on the inside except a hard wooden bench, but Jan didn't care. He sat in and they took off promptly.

He noticed as he was going through those grubby streets that there was very little difference between London and Paris as regards the hardships of the common people and the foulness of the world in which they lived. He saw the same grime that stuck to everything and the same wretchedness in the gaunt faces of people who looked out at the world with lost eyes. They were a vanquished people, colonised and oppressed, rummaging in every nook and cranny of the city for the most meagre of gains. There were other people there as well who seemed wealthier, but that was all part of the same trap. One cannot, according to the rules of colonisation, take everything from the people. One must leave them a small amount so that they can fight over it. In the end, they'll oppress themselves.

But it wasn't the conditions of the common people which was on his mind now as he moved slowly through the grimy London streets, but rather the reason that had brought him over from France. Thévenot had told him at Christmas that there was a man in England who, like himself, had looked through the lens of a microscope and seen the same little men. His name was Robert Hooke, and he was a scientist who had made a comprehensive study of insects. Hooke published a book some months later called *Micrographia*, and Jan was excited and hopeful that he would write the truth of what he had seen. When he finally received the book, he saw that it contained many wonderful drawings of insects, one with the head of a fly. It was a very special book academically, but there was no mention of the little men in it. Thévenot made contact with Hooke then and told him of Jan's story. Hooke was very happy to hear this and a correspondence arose between them. He wrote to Jan to express his delight that someone else had also seen them, and asked that he come to England so that they could properly discuss the matter. Steno thought that the plan was devilry, however, and Jan saw the fear in his eyes every time the subject was mentioned. It appeared that it was wearing away his natural inclination for knowledge and driving him towards religion instead, even towards Catholicism.

But Jan felt this conflict within himself as well, and he couldn't deny it. How could he say that it wasn't the Devil who had looked up at him through the lens of the microscope that day? He always regarded knowledge as something that worked in the service of God. He believed that it would function to dispel error, that error would be pared away as one pares the skin of an onion, layer after layer, until one comes upon the pure absolute truth in the centre. And was that not God as well? Absolute truth, a truth on which all other truths depend. But now every absolute was lost in the grimy twilight of that liminal space between truth and falsehood.

The carriage stopped on the street, and he heard agitated voices competing with one another outside. He looked through the window and saw a ragged crowd of people there incited by some awful energy. Some of them were looking to the sky, raising their hands and pointing at something, grabbing the shoulders of the person beside them, enthusiastically affirming and proclaiming that it was true, whatever it was. He thought that he saw real madness in these eyes. Some of them fell on their knees and prayed devotedly, their hands clasped tightly together, their frozen faces directed to the heavens. There was a half-naked man with a short piece of rope in his hand, scourging his own back with it and shouting some unintelligible phrase with every lash. There were ugly, red marks stretching across his shoulders now, but he still carried on with his torment. Then Jan saw that the very walls of the street were covered with leaflets and signs that made prophecies and spoke of omens. There were mysterious symbols everywhere as well, but he couldn't understand them.

After a while, the driver was able to find his way through the crowd and the carriage pushed on again slowly, but Jan saw that these terrible sights continued all the way up the road. There were groups gathered together in agitation on every street and corner. He saw a tall man, dressed in a velvet jacket and black cloak, as he walked boldly in the street with a band of people following him like pups after their mother. There were others giving orations to groups and one would think that they were calling the stars down from the heavens. Other people prayed in the street, their raised voices mixed into one fearful noise like a bell ringing ceaselessly in your ears.

When the carriage eventually stopped, the driver came down and opened the door for him. 'This is Gresham House now, sir,' he said with a strange merriment in his voice.

Jan saw the big house standing on the left-hand side of the road, but on the other side was a church with a large crowd gathered outside. He heard cries of horror coming from this group and the voice of one man in particular.

'Can you take down my trunk and wait one minute for me please,' Jan said to the driver, and he walked across the road towards the church.

Terror ran like a rabid dog through the crowd. They were all listening very carefully to this one man who proclaimed something to them at the top of his voice. He was looking into the graveyard, screaming and pointing his finger at one place and then another. Jan understood well what he was saying: there was a ghost in the graveyard, walking in between the headstones. 'Look! He's over there. Don't you see him?' he screamed. And they saw him, right enough, some of them anyway, and the horrible cry of their voices rose again into one sound in the street.

Jan went directly back to the safety of the carriage. He felt a quiver rise in his body and hands. He saw nothing in the graveyard except headstones, but still the incident had shocked him. The driver took his trunk to the door. This was Gresham House, or Gresham College as it was now called, the headquarters of the Royal Society. Robert Hooke was curator of experiments there, which came with a residence within the building. Jan gave money to the driver, a tremble still in his hand, and knocked on the front door. The driver waited until someone came down, and then he left quickly. 'Take care of yourself,' he said as he turned about.

The servant who stood at the door was an old man with long, noble features. 'Mr Swammerdam, to see Mr Hooke,' said Jan half-bewildered.

He saw confusion on the old man's face for a moment, but he called then for someone else to take the trunk inside. 'Please follow me, Mr Swammerdam,' he said and walked up a broad staircase. It was an elegant house but Jan hardly noticed. Before long, they were standing before large double doors and he knocked now, opening them when he heard the voice from within. It was a laboratory with scientific instruments that Jan recognised very well. There was a short man sitting there: about thirty years of age with black curly hair down to his shoulders. His face was thin and haggard, and Jan noticed that he was slightly hunchbacked. This was Robert Hooke.

'Mr Swammerdam, sir,' said the servant.

Hooke jumped up from his chair when he heard the name. 'Swammerdam! In the name of God, you're here! But didn't you receive my letter?' he said in great agitation.

'I received a letter … asking me to come here alright,' said Jan awkwardly, hoping there had not been some misunderstanding.

'But I sent you another letter after that to stop you. Mr Swammerdam, you are welcome here, and will always be, but I must admit to you that I am not at all happy that you are here now. The plague is in London. It's bad, much worse than was thought at first.'

This was a heavy blow to Jan, and he felt a weakness in his legs. He knew that the plague had been reported in London a few months before, but it was said to be only a few cases in the west of the city and that it would soon abate. In truth, he was much more worried about Amsterdam when the plague had appeared there a year earlier. That would explain the madness in the streets of London anyway, but this was worse than anything he'd ever seen. The plague in Europe was like a constant black cloud, a demon that lived in the darkness around them. But if the plague was a demon, then yet another demon was the terror that ran before it, putting panic in the hearts of the people, driving them mad. The ebb and flow of the disease was reported in places every couple of years, but he had never seen a great city like London in the grips of that terror. It was horrible.

'There were cases in the west of the city and every house in which it was found was shut up,' said Hooke, speaking with deliberation. 'But I fear that this was a device which added to the problem. They kept the people who were sick with the plague in their own houses and put guards on the doors. But they kept their families in the house with them as well, those who were sick along with those who were still healthy and, of course, this was a death sentence to them all. I went to the west of the city a couple of weeks ago and saw it with my own eyes. It was horrendous. I heard the piteous cries of poor people locked in their own houses, suffering the torment of the disease. There was a woman who implored her neighbours to take her child from the house, and the neighbours then began to threaten the guards. A great commotion began in the street and the authorities came down heavily on the neighbours. But of course, it wouldn't surprise the most naïve of simpletons that people would be reluctant to report the plague to the authorities if this was the outcome – and that's exactly what happened. They thought that they had the plague under control, but it was spreading before their eyes. Now I believe it's too late. It isn't here in the east of the city yet, but it will not be long coming. People are escaping – those who can anyway.'

'I am here at the worst of times so,' said Jan despondently.

'But I am sorry, Mr Swammerdam,' said Hooke, becoming more relaxed. 'This is a terrible welcome. I have been very much looking forward to meeting you for a long time, and now you're here. I would have hoped that it were in more favourable circumstances, of course, but that cannot be helped now. You are very welcome, sir! You must be hungry after your journey.'

They walked through the extensive house until they came to Hooke's own residence, and found Jan's trunk already there. The servant was waiting for them.

'Well done, Fuller,' Hooke said to him. 'Prepare a meal now for our guest.' Fuller inclined his head and left. 'We have our own business, and it's a business that no one else can undertake,' said Hooke, pouring out two glasses of brandy. 'Drink this, my friend. It will give you courage in these dark days.' Jan drank it eagerly, and it brought the colour back to his cheeks.

Fuller was not long returning with the food, and if it was simple enough, it was wholesome. Jan was hungry after spending the day at sea, and he ate greedily when it was put before him. With a full stomach, and a few more glasses of brandy, there was a new sheen to the world and he lost some of the worry he had felt on his arrival. 'Tell me about your book *Micrographia*,' he said. 'My congratulations first, of course. I've never seen anything like it. The accuracy which you have in your drawings is incredible. But wouldn't it have been the perfect place to disclose the knowledge of the little men to the world? What prevented you from doing that?'

'One moment,' said Hooke, and he left the room. When he returned, he had a bundle of papers in his hand and he laid them down on the table, saying: 'I wanted to put these into the book as well.'

Jan beheld the bundle before him, seven drawings and one engraving, all done with an extremely high level of precision. They were so precise that he felt a moment of terror as he looked at them. It was them! There were the little men, as large as life on the page! He found it strange in one drawing that they were both looking directly at him with questioning expressions on their faces. They had the proper human form, of course, but Jan remembered the one-piece suits they wore as he looked at them.

They had a white band around their waists and high boots of the same colour. He closed his eyes for a moment and saw them struggling in the water.

'At the time, I didn't realise that there was another living person who could say that he had seen them,' said Hooke. 'When I first saw them, I went to Robert Boyle and told him about it. He's a wonderful scientist, a learned man in many fields. I told him what I'd seen, but he was reluctant to accept it. I was working for him some years ago and I helped him with his experiments and his discoveries. He is one of the founders of this Royal Society which published my book. He is the only person in England to whom I have told my story. But when I went to him with these drawings, he recommended, as strongly as he could, that I not put them in the book. He said I had seen them only for a moment: there wasn't a scientific basis for including them in the book because I could not repeat the experiment. All very good reasons, of course, and I yielded to them in the end. If I had known that you had seen them as well, maybe it would have been a different story. He didn't tell me out straight that the Royal Society would not publish my book if it included references to the little men, but I could imagine that it wouldn't have.'

'They're perfect,' said Jan, looking again at the drawings. 'There's no difference between these two men and my own, except the faces. It was two other men that I killed.'

'Do you feel responsible for their deaths?'

'I don't know if I could actually have saved them, even if I'd had the presence of mind to attempt it. I understand that they're not members of the human race, our own human race anyway. But still, I looked at them as they died. I don't like that.'

'I understand completely,' said Hooke pensively. 'It's a horrible thing to remember.'

'But what can we do now?' We have no proof that we saw them. We only have our own affirmations that this is true, that such beings as this exist in the world. Maybe Boyle is right. Is there a scientific basis for our opinions without proof?'

'It's true that we don't have proof, and if one of us released the story on his own, no one would believe it. But if the two of us are of one voice and say that we both saw them at different times, in different countries, I believe that they would have to pay attention to us. We can work together on this, and as soon as the story is out, it cannot be put back. We have a duty as learned men, as scientists, and if I am involved in releasing this information to the world, I believe I will have done my duty.'

Jan did not speak for a while but he looked closely at the drawings. It was clear that there was a conflict going on in his mind, but in the end, he turned to Hooke and spoke to him clearly. 'You're right. Let's do it!' he said, stretching out his hand.

Hooke shook it, and a broad smile broke across his face.

The following day, the news arrived of the first case of plague on that side of the city.

Scene Three

Salvadóir parked the van some distance up the road, and we walked to the house. We must have seemed a peculiar group to anyone in the street. I have to admit to being nervous, but I knew that there was no getting out of it now. I had never imagined that I would break into someone's house, but similarly, I hadn't imagined the circumstances behind this act either. If there were answers to be found to what we saw that day, we would have to break in and take those answers. Anyway, Salvadóir had said that anything that was in the *magic box* was his by right, and so we weren't actually stealing anything. I was happy that Aogán was with us, even though I felt guilty for dragging him into this whole business. He asked Salvadóir to show him his tool box before we left the van, and he took a few things with him.

'We're here,' said Salvadóir quietly.

We were standing before big double gates, made from wrought iron and set into a semi-circular recess in a high wall. It was one of the big houses built by the upper classes in Glanmire back in the day. There was no view of the house from the outside because of a line of trees directly inside the gates. There was a dark path that turned sharply right then and created a mysterious appearance as if you were entering an enchanted forest. Salvadóir laid his heavy hand on the latch of the gate, and it swung in easily and silently. There was something eerie about that lack of sound, and I felt as if I was in a fairy tale. As we went through the gates together, my nervousness increased. The smell of pine came to me on the air as we walked along a path completely covered by the trees. We turned right, and I saw that we would come out into the garden and into the light again in twenty metres. It was a lovely garden, neatly laid out with flowerbeds and bushes. I noticed that the grass and the leaves on the bushes were a little too long, but not as if they had been abandoned for years. Someone was living in this house. We walked carefully up the gravel path, our feet announcing our arrival with every step. It was a large, square, two-storey house with elegant bay windows on the ground floor and a semi-circle of stained glass above the front door. I imagined croquet on the lawn with a peacock poking its head through the chrysanthemums and the dahlias.

I understood now why Salvadóir couldn't break in on his own. It was a large heavy door, and even though I was sure he could have done it, it would have made a lot of noise and that would have been like a burglar alarm. This was a big house on its own grounds, but there were other grand houses on either side of it and it wouldn't be long before someone called the Guards. There were old-fashioned sash windows in the house, and right enough, they were too small for Salvadóir.

'Isn't there an alarm?' Aogán asked, and I could hear doubt in his voice that there was any plan at all for this event.

'Don't worry about it,' Salvadóir answered calmly. 'I found a way in the last time I was here.'

We walked around the house and saw what he meant. There was a basement in the house, even though you couldn't see it from the front. It had a window that let in sunlight, almost at the same level as the ground, and this was open. It was a little window and it wouldn't be easy to slide through, but someone who was thin enough could manage it.

'I'll do it,' I said before I had the chance to think about it. 'I'm the thinnest person here.'

'Are you sure?' said Peadar. 'I'm thin enough myself.'

'Maybe you are, but you're taller than me and there's a chance that you'd get stuck in there. We don't have much time. I'll do it, and then I'll go upstairs and open the front door.'

'Good man yourself!' said Salvadóir, giving me a slap on the back.

'Don't open anything on the inside until you're certain that there isn't an alarm,' said Aogán sensibly.

I tried to go in feet first at the beginning, but it was very awkward for some reason. Then I got down on my knees, pushed my head and shoulders through the narrow gap, and lowered my body into the basement, the three outside keeping a grip on my legs. It was difficult for me to see anything on the inside, as if I were going into a dark cave, but there was a frame of some sort that was able to hold my weight. When I was halfway in, I thought of poor Oliver Twist when Bill Sykes took him out thieving. I saw that there was a table under the window with different, unrecognisable things on it, and I laid my hand on this. Bit by bit, I slid through the narrow gap of the window until I was almost inside, and then down, like the serpent entering the Garden of Eden. I was almost safe and sound until the table gave way beneath me and I fell with a thud amongst its shattered pieces on the floor.

'Are you alright?' came down to me from the real world outside.

I couldn't answer the question at first. I wasn't badly hurt, even though I'd hit my shin on the way down, and I was a bit winded. There was a musty smell, and I lay on the flat of my back looking up at the basement ceiling. 'I'm ok,' I said eventually.

I stood up and looked around. It was clearly a storage space, and everything there was jumbled together. There was furniture from some bygone age, as well as boxes and cases with things piled haphazardly on top of one another. I saw hat boxes like you'd see in the nineteenth century, a manikin with a mandolin hanging around its neck, great landscape paintings in ornate frames, and stuffed animals frozen forever in dramatic poses. I looked at the things that fell from the table I'd broken on my way in. My eyes were getting used to the darkness now, and I saw old black and white photographs scattered on the ground. I did my best to pick them up, and looking through them, I saw that they all appeared to be from the 1920s, posed pictures of people on their own or in families, frozen forever in their own dramatic gestures just like those stuffed animals.

'What's going on?' came to me from outside.

'Wait a minute,' I said. I saw stairs that would lead me up to the ground floor, and I walked towards them. For a second, I wondered what I would do if it were locked. I turned the doorknob quickly and it opened with a short squeak to show me the hall upstairs. I went back to the window and shouted to the three outside. 'I've found the way up! Go to the front door and I'll open it for ye.'

'Right so!' I heard footsteps as they went around the building to the other side.

I went back to the bottom of the stairs, and was about to go up when I saw something out of the corner of my eye. There was a man standing there looking at me. I remember that I felt the terror physically like an icy finger going down my spine. He was a small, portly old man in a black suit with a waistcoat and dicky bow, and he had a cross look on his face. He stood there, a stick in his right hand and his left hand positioned behind on his lower back just above his hip. I saw all these things, but he was staring directly at me without moving. I felt as frozen as the stuffed animals or those people in the old photographs, but it occurred to me that I should speak to the man.

'Excuse me,' I said at first in Irish before I remembered that he probably only spoke English. '*I'm just here to… ehm…*' I don't know why I was looking for an excuse. I was after breaking into his house. Could I begin with the story about little men in a fly? I wanted to run but for some reason, I couldn't. '*Sorry about this now. I'm actually not a burglar. I know you probably find that a little difficult to believe, given that you've just found me in your basement but… eh.*'

He didn't answer or even move a finger, a scary enough thing in itself. I walked towards him anyway. When I was halfway across, a horrible thought occurred to me that stopped me in my tracks. He was a ghost! That was the reason why he didn't move. He was a ghost and now I was with him here in the basement. The others were gone and I was on my own. Things like that happen in horror films all the time. But I straightened myself up and carried on.

I walked slowly until I was standing directly before him, until I recognised him. I recognised his face and involuntarily called out his name: 'Winston fuckin' Churchill!' Of course, it wasn't Winston Churchill in the flesh – the old bastard, divider of nations and enemy of the people – but a waxwork dummy. It occurred to me how strange it was that something like this would be in the possession of the person who owned this house, but I didn't have time now to think about it. I turned on my heels and headed up to the lads at the front door.

But as soon as I stood in the hallway upstairs and looked around me, I saw the style of this house properly. It was an old-fashioned style, as if I had travelled back in time to the Edwardian period. I saw pictures and animal heads stuck to the wall, a musket in the corner, a bugle, an ostrich feather, and an ornate vase from India. There was even an umbrella stand made from an elephant's foot. But there was no order on the place and things were thrown haphazardly here and there. I was in the untidy hallway of the British Empire, and I walked quickly through it to open the door.

But then I remembered Aogán's warning, and made a good search first to ensure that there wasn't an alarm. Then I opened the front door.

'What took you so long?' asked Aogán.

'You won't believe this,' I said half-laughing. 'Winston Churchill is in the basement. Well, a waxwork dummy of him anyway.'

'A waxwork dummy of Winston Churchill? What sort of bollocks owns this house? Where's the door to the basement?'

'Down the hall and turn to the right,' I said, and with that, Aogán headed off in that direction.

'Birdy's cabinet is right here in the sitting room,' said Salvadóir. But when he turned the doorknob, it was locked. He took a quick glance at us and laid the great mass of his shoulder against it. It opened with the sound of breaking wood to show us a room from another age. There was the same 1920s' style, but it was much neater: gaudy wallpaper, a carpet in the centre of the room that didn't quite reach the walls, and a voluptuous sofa in front of the window. But Birdy's press itself stood out like something different, something far older than anything else in the room. I saw that there were animal faces carved into the dark wood. It was a piece of furniture that you'd imagine in an Elizabethan castle. It stood about two metres tall, and was divided vertically into three parts, bookshelves in the centre, with doors and drawers on either side. My first impression of it was that it was like a confession box. Salvadóir opened the low door on the left-hand side and dragged out everything that was in it. Then he went to the door on the right and did the same, but now he began rummaging around in the corner as well. 'Damn it!' he said. 'My fingers are too big now. Peadar, come here. Put your hand in here and feel around in the top right corner.'

Peadar went down on his knees and put his hand inside.

'Can you feel a small cavity in the wood?'

'I can.'

'There should be a small metal latch in it.'

'I have it.'

'Wait a minute now,' said Salvadóir, and he went back to the door on the left-hand side of the press. I followed him and looked inside, waiting for the wonders that would come from it. 'Press it now, Peadar,' he said.

Peadar pressed the latch, I heard a click from the bowels of the cabinet, and saw a panel open inside at the back. Salvadóir thrust his hand into this hole and it was big enough this time. He pulled out a leather satchel, and the three of us looked at each other with a tense giddiness. When he opened it, there were three things inside: a hefty old Bible in English, a manuscript of some sort, and an envelope. 'It's my inheritance from Birdy!' he said with elation in his voice. 'I have it at last!'

We were about to look through them when we heard a horrible sound from outside, the sound that a car makes on a gravel driveway. We ran to the window and looked out through gaps in the curtains. 'Christ!' said Peadar. 'It's the Guards!' We heard a robotic voice from a walkie-talkie as four of them got out of the car and began walking around the house.

'I've been waiting on the things in this satchel for years, lads, and I won't give them away easily now,' said Salvadóir.

'Maybe they'll just look around and go away again,' I said hopefully.

But, with that, I heard footsteps to the door and three loud knocks. We stood there quietly, frozen to the spot. I still hoped that they'd go away, but then I heard an authoritative voice in the hall, as if he was shouting through the letterbox: '*We know that you're in there.*

You were seen entering the premises. The house is surrounded. Make it easy on yourselves now and just come out.'

'There are four of them, and four of us. Can we force our way through and escape?' I said in a whisper.

'We could alright, but there'd be ten more of them before we reached the top of the street,' said Salvadóir.

'That's it so. We're going to prison.' Peadar said in despair.

'You're not going to prison,' a voice said from behind us, and we all turned around quickly. It was Aogán, back from the basement. 'I have a plan. Come with me quickly.'

We followed him out through the hall and down to the basement, that dark room under the house.

'You're not suggesting that we escape through that little window, are you?' I said. 'It was hard enough for me coming in through it.'

'I'm not. We'll escape with the help of this old bollocks,' he answered, referring to Winston Churchill.

'Winston Churchill is going to help us escape from the Guards?' Peadar asked with astonishment.

'He will. Grab him quickly. We haven't much time.'

So we carried the ex-British prime minister upstairs.

'Leave him here, looking forward in the direction of the door but a good distance back and in the darkest part of the hall,' said Aogán. 'Now go down to the kitchen, and wait at the back door until the way is clear to escape through the gate at the back of the garden.'

'That gate is locked,' said Salvadóir.

'It isn't locked anymore,' replied Aogán, pulling out the two spanners he had taken from Salvadóir's tool box in the van. 'When the two of you were looking in through the basement window, I went around to find an escape route in case we needed it.' He took the bugle from the wall, walked to the front door and opened it a little. He came back to us then and stood behind Winston Churchill in a way that he wouldn't be seen from the door. 'Go quickly!' he said, and blew loudly on the bugle.

'But what about you?' I asked.

'I'll be fine. Go on!'

The three of us ran down the hallway towards the kitchen at the back of the house and looked carefully out the window. There were two guards there and they were looking around trying to find out where the sound of the bugle had come from. Then we heard the voice of the first guard from the front door. '*Hello?*' he said carefully.

Another voice reached us then, and you could imagine it coming down through the ages. It was a loud English voice. The voice of Empire, a voice from the age of the old news reels of the Second World War. It was the voice of Winston Churchill. '*What do you think you're doing, entering my house. Get out this minute. How dare you!*' it bellowed.

There was silence for a few seconds and I imagined that the Guards were confused as to how they should respond. '*Excuse me, sir. Is this your house?*' the guard asked. He was speaking now as if he was standing just inside the door.

'*Of course it's my house, you bloody imbecile!*' Winston answered.

'*It's just that we had a report of some suspicious individuals entering the premises.*'

'*Those were workmen that I plan to employ during the week. Nothing for you to be concerned about.*'

'*That's fine, sir. If you could just come towards the door so that I can verify that this is actually your house.*'

I heard a shout then and the two guards who were at the back of the house went around to the other side of the building. We opened the back door and looked out carefully. Our escape route was before us.

I heard Winston's voice once more before we headed off out through the garden. '*Very well, very well! Just give me a moment. My legs are not quite what they used to be.*'

Salvadóir directed myself and Peadar through the elegant garden to a little gate in the high wall behind the house, and as Aogán had said, it was open. We escaped out to the lane and down to the road. In a couple of minutes, we were at the van and we jumped in with great relief.

'Wait!' I said to them. 'Wait for Aogán.'

They waited, even though I could see that they wanted to be away from that place as fast as possible. But Aogán wasn't long after us anyway, and he jumped in quickly. Salvadóir started the engine, and soon we were darting through the Jack Lynch Tunnel towards Ballyphehane.

'I really liked your impression of Winston Churchill,' Salvadóir said, laughing. When we were heading west along the South Ring Road, he took up the satchel and threw it to me. 'Open it!' he said. 'Look at the manuscript.'

I took it out carefully. Its yellow pages had the appearance of having been in this world for a very long time. There was something written on the cover that I didn't understand, but then through the ornate penmanship, I saw a name that I recognised: Jan Swammerdam.

'Jesus Christ!' shouted Peadar. 'This is Jan Swammerdam's diary.'

Scene Four

Chalfont St Giles, Buckinghamshire, England
11th June 1665

The carriage moved along at an easy pace through the country roads, the broad fields trotting lazily past the window in the heat of the sun. The pale green landscape stretched its curved flanks up and down like great waves in the Chiltern hills. Now and again, a shade of dark green was placed over this view as the carriage was immersed into the thick beech woods. Ancient hamlets would also leap into the frame with their thatched cottages of warped wood, but they would be swept away just as quickly, like half-remembered dreams.

There was one man in the carriage and he sat there quietly, looking out at visions of England that darted past aimlessly. He was a man of English descent, although born in Ireland, yet he was a long way from Waterford now. He had left Oxford at about eight o'clock in the morning and now, approaching midday, it would not be long to his destination. The horses sped up, and you would imagine they knew the way, even though they had never made this journey before. They were sturdy horses and it was a fine and comfortable carriage, but no one who looked at it would say that it belonged to a wealthy man. There was none of the gaudiness that you would see on the carriages of the grandees of London, for example. This man was a scientist, a learned man who directed his life to objectives higher than commerce, business or the accumulation of wealth. He preferred the study of the material of the world, the material from which everything is made. His mind was incited to ask the most basic of questions of the world that God had created. What were the raw materials that he used? What were the everyday things around us made from? Metal, stone, the air itself: were they compounds or basic elements? He was searching for God's building blocks, and he well understood that it was never going to be an easy task, and yet, that was his goal and he was sworn to it. But he understood as well that he would fail in the end, that he would cut a path through the woods to a certain point and then he would fall as everyone does. As such, he wanted to make a new system so that others could follow his path and extend it. He rejected the secret methods of the alchemists in days gone by, and published all his discoveries.

But he was lucky that he had money and a certain status so that he could devote his life to this work. He remembered writing of this in his diary when he was young and had recognised that he had the good fortune to be born 'in a condition that neither was high enough to prove a temptation to laziness, nor low enough to discourage him from aspiring'. He gave himself the name Philaretus in this diary, named after Saint Philaretus of Byzantium who had given up his money for the poor, even though he himself was of the nobility. He would likewise spend his own life modestly, and could also be generous with people. He could spend his wealth in the service of learning and the glory of God. He could do these things because he had the resources to do so. The money would arrive over from Ireland as it always had. His name was Robert Boyle, and he was born in Lismore Castle, the youngest son of the Earl of Cork, Richard Boyle. When his father died, he inherited a substantial estate in County Limerick, and now the money would flow forever across to him like an eternal river.

They were not an old family, of course. His father, the Great Earl himself, went to Ireland with £27 in his pocket when he was just twenty-one years of age. But Queen Elizabeth was looking for people to take possession of this inhospitable land at the time, and there was a good life waiting for the right people. Boyle married well, and when his first wife died, he married better again. He was able to buy large tracts of land with these two dowries, especially in Cork and Waterford, and the title of Earl of Cork was thus conferred upon this wandering adventurer. The Earl had married Robert's mother when she was about fifteen years old, and she gave him fifteen children before her death.

Robert himself was born three years before his mother passed away, and he spent most of that time being fostered. He came back to Lismore Castle then until he was eight years of age, and was subsequently sent to school in Eton College. He couldn't truthfully say therefore that he knew his father well (and his mother even less, of course), but he had spent a summer with the Great Earl a few years after that and felt that the old man was quite fond of him. And he didn't forget him either in his will, even though Robert was the youngest son of the family. The estates in County Limerick were bestowed upon him, as well as Stalbridge Manor in Dorset.

Robert's brother Richard was fifteen years older than him, and he was the second Earl of Cork now and also the first Earl of Burlington. He also sat in the Parliament in Dublin as Lord High Treasurer of Ireland. He was an important and distinguished man, and had fought on the right side when he was called upon, as had many of his other brothers. Their loyalty added to their wealth as well, of course. In that world, the gratitude of the King was always a valuable commodity. But Robert never liked that life, and always avoided it.

He thought of his brother Richard now as he sat in the carriage. He had a son who was also called Richard. Robert had received a letter just a few days before to say that this young nephew of his had been killed in battle. He was on board the Duke's flagship when it was struck by a cannonball. The cannonball killed Richard as well as Viscount Muskerry and the Earl of Falmouth. It was said that his blood and brains were thrown into the Duke's face and that poor Richard's head had even knocked down the Duke. Robert remembered his nephew now when he was just a four-year-old boy, and a shiver ran down his spine.

That was their life, of course. They had great wealth, and if they could remain on the right side of whatever trouble was going on around them, then they would be rich forever.

Some riches would undoubtedly come from the thankful purse of the King in recompense for the loss they suffered with poor Richard's death. Twelve of the children born to Robert's mother had lived, and they all got their share. All were interwoven in the Anglo-Irish world and in the world of the nobility in England. Robert had another brother called Francis whose wife had a daughter who was acknowledged openly as the illegitimate child of the King.

But, of course, life was not always kind on this poor King either. During the Civil War when he was eight years old, his father had been beheaded before the mob on the orders of Parliament. He lived as a king in exile then in the Netherlands with his own country under the control of the Lord Protector, Oliver Cromwell. But then Charles II was put back on his father's throne in 1660. It was strange for Robert now that he was about to visit the house of one of the most steadfast of republicans: John Milton.

Milton was a writer, and had often used his pen to strengthen that devilish republicanism during Cromwell's rule over the country. Robert had read the *Eikonoklastes* that he wrote, and it disgusted him that he openly defended regicide in it. He was a lot older now, and blind as well, but Robert remembered him twenty years before. He had been given the position of tutor to his nephew Richard Barry, his sister Alice's son. Robert recalled that he was a headstrong man, full of righteous indignation and spitefulness towards the reign of the King. He and Alice eventually fell out because of his outspoken opinions, and that was the end of those classes. Milton was the kind of person who would not mince his words when discussing something that was close to his heart, and he received a good position during Cromwell's reign because of it.

But life was different for him when the Restoration came, and he had to go into hiding. His books were burnt and he was imprisoned for a while, even after the general pardon. Robert remembered that it was his own other sister, Katherine, who came to Milton's rescue then, but she was always very impressed with him for some reason. It was she who had introduced him to Alice as a tutor and she sent her own son – yet another Richard – to him as well. Even though Robert didn't like Milton's politics, if Katherine had a good opinion of someone, then that was often enough for him as well. She was very clever, and had she been born male, he was certain that she would now be a renowned scientist. He knew that Milton had great respect for her as well, and this thought softened any ill-will he bore the old rebel.

After that, Milton lived quietly in London, and Robert heard a year or two ago that he had married for a third time. But then recently, everything changed and he had to escape and go into hiding again – this time from the plague that was scourging the city. Robert worried about what lay in store for those who were still in London now. He received news regularly in Oxford and heard that things were getting worse there. But it was neither the plague nor Milton's republicanism that set Robert travelling for four hours now to speak with him. It was one strange thing, a sentence he had said in London almost twenty years before, and he needed to find out now what he had meant by it.

He well remembered that day in Alice's house in Barbican. The classes with his nephew had finished for the day, and a lively conversation arose between them. Robert was about twenty years old at the time and it was clear to him that this tutor was an extremely learned man. He was amazed when Milton told him that he had once met Galileo. Robert told him then that he himself had been in Florence, a couple of miles from Galileo's house in Arcetri, when that great pioneer had died and that this occasion had a huge effect on him.

They were talking together pleasantly when Milton said something very strange: 'Alas, it is clear that little men do greatly rule this world.' He said with disgust in his voice.

'I agree with you, Mr Milton. Too much power is given to those of weak intellect,' Robert replied carefully.

'That's not what I mean. Little men! Men so tiny that you could not see them with your eyes.'

'I have heard, right enough, that the scholasticism of the Catholics could discuss how many angels would stand on the head of a pin,' Robert said, trying to introduce some sense into the conversation.

'Maybe they were right,' said Milton abruptly, and that was the end of it.

Robert thought at the time that it was a peculiar thing to say, and for some reason he never forgot it. Maybe it was the way in which it reminded him of something he had seen in an old book many years before. But, in truth, he didn't think of it often. That is, until Hooke came to him that day in London with his story.

It was an dreadful story, and he had never seen anything quite like the expression on Hooke's face as he told it. It was terror, terror and panic in his eyes, his mouth shaking, his hands squeezed together tightly. He was breathless from running in the street and wisps of hair were stuck to his forehead now with sweat. He was a small man with a hunchback, and when Robert looked at him that day, he imagined him as some sort of gargoyle. But this wasn't the Robert Hooke he knew. He was a sensible and intelligent man, a man with a sharp intellect that was always able to find answers to the most difficult questions. Boyle had employed him at first to help in his laboratory, but it was clear before long that he was just as astute and progressive as himself. It was Hooke who made the vacuum pumps when he did the experiments from which his gas law were made. In truth, it was he who actually carried out the experiments themselves at the time. But now he was like a madman before him.

Hooke told him his story. It was difficult for Boyle to accept it, of course. Was he drunk? Had he lost his mind? Hooke wasn't working for him then, because he had found another position as curator of experiments in the Royal Society, but yet it was to him that he came now with this disturbing story. He said that he had looked through the microscope at a fly and saw tiny men there. He asked him if he was sure that they weren't animals of some sort, but he told him that he was certain that they had a human form. Then he told him that thousands of flies came all around him, an immeasurable amount of them, and he escaped with his life.

What can one say to such a story? Could it possibly be true? Maybe Hooke was working too hard. Boyle recommended that he redo the experiment, and saw the fear rising in his eyes again. He agreed to do it eventually, because that was the type of person he was. Unanswered questions bothered him. But Boyle could see that it took every ounce of courage he had. Hooke asked if he could do it with him, however, or at least to be present when he did it, and he agreed to that. They did the experiment the following day. Then they did it again, and again. They killed twenty flies, but there was no sign of the little men in any them. Boyle saw both disappointment and relief mixed together on Hooke's face. 'I don't know what you saw yesterday,' he said to him then. 'You are certain of it, and I accept that. You are a prudent and level-headed man, and I do not need to tell you how great my respect is for your intellect. But, as learned men, we need to include every possibility and to measure and weigh each one of them against the other. That is the scientific process and we must adhere to it. Are you certain that you are not in error about this?'

Hooke lowered his head and spoke softly. 'I must accept that possibility,' he said.

Boyle recommended then that he say nothing to anyone about this until they had more information. As he was leaving Hooke's house that day, he believed that he had dealt well with the problem. The poor man! What an terrible shock for him? That sort of mental breakdown can happen to people who work too hard. A person's imagination is a powerful engine. Maybe those little men were nothing more than a chunk of indigestible cheese that didn't agree with his stomach.

Boyle walked out onto the street. It was a fine day and he decided to take a stroll around the town. He was only a minute down the road, however, when the words came to him, and he almost collapsed. He had to lay his hand upon the wall to steady himself. Why had he not thought of it before? Milton's words ran through his mind like a barking dog: 'Alas, it is clear that little men do greatly rule this world ... men so tiny that you could not see them with your eyes.'

But how would that old republican know? He remembered then that he had said this after they had spoken of Galileo. Maybe he had seen them as well, and had told the young Englishman who had come to visit him. Milton himself was blind at this stage. Should he go and speak to him? He was living in London. He could go there now directly, but he wouldn't do it. He didn't want to. It was an abominable thing and he couldn't face it. He would go home and he would not think about it again.

Of course, that was difficult to do, and worse still, it was clear that Hooke could not remain quiet about it either. He wanted to mention it in his book, and Boyle had to persuade him not to do it. But, as well as that, he had exchanged letters with Melchisédech Thévenot in France, and he had made him aware that the existence of the little men was known to other people as well. Hooke had told him nothing of this until recently, and then he came to him with news that he had received a letter from Thévenot to say that a learned man in the Netherlands had also seen these little men, someone called Jan Swammerdam. But still Boyle revealed nothing of what Milton had said to him. It was nothing but a stray comment at the end of the day, wasn't it? For some reason, he didn't want to be a party to this affair at all.

The war began then between England and the Netherlands, and he could put it out of his mind for a while. But then a letter came from Hooke to say that Swammerdam was to travel to England to meet him. The letter took some time to arrive, and maybe he was even already in England. Boyle had no choice now. He would have to visit Milton's house and get the truth from him. If it was only a stray comment, there would be no harm done and this business would not involve him any longer. As luck would have it, he was not far away. He had already heard that Milton and his family had fled from the plague and that they were living in a little house in Chalfont St Giles, four hours from Oxford. This was the journey he was now on, and he hadn't the slightest idea how he would begin such a conversation with the old man.

The carriage entered the sleepy village and it didn't take the driver long to get directions to the house. It was a neat box on the street, made of red brick on a wooden frame. The sturdy footing of the chimney stuck out from the wall beside the front door, and it narrowed as it extended high into the air. There was a window in the gable wall at the side of the house which looked out onto a fine garden, filled with flowers. It was a charming house and Boyle liked it very much.

He knocked at the low door and it wasn't long before he heard a noise from inside. An attractive young woman opened it with a sudden tug, black curly locks of her hair falling from her bonnet. He imagined her to be a woman of about twenty-five and wondered whether she was Milton's daughter or a maidservant. She had a cross expression on her face at first, but this softened a little when she recognised that Boyle was a gentleman. 'Good day to you,' he said. 'Is the master at home?'

'He is, sir,' she said, and stood there without saying another word.

'Tell him that Mr Robert Boyle is calling on him, the brother of Lady Ranelagh.'

He saw that she curtsied a little on hearing that title, but was still reluctant to let a stranger into the house. He wondered if she imagined him to be a royalist who would thrust a dagger into the heart of the regicide within. 'You're very welcome, sir,' she said eventually. 'Please come in.' She stood to one side to let him enter, but he still had to lower his head to come through the door. It was a narrow space on the inside as well, but the house was neat and clean. 'I'm Betty, the master's wife and lady of the house. If you would kindly wait a moment, I will tell my husband that you're here,' she said assertively and went out to another room.

He had heard, indeed, that the old agitator had married again, but he wasn't expecting this spirited young woman, about thirty years Milton's junior. He looked about him at the little house as he waited. There were roughly hewn beams running horizontally in the walls and over the fireplace which formed part of the frame of the house. He heard a man's voice coming from somewhere and it was mixed in places with a different female voice.

It wasn't long before Betty returned and spoke again in the same assured tone. 'You can see the master now, Mr Boyle. Follow me, please,' and she directed him down to another room.

Milton was sitting on an armchair in the corner. His eyes were closed and he was a lot older than Robert remembered him, but he recognised the solemn features immediately.

'Mr Milton, please forgive this unexpected visit. Do you remember me? I am Robert Boyle, brother of Katherine Jones, the Lady Ranelagh,' he said, more humbly than he had expected.

'I remember you very well, Mr Boyle, and you are most welcome,' Milton said. With that, he turned his head a little in the direction of the young girl who was collecting papers at the table. 'Finish with that now, Mary, and be careful that you put everything in the correct order.'

'I will indeed, father,' she answered humbly.

'This is my daughter, Mr Boyle. She is helping me to write my literary work now that I have lost my eyesight. And, of course, you have already met my wife Betty.'

Mary turned her face to Robert but kept her eyes on the ground. He estimated that she was about sixteen years of age. 'Sir,' she said as she curtsied to him.

'It is very nice to meet you, Miss Milton,' Robert said. 'And indeed, I have already had the pleasure of meeting the lady of the house today as well.'

'Out now quickly, Mary! You have not done your chores yet,' Betty said curtly, and the two women went out, leaving the men on their own. Robert wondered what sort of strife there was in this house between a new young wife and the old man's daughters, particularly someone as wilful as this Betty. How many daughters did Milton have again? Three or four, as far as he remembered.

'I am very pleased that you would call on me like this, Mr Boyle. Forgive us that we are lodged in this humble little house, but as you know, the cursèd plague has driven us from London.'

'It is a charming house, Mr Milton, and I am delighted to be able to visit you. I hope that you are well?'

'As well as God permits me. He took my eyesight years ago, as you see, yet still his eternal mercy allows me life.'

'And did I hear correctly that you are embarking on a new literary work?'

'It is poetry, Mr Boyle. My first love. The air in this country is no longer suitable for my political opinions. It would be an unhealthy venture for me now, even though cares for my own well-being have never hindered my pen before. But I am old and blind now. That race has been run, but I have another yet to run.'

Milton was always a fiery agitator, a warrior that would not lay down his sword till death. His sword was his pen. Robert looked now at this quill as it stood faithfully on the table beside him, always within arm's reach of the old hero in case assassins would come in the night, and he wondered about this new race he had to run.

'But let us not speak of the old days,' Milton said. 'Tell me of yourself, sir, and about your wonderful sister Katherine. She is the best of women! Is she well in these dangerous times?'

'She is in fine health, and sends you her blessings,' said Robert, lying to him. He hadn't told his sister that he was coming here at all.

'Wonderful! I will be in her debt forever. And your nephews, the two Richards. I hope they are also well?'

This question grieved Robert deeply. Certainly, those two Richards were in the best of health, as far as he knew, but what about the other poor Richard? The Dutch had made a bowling ball of his head so as to flatten the Duke. 'They are very well, Mr Milton,' he said.

But now that they had finished the well-mannered chat, Robert perceived a change coming across Milton's face, even with his eyes closed. 'But you didn't come all this way to make pleasantries with me, Mr Boyle,' he said.

Robert stopped now, because he didn't know how to start this conversation, a conversation that would have to be broached. Milton was too sharp to be blind to the fact that there was something up with him. 'Forgive me, Mr Milton, but I need your advice on an important matter.'

'My advice? What sort of advice would you want from me?'

'Advice regarding scientific questions.'

'I have no knowledge regarding such questions. I leave matters of that nature to God.'

'But did you not tell me that you once visited Galileo?'

'I did, but what of it? It's not to say he shared the secrets of the stars with me. I visited a blind old man in his house, just as you're doing now. The authorities had persecuted the poor man. That was the Catholic Church, of course, the cursèd whore of Babylon. I was a young man on a tour of Europe, as many others have done, and I got the opportunity to go to Galileo's house and speak with him. He was a wonderful, spirited man, the kind of man that you meet only once in your life. But, beyond that, I have no knowledge of this science you require.'

'Do you know, I was in Florence when Galileo died,' said Robert. 'Of course, I never met him, but I was just a couple of miles from his house in Arcetri. The news came to us the following day. My father had sent my brother and me on a tour of Europe, but I was very young at the time, just fifteen years old. That tour opened my eyes. It gave me the call of learning, the call of science, and Galileo's books were extremely important in that regard.'

'And you stayed in the house of that great man Giovanni Diodati in Geneva,' said Milton, cutting across him abruptly. 'He was an uncle to my great friend Charles, who is no longer with us, unfortunately. I stayed in the same house when I was there. I remember you telling me this story twenty years ago. But forgive me: I still don't understand what advice I might have to give you on the subject of science.'

'You remember our conversation about your visit to Galileo's house?'

'I do indeed, as if it happened yesterday.'

'Do you remember something else you said to me on that day?'

Milton didn't reply immediately. He turned his face to Robert in a way he would have done if he'd had eyes. He took in a deep breath and let it out slowly. 'Say your piece,' he said calmly.

'Alas, it is clear that little men do greatly rule this world, men so tiny that you could not see them with your eyes.' That's what you said. Did Galileo tell you about these little men?' Robert said it out straight, and it was a relief to him now that it was done. Like a person about to dive into cold water, it's the waiting beforehand that's the worst.

Milton remained quiet again for a while, as if he himself were uneasy before plunging into the same cold water. 'Yes,' he said in the end. 'Galileo told me that he had created an instrument for looking at the smallest things in God's creation, but he saw something he wasn't expecting. It was a great error that I spoke to you about this. I don't know what sort of stupor came over me that day. But anyway, you wouldn't be here now questioning me about something that I said twenty years ago if you hadn't received information on this matter from somewhere else. Did you see them with your own eyes?'

'I didn't. It was a colleague of mine who saw them some time ago. Now there is correspondence from France to say that someone else has seen them as well. I don't understand how such a thing can be true. My colleague said that they had human form, but did God not create us – and us alone – in his own image?'

'But this is the form of the angels as well, Robert … and of the devils. I will tell you the story, even though I do not wish to speak of it. Woe that I ever learned this cursèd knowledge, that I was made aware that such things exist. We are astray now from the normal path of life and wandering in the dark woods. I recommend that you guard your soul before you lose it forever. I will tell it to you, but first let us beseech God that he may give us his help and protection in this our time of peril.'

Milton put his face in his hands and didn't move for a while. Then he raised his head and spoke in a low voice, like someone in a dream: 'Yea, though I walk through the valley of the shadow of death, I will fear no evil: for thou art with me; thy rod and thy staff they comfort me. Thou prepared a table before me in the presence of mine enemies that night in Rome, oh Lord. But my trust will always be in you.'

'Amen,' said Robert awkwardly, even though he didn't understand that last part which Milton had added to the psalm.

Then the blind man began speaking again, slowly and steadily: 'It was 1638 and I was still a relatively young man, twenty-nine years of age, when I left England to go on a tour of the Continent. A young man, full of education but yet with no prospects in life. I went abroad, as such, looking for inspiration, trying to find something that would give me direction. I went to France first and then on to Italy. If I was looking for inspiration, I found it in Florence.

That beautiful city was like a heaven to me, a city filled with culture, music and learning. It wasn't long before I had met a good many learned people and they inspired the poet in me. I'd spent long years before that reading and studying. Now I was in a place in which respect was given to that learning, a place in which there was a circle of scholarly men who were immersed in art, in poetry and in every form of study. The news went around that a learned young Englishman had recently arrived and the intellectuals of the city made themselves known to me. I was given respect as a writer far beyond anything I had received in my own country. My eyes were opened in Florence to what art is and they have never closed since, even though I have lost the physical sight of everything else.

'I received an invitation to visit Galileo's house then, through connections I had made in the city. I was worried because I knew the story of how the Catholic Church had placed him under house arrest when he implied in his book that the earth went around the sun as opposed to the other way around. I was not a scholar of that type and had no understanding of the mechanics of the heavens, but yet I understood that the theory was contrary to that which was written in the Holy Bible. Even though I had respect for Galileo's intellect, I was still worried that his opinions were wrong in the eyes of God.

'But yet I was excited when I met him. The first thing I noticed was his enormous intellectual presence. I noticed it as soon as I walked into the room, and I don't believe that I've ever met another person who has so affected me. And I received a wonderful welcome in his house, so great that I was fully at ease within a few minutes in his company. Did you know that he was also a musician? He played excellently on the lute. Both our fathers were musicians and that created a bond between us, I believe. There were two other people there as well: a clever mathematician called Evangelista Torricelli, and a young boy with him about fifteen years of age. Vincenzo Viviani was his name. The night progressed pleasantly with a lovely meal and inspiring conversation, and Galileo asked me about my own writings, as well as my political and religious opinions. As you know, I am not a shy person as regards conversation of that sort and I spoke candidly, but Galileo was an open, understanding and mannerly man and listened carefully to everything I had to say.

'Anyway, outspoken as I am, I asked him about his imprisonment, about his troubles with the Church, and that theory on the heliocentric system. A wry smile came across his face and he said to me: 'That's not the reason I'm in prison. That was the excuse they used to shut me up. It was something else, something that I saw one sunny day in this very house. Maybe that's the reason they put me under house arrest, that the imprisonment be in the same place in which the crime was committed: that's the humour of the Barberini.'

'The master is tired now,' Torricelli said anxiously, but Galileo silenced him. It was clear that Torricelli had heard this story already and there was alarm in his eyes. I remember that the face of that boy Viviani was white with fear.

'Be quiet,' Galileo replied. 'I will say my piece. What will they do to me? Whatever it is, I don't care now. The truth is all that's important now, to me and to God!'

'He turned to me and spoke calmly. He told me that he had created a telescope to look at great things in the heavens, and that he had also created another instrument to look at the smallest of things, a backwards telescope, or a microscope. He told me that he had used it about ten years before to examine a small insect, a fly, and that everything changed in his life after that. Apparently, this instrument can greatly magnify small things, and Galileo thought that he could see the face and the eyes of the fly clearly with it. But he saw something else, something terrifying and dreadful. He saw two tiny men inside the head of the fly, men so tiny you could not see them except with the help of this instrument. Then thousands of other flies came all around him. They attacked him and he had to flee from the house.

'He told me that it was difficult for him to believe at first himself. This was not a realm of knowledge with which he was familiar. They weren't insects or animals. They weren't stars or planets. They were people – little people. Was it true that such beings existed in the world? Why was it not spoken of in the scriptures? Could it be that the Church was unaware of their existence, or was it some obscure secret of theirs? Anyway, Galileo understood that it was important information and that he would have to speak to the most important of people about it: the Pope himself.

'He was lucky that he knew Maffeo Barberini well before he had been made Pope Urban VIII. Galileo had been a friend of the family for years, and had even given lessons to Barberini's nephew Francesco. So he went to Rome and the Pope gave him a great welcome. It was clear that Galileo had respect for him, and that they were friendly with one another.

But when he told him the story, the Pope's face changed immediately and he looked sharply at Galileo. He said that he already knew of these little men and told him how. This was a mistake, according to Galileo. If he had told him that he had learned this information through the office of the papacy, he would have gone back to Florence with his mouth shut forever.

But the Pope told him the truth. Maybe he did this because he was fond of Galileo or because he trusted him. Anyway, he thought it better to tell him the truth and let him in on his family secret.

'The story related to the Medici family and went back to the end of the fourteenth century. According to Maffeo, there was some contact between Giovanni di Bicci de' Medici and the little men in the 1390s, and they gave him help and advice. Within a few years he was in charge of the papal account, and his power and the wealth of his family grew then until his descendants sat on the thrones of Europe. There was history between the Barberini and Medici families and it wasn't always very friendly. The Barberini family were merchants in Florence and they had accumulated a substantial wealth early in the sixteenth century. Carlo Barberini (the grandfather of Maffeo) and his brother Antonio were doing well for themselves, but Florence suffered regularly at the time under the hand of the Medici, and Antonio himself fought against them for the Republic of Florence in 1530. He lost that fight but won something else that was more important: the knowledge of how the Medici had gained their power. Maffeo didn't tell him how Antonio had come by this knowledge, but said that he had made the same contact himself with the little men and every benefit that went with it. There was one difference, however, because the Barberini made contact with those who were in bees, as opposed to those in flies. The Medici family killed Antonio in 1559, but the Barberini were very strong by then. They afterwards put bees on their family coat of arms and on statues and fountains all over Rome.

'Galileo was disgusted when Maffeo told him the story, and said that he would bring it to light. Whatever those little men were – devils, angels, or a new species of human beings – he believed that it wasn't right to use that knowledge for the ugly accumulation of wealth. They fell out, and he saw a side of Maffeo that day that he had never seen before. It was clear that those bees had a poisonous sting. He escaped with his life from

Rome under the cover of darkness a few hours later and went back to Florence.

'But this was a complicated political affair. If Galileo had a personal history with the Barberini, he had an even stronger connection with the Grand Duke of Tuscany: the Medici family themselves. He had been a tutor to the youth of this family as well. The Grand Duchess of Tuscany, Cristina di Lorena, had sent her son Cosimo to him, and it was not long before he received a full patronage from them, as well as the position of court mathematician.

It was a key to that elegant world – but better again – it gave him freedom to do his own work. He understood now, however, that he was in danger from all sides.

'It was no surprise to him then when he received in invitation to go to Palazzo Pitti, chief residence of the Grand Duke, Ferdinando II de' Medici. But this Grand Duke was still only a young man. His father Cosimo had died (the same Cosimo whom Galileo had taught years before) and he was put in his place when he was only ten years old. His mother and grandmother were made joint regents at the time and now, eight years later, the invitation came from this grandmother, Cristina di Lorena herself. It was clear to Galileo when he was shown before her that she still very much held the reins.

'Galileo described her as woman of haughty bearing, even though she could be well-mannered in her own cold way. I found out that she had died only five months before I came to Florence, and she had kept her power all that time. Ferdinando was there as well, and Galileo was very taken with the young Duke. Cristina wasted no time, however. 'We heard about what you saw, and we would like to say to you, as a friend to this family, that we will continue the patronage we bestow upon you, and more than that, will provide you with protection from the vengeance of the Barberini.'

'Galileo thanked her heartily.

'But we hope that you can do something for us as well.'

'Galileo told her he would do it gladly.'

'We hope that you can stay in the heavens with the stars, and leave the affairs of the flies to us. Can you do that? I trust that this is within your capabilities, a man as clever as you. I believe that we can protect you from the dogs of the Barberini as long as your mouth and your pen, remain silent on this matter.'

'Galileo inclined his head and said that he was forever a loyal servant of the Medici family. He understood now that he would have to be very careful with every step he took from now on. But Ferdinando himself accompanied Galileo to the door, and shook hands with him warmly as he left. 'You will have a friend in me always, whatever else happens. I can say no more than that,' he said and went back inside again quickly.

'It is true that Galileo did not write one word about the little men he had seen. But he was a stubborn man and had told people the story. Then in 1632, he published *Dialogo sopra i due massimi sistemi del mondo*, his book regarding different understandings of whether the earth or the sun is at the centre of the universe. He dedicated it to his patron Ferdinando de' Medici, and received full permission for it as well from the Inquisition and the Pope himself. But when it was published, they came down on him heavily. Cristina did not protect him, and even strengthened the ties between the Grand Duchy of Tuscany and the Barberini Papacy, giving them lands that should have been left to Ferdinando himself. It was clear that his grandmother still held great power, but Ferdinando remained true to his promise and was always a faithful friend Galileo. He gave him every help he could in his predicament, but the Barberini were too strong. At least, he didn't suffer in prison under the hand of the Inquisition, and he believed Ferdinando's help was instrumental in that.

'The Grand Duchess Cristina died five months ago. Did you know that?' he told me. 'The Barberini are fond of me, I know they are, yet they will leave me here until I die. But I promise you one thing: I will not take their secret with me to the grave.' And with that, Galileo finished his story.

'It was difficult for me to believe, of course, but the intensity of his voice impressed upon me that I should not discount it. Was it possible that he was out of his mind, that he was a bewildered old man, pouring forth his ravings about those who had imprisoned him? Somehow, I was certain that wasn't the case. I believe that he was sharper than any person I had met before or since. But if that was true, what were these beings? Was it angels or devils that looked down upon humanity from the eyes of flies? Maybe there is no difference between the kingdom of Heaven and this world except the size. It's possible. I felt a great confusion that night on leaving the house.

'I left Florence the following month and set out for Rome, or *Urbs Aeterna* as Tibullus called it. It was there that I got the next part of this story, and saw that what Galileo had told me was the truth. But I wasn't ready to accept it at first. I remember walking around the city, and seeing stone bees everywhere, like gargoyles, looking at me, every one of them put there by the Barberini. I tried my best not to think about it and, as in Florence, I made the acquaintance of the learned people of the city. Amongst them, I met Lucas Holstenius, the Vatican librarian at the time, and a very honourable man. It was this Mr Holstenius who organised an invitation for me to a concert of Leonora Baroni, the renowned singer, and where would she be singing that night but in the Palazzo Barberini. It was the opera *Chi soffre, speri* by the composer Virgilio Mazzocchi, and I was looking forward to it very much.

I went in Holstenius' carriage and we stopped before that beautiful building. There was a special servant waiting for us there who directed us in through the elegant doors, and who should be right inside but the nephew of the Pope himself, Cardinal Francesco Barberini: the same nephew whom Galileo had taught years before. He seemed like a prince and gave me a huge welcome. You would imagine from such a reception that I myself was a prince: he took my elbow and directed me through the ornate hall, filled with the finest statues and paintings.

That disgusts me now, thinking back on it, because what that house must have cost is immeasurable. Pomp and ostentation, that was all it was, but I had eyes that time and it's easy to beguile the eyes of a young man with gaudy colours. Still, I must admit that it was more beautiful and luxuriant that anything I have ever seen. And the music! The music affected me greatly and I felt as though I were floating on warm breezes in the great hall, blown by the indescribable voice of Leonora Baroni. The extravagant drama was magical as well, actors in elegant costumes, and the wonderful set brought you to another world. For a while I felt as if I was in heaven. Whatever qualms I have ever had about the flamboyance of the Catholics melted and I fell into a dream of happiness.

'But then it all burst like a soap bubble, and I fell from the dreamy air and landed on the hard ground. I heard one word in the libretto of the opera that woke me from that dream as if a bucket of cold water had been thrown in my face. The libretto tells the story of a young man called Egisto who is in love with a young widow, Alvida. At the end of the drama, they marry and Egisto finds buried treasure and a heliotrope, the healing stone that saves Alvida's son. It's a simple enough story, but Egisto has a servant who helps him, and the word that so disturbed me was the name of this servant: Moschino, another word for *mosca* or fly. I thought then of the wealth that Egisto had found and the wealth of the Barberini. Was it all an allegory for the family's history?

'It must be a coincidence, I thought. Then I saw Francesco Barberini sitting next to Giulio Rospigliosi, the writer of the libretto, and I remembered being told that he was also very close to his uncle Maffeo, the Pope himself. But still, what did that mean? It was a coincidence, I said to myself. Leaving the palace that night, I felt the same sense of bewilderment as I did that night at Galileo's house. But the Cardinal came to me again, full of generosity and manners. Did I like the opera? I liked it very much, I answered. Would I come to dine at his residence the following night? I would come with much gratitude for the Cardinal's generosity. And that was it. I felt as if I had accepted an invitation to the house of the devil.

'I will not bother to describe the beauty and riches of the Cardinal's residence, or the succulence of the meal. Holstenius came with me because he had received the same invitation. I also met that night with Angelo Giori, who had been in the service of Maffeo Barberini for years. I have to say that Giori had a strange effect on me from the beginning. He was a small, thin man, in his fifties I would say, with sharp eyebrows like arches over cold, black eyes, and his hair was cropped short. I found out a few years later that he had been made a cardinal as well. The evening was very pleasant and Francesco's generosity was beyond anything you could imagine: even a rich man like yourself, Robert. But the question was on my mind the whole time and, as you know, I've always been an outspoken man.

'Tell me about the bees on your family's coat of arms,' I asked the Cardinal politely. He began to tell me some story about it, but I cut across him: 'Aren't those little men wonderful?' I said, 'and the great abundance that they bestow upon us.' The air suddenly changed in the room. I can't explain this, but I felt that it became colder. Giori stared at me, at Barberini, and then back to me again. I was certain at that moment that he knew as well.

'But there was no change at all in Barberini's face. He had the same gentle smile, but when he spoke there was an undertone of coldness in his voice now. 'You were in Florence before you came to Rome, weren't you, Mr Milton?' he asked me. I told him that I was. 'I hope that you enjoyed your conversation with our friend Galileo. I love that man,' he said heartily. 'He helped me a great deal when I was a student, and has been a friend to my family for years. Do you know, I was a member of the tribunal of the Sacred Inquisition when he came to trial. I am the Grand Inquisitor, of course, but yet I was unable to cast my vote against him. There were three of us who refused to condemn him. It didn't matter, of course: I knew he would be condemned in the end, and that's the most important thing. But I still wanted to show him my friendship. I would like to show you my friendship as well, Mr Milton.'

'I tell you now, Robert, that last sentence was the most terrifying thing I have ever heard in my life. His eyes looked directly into me like the eyes of a serpent.

'Do you know what I am,' he said, carrying on in his cold, calm voice. 'I am a politician: that's all. My uncle, the Pope, is a politician as well. We do our best to ensure that the world moves along as smoothly as the waters of the river. When Satan and the other angels were expelled from heaven, it happened simply because of a political conflict. A political conflict between God and Satan. God was stronger and more powerful than Satan, and he failed because of that. Weak people always fail. Be careful that you don't fail, Mr Milton. It would be better to be a good politician than a bad rebel.'

'The conversation changed quickly then and, strange as it may seem, I felt that the air in the room warmed again. It was clear that Holstenius hadn't the slightest understanding of the conversation, and I was glad of that. Barberini bid us farewell in the great hall at the end of the night, and Giori walked with us to the door. Then he stopped and looked directly into my eyes. He had a very strange voice and a peculiar look on his face. 'We all speak with one voice here, Mr Milton,' he said to me. 'We are stronger than you could imagine. Be sure that you recognise our name and stand back from the peril.'

'And what is *your* name, Mr Giori,' I asked him suddenly. I don't know why that question just fell from my mouth, but I saw it created a twisted, burnt smile on his face.'

'My name is Legion, for we are many,' he answered, and closed the door on us. That sentence struck me heavily because I understood what it meant. It comes from the Bible, of course, where Jesus meets a man possessed by demons. What meaning could that sentence have in Giori's mouth but to say that those devils, the little men that Galileo saw, were inside him: that they spoke through him? That was how they communicated with the Barberini.

'Are you alright, John?' asked that good man Holstenius as we walked to the carriage.

'I am, my friend,' I answered, but I understood that nothing would ever be right again. I stayed in Rome for a while after that, but received news then from England of the Civil War and had to return.

'You are the only person to whom I have told this story in its entirety. I give you a warning, Robert. Do not open this box. It is Pandora's box. There is no goodness in this science of yours.

These things are God's alone and humanity has no right to look into them. Keep out of it. I was never able to forget this story, but I am trying to deal with it in my own way now: through the medium of poetry. I am writing a long poem now on the subject of the conflict between God and the Devil and the fall of humanity that followed it. I will give it the title *Paradise Lost*.'

Milton stopped here and there was a deep silence between the two men in the room for a while. Robert understood that the story had finished. 'I am no poet … but I understand your warning,' he said in the end.

He had listened quietly to Milton as he spoke. The story grieved him deeply, but it wasn't as if he hadn't been expecting it. Wasn't Beelzebub Lord of the Flies? He wanted to put a stop to everything now, but Robert Hooke had his own opinions and it would be difficult to dissuade him. And what of that Dutchman Swammerdam? Perhaps they could open up the gates of Hell. A cold shiver ran down his back and he stood up.

'Thank you very much for your honesty and your openness with me, Mr Milton. I will be honest with you now. Two others have seen these little men within a few years. Robert Hooke is one of them – that's the colleague of mine I spoke of – and another man from the Netherlands called Jan Swammerdam. Hooke's tale of how he saw them is exactly as you described Galileo's incident. It can only be that they are the same beings. I will inform them of everything you have told me, and I will ask them to cease their studies on this matter and forget it, as much as they can. I will go now. May God help and protect you … and may He strengthen your pen. Farewell.'

'May He be a shield to you in the darkness, Robert,' replied Milton, and he heard him leaving through the house without a word. He sat then in his own darkness for a long time. It was hard on him to tell that story, and he felt an abyss around him darker than the blackness in his own eyes. He felt it inside the room with him and squeezed his hands together to expel the fear. But it was still there. He saw the faces of Galileo, Barberini and Giori in his blindness coming to him through the years. Betty and Mary came in then, but he drove them out. He didn't want food or anything else. He would stay where he was and it would go hard on anyone who disturbed him before they were called upon. He had to think. He would put a message in his poem so that it would be a warning, evidence to the truth. He would insert it as the last line of the poem. Though he could not use a pen to count the letters, still he would do it.

He sat there for the whole night and by the time he heard the birds singing, he had it. He was certain that it was right.

He heard steps in the kitchen and called out. It was Mary who came to him. 'Take out paper and a pen, girl,' he said to her calmly, and told her the two sentences. 'Now, look at those letters. Can you reorder the letters in the first sentence to make the second one? Do you understand what I mean?'

'I do, father. It's an anagram, is it?'

'It is, girl. Well done.'

It took her time to do it and to be certain that she was right. In the end, she spoke. 'It's a perfect anagram, father.'

'Are you certain?'

'I am.'

'Read the first line to me then.'

'*Through Eden took thir solitarie way.*'

'And the second line?'

'*They who are do talk in true host Giori.*'

Scene Five

I said earlier that I would tell you, when the time was right, how I knew of the events in the historical parts of this book. Well, you understand now where all this information about Jan Swammerdam, and those who have a part in his story, came from. He had written everything in the manuscript that was now in our hands as we darted west along the Ring Road. It wasn't exactly a diary, but an account of everything that had happened to him from when he first discovered the Firíní. He wanted to better understand these events and believed he could make some sense of it if he were to write it all down. In many ways, I'm doing the same thing here myself in this account of mine.

Salvadóir drove at breakneck speed back again along the Ring Road to our house in Ballyphehane. The four of us stood around the kitchen table and opened the satchel, laying the three items onto it. I felt that each of us took a deep breath before diving into the dark waters that we would find in those three documents. Salvadóir opened the manuscript first and, with Peadar looking over his shoulder, began searching through it. Both of them spoke Dutch perfectly, and I could see amazement on their faces.

Salvadóir lifted his head with a broad smile that soon turned to a laugh. With excitement in his voice, he said: 'It's not a normal diary! It's an account of everything that happened to him as regards the Firíní!'

This excitement was infectious, and I could even see a little of it on Aogán's face. It wasn't, of course, that he believed a word of the story about the Firíní, but he couldn't just dismiss what was happening around him either. Whatever part he played in these events, I knew that he did it on my behalf, and I was grateful to him for that. I think as well that he had enjoyed his role as Winston Churchill with the guard. 'I have a little Dutch from the time I spent in Amsterdam, but I only understand a word here and there,' he said. 'Translate part of it for us.'

Salvadóir opened the first page again and began reading:

> I, Jan Swammerdam, do solemnly swear that this account is a true representation of the events that happened to me from 1663 to the present day. I have gathered the details of this story from my diaries over the years and I will lay them out now as precisely as I can. I am writing this account in the hope that I may better understand that which has happened, but if anyone else reads this book after my death, know that in spite of the strangeness of the tale itself, that I was always faithful to its truth and to God.

He carried on then with the story, telling of that sunny day in Steno's garden when he first saw the Firíní. I thought it striking when I heard that the flies had attacked him in the garden, and was glad they hadn't done that with us. But beyond that, it was the similarities between his story and our own that had the greatest effect on me.

Peadar looked at me when we read about the one-piece suits of light blue. 'They clearly haven't changed their clothes in three hundred and fifty years anyway,' he said with a smile.

We could both identify with him as well when he told of the terrible effect that this incident had on him, and I was happy then that I hadn't seen them on my own. I have to say that I liked him from the start, and felt that he was an honest and courageous man. I just hope that I'm doing him justice here in this account of mine.

When Salvadóir had finished reading the part where Jan and Steno were speaking in the garden, he stopped. 'I'll translate the whole book to Irish so that you can all read it for yourselves,' he said.

'I'll help you,' said Peadar. 'I'll take pictures on my phone and I can read through it then on the laptop.'

'Ok! So what are the other two things in the satchel?' I asked.

The three of them were laid out on the table, and the envelope was the next document that Salvadóir opened. It was a single page and appeared to be very old indeed. It had only eight lines, and it was clear that it was the last page of a letter written in English. 'This is brilliant!' exclaimed Salvadóir.

'What's that signature: JS Nolan?' I asked.

'That letter is a W,' said Salvadóir, pointing his finger at it. 'And this isn't JS but rather Is, short for Isaac. This is the last page of a letter that Isaac Newton wrote to Robert Hooke. They hated each other, and it has even been said that Newton destroyed the only portrait that ever existed of Hooke. Maybe that's a myth, but the animosity between them is very well known.'

We read the letter carefully then, and even though the handwriting was difficult for me at first, I could make it out with Salvadóir's help:

> *...machinations. Be certain, Mr Hooke, that these conspiratorial endeavours will not go unrewarded as I shall make it my solemn business from this day hence to besmirch your name amongst the learned community. You may keep the knowledge of these beings private and even the conspirator Boyle may ensure the silence of others by installing them, despite utter unsuitability, in the Royal Academy, but the enmity which this engenders in me will live till one or both of us ceases to draw breath.*
>
> *Is. Newton*

'Lovely man,' said Aogán when we had read it.

'Newton's hatred of Hooke therefore stemmed from the fact that he would not share his knowledge of the Firíní with him,' said Peadar.

'It appears so anyway,' said Salvadóir. 'That's strange as well about people being allowed into the Royal Academy in order to keep them quiet: '*installing them, despite utter unsuitability.*'

'What about the last thing? That Bible,' said Peadar.

We took it up and examined it carefully. It was a big, heavy book, and clearly very old, though still in good condition. We opened the title page and saw intricate artwork in the pictures there of biblical characters. The words "*The Holy Bible*" was written in the centre and "*Anno Dom 1611*" beneath that. 'This is a first edition of the King James Version. You'd get €70,000 for this on the open market,' said Salvadóir.

'A good day's work so,' said Aogán. 'And I'd say we'd get ten years for it in court.'

'But is there anything in it about the Firíní? Why was it in the *magic box* with the other things?' I asked.

'I don't know. Maybe it was only there to keep it safe. Perhaps it doesn't relate to the other things at all,' said Salvadóir.

But we looked through it anyway to see if there were any clues at all to be found. It was a beautiful book and I was very impressed with the craftsmanship on every page. But we saw nothing in it until we came to the end. There was a white page at the back of the book with a poem written on it in elaborate handwriting. It was written in English but I still found it difficult to read. Again, though, Salvadóir went over it and I could see the letters with his help. There were two verses, and two references to verses in the Bible itself on the margin of the page beside them – except that there was damage to the page in one place and the reference for the second verse was illegible. There was a name then written on the bottom of the page: Robert Tighe.

'Who's Robert Tighe?' I asked.

'I don't know,' said Salvadóir. 'I've never heard the name, but the handwriting appears to be as old as the book itself.'

This is the page, exactly as it was written:

Exilium

El hath damned Lord of Flies *Exodos 8:31*
and Athar, Star of Morn
Shem drove north oppressèd Hamm
to chase the Fingin tome
He rids Empire of woe,
Sworn dove of cries adorned.

Banish to colde and bitter climes *Exod-*
Usurper to the throne
Lake isle where Tondolus did dine
On anguishe to the bone
Where Bara fair did make
A churche of high renown

Robert Tighe

'Let's look at that reference to the line in the Bible: Exodus 8:31,' said Peadar. We turned the pages back to the book of Exodus. These are the lines as they were written in this version of the book:

And the LORD did according to the word of Moses
and hee removed the swarms of flies from Pharaoh,
from his servants, and from his people: there remained not one

'*Flies*! More flies again,' I exclaimed. 'It has to relate to the Firíní.'

'Yeah,' said Salvadóir with a smile. 'And I won't be a fool again. I bet it's another anagram.'

Peadar took the phone from his pocket and photographed the lines from Exodus. 'You count the letters in the first verse of the poem, and I'll count the letters from Exodus,' he said to Salvadóir.

They both did it carefully and in a little while, they raised their heads again. 'What have you got?'

'One hundred and twenty-eight.'

'Me too. It's an anagram alright.'

'It must be, but let's be certain. Do you have a piece of paper?'

Peadar went to a drawer and took out paper and a pen. He sat down and wrote the verse from the Bible and the verse from the poem on it. He went through it then, letter by letter, with the three of us looking over his shoulder, until he had scribbled out every letter in the two verses. It was a perfect anagram.

'But what about the other verse?' said Aogán. 'The reference to the Bible verse is illegible.'

'It's a great pity,' said Salvadóir. 'It's from Exodus again but it could be anything at all. Maybe we'll never know.'

'But what about the poem itself? What does it mean?' asked Peadar. 'It mentions Lord of Flies: that's Beelzebub. The devil!'

Salvadóir examined the poem and scratched his beard to help his thinking process. 'Well, that's true, but it depends on your perspective. It came about in the Christian tradition that the Devil and Beelzebub are synonymous with each other. Beelzebub can be translated as "Lord of the Flies" right enough, but the name itself goes back to the ancient religion of the Canaanites. It's said to be associated with the god Ba'al. But there are other things in the poem that I find interesting too. El is mentioned here. That was the name of God for the Canaanites: the supreme god, father of all the other gods. The Jewish religion sprang from the ancient religion of the Canaanites, and if you read the Hebrew Bible, El is commonly used as the name for God.'

'I thought they called God Yahweh,' said Peadar.

'They did, but the Canaanites had a polytheistic society, with gods who were often specific to certain regions. When those who worshipped Yahweh became dominant, they declared that El and Yahweh were the same, and then that there was only one God, and all the others were false gods.'

'But who's '*Athar, Star of Morn*' so?' I asked.

'That's very interesting as well,' Salvadóir replied. 'It's another Canaanite god. It's often spelled *Attar* or *Athtar*, and he was worshipped extensively in both male and female form throughout the Middle East. The Babylonian goddess Ishtar is another form of him. He is imagined as the "star of morn" or the planet Venus because stories about him are often related to the movement of Venus in the sky. It stands high and bright in the sky in the morning, but then it falls and yields to the supremacy of the sun. So he is imagined as a proud character who tries to gain power for himself before he fails completely and falls down into the darkness.'

'Lucifer,' said Peadar. 'The word lucifer means star of morn.'

'That's true. But the term is used in the Bible to refer to different characters, even to Jesus himself. It was this book, the King James Version of the Bible in English, that made a personal name of the word lucifer when they left it in Latin in the Book of Isaiah and gave it a capital L. They turned lucifer, the star of morn, to Lucifer a specific person: the Devil himself. It's not found in the Bible in any other language. Lucifer as an individual is an English invention.'

'What do ye have so? Lucifer and Beelzebub were damned by God. That's hardly news!' Aogán said. 'And who are Shem and Hamm?'

'They're the sons of Noah. Shem was the favoured son, and Hamm the cursèd one.'

'What about Fingin?' I asked.

'I don't know. I've never heard of it.'

'*Sworn dove of cries?*' asked Peadar. 'I don't know.'

'*Tondolus?*' I asked.

'Again, unfortunately, I don't know. I have knowledge of the ancient religion of the Canaanites from my father's studies on the subject and because the phrase "Lord of the Flies" sparked my interest, for obvious reasons, but that's the end of my understanding of this poem. I'm sure that there are answers, but we'll have to do some detective work.'

'Maybe Swammerdam's diary is the most urgent thing for now,' said Peadar.

'You're right, and it's a good thing that two of us can speak Dutch. Let's both read it as quickly as possible and translate it into Irish.'

'Great! I'll tackle the poem,' I said. 'My own training is in literary criticism and maybe I'll be able to make sense of it.'

'Fantastic!' said Salvadóir.

'Absolutely fantastic,' said Aogán and he got up to leave. When he reached the door, he turned back to me: 'Give me a shout if you need anything.'

'Aogán!' Salvadóir called after him, and he turned back to us again. 'Thank you. You're a good man in time of need.'

Aogán shrugged and left without saying another word.

Peadar began taking photos of the diary, and Salvadóir examined each page carefully. I took up my laptop and went on the internet to see if I could find any insight on the poem. Isn't it a strange and wonderful world in which we live? If we had seen the Firíní twenty or thirty years before, we would have been rummaging through texts forever, but now I had an answer within two minutes. I went on the internet, put in his name, and there he was: waiting for me with his information. 'Sorry now, lads, but I think I've found Robert Tighe.'

Peadar down put his phone and they both came over to me.

'Robert Tighe, 1562-1620. He was one of the translators who wrote the King James Version of the Bible, that book on the table. He participated in its creation and, not only that, he was part of the First Westminster Company that translated the part from Genesis to Kings II – and Exodus is included in that.'

'That's amazing,' exclaimed Peadar. 'So maybe he wrote both texts: the poem at the back of the book, as well as the verse in the Bible itself.'

'Incredible,' said Salvadóir.

'Now that I'm thinking about it,' I said, 'isn't there a strange connection between the two texts: the poem "Exilium" at the back of the book and the line from Exodus? They relate to banishment, to people who are expelled and exiled from their own country. It's El, king of the gods, who does it in the poem, but in the verse in the Bible Pharoah is trying to keep people in the country against their will. Both extracts entail exile, but they look at the case from different sides. I don't know. I'm just thinking out loud.'

'Well, keep it up,' said Salvadóir. 'You're the literary detective now.'

'Let's carry on so,' I said, and I wrote another name into an internet search: Tondolus. I was only waiting a couple of seconds before I had another answer. 'I have it!' I said reading down through the text on the screen 'This is almost too easy,'

'What is it?' asked Salvadóir.

'It's a story from the Middle Ages: *Visio Tnugdali* it was called. It was written in Latin. This story was famed throughout Europe and translated into many other languages as well. It tells a story about a man who goes down to Hell, as happens in Dante's *The*

Divine Comedy, but this is much older. Someone called Brother Marcus wrote it in the Scotus monastery in Regensburg. He said that he got the story from the knight himself and – you're going to like this – that the original version was in Irish. That word *Tnugdali* comes from *tnúdgal* in Middle-Irish, or *tnúth gaile*: "longing for valour". The story itself is set in the year 1148, and *where* do you think it's situated?'

'In Ireland?' asked Peadar with excitement.

'Better again! It's set right here in Cork.'

'That's brilliant,' said Salvadóir. 'I always thought there was some link between this place and the whole thing. What do we have so?' He went back to the poem and read the second verse:

Banish to colde and bitter climes
Usurper to the throne
Lake isle where Tondolus did dine
On anguishe to the bone
Where Bara fair did make
A churche of high renown

'And who is this "*Bara fair*"?' I said. I was flying with it now. 'Fionn barra. Saint Finbarr. And Guagán Barra has to be the "*lake isle*" where he built his *churche of high renown*.'

Salvadóir started laughing and his gold tooth shone over the whole room. 'Well done, Seán. Have you ever thought of applying for a job with Interpol or the CIA?'

'I'll give them a call as soon as we've finished this case. About lunchtime tomorrow, I'd say.'

'But what does this mean?' asked Peadar. 'Beelzebub and Lucifer were expelled … to Guagán Barra?'

That put a stop to my flight for a moment. Was that really what I was suggesting? 'Well, we don't know for sure,' I said. 'That's one way to read it, anyway.'

'We have work to do yet, Seán,' said Salvadóir. 'But we'll study everything carefully, and come together again to discuss things and make a plan.'

Peadar finished the photographs and uploaded them to his laptop. Salvadóir collected the three things that were in the satchel and readied himself to leave. 'I'll head off so,' he said. 'I'll read everything as quickly and as carefully as I can. Thanks very much. I couldn't have done anything without ye. We've done great work today. Better than any progress that I've ever made with this in my whole life.'

With that, he left. Peadar went up to his own room with his laptop to read the diary, and I was left on my own with the photographs I had taken of the poem and of Isaac Newton's letter. Now that I was alone, I felt as if the wind had been taken out of my sails a little. I looked at the poem again and started to put phrases and words into an online search: "*Fingin tome*" or "*Sworn dove of cries*", but there was nothing. Then I started with Shem and Hamm, the two sons of Noah.

But I felt uncomfortable with it all. This wasn't an academic study. I had seen the little men with my own eyes, and now I was looking for information from people who had written about them in the context of Beelzebub and Lucifer. I was raised Catholic, though I hadn't believed in God since I began thinking about such things for myself when I was young. But I was never so arrogant as to think that my lack of faith sprang from my intellect.

I think people believe in the things that they want to be true. Certain people like the belief that an all-powerful father is taking care of them, but I'd hate that very same idea, that the whole universe is controlled by just one being. I was an agnostic because I thought this to be a more reasonable attitude, but as well as that, I had to admit that I didn't want any "supreme being" either. Yet I was raised in a Western Christian society, and even the most reasonable of people cannot completely escape from the horror stories that are woven around us. I felt now that my natural disposition for reason was under attack from the Christian mythology of the Middle Ages: the Devil and his demons waiting for me with their snares. My own pride would be my undoing in the end, of course. I would be cast into the flames of Hell because of my pride and my enthusiasm to uncover this secret.

I went to the kitchen and threw water on my face. I would have to put a stop to this superstitious nonsense. Robert Tighe must have been a very religious person. How else would he look at these matters except through the lens of religion. That's not to say that the Devil and Beelzebub were actually part of the story. I would have to be objective.

But even though I was never a religious person, I still liked the Bible as a work of literature. It was an enormous achievement for the Jews to create these stories, and human society has been hugely under their influence ever since. I thought of the hero Samson who killed an army with the jawbone of an ass, or Jonah in the belly of a whale, or the young boy David who killed the giant Goliath with a sling and was later made king, chariots of fire flying through the air, a boat with a pair of every living creature, the walls of Jericho falling under the roar of the Israelite trumpets. They're wonderful, vibrant stories that will live forever.

I imagined the storytellers of the oral tradition and the scribes of the ancient Israelites who composed these stories under the heat of a Middle Eastern sun. They created them to illustrate their faith, which was to them like the blood in their veins. But there was much more to these tales. They were political stories as well, stories that fortified and illustrated their rights as the people of God. The walls of Jericho fell through force of arms, but if you create a narrative that they were knocked down by the sound of trumpets through the will of God, you then proclaim your right before the world to keep that land forever. The ancient Israelites were very clever people. Those old scribes were the spin doctors who invented nationalist political propaganda and gave it to the world.

But when they proclaimed that there was only one god and that he had selected them as his chosen people, they then had to show the power of this god in their stories. He was a god who would burn and drown people, who would kill the children of the unbelievers in their beds, a god who would judge them always. He was an angry god, a vengeful god, a jealous god. Was that El, god of the ancient Canaanites? I didn't believe it was. He wasn't a jealous god in that polytheistic religion, but something had happened to him. He was altered, under the pen of the old Israelite scribes, into a tyrant who demanded absolute submission because he was an absolute god, the basis of everything, the beginning and the end, the source of all truth.

I went to my own room and took a Bible from the shelf. I had a plan to make a critical reading, ransacking it to find answers to what had happened to me. I turned idly through the pages, the Old Testament and the New, and I thought of how strange those two books are together. It is said that Christ was the son of God, but no Jew would ever believe such a thing. It's the complete opposite of Judaism. El was a jealous god in that tradition. But in the traditions of Greek and Roman culture, it was a common concept that someone may be the son of a god, and it was no coincidence that Christianity arose amongst the Jews after they had fallen to those empires. Jesus does not follow in the footsteps of Moses or Abraham: he follows Alexander the Great.

I remembered that the philosopher Friedrich Nietzsche liked one particular phrase from the Bible. It was a question that

Pilate put to Jesus when he was brought before him. Jesus said at the time that he was there to 'bear witness to the truth' and Pilate asked him 'what is truth?' – a reasonable question, I always thought, after such an obscure statement, but he got no answer to it, at the time anyway. Of course, Nietzsche was an atheist, but he felt that this was the only sentence in the Bible that was of any value. It's a big question. The biggest question of all perhaps. I looked through the Bible now and imagined Pontius Pilate as the only person with the courage to ask that question, the voice of one crying in the wilderness.

Forgive me, but I'm trying to show you the type of rabbit hole that I had fallen into with all these narratives flying through my mind. It wouldn't be difficult for you to understand that my own notion of the truth took quite a battering from that day with the microscope, but when I saw then that the strings of the spider's web that we call history, culture and religion were coming together to prove everything – to prove that little men fly around inside the heads of flies – you'll see how I began thinking of how we create the notions of truth we live with every day in this world. I saw that rabbit hole in which we all live, planting our feet firmly in the sandy ground of truth. I looked back through the ages and I saw the prophets struggling through the burning wind of the desert to proclaim God's truth to the believers and the unbelievers. I saw the sunburnt hands of the scribes writing down that truth, the truth of the invisible king who would judge each moment of their lives and destroy them, as he had destroyed their enemies, if they did not properly show him their endless devotion.

Scene Six

London, England
27th June 1665

The city was sweltering in the intense heat, even at that time of day. It was approaching six o'clock now, and Jan still felt the stifling air around him like thick soup. There was no escape from it even in the street, as there wasn't the slightest breeze to be felt there. That's how it had been every day and every night for almost a month. But at least he was out of the house now. It was fear of the plague that had kept him locked up in Hooke's house for all that time. During this confinement, he would often look out of the window at the madness in the street below. He would look at the prophets, the quacks and the charlatans, and he saw the poor people who would follow them like lost children so that they might possess the special potion that would save them from the plague, or hear of their fate in the form of secret messages from the spirits. But gradually, these crowds were decreasing. It wasn't that they were dying in great numbers from the plague, because that slaughter was still only just beginning on this side of the city. But many people saw now that there were no answers to what was coming, that grotesque monster that slid through the city towards them, street by street.

But he was not idle in Hooke's house either, because they were both working diligently on the book. Jan had made his own drawings of the little men and had written his account of the event as it had happened to him. It was difficult for him at first to be locked in a house with someone he hardly knew, but they worked well together generally and he looked at Hooke now as a spirited, intelligent and highly talented person. Jan saw his energy when he set himself to work and felt a glimmer of hope for the first time in a long while. Outside of their efforts on the book, Hooke also showed him his laboratory, and he was very impressed with the level of work he had done there.

As such, things progressed well until Boyle's letter came and then everything fell apart. Hooke was like someone possessed when he read that Boyle had known about the little men all the time but had said nothing. It was Jan's coming to England which had prompted him to go to Milton and get the full story. It was a long letter and it told Milton's story in its entirety, his description of his visit to Galileo's house, Galileo's story about the Medici and the Barberini, and Milton's own visit to Palazzo Barberini. It was a description of the power that the little men had in the most illustrious houses of Europe, and Boyle believed that they were dealing with the Devil himself. He made it known as strongly as he could that any business or interference they had in mind with these little men should immediately stop.

But there was more than that in the letter. Boyle said that his family had taken possession of extensive lands and grand houses in Ireland. In one of those houses they came upon a wonderful acquisition, a manuscript in the language of the Irish. It was a collection of different stories, but one extract told the tale of a saint in Ireland in the seventh century who had fought with a devil so small that he could ride on the back of a fly. Boyle had very little of that language, but he had a translation of the story, and was certain that it could only be the same little men. He said that he tore those pages from the manuscript and burnt them in his enthusiasm to keep this knowledge a secret.

'Why couldn't he have said all this to me before!' Hooke shouted. 'He's a blackguard!' He didn't speak for a while then but stood rigid with temper, staring at Jan with a fierceness in his eyes. 'Did you know about this?' he said angrily.

'I didn't know about that book in Ireland, and I've never heard of this man John Milton. I knew that Galileo was connected with the matter, of course ... but we spoke about this already, Robert,' Jan answered as calmly as he could.

'Yes but ...' Hooke began again testily. 'But the connection that the Medici have with it?'

'Melchisédech Thévenot told me that the Pope came down on Galileo because of the information he had on the little men. I had heard alright that his name was Barberini, and I understood that the Medici had intervened as well but ... forgive me, Robert, we have spoken of this already.'

'You never mentioned the Medici!' Hooke shouted gruffly.

'I don't remember whether I mentioned the Medici directly or not, but I certainly mentioned that there were important people behind this conspiracy.'

'You knew! Thévenot, Boyle and even that mongrel Milton knew. Maybe I should ask the woman who brings milk to us in the morning. Maybe she'll have something new to add to the story.'

Jan understood that Hooke's anger was really directed at Boyle, but he wasn't there now and so that just left him to suffer the spite.

'Do you not think that the Medici have agents here in England? Money like that buys anything you want, even assassins in other countries!' Hooke said.

'We both understood from the beginning that we would have to deal with powerful people, even dangerous people.'

'Boyle believes that we are dealing with the Devil himself in the flesh. Maybe he's right. Maybe it's the Catholics in Rome who are behind everything. What political ingenuity did the Catholics in France use to send you over here to me?'

In the end, Jan left the house and walked out onto the street to collect his thoughts. It was difficult to stay in Hooke's house when he was that angry. He was incensed and it was impossible to speak to him reasonably. Jan felt that things were falling apart, and this grieved him very much. He could see that the glimmer of hope was diminishing with every sentence that Hooke uttered. But there was more than that. How did he himself know that they weren't actually dealing with the Devil all the time? A sort of recklessness overcame him as he left the house. At that moment, he didn't care about the plague or about anything else.

The sun still stood high in the sky, glaring down pitilessly on everything. The church was directly across the road from him, but if he turned left he would soon come to Bishopsgate and the city walls. On his right, the main road stretched south, the road he had travelled on that first day in the carriage from the river. There was another road that led west, but before long it ran into a mesh of lanes and little houses. That was the direction in which the plague was currently slaughtering the people, both young and old. He understood the terrible danger that was there, but yet there was a curiosity as well that incited him in that direction. He was a doctor who had received an education in medicine at the University of Leiden. Didn't he want to put his training into practice to help the poor in this terrible ordeal? He thought of the two little men drowning in a drop of water, and of himself as he looked at them.

A man's voice came then from Bishopsgate, a solemn voice like someone reciting verses from the Bible, and in between those verses he would shout out some phrase again and again. Jan saw him when he came closer. He was naked apart from a dirty rag around his waist, and his beard and hair grew down to his chest. Cuts, bruises, dirt and blood could be seen all over his body, but the most remarkable thing about him was the fire on his head.

He carried a pan or metal basket of some sort there, tied down with straps around his chin, and with a charcoal fire burning inside it.

Jan had seen him before from the window, but he was always too far away to hear properly. He felt a strong impulse now to go and speak to the man. He walked over and stopped before him. He could smell burning hair and noticed ugly scorched skin on his forehead. The wild man stopped to look directly back at him with big, deranged eyes. 'Repent!' he screamed hoarsely. 'Repent before you are lost forever.' He raised one hand in the air as if he was about to pull down the heavens.

'I will, sir,' Jan said politely. 'My sins are great and I thank you for your advice.'

'Repent!' he screamed again. 'Repent before you are lost!'

He knew that this man was mad. But perhaps because of that, it was easier to tell him his story straight out. 'I see the suffering in your eyes, my friend, but maybe God would speak through your tormented mouth. I thought that I was in his service, but I am no longer certain. Maybe I have committed an offence against God. I looked through an instrument, an instrument made by the hand of man, but I don't know now if it was the world of the angels or the devils which I saw that day. Maybe it was Hell.'

'I am the voice of one crying in the wilderness. Make straight the way of the Lord!' said the wild man, calling out to the street again, as if he hadn't been listening to Jan at all.

But Jan recognised it as a verse from the Bible. 'You are a preacher, sir. You speak in the voice of John the Apostle but – forgive me – you appear more similar to John the Baptist. Who are you?'

'I am Solomon Eagle!' he exclaimed triumphantly as he turned back towards him. 'I come here through the streets of Gomorrah to force repentance upon the rabble of the lost city, those who went astray and drew the terrible plague down upon us, that they may accept his law. He that is the Alpha and Omega, the beginning and the end, the first and the last. I saw another sign in heaven, great and marvellous, seven angels having the seven last plagues; for in them is filled up the wrath of God.'

Jan recognised these as verses from the Book of Revelation and the words incited his heart with a fever that he didn't understand. He grabbed the man's hair and looked deeply into his eyes. 'Help me, brother! I understand that your mind is deranged with suffering, but I believe that God would speak through your mouth if he would permit it to me. If I have committed a great sin, tell me, Lord. Tell me through the mouth of this poor man.'

Some of the burning charcoal fell on Jan's hand and burned it until he let him go.

'Babylon the Great, the Mother of Harlots and Abominations of the Earth!' Solomon screamed at the top of his voice, and fell on his knees.

Jan regretted his foolish impulse now and looked at the madman with pity. He was a lost man, a lunatic amongst the other lunatics who suffered the horrors around them and the demons in their own minds. His eyes were rolling in his head and he appeared to have lost his senses.

Jan turned to leave, but then he heard Soloman Eagle's voice again, calmer now, and the change disconcerted him: 'The first beast was like a lion, and the second beast like a calf, and the third beast had a face as a man, and the fourth beast was like a flying eagle. And the four beasts had each of them six wings about him; and they were full of eyes within: and they rest not day and night, saying, Holy, holy, holy, Lord God Almighty, which was, and is, and is to come.'

Jan turned back to him quickly. He recognised the verse from the Book of Revelation, but it was a verse that spoke of wings on the beasts and that they were full of eyes within. Was that not a description of flies? Was God actually speaking to him through this poor man? He ran to him again. 'What did you say? What did you say just now, my friend? Say it again!'

But Solomon had nothing more to say. He sat where he was, mute, his eyes still rolling in circles in his head.

'Again, my friend. I implore you,' said Jan, but it was hopeless.

The wild man stood up unsteadily and Jan saw blood on his knees that had not been there before. He walked away down the broad street towards the river without saying a word to him, or even recognising that he was there. 'Repent!' he screamed out again.

Jan followed him for a while but saw that it was pointless and he let him go his own way. But what had he said? Was it an answer from God, an answer to Jan's own problems? He had asked God to speak to him through this man, but had he actually answered him? And if it was an answer, what sense could he make of it? Those Four Beasts in the Book of Revelation stood beside God. They weren't demons. Was that to say that the little men he had seen that day were angels, beings on the side of God? There were too many questions and they wearied his mind. He walked down the road in the same direction that Solomon Eagle had gone, but then turned right and headed west. Leaving his destiny in the hands of God, he went in the direction of that side of the city in which the monster resided: the plague.

The sun was still high in the sky over the ramshackle roofs of the houses on the main street, but it was cooler here in the narrow, dark lanes. The houses had two or three storeys as well, but they were only twelve feet apart in places. The upper floors of some of them were sticking out over the lanes, colonising the air in ways not available to them on the ground. Some of them were made of wooden frames with red brick, but wattle and daub and thatched roofs were to be seen as well. It was a jumble with each house different from the one beside it, and the lanes turned at sharp angles so often that it became a maze. It wasn't long before he was completely lost, and he didn't believe he could return the way he had come. People avoided him as well, staying back on one side of the lane for fear of the sickness.

Then he saw the red crosses on the doors and 'Lord have mercy on us' written alongside. These were the locked-up houses with guards sitting lazily in front of them. Inside, he knew there were people waiting in that final prison until the disease gnawed the life from them. There would be no mercy on the inside of those houses. There would be swollen ugly buboes on the groins, necks and armpits of those poor people, agonising boils that would put them clean out of their minds with pain. There would be fever, terrible headache, muscle pain and fatigue as well. Those houses were dungeons, torture chambers, but the worst thing was that people had to look at their own families and children in the same plight.

There were less people in the street now as he walked on. He didn't know if he was still travelling west, but he hoped he was. If so, it would be possible to turn right at any time, reach the city walls, and then follow them back to Bishopsgate, if he wanted to go back.

He was still inside the walls, and it was said that the districts most afflicted with the plague were outside. He felt the fear rising in his heart. After an hour, it was darker again in the lanes but he carried on. He didn't know how long it would be before night came, or how difficult it would be to struggle through these diseased alleyways in the darkness.

Then he heard the first scream. It was a girl's voice, and it was clear that she was becoming frantic with agony and fear. It came from a little house just as he was walking past, and it shook him terribly. She screamed again and again, and he heard her beating on the door. She was crying piteously as well in between her pleas, and the sobbing came out through the cracks in the door.

'Let me go! I beseech you. Don't leave me like this. The pains are awful. I … can't suffer them any longer. I'm afraid. Please help me! Have pity on me … I'm a good girl … I was always a good girl. Don't leave me like this.'

Jan had never heard anything so piteous in his life. He wanted to run to her and break the door down, tear it apart.

But when he approached the door, a great lump of a man who had been sitting before it stood up and threatened him with a heavy cudgel. 'Get out of here! You've no business with this house,' he said angrily, and raised the cudgel before his face. Jan stood back from him in fear; he could do nothing against a man so huge.

But the girl in the house realised that someone else was there and she directed her voice to him now. 'Who's there? Is there someone else there? Help me! I beseech you! Don't leave me here like this! Who is it? Is that you, Charles? Charles my love – help me. Don't leave me like this, Charles!'

The big man swung his cudgel suddenly and swiftly at Jan's head and it came within an inch of his nose. He jumped to one side and moved back from the house. 'Didn't you hear me? I'll split your skull if you come back this way again,' and with that, he raised the cudgel again to strike down on him with a deadly blow.

Jan ran for his life up the lane, but stopped when he saw that the guard wasn't following him and looked back at the horrible scene. This great lump of a man was sitting on his chair again in front of the house. Jan could do nothing but leave. He walked away up the lane, but the crying and pleading of the young girl still followed him. 'Don't leave me! Don't leave me, Charles!' she pleaded with the lost love who wasn't there. There was no one there but Jan, and he was leaving now. But he felt her pleading like a heavy weight on his shoulders, and tears filled his eyes as he struggled through the lanes again. He wanted to be away from that voice, but he knew now that he would hear it forever.

He stumbled on, becoming more lost with every step in the maze. If it had been his intention at first to go directly on, he failed with every twist and bend in those narrow streets. They constantly directed him left and right. He would reach a little square here and there, but then be immersed again into the interwoven streets. There were very few people out now and they all avoided him. He didn't know what time it was either, but he could see that darkness was coming.

Then he heard voices from somewhere. He followed them, but the sound travelled its own entangled way in those lanes. There were many times that he believed that he'd found them but he hadn't in the end. It was a sharp murmur. He heard boastful shouts mixed with complaints and yells, and through that, weak, pitiful screams came to him on the air. After a while, it became clear that the voices themselves were moving through the streets before him, and he hastened his step to catch up with them.

He was disgusted and horrified when he came upon them in the end. They were whipping a young man through the streets. In truth, he was only a boy of about eighteen years, his hands tied with a rope around his neck in the way that they were tight up under his chin. His shirt had been removed, and Jan saw the torn skin and flesh on his back. A small crowd followed him like an ugly procession, but there were five men central in this group walking step by step behind him. One big man with a whip lashed him with pitiless enthusiasm, and another man –

perhaps a sergeant in charge of this horror – called out loudly to everyone around. Behind him, walked three armed men, one with a musket and two others with lances. The young man let out a whimper with each lash, but it was clear that his strength was almost exhausted.

The sergeant called out: 'In accordance with the orders of the King! That anyone who besmirches his position as a lawful agent of the King through illegal acts shall be whipped through the streets of London; and that being specifically as it relates to rules and laws against the offence of bribery, particularly in cases in which money is accepted or others are allowed to accept money in order to break the King's law. As such, this law shall be imposed upon William Hanbury here and directed, in accordance with the King's law, that he shall receive the suitable punishment!'

The young man fell in a weakness on the ground but the whipper kept at him. A woman stepped in to help him, but she felt the whip as well, as an answer to her pity. She was a woman of about forty-five with a haggard, white face. She was crying, and Jan thought perhaps that she was his mother. He came closer to the group, even though a dread ran down his back with every lash.

'Get up, you rogue, or I'll skin you alive on the spot!' shouted the whipper with gleeful ferocity. The young man got up slowly and carried on with his journey. Jan saw real venom in the eyes of those who followed this ugly procession, though it wasn't directed at the young man himself but rather at the five who tormented him. It was like a hideous drama that you couldn't take your eyes from. Jan walked with them through the twisted streets, and within two minutes the boy was on the ground again. Everything happened then exactly as it had done the first time, and it occurred to Jan that he himself was in Hell and caught in a loop, damned to follow this procession for eternity.

To look at him, he appeared to be moving calmly along with the crowd, but in his own mind he was a panicked animal, caught in a snare.

But an end did come eventually. A young man stood out from the crowd and faced the tormentors, speaking directly to the sergeant. 'He wasn't sentenced to death,' he said brazenly. 'He was only sentenced to be whipped, but you'll kill him if you don't stop now.'

The march stopped and the sergeant looked calmly at the three armed men. As if a secret signal had passed between them, they stepped forward and grabbed him. 'Are you interfering with the orders of the King?' the sergeant asked.

'You will exceed the orders of the King if he dies, and then it's you that'll pay for it. Be careful that the law doesn't fall upon your own head,' said the young man boldly.

It was clear from the sergeant's expression that he would have been very happy to put this impudent rogue in place of the boy and teach him some manners. But still, he wasn't a fool either and he knew that there was some sense to his argument. There wasn't an ounce of strength left in the boy now, and if he died, the sergeant himself would be answerable for it. Not only that, but there was a spirit rising in the mob now with this man's boldness. Could he control them all with three guards? 'I am a servant of the King. But I do know that the law can also be compassionate, and so you may take him,' he said with greasy articulation. But then he looked sharply at the young man who had challenged him: 'But I believe that I shall not forget your good advice, or you yourself, young fellow.'

The five of them moved off then and left the crowd to take care of the boy. People came out of their houses to help, and his mother called for something that they could use as a stretcher to carry him home.

It was a great relief to Jan that the horror had ended at last and he spoke to some of the people who were there. 'What did this poor man do? It was said that he accepted a bribe. Is that true?' he asked an old man who was hanging around amongst the crowd.

'Not at all! If he took money, it was only a tiny amount, and who would begrudge it to him in days like this? He was employed as a guard on one of the plague houses that are locked up now. The people there implored him to let them go and, in truth, only one of them had the plague. The others were free of it, and there were children amongst them. That's how it happened. He released those who were healthy. It was an act of mercy, but he got no mercy himself for it. I've known that lad since he was a young child, and he was a kind and honest boy always.'

A door from one of the houses nearby was given to the boy's family to make a stretcher, and he was laid face down on it. Jan heard that the young man who spoke out on his behalf was related to him in some way. He looked at the small group now as they disappeared into the dark lanes. They left together through the narrow streets, and his mother kept a grip of his hand, even though he was unconscious at this stage.

Night was falling now and he looked around at the people who remained there, talking together on their doorsteps. He saw a small fire in the corner of the little square with people roasting some fish over it. There was no cold at all on this muggy night, and Jan wasn't hungry after the horror he had just witnessed, but yet the light of the fire drew him and he sat beside it looking in at the flames.

'Are you lost in the streets, sir?' a young girl asked him, recognising the quality of his clothes.

'I am lost, right enough, girl,' he said sorrowfully, 'and not just in these streets.'

A look of surprise came on the girl's face and she went over to one side to speak to a man there. She pointed at Jan and was clearly talking about him. He thought at first that she wanted to give him directions or help, but when she came back, her question surprised and worried him. 'Are you Dutch?' she asked in a curt voice.

The warm light of the fire had lured him into a trance, but this blunt question awoke him suddenly, and reminded him that he was an enemy in this country. 'Of course not,' he said as assertively as he could. 'I am French.'

But there was a vindictiveness in her eyes and it was clear she didn't believe him. He stood up quickly to leave but she followed. The man to whom she'd been speaking came over now as well. 'You're not French! I recognise your accent,' she shouted. 'That's a Dutch accent, and you're Dutch. You're at war with us. You killed my brother! Why are you here? To give us more plague, is it?' The man grabbed his shoulder but he released himself easily enough.

'I promise you that I'm not Dutch! I am a Frenchman from Paris. I know nothing about Holland. I've never even been there,' he said in agitation.

But there was a crowd gathering around him now. They grabbed him and he realised he was in great danger. 'They weren't able to get the better of us in a fair fight, so they gave us the plague to kill us in our beds,' screamed the girl now, inciting the rabble.

'Let me go!' he shouted at them wildly. 'I've told you already that I'm not Dutch.' But they had a firm grip of him and he couldn't escape, no matter how he struggled.

'Hang him!' the girl screamed and she struck him heavily across face. This was the incitement the crowd needed, and they attacked him now with their fists and feet. At that moment, Jan believed they would kill him. There was a fury in them, a fury born of the terrible injustice that surrounded them every day of their lives, of an oppression that was carried out in accordance with the 'orders of the King' and the demonstration of those orders as they had just seen with the whipping of the young man.

Then he heard the call, the call and the bell. They all heard it and stopped. 'Bring out your dead! Bring out your dead!'

Some of them ran back to their houses. With the rest distracted by the call, Jan took his chance. He freed himself from their grip and ran for his life back into the narrow streets again. It was dark now and he knocked against the walls as he ran, hurting himself again, but the fear and the harsh voices behind him drove him on. He ran in the direction of the call, and maybe that was why they didn't follow him too far. That call was a death threat to anyone who came too close. Before long, he was on his own again in the lanes, but he had to feel his way in the darkness now with his hands. He heard the call before him all the time, the call that had saved him from the mob, and he ran towards it without thinking. Then suddenly, he stumbled over something on the ground, lost his footing and went down heavily, striking his head against a wall.

He didn't know how long he'd been unconscious, but there was a light there when he came to again. Rough hands lifted him up and carried him as if he were a sack of rubbish. Opening his eyes, he saw that they were carrying him towards a hand cart on which a pile of bodies had been crudely thrown. The faces of these people shone in the light of the torches that were tied to the upright posts of the cart, the white faces of death with their frozen eyes looking directly ahead. There was one face there, the face of a woman. Unimaginable fear struck him when he realised that he recognised her. His own mother! But how would she be here now having been dead for the last four years? He let out a terrible wail and fought against the rough arms around him.

They let him go as soon as they realised he wasn't dead. 'Oh God, this one's still alive!' one of them shouted.

'We're sorry, son,' said another man. 'We thought you were a body thrown out with the plague. What happened to you? Are you drunk or were you attacked?'

Jan didn't hear the voices but stood staring at the face of the woman on the cart. He took a step forward but they grabbed him again.

'I wouldn't recommend you go too near that cart, if you haven't already got the plague. We wouldn't do it ourselves only that the hunger will do us in before the plague would. But why are you lying here in the darkness? Speak up, son!'

But Jan's mind was frozen now and he couldn't speak a word. He retreated from them and from the awful cart, back into the darkness of the lanes. After a while, he heard them moving through the city again, their call and their bell proclaiming their trade. 'Bring out your dead! Bring out your dead!' He stood there alone and motionless now in the darkness, not wanting to take a step left or right, but letting the darkness cover him like a thick blanket, as if it was death itself. He even closed his eyes and allowed the silence to come about him.

There was pain all over his body and rubbing his hand to his face, he noticed it was wet. It had to be blood, he thought. It didn't matter now. He wanted nothing but the silence. Sitting down in this silence, he felt that time itself had stopped around him, that the world had been swept away, the lanes, the houses, even his own body, and that only his consciousness remained in the vacuum.

He didn't notice the change at first, but gradually the blackness softened and he perceived a greyness about him through which he could recognise things nearby: doors and windows, a box in the corner. Eventually, he realised that while he'd been sitting there, the moon had risen, and was now spreading milky grey light into the city's lanes. Another while later, and he saw it shining over the rooftops, its full silvery face standing boldly in the sky. It gave him courage, and he rose again from the ground.

It was as quiet as the grave around him, and he walked alone though the streets and lanes now. He went past houses and, even in the moonlight, could see those that bore the mark of the cross upon the door. The living bodies of the guards sat before them like ghosts in the darkness, but he avoided them. He had no idea now in which direction he was walking, but kept his own course moving forward.

Then he heard voices up ahead, a gleeful sound of people laughing and shouting, and following the noise without thinking, it wasn't difficult this time to find. Before long, he was standing before a big stone house and the sound of those voices coming out through front doors that spread open in a welcoming manner. Like a person in a trance, he entered through them and down the dark hall directly towards heavy oak doors and the source of the noise. When he pulled at them, they opened easily onto a grand, elegant hall and a group of people within it.

In the centre of the room, he saw a man sitting on an armchair that had been placed on top of a large wooden table. The man gazed down from that stage like a king with a satisfied look on his face at those who were gathered before him. He wore a big fur hat on his head, but his clothes were torn and dirty. Suddenly, he noticed Jan and stood up from his chair: 'Look! He has come,' he shouted in a commanding voice. 'He has come to us at last. Was his coming not prophesised and is it not now he that is before our very eyes, as was foretold in the prophecy of Moses!'

They all turned towards Jan and looked at him. There was a short man with the face of a little bird and a conical hat on his head. There was a pretty girl in a lovely dress with braids and ribbons in her hair as if she was a child's doll. She was standing on a chair for some reason and squeezed her hands in fear when she saw Jan standing there. He saw an obese man with a face so bloated that his eyes were almost lost in it, and another man crawling on his hands and knees. There was an elderly woman and a young man dancing together. She wore an elegant gown, but he had only a cloth around his waist like Jesus had on the cross, and it was clear that he was so drunk that he could hardly stand, let alone dance. He saw a bearded man under another table beside the wall, defecating and peering out, a questioning expression on his face.

Another woman approached him then, an elegant, attractive woman with Mediterranean features and curly black hair. 'Stop your nonsense, Baltasar!' she said in a gentle voice. 'It's only a sailor come from the sea looking for peace. There are more things in heaven and earth than are imagined of in your dreams, Horatio.'

'I hate to mention it, Queen Circe, but you are wrong again,' said the man in the high chair. 'You've used up all your sailors now.'

The man on all fours came towards Jan and smelled his trousers.

'But I see that he is injured,' she said, 'What happened to you, sailor?'

'I don't remember,' said Jan inattentively.

'You have your own troubles and your battles fought. We are escaping from the world, and you are welcome here,' she said.

'But stop now!' said the man on the high chair. 'It's obvious that he's a clear fulfilment of the prophecy of Moses which states that a man bathed in blood would come amongst us and it would be Daniel in the flesh. It is as clear as that I myself am Baltasar sitting here on high above the party. But you yourselves are a fulfilment of the prophecy as well. We are all part of it, my friends. Is it not clear that he has come here to give us answers – he that understands things, he that is learned beyond the wise men of the King? He that has seen things that no one else has seen. Come in to us, Daniel.'

'What do you know?' the girl standing on the chair asked cautiously.

'While once alone, I peered into the darkness of the day,' said the obese man. 'Did you ever see that?'

'Leave him be,' said the Queen with frustration. 'Come here, sir, and drink with us,' and she offered him a full glass of brandy.

'Be careful, lad. Look at that man with the appearance of a dog,' said the little bird, pointing his finger at the man on all fours on the ground. 'It was she that did that to him. She is Circe, queen and sorceress, who'd steal your humanity from you if you're not careful.'

'That's Nebuchadnezzar, granduncle of Baltasar there,' she said in response. 'I stole nothing from him that hadn't already been stolen by life. But I see that you're hurt? Come to me and let me help you. Take off your shirt. It's soaked in blood.'

Jan looked down and saw that his shirt was sodden. He was light-headed as well from the loss of blood, and he let this woman remove it. She took water and a cloth then and washed some of the blood from his face. 'That's better. Now, take this,' she said, offering him some brandy again.

'Don't drink it! Beware, brother,' said the big man. 'That's Circe, daughter of the sun. You will be under her power in a moment. This room is full of brandy. Here, take some of mine.'

'In the name of God!' said Circe with frustration.

Nebuchadnezzar was walking around smelling Jan's trousers again, and he had to give him a kick to get rid of him.

'Tell us the prophecy, Daniel,' said Baltasar.

'I have no prophecy,' Jan replied.

'Of course. You will have to wait for the writing on the wall. Then you will be able to read it and give us an answer.'

Jan recognised the story from the scriptures. 'You believe that I'm Daniel from the Bible?'

'It is written in the prophecy that you would come soaked in blood and give us understanding, that you would read the words on the wall when they are written.'

'Who said that?'

'That's the prophecy of Moses.'

'I've never read that prophecy.'

'It isn't in the Bible. Moses told it to us a little while ago, didn't you, Moses?' said Baltasar, and with that he turned to the man who was defecating under the table. He was having trouble with this act apparently, and kept himself on his hunkers with his britches around his ankles. 'Unfortunately, he is troubled with a stopcock,' said Baltasar, laughing a little. 'But maybe that's a good thing for us. It was a horrendous smell that we suffered a while ago with Nebuchadnezzar doing his business as he liked. But, anyway, he predicted your coming and we made Baltasar's party then in order to be ready for you. I am Baltasar and you are Daniel. Now, we need nothing but the hand of God on the wall.'

'And you believe that this will happen?'

'How would we not believe?'

'Did you see me before I came, Moses?' Jan asked the man under the table.

'I saw you in a dream,' he answered shyly. 'I saw a man bathed in blood coming before the King. The hand of God wrote upon the wall, and that man understood that which was written and told it to the King.'

'And it was me?'

'Oh God! The shit is coming now!' said Moses, growing restless.

Queen Circe offered him a glass for the third time. 'I promise you that I will not do you harm, sir. It's only brandy. You won't turn into an animal afterwards, unless you drink too much of it as that poor man did,' she said, pointing a long slender finger at Nebuchadnezzar.

Jan took it from her and drank it. It was only brandy, or that's how it tasted anyway. The girl on the chair began dancing and Nebuchadnezzar started barking. Baltasar stood up and his head almost touched the ceiling. 'Come to us, oh Lord!' he proclaimed loudly. 'I will repent, even if I may lose my kingdom for it. Write your piece on the wall. Tell us your truth so that we may be spared from the darkness of the world. You, oh Lord, speak to us! Speak to us now and tell us your truth!'

The obese man grabbed Jan and spoke loudly into his face. He smelled the foul odour of brandy from his breath, but didn't understand a word of his English. The girl on the chair was singing now as well. The man with a face like a little bird came to him then. 'Isn't it wonderful that you've come, that you are with us! The world outside has ended now. You noticed that, didn't you? It happened in the darkness before the moon rose. The world ended at that minute, and now nothing is left but us in this room forever. There's no escape for us.

But maybe the hand of God will come and give us an answer on the wall. Moses spoke clearly and then you came. I think that's what he said, anyway. What did you hear? Isn't that what he said? Why else would Baltasar be up there? It's clear. But still we'll have to wait, waiting forever. We have no choice anyway. The world is ended. We that are still alive, we are like the family of Noah after the flood and every other living thing dead. Maybe God will begin the world again afresh, but I don't believe it. That was the last chance. He gave us the plague as a sign of the coming of the end, didn't he? If you walk in the street now you would find nothing but destruction. Was it not said in the book of Daniel, in your book, that there would be 1,290 days left at the end. Surely that's been used up by now.'

'I'm afraid of the end of the world!' the girl on the chair screamed.

'Don't be afraid, Florry,' the old woman said. She was still dancing with the young man dressed like Jesus. 'Drink your fill and you will have no pain. Grab a nice man to dance with at the last moment. It is coming, be certain that it is, and don't be afraid.' Jan saw that she had only a few broken teeth in her mouth. The young man was blind drunk, and suddenly he fell in a heap on the ground. With that, his dancing partner cried out: 'Oh Lord, he is lost! The end has come.'

The girl on the chair screamed when she heard this, and Moses came out from under the table with his trousers still around his ankles. 'Baltasar!' shouted the man with the face of a little bird. 'Where is the hand of God? You said that it would come.'

'Listen!' shouted Baltasar loudly. 'I hear the horns of the angels.'

For a second, there was complete silence in the room, and then a frightful cry arose from them. It was a terrible sound. Jan thought he was in a dream and he wanted to wake up.

He thought about leaving, but wasn't sure if the world was still there, as the little bird had told him. The girl started to sing maniacally:

I am a fair maiden from London
London, London of the sun.
And I come here at the end of the world
To give yellow flowers to everyone

'Oh Lord, come in. Show us your hand. Drink! Drink! You haven't drunk enough,' said Baltasar, compelling them to drink more, which they all did except Nebuchadnezzar, who carried on barking.

Circe put her slender arm around Jan's waist and put her lips close to his cheek. The blackness of the night was in her eyes, the blackness of the abyss in the depth of the ocean. 'You are a pig, a beautiful, strong pig,' and then he felt her tongue in his ear.

He jumped back from her. He'd had enough of this madness. He grabbed the leg of the table under Baltasar's chair and pulled it hard. Baltasar fell onto the ground. Everyone stopped and there was silence in the room. Jan grabbed his bloody shirt then and screamed at them: 'Do you like your madness? The end of the world? Wouldn't that be a wonderful day? But I have seen the devils in the flesh. They are small, so small that they live inside flies and fly around looking at us. But do you think that means they care whether we live or die? I wouldn't believe that even if the end of the world was to come. I understand nothing, but I won't be in your prophecy.' And with that, he scraped his bloody shirt on the wall, a broad red smear without form or sense. 'Look now! What does it say? Nothing. It says nothing. There is nothing to say, and maybe there never will be.'

There wasn't a sound in the room now but they all stared at him in surprise. He walked towards the door but Circe followed him. 'Odysseus, Odysseus!' she shouted, and he stopped at the front door when he realised that she was speaking to him. 'I'm sorry. Forgive me. I understand that you have to leave this lunacy. But tell me, where are you going?'

'I'll go to Bishopsgate. I'll go back.'

'Do you know where it is?'

'No.'

'The night is almost spent now and the end of the world will come to us here with the rising of the sun, but I will give you directions before that happens.' She walked out of the house with him and pointed up the road. 'Take this street. When you reach a big stone house, take the lane on the left. Follow it until you come to a little square. Take the broadest street that comes out of that and go straight ahead. You will come to the city walls then, and if you turn right and follow the wall, you will come to Bishopsgate. If you go outside the walls, you will meet with the dead. I go there from time to time to speak with them. I don't recommend you do that, but it's your own choice. Anyway, goodbye now. I won't see you again.' She kissed him on the cheek and went back into the house.

Jan turned in the direction she had shown him and started walking. The full moon was still in the sky, but there was another light coming now, the pallid light of the new sun. He came to the big stone house before long, and on then to the square. She had given him perfect directions and he felt safe now in these empty streets. At the square, he saw the broad street stretching from it. It was a straight road, and it was only a few minutes until he saw the high stone wall of the city. He turned right and followed it, but within ten minutes he reached another gate. This wasn't Bishopsgate, but he remembered what she had said about speaking with the dead. He went out through this gate and walked past the little houses that were gathered around it until the sky opened up. The first hints of the dawn appeared ghostly to him over the little fields. The path before him was easy to see now, and he followed it without difficulty. This open country was inviting after the confinement of the streets in which he'd spent the night, and he heard the birds begin their morning song. He saw torches lighting a short distance away and walked towards them now, even though he didn't understand why they would be put here in the middle of the night.

But the dead were waiting for him. Some of them looked at him with cold eyes, men and women, both young and old, lost children amongst them with their white, frozen faces. There were about a hundred of them thrown in one pile into a great hole in the ground. It was a long trench and about twenty feet deep. Some of them were naked, and he saw the ugly boils on their bodies. There they were, those were the dead, but what would they have to say? How could he speak with them? What enlightenment or solution could they provide on the matter? Their own stories had been told now and they would never have anything more to say.

But then Jan saw the flies, millions of them. He hadn't seen them at first in the half-light, but they looked up at him now with a billion eyes. Was that the message that was waiting for him, that it was they who had done this, the little men, that they had given the plague to the people of London? He didn't want to accept this, but now they were there, waiting for him so they could show him their truth, and scoff. 'Hello ... It's us, Jan ... Can you see us? ... Where's your microscope now, Jan? ... Where's your drop of water? ... What's you educated opinion on this work of ours? ... Isn't it nice? ... Aren't our methods thorough? ... Every case done precisely ... Every specimen counted and measured. We're scientists, Jan. We're like you. We're the same.'

He turned and ran in the direction of the wall, the ugliness burrowed like a worm into his mind. He went back in through the gate again and turned left, walking beside it and east towards Bishopsgate. He walked past houses in which slept thousands of people, those who would be a meal for the coming serpent. It wouldn't be long before they slept out in the fields, in a big hole that was waiting for them, every one of them a new specimen.

Then he was at Bishopsgate. He walked down the road towards the church, across to Hooke's house and knocked on the door. It was soon opened and Fuller stood there, looking at him with an expression of horror on his face. 'Mr Swammerdam! In the name of all that's holy. What happened to you? Were you attacked? Are you hurt? Come in quickly. I'll call the master.' He tried to help him but Jan told him that he was alright and would go directly to Hooke's rooms. So the old man directed him up the stairs to the sitting room, and he himself ran to the bedroom to call Hooke. Jan saw the cause of the old man's fright when he looked in the mirror. His face was reddened with blood, a deep cut on his forehead, his clothes torn, and cuts around his arms and legs. Hooke came in and was shocked at his appearance, but Jan quietened him, telling him that he wasn't badly hurt. He told him of the events of the night: his conversation with Solomon Eagle; the girl suffering her cruel death locked in the house; the whipping of the boy and the attack upon himself; the cart of the dead; the plague party; the pit of bodies and the hordes of flies.

Hooke listened to every word carefully, and when he spoke, his voice came out in a slow, measured tone. 'This city is no longer safe. The plague is coming now unhindered and the people are demented with fear. I heard that they attacked some of the Quakers as they were trying to help people. Anyone who is out of the ordinary will be in trouble from now on.

He stopped here for a little while to collect his thoughts. 'I am sorry, Jan, for my outburst yesterday. I was enormously angry at Boyle, but it was you who suffered for it. I heartily apologise and deeply regret if I put you in danger. But I was thinking about our project last night as well, and I decided upon a new plan whereby we shall carry on with the work but much more cautiously. Looking at you now and the danger around us, I am even more determined than I was last night. We have no choice now because we do not know the full story. How could we publish a book without the full story? As learned men, we must follow the scientific methods and collect credible evidence before we publish anything.'

Jan nodded his head but said nothing.

'And you, Jan. I believe that you will die if you stay in London. Can we say with confidence that the little men themselves did not start the plague? There's not enough evidence to say that, but we cannot, as learned men, discount it either. I will go soon to Oxford, and you are welcome to come with me, if you want.'

'Thank you, Robert,' said Jan, 'but I will return to Paris. You are right that we should wait until we have more information, but I don't want to lose the chance either. I don't know what those little men are, but I know that God still exists in this world too.'

And that was the end of it. Hooke got him a letter of health so that he could leave the city, and another letter of introduction to friends of his in Dartford. If he took a small boat down the Thames, they could help him get to Canterbury and from there to Dover. He would have to wait for a while before he could sail across the Channel, but he was happy with that for fear that he had contracted the disease on the night out in the streets of London and that he'd bring it back to Paris and Thévenot's house.

He looked at the white cliffs from the deck of the ship as he left England. He remembered the hope that this same sight had given him on his voyage over, the hope that there would be a light in the abyss. These high walls stood like a glistening city, shining in the sunrise. But he knew now that it was a chalk castle, a chimera that would shatter to pieces as soon as it was touched, and he felt the abyss around him once again.

Act Three

Scene One

The sun was setting over Cork City, filling the horizon with a golden light that spread over the houses and the buildings like honey. I looked down on it from an eagle's nest up on a hill at St Luke's cross, up again to the big old houses in Adelaide Place, and up farther to the top floor with its rough windows that gave this beautiful view of the hilly city to anyone who might travel up here. At one time, the elites of society had lived in these houses on the hill, but they dispersed long ago to the suburbs and left them like the bodies of great giants, dissected into strips for the poor to live in. If they were once elegant houses, then the years of neglect took that lustre from them and this rough state could be seen now in every corner. But nobody could take away that view: hilly Cork City under the golden sunset.

I sat on the floor under that window looking out, a bottle of red wine beside me and a glass in my hand. That wine gave me a warmth in the same way that the sun gave warmth to the golden city. I felt peaceful at that moment, and I remembered that the city would continue ticking like a beautiful clock whatever happened to us. I remembered the precise account that Jan had written in his diary of the events that occurred that night in London. Salvadóir and Peadar worked together tirelessly to translate it into Irish as quickly as they could, and I had a complete copy of it my hands within two weeks. It was a remarkable book in which he laid out everything that happened to him in relation to the Firíní from that first day he saw them. As well as that, there were letters from other people which he had written into it, and poems of his own that showed his feeling on the matter. It was a summary of all the knowledge he had gathered, and a fantastic window on the world around him at that time. Maybe he was just trying to find some understanding on what had happened, but the precision of the scientist could still be seen in its narrative.

The sun's rays were nearly spent now, and I looked towards the horizon as it went down into the bowels of the earth. The sunset would not be at the same time tomorrow because the clocks would go back overnight, and everything would be different afterwards. The winter was coming, and I was in that liminal space between one thing and another.

It's strange the way things have come about, because I'm now at a liminal point in this account, this book in your hands, readers. I wanted the contemporary and historical parts of this book to follow each other consecutively so that you would understand it as one story that has been going on for centuries. That's how I did it, but I recognise now that we are at an important point in this book. I didn't know about Jan's account until this point in my own story, but you *did* know, readers. From here on I will have Jan's story in its entirety in the contemporary part, but you won't have it all until the end. You'll get it bit by bit, as normal. But it doesn't matter, everything will come together sooner or later.

So we got a great deal of information from Jan's diary. I was very happy to find out that my instincts were correct regarding the anagram of the last line of *Paradise Lost*, even though my own attempts at it were wrong. But there were still huge gaps in our understanding of the other texts, and I hadn't made a lot of progress with the poem at the back of the Bible. I spent a long week wallowing in that rabbit hole, wrestling with the Old Testament and the New, falling further down all the time with no answers for my efforts.

Robert Tighe and Jan himself were religious people who saw the hand of God in everything, but that was the world in which they lived, I suppose. Yet it was difficult for me to deal with this. It's hard to keep a grip on the objectivity of our own age when you're looking for insight on the world through the mythology of the past.

I got a copy of *Visio Tnugdali* as well and read it. It's the same basic story that Dante Alighieri told in *The Divine Comedy* one hundred and fifty years later, and he was clearly influenced by it. An Irishman called Brother Marcus wrote it in Latin and said that it had been told to him through Irish. I don't speak Latin but I got a translation of it in Middle-English, and was just barely able to understand it. There's a difference between this story and Dante's in that the main character has to go through the torments of Hell again and again, but he is cured each time by the hand of the angel who guides him. The character in Dante's story fares much better in the company of Virgil. But I found it strange that Brother Marcus was able to illustrate the torments of Hell with such wonderful imagination, yet he could say nothing about the wonders of Heaven, except that people walked around in golden palaces with crowns on their heads.

But whatever progress the three of us had made, there was still someone missing. Aogán hadn't liked this business from the beginning, but whether he liked it or not, he was still part of the story and I would have to share the information with him. He'd been lent an apartment for two weeks by a friend who was going on holiday, and that's where I was now: sitting under the window waiting for the last moment of the sun.

'Are you here to convert me?' he said when he opened the apartment door a few hours earlier.

'I am the light of the world,' I answered. 'Whosoever shall follow me will not walk in darkness, but shall forever have the light of life.'

'Be careful with your blasphemy now. Your sort can't be too careful with the kind of things that you've seen,' he said with a smile.

'Don't say you believe me now at long last!'

'I wouldn't say that at all. Come in.'

The ornate plasterwork was falling from the high ceiling in the living room, but you could still imagine how elegant it had once been. I sat on the sofa and Aogán sat on the armchair before me. I could understand why this story grieved him so much. How could anyone believe it? Our fathers were brothers and they had both died in a car crash when he was seventeen and I was five years old. His mother was dead by this stage as well, and he went a bit astray after that, but we were always very close in spite of the fact that there was twelve years between us.

'I know, Aogán, that you don't like hearing all this stuff, but I can only believe the evidence of my own eyes. I'm trying to find answers to what happened. If you can give me another answer other than the fact that there were two little men in the head of that fly, I'd be very happy to hear it. But listen to me first. We have more information now from the things that we took from the house. I'm only asking that you listen to me.'

'Ok, go on.'

I told him then about Robert Tighe and *Visio Tnugdali*, the two things that I'd found out after he'd left the house that day. Then I gave him a copy of Jan's book. It was a big bundle of paper, bound together with staples. 'This is the diary of the person we were talking about at the start, the man who made the anagram Peadar found in the book. Jan Swammerdam was his name, a Dutchman who was born in the seventeenth century. He said that he saw the little men too, and there were two other people at least who saw them as well. Peadar and Salvadóir translated it into Irish. Read it, Aogán, please.'

He took it from me cautiously, as if he thought there was a huge spider hiding in between the pages. He looked through it and then he stood up, went to the cupboard and took out a bottle of wine and one glass. 'Turn on the television and drink that,' he said, giving me the bottle. He took the bundle of paper with him to the bedroom then to read. I understood that this wasn't easy for him and I was grateful for it.

As he'd ordered, I opened the bottle of wine and poured myself a glass. I pushed the button on the remote control to switch on the television, and before long I was very comfortable there. I looked at a television programme about politicians around the world, the kind that Kate was discussing for her thesis. I won't bother naming the individuals; it doesn't matter. If someone reads this book in fifty years' time, there'll be another group of such politicians in the world. Someone on this programme said that we were living in the age of post-truth. Fair enough. It's clear that the internet has had a huge effect on the world, what with people spreading lies everywhere and politicians taking advantage of those lies – but wasn't it always like that? It was Adolf Hitler in his book *Mein Kampf* who created the concept of the 'big lie'. According to him, people would believe you if you tell them a gigantic lie because they wouldn't believe you'd be so bold as to concoct such a story. In truth, we're fairly gullible as a species really. If I tell you that there's a terrible conspiracy going on in the world, if I tell you that no one sees it but me, you and a small group of other people, wouldn't you be proud that you have an understanding of things beyond that which the majority of the human race possesses? People like the personal empowerment they get from conspiracy theories, especially when they're feeling low. It's an enticing feeling and some people will believe anything to have it.

I turned off the television and went to the window to look out at the beauty of the city as the sun set. That was real, at least. It was a Saturday night at the end of October, and you could feel the earth as it turned beneath your feet towards winter. The sun went down as it does every day, and I poured another glass from the bottle. Jan's diary was a big book and it was a dense text as well. I looked down at the darkness spreading over the city and drank greedily.

Aogán took a long while reading, but eventually, he came out with the bundle of paper in his hand. 'It's interesting,' he said. 'But it's very hard for me to believe that this story is true.'

'What is it so? I'd be happy to hear an alternative explanation.'

'It's a forgery.'

'And who made it?'

'I don't know. Salvadóir maybe? You only barely know him.'

'But if he himself created Jan Swammerdam's book, if he got a copy of the King James Bible, and made an anagram of a verse from it and wrote it then on the back page, if he created the anagram that Peadar saw in another of Swammerdam's books, if he did all these things, two questions remain: Why would he do it? And how did he create the vision that myself and Peadar saw in the microscope?'

'I don't know. Maybe it wasn't him who did it at all. But *somebody* did. As regards the thing that you saw, it hurts me to say this to you, Seán, but maybe you have some sort of mental aberration.'

'Maybe that's true. That was the first thing I thought myself. But if it's a mental aberration, how is it that all those books are there as well ... and how did it happen that Peadar saw the same thing?'

'I don't know ... maybe ...' he said and a sad look came across his face.

'What is it? Say it out!'

'Maybe it's you that's lying to me. Maybe you created all this.'

It was hard for me to hear this from Aogán, but I understood why. That was the only possible reason that he had left, and he had to say it out loud. 'I'd never do that, Aogán.'

'I never believed that you would, but this is too strange and too demented to be true. I'd never call you a liar, Seán, but I can make no sense of this.' At that moment, we both looked down at the coffee table between us. A fat, black fly sat there, rubbing its front legs together. 'It's a strange thing,' said Aogán. 'I was only thinking the other day that I haven't seen any flies since this story of yours started.'

'Now that you mention it, I haven't seen many of them either since that day with the microscope.'

'Well, there's a big bastard there now on the table,' he said. He looked at it for a while, and then, with one swift movement, struck at it with Jan's diary. He failed, however, and it flew mockingly up under the lampshade. 'All that work poor Jan Swammerdam put into this book, and we can't even kill one fly with it,' he said with a laugh. 'Let's get out of here, Seán! We'll go for a pint.'

'Right so,' I said, jumping up.

We went down to St Luke's Cross and along Wellington Road. It was dark now and I felt the strange energy of autumn nights around me, hanging in the air like static electricity. We walked on without speaking for a while, past the old hospice that had cared for those who were not far from death. Down again and back in time for me, past a gap in the wall in which there were narrow, winding steps stretching up to other big houses that were also divided into apartments. I heard rough voices coming down those steps, and remembered that I myself had lived up there once. We carried on. The footpath here is raised about a metre from the road with a railing, so that people don't fall, and I grabbed it. It was strange how quiet the road was because I'd seen the clamour of the city on my way across earlier, but now it was like the grave.

Then something strange happened which I still don't understand. The street lights went out and we were left in darkness. There wasn't even a car on the road at that moment. I stumbled over something and fell hard. Lying there on the ground, I remember feeling for a second that I was dead, but then I felt a hand on my shoulder pulling me up. It was Aogán, of course. 'Are you ok?'

'I am. What happened?'

'The street lights went out. For some reason, it's only happened on this street. Grab that railing and we'll carry on.'

We did that, slowly and carefully walking the length of the raised footpath. Apparently, the lights in the houses went out as well, and there wasn't a living soul to be seen anywhere. But then we heard voices before us and saw little red lights dancing in the air.

Coming closer to them, I heard that they spoke a language I didn't understand, and I felt bewildered. We stopped when we reached that place and, to my astonishment, Aogán began to speak to them in this language. It was Arabic, and I saw that the red lights were the tips of cigarettes that glowed with every drag they took on them. I listened in wonder to the conversation between Aogán and one from this group and I heard excitement and joy in that man's voice as he spoke. They were talking for a minute or two, and then Aogán lead me on again, farther down the dark road.

'I recognised the Moroccan Arabic they were speaking and I wanted to say something to them,' he said. 'That's a direct provision centre, and those poor unfortunates are in Limbo.'

We went on then and I heard some noise up ahead. It was the sound of the city, grinding slowly down before us. Then the street lights spluttered around us and came on again, so we could see our surroundings. A strange feeling struck me for a second as if I didn't recognise the place at all. We were on the corner of Wellington Road and Patrick's Hill and we turned left and down into the city centre.

It was a different world. As I said, I'd seen the clamour of the city as I was coming across earlier in the day, but it was an entangled jungle now with the streets filled with revellers and partygoers out to enjoy the Saturday night. And it wasn't a normal Saturday night either. This was the Saturday night of the Jazz Festival and its gaudiness was increasing by the second. There were people with straw hats and flamboyant clothes and it was clear that many of them had been out drinking since the afternoon. There was a group of them struggling up McCurtain Street with their arms around one another, singing some old song.

The sound of a saxophone burst from the bar on the corner like a wind, and a big group of people crowded in front of it, adding to the noise with their voices.

We stood on the slope at the end of Patrick's Hill looking at the boisterous celebrations around us. There are concrete steps on that slope on which generations of Cork people have walked, and I saw them now as if they were an old ruin from an ancient age. A group of young people sat on the steps, having their own party. In spite of the cold, there were young men with no jackets, and girls in short skirts and high heels. Some of them had cans and I thought perhaps they were too young for the pub. They spread out in one big group from there to the steps on the other side of the road. A young man and woman sat in the middle of the road, kissing one another as if no one else was around, until a car came down the hill and blew the horn at them to move. Their friends called out to them, joking, and they got up bashfully and moved to the footpath.

We walked past them and turned left at the bottom of the hill and onto McCurtain Street. There was a chipper a couple of doors up on the left and I saw people gathered outside it. A man was standing there, chicken curry and chips piled up on a bundle of paper in his hands as he shovelled it greedily into his mouth. I looked into the chipper itself and saw two men behind the counter. They were men of Indian origin, I thought, and they were struggling even now with the waves of the crowd that would break on the shore of that counter tonight. We turned from this sight and looked across the road.

'Do you know?' I said to Aogán. 'I like jazz, but I have to admit that I've never really liked the Jazz Festival.'

'Me neither, but we're here now,' he said apathetically. 'Pick one of the bars there and we'll try it. They'll all be the same tonight anyway.'

I picked one and we walked across to it. On opening the door, we looked in at the crush of bodies like a human stew, arms entangled and shoulders pressed against one another to gain an extra millimetre of space. We saw the distracted faces of people who were doing their best to tell themselves that they were enjoying the evening as they pressed on eternally towards the counter. There was no band playing now, but the music on the stereo filled the room with a mad energy. Aogán and I looked at each other once more and dived in.

I would have loved if there was a boat to row across that lake of bodies, but we had to swim like everyone else. They were three deep at the counter, and we had to weave through them like worms. A tall man raised his hand and shook a fifty euro note like a flag to attract the barman's attention, but it was a futile attempt.

Money was poured over the counter and drink was poured back in its place, but everyone, barmen and customers, were stopped at this point, as if it was a great reef between the sea and the land. Grotesque creatures lived in this soup, conger eels and crabs with sharpened claws. Somehow Aogán pushed his way through this and won two bottles of cider. He paid heavily for them though, much more than normal, and the money was taken in greedily. We retreated from the bar in search of a place to stand and found a ledge at the wall. I looked back at the counter and at the eternal struggle between those two sides.

We weren't at ease there, of course, with shoulders pressing on us all around, but we drank the cider to blunt our discomfort. I was better off than Aogán, having drunk wine before coming out, and was getting a bit used to the space now as well. I went up to the counter again to get two more bottles, and didn't feel it was so bad this time. It appeared that everyone in the room was drunk. A few people wore straw hats or a feather boa and, in spite of the crush, some of them were dancing enthusiastically in their own space. Gales of laughter erupted from groups here and there as I was going past.

On my way back to our ledge, I saw a woman approach Aogán with a big smile on her face. She gave him a hug and I saw that he was happy to see her. She was a woman in her late thirties, I'd say, and had short, black, curly hair and a big round face. '*Síle, this is my cousin Seán,*' said Aogán introducing us.

'*How are ya, Seán?*' she said. '*I think I know your face alright. Myself and Aogán go way back. We were going out with each other when we were teenagers. I had to sneak out of the house 'cause me father wouldn't let me see him.*'

'*He had great sense alright, your dad, to give him his due,*' said Aogán.

'Well, there were no flies on him definitely, but I always thought he was too hard on you, though. But what are ya doing these days? I haven't seen ya in years.'

'I'm living down in Morocco all the time.'

'Jesus, you were always very exotic, weren't ya! You're like a pirate or something. I'm very boring. Cutting people's hair now for almost twenty years.'

'Sure, how bad?' said Aogán. *'As long as they keep growing it back, then you're guaranteed work.'*

'I suppose. And what about you, Seán? Are you down in Morocco too?'

I was about to answer her question when Aogán interrupted me. *'Oh, he's not. Seán's the scholar. He's writing a book about tiny little men that are inside the head of a fly.'*

I was surprised that he'd say it straight out as easily as that. By the way, that was the first time that I thought I should write a book about these events.

'Tiny little men in a fly's head,' she said to me. *'And is it a work of fiction?'*

'Eh … yeah, I suppose so.'

'Well, we think so anyway, Síle,' said Aogán.

'But, sure, some people think that's true,' she said confidently.

'They do?' we both asked.

'Well, maybe not in flies' heads. But what's your man's name again? The lightbulb fella? Thomas Edison. He believed that tiny little men lived inside our brains and controlled our memories.'

'He didn't!' said Aogán.

'Oh, he did! So they say, anyway. I never actually met the man myself, so I suppose I could be wrong. But that's brilliant anyway: fair play to ya, Seán.'

An uneasy feeling struck me with this random piece of information. The idea that the Firíní were inside my own brain was too strange to deal with.

'Anyway, c'mere, I'd better go back over to them,' she said and she gave him another hug. *'Aogán, lovely to see ya again. Take care out there now in Morocco. Nice meeting ya, Seán. Good luck with the little men!'* We both looked at her as she disappeared from view, swallowed again by the crowd.

'What did she say about Thomas Edison?' Aogán asked in bewilderment.

I took out my phone, went on the internet and had an answer within a few seconds. 'It's true, apparently. He thought that little men kept our memories somewhere in the brain that he called the *fold of Broca*. It says here that he wanted to create a device to speak with the dead as well. Maybe he was just mad.'

'Maybe we all are,' he said dryly. 'Come on, throw that back and we'll go somewhere else.'

As soon as we went out onto the street, we heard voices raised in an argument. It was a man and a woman: a couple, I thought, but maybe not. The woman in particular was shouting aggressively at the man. *'You're nothin' but a useless fuckin' cunt!'* she said fiercely.

We left them to their troubles and walked back to the corner, down over the bridge and into Patrick's Street. Everywhere was packed with people, and we carried on aimlessly, drinking in the atmosphere. It was rough, unmannerly and disrespectful to the rules of normal life. But still you could get the smell of the human race there, that beautiful, eternal humanity that lives through the ages with the awareness that every one of us is part of that force from which history is made. It was an earthy smell.

We heard a man's voice coming to us then, as if it was on a loudspeaker. It was calm and steadfast, yet passionate as well. It stood out over the bedlam like the word of God in one of those old Hollywood films. We understood what was going on before we reached them. 'Christians? Out here, tonight?' said Aogán with surprise. 'Aren't they brave.'

'You can't get into Heaven without a bit of masochism. You get fifty points from a night like this,' I said to him.

There's a sports shop on Patrick's Street, and this man was standing in front of it now with a microphone in his hand, his soft voice blasting out from the loudspeaker on a stand behind him. There was another man giving out leaflets. 'Jesus has promised that he will save us. He is the surest friend that anyone can ever have. When all others desert you, he will be there. He will guide you when you are lost.'

Three young men stood there, laughing and calling to him. They didn't pay much attention to the man with the leaflets. It was the attention of the man with the microphone they wanted. '*Do you know 'The Fields of Athenry'?*' one of them said.

'*Hey, mister! Mister! C'mere a second will ya,*' said another.

The man with the microphone didn't want to stop, but in the end they broke his concentration and he had no choice.

'*Ya know that in the Bible they say that John was the apostle that Jesus loved.*'

'*Yes.*'

'*Does that mean that they were gay?*'

'*No, Jesus's love for us is greater than any earthly love.*'

'*But didn't he love the other apostles at all?*'

'*He loved them all. He loves all of us.*'

'*But he* really *loved your man John, did he?*'

Then the third man who had been quiet up to now began singing: '*John and Jesus up a tree, k-i-s-s-i-n-g.*'

'*That's not true. That's not what was meant.*'

'*Are you being homophobic?*'

We walked past them and down the lane in the direction of Paul Street, a narrow lane thronged with people now, and with a busker playing a jazz song on the guitar. Aogán gave him some money and we carried on. In Paul square, there was a man on stilts in flamboyant clothes, someone else juggling, and girls in gaudy masks. It was like a little carnival, and I thought it was brilliant.

But then two men with a rough, angry appearance came down the street. One of them approached the stilt walker and shouted up to him: '*You're the big man around here, are ya?*' he said, thinking himself very funny indeed. Then he kicked one of the stilts. The stilt walker nearly fell, but he grabbed on to a drainpipe and did his best to steady himself. When he had done that, he kicked this man back himself, and that stilt was a heavy enough baton. But he was in trouble now. He couldn't release his grip from the drainpipe in order to take off the stilts because these two would knock him. They both grabbed the stilts now and his friend, the juggler, came over to help but one of them punched him in the nose.

Everything happened very quickly, and we were about to help them when two guards came around the corner and saw the commotion. They ran and stopped it immediately, grabbing the two who had started everything. Myself and Aogán walked past them like ghosts on the street, invisible to everyone. There was an argument going on at the corner between a man selling straw hats and another man. There was a straw hat on this second man's head and a disturbed angry look on his face. I heard one sentence from their conversation as we were going past: '*But I gave you a fifty euro note … Fifty euro … not twenty!*'

We went up to Emmett Place then, past the art gallery, and sat down by the railings in front of it. There were big jazz gigs going on in the Opera House and people gathered here and there on the broad pedestrian street. Two men with a clarinet and a guitar stood busking by the railings a short distance from us. They played very well and it softened some of the ugliness that we'd just witnessed.

'I have something to tell you,' Aogán started in a confessional voice. 'I wasn't able to say it to you tonight when you gave me Swammerdam's book. I don't want to encourage this madness of yours, and this is not to say that I believe one bit of it, but I know what that "Fingin tome" is in the poem at the back of the Bible.'

'You know what it is?' I said excitedly. 'Tell me!'

'I was never a scholar like you, but I remember things when I hear them. I was in a bar in Marseille a couple of years ago and started drinking with another Irishman: he was from Limerick, I think. Anyway, this fella starts giving out about the things the English stole from the countries that they colonised – the Elgin Marbles from the Parthenon, and so on. Then he started on the Book of Lismore, a manuscript from Ireland that's over in England now in the possession of the Duke of Devonshire. The correct Irish name for it, however, is *Leabhar Mhic Cárthaigh Riabhaigh*, because it was Fínghin Mac Cárthaigh Riabhach who originally commissioned it early in the fifteenth century. I remembered this when I saw the "Fingin tome" in the poem at the back of the Bible that day, but I didn't want to say anything. I didn't want to add more fuel to the fire. But I left that day and did some detective work of my own. I thought at first that it couldn't be true, but when I read tonight in Swammerdam's account about Robert Boyle, I realised that I *was* right. Fínghin was an important person, a Prince of Carbery who married Caitríona, the daughter of Thomas Fitzgerald, Earl of Desmond. The book was a commission that was done on the occasion of their wedding. It's a collection of a huge number of stories on lots of subjects: the stories of the saints, stories of the Fianna, even the story of Marco Polo. It's called the Book of Lismore in

English because it was found hidden in a wall in Lismore Castle early in the nineteenth century.'

'The same place where Robert Boyle was born?' I said.

'The very place! Boyle's father was the Earl of Cork. He had an enormous estate that stretched from Cork to Waterford and Lismore Castle was his headquarters for a long time. Robert had a brother Lewis, and it was he that took possession of the book when he plundered Kilbrittain in 1642. The book is over in England now, and there are some pages missing from it. It's mentioned in Swammerdam's diary that Robert Boyle had said that there was a reference to the Firíní in an Irish language book in the possession of his family but that he tore those pages out. Some pages were lost in the nineteenth century after it had been mistreated, but I'd say that there were pages ripped out even before it was hidden in that wall and that it was Robert Boyle who did it.'

'Aogán, this is great!' I said, overjoyed with this news. 'Well done! Have you any idea then what connection Robert Tighe had to the Boyle family?'

'There was no connection in the slightest between them. Robert Tighe died twenty years before Robert Boyle's father even came to Ireland. But I think that I've found a more important connection. Fínghin Mac Cárthaigh Riabhach was a big lord, but his cousin is interesting as well, the Lord of Muskerry, Cormac MacTeige.'

'Brilliant!' I said in amazement.

'Think of this now,' he said conspiratorially. 'If Robert Teige was related to Cormac MacTeige – his grandson perhaps – he could have got information on the Firíní from his own family in Ireland. It was said that he left a great deal of money in his will to his son, and people at the time wondered where he'd got it from. Maybe it was because he was related to the Irish nobility.'

'And then when he translated his part of the Bible into English and made his own anagram with that poem, he put in a reference to *Leabhar Mhic Cárthaigh Riabhaigh*, the book of his own people in Ireland!' I said, finishing the story for him in excitement. I felt awestruck by this news.

'That's all I have, anyway,' he said, like a person who had just made a confession. 'I don't want to add to this madness, but I had to tell you.'

'Thanks very much, Aogán. I realise that you don't like this stuff, but you've no idea how grateful I am to you for your help.'

At that moment, we felt a presence standing behind us. We turned around and saw a slouching old man with long grey hair that straggled down to his shoulders, even though the top of his head itself was bald. His cheeks drooped, as if he was an old bloodhound, and he looked down at us through watery eyes. He had a paper bag in his hand and wore a dirty raincoat that would have been expensive enough once, I'd say. He sat down on the ground beside us, opened the bag and took out two pieces of chicken, one for each hand. '*Do you know that I'm immensely fond of fried chicken,*' he told us in a calm, measured, well-to-do accent, and then he began gnawing at them, one by one. His voice surprised me because I didn't feel it suited his general image at all.

'*Yes,*' answered Aogán. '*But surely everyone is aware at this stage of your fondness for fried chicken.*'

He stopped eating for a moment then. He looked closely at Aogán and an indifferent smile broke on his face. '*Oh, yes, very droll. Very droll indeed,*' he said. He finished the two pieces of chicken quickly, licked his fingers, and threw the bones into the street. '*Please don't think me a litterbug. I'm simply thinking of the birds, you see.*'

'*It's good to think of the birds,*' I said.

'It is, indeed. They teach us so much, you know.'

'Do they really?' I asked.

'Oh, yes. Have you never heard the expression 'A little bird told me'?'

'You know,' Aogán said to him, *'there aren't many people who would think to take that expression literally.'*

'Yes, well many people are often wrong about a good many things,' he said, standing up. He turned to leave then but when he was a couple of metres from us, he turned back again. *'Perfection is God; simplicity is perfection. The curse of curses is that men will not let truths like these alone,'* he said solemnly. *'Do you know who said these words?'*

I shook my head to tell him that we didn't.

'It's a line from Ben-Hur by Lew Wallace,' he said in the voice of someone who is revealing some dark secret. *'A line that he gave to Balthasar, one of the Magi … the Three Wise Men. Farewell until we meet again, my friends.'*

We looked at him as he walked slowly in the direction of the bridge. 'That's why I never liked the Jazz Festival,' I said to Aogán when he'd gone.

Scene Two

Letter from Robert Hooke
to Jan Swammerdam
28th June 1666

My friend Jan,

You have undoubtedly heard by now of the terrible disaster that has recently befallen our beautiful city, London. Much of the city, as you remember it, has been burnt in an awful fire and is lost forever. I myself was a witness to this abominable scourge and, even though Gresham College itself was saved by the grace of God, broad tracts of the city were left as charred rubble on the ground. I believe there has not been a destruction so great in the history of humanity since the Romans destroyed Jerusalem and its temple.

Let me give you my own account of this terrible time. Fuller woke me shortly before sunrise with the news that there was a great conflagration in the south of the city near the river. I got up at once and could clearly see a reddening of the sky in that direction, estimating it to be some distance from us yet and perhaps in an area directly north of London Bridge.

Around nine o'clock, I went in a carriage to examine the damage, and saw that a great many houses had been destroyed at that point and that the fire was growing and spreading westwards with the wind. You will remember from your visit that lots of houses were pressed together and made from inflammable material such as wood and thatch, materials that were illegal in the city but still widely used. I made my way to the river through streets that were still spared from the flames, and hired a small boat that would take me out onto the water to get a better view of the damage. It was a terrifying sight, and I was horrified when I saw that the fire was spreading out of control.

This was still only Monday morning, but the following days would burn themselves into my memory forever as I looked at the jewel in England's glory, the noble city of London, reduced to ashes. Those days were like a horrible dream, days in which hurried events crowded on top of each other, trying to surpass one another in their atrocities.

Great efforts were made to knock down houses to create firebreaks, but alas, because of the inaction of the Lord Mayor, this was left until the intensity of the flames had gone beyond the effectiveness of this resource. Great was the rush that occurred then to take valuable items from houses before the flames would reach them and so the streets were thronged with every sort of cart or wagon, with people carrying their belongings on their backs and the infirm on stretchers or beds. They made their way down to the river in the hope that they could load everything onto whatever vessel or boat would be available but, as you can imagine, it was not long before those became quite scarce. But still the flames and the smoke drove the people on, laden with their belongings. When I was trying to help a friend, I myself was almost overcome with the suffocating smoke, the searing heat and the multitude of fire sparks that would burn your eyes and skin. Alas, it was all in vain, and we could but watch as the voracious flames engulfed my dear friend's house.

I believe I shall never have to imagine Hell because I have already been granted a vision of it in that terrible week. I went on the Thames again on the second or third night and saw the city as one great inferno, a malicious fury that spat its poison with great eruptions from oil, tar and gunpowder stores which scorched the air and the earth itself. There was nothing missing from that hellish vision but the giant Lucifer himself walking proudly through the flames.

Many looked for answers which could explain this great loss, and the blame was put on the enemies of the country: the Dutch, the French and the Catholics. I myself saw a great crowd of people, incited by their loss and fear, who believed that the armies of the enemy were ready to attack the city and to murder and defile the people. And so they set out to face this threat, beating and hanging anyone who appeared in any way out of the ordinary. I saw one poor man, an innocent Catholic as far as I know, who was cruelly beaten before being hanged from the frame of a burnt house.

By the end of the week, the flames had all but abated, and I walked through the burning embers of the city. Many people gathered near Gresham College because food was being sold there by order of the King. By the will of God, the college and the area around Bishopsgate was spared from the blaze, even though a suspicious fire started there on Thursday when the fires in other places were easing. With great wildness, the crowd again began their search for the cause of all their loss. Again the blame and curses were placed on the Dutch, the French and the Catholics. As a reasonable man, I cautioned them not to spread baseless rumours. I myself was not in favour of the attacks on innocent people which happened during the fire, and I know as well that you yourself suffered at the hands of a mob like this when you were in our country.

But we English are a proud people, with our enemies around us on every side. We have always faced these enemies courageously. But however much we are besieged by the Dutch or the French, I know that our real enemies are those who would enter the head of a fly, and it's clear to me that this enemy reigns now in Rome. If I was of the opinion that these beings were behind the great plague that struck the city last year, then this new calamity has greatly strengthened that view. I believe that those same beings, which we both saw, are responsible for the destruction of this noble city and that it was done as a warning to me not to publish the book.

I have thus decided that I shall never publish it. I shall destroy all the drawings and the written work I have produced to date. I recommend that you do the same and put this terrible period behind you. As men of science, we are permitted to glance into the kingdom of God, but I believe that we went astray, onto a forbidden path. If we choose to continue, it will draw a disaster greater than we can imagine down upon innocent people. I need not mention, of course, that I shall deny any claim you make in relation to me if you choose to go ahead with your own book.

Let us return again to being learned men and leave the crazed vision that tormented us. You are an exceptionally talented man and I believe that you are destined for greatness. Let us be happy with these feats. The enemy is everywhere around us and, just like they were during the destruction of Jerusalem, the orders come from Rome. Maybe these beings were working behind the scenes back then as well, laughing as the temple was destroyed.

I have decided to use my skills to rebuild this city as a new Jerusalem, so that she may again be a light of hope to the world and a monument to our courage against the enemy. I pray that God may grant you that same courage and the grace to withstand this terrible foe, and that you may live a long and glorious life.

Your friend,
Robert Hooke

Scene Three

I had bought a car just the week before. It was old and rusty, but it wasn't very expensive and it still moved. Three days after our trip around the lunacy of the city, I decided to take another trip that would give an ease to my ailing spirit. I had a dire need of some sort of break, a walk in the woods or something like that, and where else would I chose but the place that was mentioned in Robert Tighe's poem: Guagán Barra. I was very impressed with Aogán's insight that night, as were Peadar and Salvadóir when I told them the following morning. I phoned Salvadóir, and he was very happy that Aogán was part of it. He said he had some news himself and that he'd tell us about it the following day. Things were coming to light, and I understood that I needed to carry my share of the weight as well. I found out easily about Robert Tighe and Guagán Barra, but I had done nothing since then but plough in the trough of mythology. I knew that I wouldn't find answers written in stone at Guagán Barra, but I wanted to go there anyway. Maybe I was only telling myself that I was looking for information, and all I really wanted was the chance to be on my own in the car and think.

The thing that strange man in front of the art gallery had said was going around in my mind as I drove through the narrow roads down past Inse Geimhleach and Béal Átha an Ghaorthaidh. I'd been immersed in the world of religion since I began trudging through the old stories of the Bible, but I was certain now that I was on the wrong track with this. Tighe, Swammerdam and Milton were religious people, and they could look at the world only through those spectacles. But still those words went through my mind: '*Perfection is God; simplicity is perfection*'. I was going down to a sacred site and maybe an echo of that was having an effect on me.

Guagán Barra is a special place filled with natural beauty. You come in on one side of the lake with the high hills, speckled with green and grey, rising to the sky on the other side. The island in the lake is only twenty metres from the bank, and, in reality, you can't actually call it an island because there's a causeway out to it. It's on this island, however, that you will find the sacred site attributed to Saint Finbarr. There's an old stone ruin that dates back to bygone days and a neat little church beside it. But it's situated in a basin of water that shines like a stained-glass window, and amidst the hills that rise around it higher than Notre Dame in Paris. This is where Saint Finbarr built his religious site in the sixth century. It's from this lake that the Lee flows, the river on which Cork City is built. I decided I'd go walking in the woods after examining the church. Crystal clear waters of the stream meander through the trees here. This is the Lee in its infancy, even before it enters the lake, and it's possible to imagine that you're back in time when that river was young.

I went to the old ruin first. There's no roof on it now, and the walls are made of grey stone of every tint, dark grey and light grey speckled together in an irresolvable jigsaw. There are stone steps up to the entrance, and down into it as well. A big, wooden cross stands boldly in the centre of the space. It is square on the inside with cavities built into the walls, cells of some sort for the holy inhabitants. Higher up on the wall are tablets of carved stone with a different image of the stations of the cross shown on each one. A description of the event is written in Irish under each tablet: 'Jesus falls the second time under his cross', 'Jesus is crucified'. They were artistic, elegant and brutal. I ascended the steps again and left poor Jesus to his torture chamber.

There's more of a modern appearance in the little church which is beside the old ruin, but it's still a beautiful building with stained-glass windows and an altar of carved stone. I walked in quietly and sat down on the front pew before the altar. You don't have to be religious to enjoy places like this. They were built specifically with the aesthetic vision of calming tired souls. I felt a spiritual calmness around me that was very pleasant. There are two stained-glass windows behind the altar, Saint Finbarr on the right in his red gloves, and the Virgin Mary on the left in a long, blue cloak over a green dress.

I noticed that I was staring at the image of Mary in the window. I could see that she was a young girl, her face lowered humbly and gently, and I tried to imagine her as that young girl, as a human individual who would eat her breakfast in the morning, who would have her own friends. What opinion did she have of the Romans, for example? Did she like olives? I tried to imagine her, but failed. My mind was full of thoughts twisting around one another, something I had read at the end of Jan's diary, the thing that strange man in the street had said to us: '*Perfection is God; simplicity is perfection.*'

Something occurred to me. I failed to find that real girl because she wasn't there. There was nothing there but that simplicity itself. Human personality is a complicated, contradictory thing. Mary doesn't have a personality like that because she's a blank page, a personification of the concepts of purity, devotion and goodness. It's as simple as that, and I saw that this is exactly what spirituality is: simplicity. Simplicity is perfection: perfection is God: simplicity is God. The world is a complicated and entangled thing with a multitude of meanings for every utterance. Everyone has their own view, and a person's mind changes with the wind. Spirituality gives us permission to believe in simplicity. It doesn't matter how complicated the world around us is because that simplicity is behind everything, giving the same simple answer to every question.

I imagined that this simplicity was at the heart of every type of spirituality in the world. It was in the religions of the East as well, in the Brahman of Hinduism, and in the *taiji* of ancient Chinese philosophy which influenced Buddhism and Confucianism. It is the highest universal principle. But I saw at that moment that there is a special place for it in the Abrahamic religions. The Abrahamic God is a personification of the concept of absolute truth, a truth on which all other truths depend. This is the belief that there is a single, unquestionable truth in the universe: the greatest simplicity of all.

I thought again about the ancient Israelites when they swept away all the Canaanite gods except El and then worshiped this one single god as the source of all truth. I thought about the coming of Christianity, about Catholicism and Protestantism, and about Islam. Whatever differences exist between these beliefs, it is a basic principle in the Abrahamic religions that an absolute truth exists. It's a very attractive concept when you have a hard life. It's simple; it's beautiful; it's strong: a single, absolute truth from which all other truth flows. That's what the word El means; that's what El is.

Then I found out that I'm proper fool. I came to Guagán Barra to get some insight on the story of the Firíní, but I didn't think at the time that there would be anything written in stone there. But there was a plaque on the gate that I didn't see on my way in. Something was written on it in English about this sacred shrine to Saint Finbarr, and then these words:

> *From here he journeyed the river-way of the Lee to become the first bishop and founder of the church and City of Cork.*

It wasn't in Guagán Barra that Saint Finbarr founded his church at all: it was only ever a monastery, and other people put a church there later on. The church of Saint Finbarr was always in the place where Cork City is now, and I knew that very well. It's called Saint Finbarr's Cathedral and I've walked past it thousands of times. But I was led astray with the reference to the lake isle in the poem at the back of the Bible, and I thought that it had to be Guagán Barra. Then it struck me in a flash. I knew where there was a lake with an island that was within shouting distance of Saint Finbarr's church in Cork City. Wasn't I raised just up the road? The Lough! The same Lough that's right beside Ballyphehane.

I jumped into the car again and shot up the road. I won't repeat the bad language that I used and curses that I applied to myself as I drove up out of Guagán Barra.

Scene Four

Amsterdam, the Netherlands
28th June 1667

'Don't leave me … Don't leave me like this. Help me! I beg of you! The pains are terrible … Don't leave me!'

Her voice was coming from every corner of the room, crying piteously, sobs filling the air. He could hear her but couldn't see her. She circled him. She was behind him and before him, over behind the chair, but yet … she wasn't.

'Help me, Charles … Charles my love … Don't leave me … Don't leave me like this! I'm afraid, Charles.'

'Where are you? I'm coming! I'll find you!' The room was dark. A dirty rag hung as a curtain over the window, but he knew that there were wooden boards nailed on the outside as well. It was like a one-roomed, wooden cabin, with rough pieces of furniture, made by unskilled hands. Weak rays of light came through slits in the door beside the window, yet most of the room itself remained in the shade. He ran to the door and pulled at it, but it was like iron. He looked out through the narrow slits. There was someone outside, a man with his back turned to him, a big, rough man with broad shoulders and heavy arms. He saw through the slit that he had a heavy cudgel in his hand as well.

'Let me go! Don't leave me like this. I can't suffer it any longer!' she pleaded again.

He turned back to the room. Where was she? She was inside somewhere. She wasn't outside.

'Help me … Help me! Have pity on me … I'm a good girl … I was always a good girl! Don't leave me like this!'

He grabbed the table now and threw it against the wall. He put his fingers in his hair and pulled at it. Her voice was going through him, through his skin, through his mind. He left out a harsh gasp, ran to the door and beat on it. 'Open this door! Open it now!' He looked through the slit again but there wasn't even the slightest stir to the broad back of the man outside, standing there like an unclimbable wall before him. He turned back to the room. 'Have pity on me … Don't leave me like this!'

The thoughts ran through his mind now: 'This is hell. This is my hell … the hell that's been reserved for me. Locked into this house with her, listening forever to her desperate pleading … endlessly … and unable to do anything … unable to help her … nothing … nothing to do except listen to her … forever … endlessly!'

He ran back to the door. 'Let me go! Let me go! I beg of you!' He beat heavily on the door with his fists, but the wood was as hard as stone. He pulled at the ugly rag that hung from the window then, but the rough cloth was tied firmly. He raised it, but the wooden boards that were nailed over the window were more compact than the boards in the door.

There was only one narrow split, and when he looked through it, there was nothing to be seen but a little part of the street. It was a dark, dreary day with its gloom dripping like oil from everything. That was it… That was all he would have to see now … for all eternity.

'Don't leave me! … Have pity on me … I'm a good girl,' she said, imploring again, her sobbing droning in his ear like a fly.

Then he saw another split, a small slit in the wall at the back of the room across from the door. It was a little hole in the wall, the same size as a thumbnail. He ran over and looked through it. Two men. There were two tiny men drowning in the water. He saw their contorted faces as they struggled, their limbs beating.

Then they stopped. Were they dead? Their heads hung to one side and their bodies were motionless in their little one-piece suits of light blue.

But they weren't dead. They raised their faces suddenly and stared directly at him with a cruel grimace. They weren't drowning anymore, they were swimming, rising from the water. They stood up and pointed at him, their expressions fierce now, their teeth like serpent's fangs, their eyes swelling, their heads changing, metamorphosing into … into the heads of flies!

He jumped back from the hole. It took a few seconds before he noticed the difference. If the room had been dark before, it was even darker now. If the wooden walls and the furniture were brown, now they were black … the utter black of the abyss. They were there. The flies were there in the room. Millions of them. On the walls and on the furniture, the floor and the ceiling, the door and the window. They left a slit free on the door in order to let in a ray of light, so that he could see that they were there.

But still the voice came: 'Don't leave me … Don't leave me like this!'

He stood like a bar of iron, frozen with fear. He knew what was coming now, but still they left him wait on it, stretching the moment until it was ready to break. He let out a little whimper as a pup would, and then it happened. They exploded all over the room. They were everywhere, their drone like a blast of noise in his ears, their bodies themselves were in his ears too, in his mouth, in his eyes, under his clothes. He ran to the door, but there was no escape now. This was the hell that was reserved for him.

He fell heavily onto the ground from the bed, his body soaked in sweat and his eyes rolling in his head. The candle was still lit on the table but there was only a stump left in it now. There was water there as well, and his mouth was as dry as sand. He made an effort to crawl towards it. It was a dream, a nightmare, but it was worse than that. He had a terrible fear that this was exactly the hell that would await him when they eventually killed him. 'Lord, have mercy on me. Forgive me my sins. Forgive me my pride.' He reached the table and stretched his hand up to the jug, spilling much of the water as it came down to him, but still there was enough to quench his thirst. He pulled it back to the bed with him, and with a great effort, climbed back in.

Jan was dying. He was certain of it. He didn't know why they hadn't killed him in London with the plague, but they would kill him now. It was a light enough illness at first, and he hoped it would go quickly, but then the fever struck: shivering, headache, fatigue and vomiting. A terrifying face looked back at him in the mirror, as if he himself was turning into an insect. A yellow face with sunken red eyes that looked out through little holes in the skin. It was the face of death, a face that told him it wouldn't be long now.

All he ever wanted was to glorify God with his work and show the world those wonderful creatures he had created. Just to look at the insects themselves: the butterflies, the mites, even the flies. He never wanted to see little men … but they were there before him that sunny day in Steno's garden. If he could just go back and wash that moment from his history and begin again afresh, he would want nothing then but to work on his own studies. It grieved him dearly now that he would never be able to do that. With every fevered nightmare, he thought it to be the hell that he'd find when they killed him. But he told himself that God would not do that to him. Whatever kind of beings they were, God would always be stronger. God would not fail one who was faithful to him – and he *was* faithful.

But if he could do his work before he died, he could glorify God with his life. That was always his goal. Those animals were miracles, the little insects that walk around under our feet all the time. What type of life do the ants or the bees have? How do the maggots live? How does a caterpillar turn into a butterfly? He wanted to answer these questions more than anything else. They were questions that were woven into the fabric of his essence. He hated the little men because they had robbed him of that. He didn't ask them to be there in the microscope that day, but now they would kill him because of it. But maybe he deserved it. Maybe the little men had killed an immeasurable amount of people in London in order to silence himself and Hooke. The plague was in the Netherlands in 1664 and in London in 1665 – the two countries in which those with evidence on them were born. And how many people died in the fire then in London? Was that not a strong message? But he couldn't feel guilty about it. He didn't kill them. It was the little men who did that. But, still, he heard her voice in his dreams: Don't leave me … Don't leave me like this. He had heard her in his dreams, even before the fever came, but now she was there all the time. He felt her enter the room again with the heaviness that lay now on his eyelids.

Another weakness overcame him and he hoped that the candle would still be lit when he came to again, if he did at all.

He wasn't in the cabin in London this time but in Paris. He was out in the dark, gloomy streets that were thronged with the poor in their putrid, torn rags. They were covered in these tatters from head to toe with nothing visible of them except their dirty faces, faces with twisted noses and black, rotten teeth, if they had any at all, one-armed, one-legged, one-eyed people, eyes with demented stares and frenzied grins. They were like insects. They shouted out to one another to sell their foul goods, goods that were piled on carts or tables.

He was in the little entangled lanes in which the markets were held, but he couldn't understand how anyone could buy or sell anything here. He saw dead dogs in the corners amongst the offal and the entrails. He noticed that his feet were treading through a thick layer of oil on the ground, oil that had been smeared on the walls with filthy claws. He got the smell around him in the air like an acidic soup that burnt the nose and lungs. The voices were bellowing their curses at one another in one great clutter of ugly noise, and he understood only tiny morsels of that harsh speech as he wove himself through the carts, the tables and the filthy crowd.

But then he saw the blue colour down at the end of the street. There wasn't such a colour anywhere else in that grey, dirty area, and it stood out, even though it was still some distance away. He followed it, struggling through the filthy bodies and faces that appeared before him. The noise of the street increased and almost deafened him, but he carried on, keeping his eyes on that colour that was skipping ahead like a rabbit, almost out of sight. He lost it entirely once or twice and had to run to find it again. It was difficult for him to see what it was exactly, except that it was a beautiful blue colour, the pale blue of the sky. Then the streets widened and the horrible noise decreased. There was space for him now and he ran ahead. He was catching up with it, and he saw as well that he was coming out of the little streets onto the quays of Paris. It was then that he saw the colour properly.

It was them, the little men themselves, only they weren't little anymore. They were the same size as a normal person but still they wore the one-piece suits of pale blue. There were two of them again, and he saw that one of the men turned around and looked directly at him before they continued along the quay on the Left Bank in the direction of Pont Neuf and Notre Dame. Jan was running now in agitation to catch up with them, but he couldn't do it. No matter how fast he ran, they were always the same distance away. From time to time, one of them would turn around and look at him.

He saw Notre Dame Cathedral one moment, but when he looked again, it was gone. Then he noticed thick woods on the other side of the river with birds circling above the trees. There were no houses there but little cabins dotted about. A tall woman in tattered, dirty clothes stood on the quay wall on his own side and loudly blew a great brass horn. When this happened, people came out of doorways to look up at her. The men in the pale blue suits were beside the quay wall, but they went across to the other side now, one of them looking back at Jan before they crossed. They went into a shop then, and Jan ran after them and in through the same door.

The shop was as dark and filthy as the market in the narrow streets. Rancid meat, covered in flies, hung from hooks in the ceiling. There were piles of rubbish everywhere, with broken plates and torn rags. But he saw the pale blue colour at the back of the shop and followed it. He went down through piles of clothes that got higher with every step. Before long, it was like a dark wood with a narrow path going through it. He looked behind him, and the shop had disappeared. He had nothing to do but carry on, but the path was becoming narrower now. Then the path itself vanished and he was struggling through an enormous pile of rags, the top of which was ten feet above his head and squeezing on him all the time. The two pale blue men were gone, and he understood that it was a trap. They had led him here to entangle him in these rags forever. That was the revenge they wanted; that was the hell that was reserved for him.

He struggled on, but there was no way out of it now. Then he saw a hole in the pile of cloth before him, like a rabbit hole. He would soon be lost anyway, and he decided to try it. He jumped into it and went crawling down and through it like a ferret, but before long he couldn't tell up from down and was lost in a sea of cloth and rags. Then his hand struck against something hard. A handle! He turned it and a little circular door opened that was just big enough to let him through.

He fell out onto grass in bright sunshine. He was in a beautiful garden, full of flowers and bushes, and it was like a summer's afternoon. He recognised it immediately. It was Steno's garden, the place where he had first seen the little men, and they were there now again, except that they weren't little anymore. They were as big as Jan himself, sitting on chairs around a little table on the green in their one-piece, pale blue suits, one of them fair and the other dark-haired. Jan stood up and walked towards them.

'Jan, it's wonderful that you were able to come. Sit down, please,' said the fair-haired man, indicating the third chair, as if it had been reserved for him. Jan sat down awkwardly, staring mutely at the two men.

'May we offer you a hot chocolate?' asked the dark-haired man. 'It's very pleasant indeed.' He poured the dark liquid out of a little pot and into a cup that was placed before him. 'Your sailors took it back recently from the New World, as you call it. Try it.'

Jan took a sip from the neat porcelain cup in his hand. 'It's nice. Thank you.'

A satisfied smile came on the face of the dark-haired man. 'I like it very much myself,' he said cheerfully.

'May I ask you a question?' Jan said carefully.

'Of course, carry on, Jan, please! You are amongst friends here,' the fair-haired man replied.

'Who are you?'

The two men in the blue suits looked at each other in confusion. 'Don't you know who we are, Jan? We are the people that you saw in the garden a couple of years ago – with your microscope,' said the fair-haired man.

'I understand that. But who are you?'

'Oh, excuse me, Jan,' said the dark-haired man. 'I understand you now. That's a very complicated question, and maybe we wouldn't have the time to answer it here.'

'That's your scientific mind again, Jan, always looking for knowledge,' said the fair-haired man with a friendly smile. 'I like your work very much, by the way.'

'Thank you.'

'And we would like to let you know,' said the dark-haired man, 'that we understand that it was an accident and that you didn't kill them on purpose.'

'I … didn't kill …?'

'You didn't know that they were there at all, of course,' said the fair-haired man. 'How could you have? You were looking for knowledge, so as to widen humanity's narrow world a little. Your loyalty to your species and your enthusiasm are very commendable, but we understand that you feel guilty for their deaths, and want to let you know that you shouldn't feel like that.'

'But of course,' said the dark-haired man, 'you must understand as well that you cannot spread the story of our existence before the world. For reasons that we cannot explain here, we wouldn't like that.'

But Jan started to come to himself now and his courage returned. 'You wouldn't like that? Well, there are many things that *we* don't like either. What about the devastation that occurred over in—' he began.

But the dark-haired man cut across him. 'Maybe we shouldn't be making accusations against each other,' he said abruptly. 'We should focus on your own case here, Jan. How are you at present? I heard you've been a little unwell lately.'

'You are well informed,' Jan replied sullenly.

'There's no reason for us to be unfriendly, Jan,' said the fair-haired man. 'We understand that you like your study of insects a great deal. We can see that you're a very intelligent person and that you should carry on with this research. We wish you every success in your work.'

'But those are the cares of your own life,' said the dark-haired man. 'If you can remain just with those cares, maybe you'll live through the night and see the sunrise.'

'But you must understand, Jan, that we can't let you free to publish a book and spread our story before the world. You must see that we're giving you a chance here.'

'If you can focus on the insects, or on things like that, if you can refrain from any direct reference to us, then you'll live long enough.'

'But if you can't do that ...'

'I see a yellowness in your face, Jan.'

'Isn't it strange? You're not unlike some insect with that yellowness.'

'I thought that was quite appropriate myself.'

'And isn't the fever awful.'

'Don't leave me ... Don't leave me like this!'

'We're giving you a chance, Jan. Take it.'

'... Charles! Don't leave me, Charles.'

'An oath, that's all. Give us your word.'

'Take it or leave it.'

'And we'll give you our promise that we'll leave you alive and healthy enough to do your work.'

'Time... We can give you time to peer down your microscope at the insects.'

'We don't have to do this at all, Jan, but we like you.'

'Healthy enough. But you must understand that we don't have complete trust in you now. We'll leave the poison in your blood and the sickness will return to you now and again so that you don't forget our promise.'

'Take it or leave it.'

Jan had no choice. He knew if he didn't accept it, then he would die in his sleep. But it hurt him deeply that he would have to give in to them. He felt it like a blemish on his soul. 'I will give you my word so,' he said. 'There will never be one direct word regarding your existence in any book I publish.'

'Wonderful!' said the fair-haired man. 'I'm very happy to hear that.'

'You've made the right choice,' said the dark-haired man, and with that they both stood up as if to leave.

'And may you have every success with your work from here on,' said the fair-haired man.

'Every success,' said the dark-haired one.

Jan wasn't able to see them any longer, but he saw a weak, milky light around him. Through his half-opened eyes, he saw that the sun was slowly entering the room and lifted his head a little, remembering every word. It wasn't a dream; he was certain of that. He sat up in the bed. It was clear that the fever was spent and he felt a lot better, even able to put his feet on the ground and to stand up unsteadily. He walked to the mirror and looked at the face that was in it. It still had a worn appearance, but there was a new energy there as well.

'There will never be one direct word regarding your existence in any book I publish,' he said to the face in the mirror. 'But I said nothing about indirect words. You left poison in my blood out of malice, but you accepted my oath as it was, word for word. There will be indirect words as a clue to those who will follow me, and you can do whatever you like about that. I am still a member of the human race, and we have our own malice. I would recommend that you never forget that.'

He walked out of the bedroom and directly to the front door, opening it on a new day and drank in the cold air of the morning. He had work to do.

Scene Five

I sat on the grass beside the Lough, looking out at the tangled mesh of bushes and trees on the island in its centre. I had the right lake now anyway, the lake on the south side of the city, about half a kilometre from Saint Finbarr's Cathedral. I was near the broad open space on the north side of it, but I had walked around a couple of times when I arrived to try and look into the dim world of the island. I saw the birds peering out from time to time before they would disappear again under the cover of the bushes and trees. Out on the water, the swans sailed gracefully around the Lough, geese and ducks too, and a flock of seagulls in from the coast. There were fish under those calm waters. It was a cold day, but it was bright and the sun and blue sky shone on the surface of the water. It's an egg-shaped lake, a kilometre in diameter as you walk around. It's said to come up only to your chest if you were to walk into it, but I've never tried that, of course. It's situated in the suburbs with neat houses surrounding it on every side. I was raised just up the road, and sat here many times in my youth.

The island in the centre was always called 'the bog', and I had never imagined when I was young that the ground there would be dry enough to walk on, but looking at it now, it had tall enough trees growing there. I remembered the legend about it. It was said that a beautiful castle had stood there long ago with a young princess living in it. One night, she turned on all the taps and completely submerged the castle, but it was said to be still there, beneath the surface of those waters, under the tangled mesh of the bog. I remember imagining in my youth that I would go there as an explorer through the jungle of the bog to find that beautiful, shining castle, that the king and the princess would still be there waiting for someone to set them free. It was always there before me, yet always out of reach. No one could ever go to the bog. It was a bird sanctuary and people were not permitted access. Looking at it now, I felt the terrible taboo against it, and those tangled branches made me feel uneasy.

I was to meet Salvadóir and Peadar here and felt excited because I hadn't had the chance yet to tell them about how this lake was actually the one mentioned in the poem, rather than the one at Guagán Barra. Salvadóir called me to say that he had a discovery of his own. I told him that I was at the Lough and he said he'd meet me here. I hadn't seen Peadar the night before because he hadn't stayed at the house, but I called him now and he said that he'd come along as well. I called Aogán then, and there was a chance that he'd arrive too, but I wasn't sure. He'd suspended his disbelief a little that night during the Jazz Festival when he told me that he recognised what the Fingin tome was, but everything was still too bizarre for him.

So I sat on the grass waiting for them, looking out at the shimmering waters of the Lough and the birds swimming lazily across the surface. There were people dappled here and there about the place, children running after a ball, old people strolling slowly. Then I saw Salvadóir's van on the other side of the road and him getting out of it like a great giant from the fables. He saw me sitting there and raised his hand with a big smile. Then I saw Peadar coming from the other direction, through the park of the Lough and past the children's swings. They reached me together and sat down beside me, Salvadóir's bulk like a great weight on the ground.

'Isn't it grand to be out in the fresh air?' he said, his gold tooth shining in the sunlight. 'I've always liked the Lough. I used to be here often because it was only a short distance from us when we lived beside the college, when my mother was alive.'

'Is Aogán coming?' Peadar asked me.

'I don't know. Maybe.'

'That was a fantastic discovery he made with *Leabhar Mhic Cárthaigh Riabhaigh*,' said Salvadóir. 'I think it's an important key to other things. I have my own discovery to share with ye as well now.'

'Me too. I found out something while I was in Guagán Barra yesterday,' I said.

'I have thoughts of my own to share with ye,' said Peadar cautiously. 'I was thinking about everything. I wouldn't say that I found anything concrete, but I have a hypothesis.'

'Great!' Salvadóir exclaimed. 'I feel that things are coming together at last.' He raised his head and looked in the direction of the road. 'Oh look!' he said with a smile. 'Aogán is coming: d'Artagnan in the flesh!'

We turned around and saw Aogán walking across the green in his usual khaki jacket, his straight hair hanging to his shoulders, and his rough beard. I remember thinking that there was a cautious air about him.

'Great! It's good that we're all together,' said Peadar.

On reaching the point where we sat, Aogán stood there for a moment looking down at us. 'I heard that there was a meeting here today of the Ballyphehane Society for the Bewildered,' he said in complete seriousness.

'You're in the right place and in time for the meeting,' said Salvadóir. 'And if I may say, the Society wouldn't be complete without you.'

'Hang on now! I'm only here as an observer. I'm from Mayfield originally,' he said, a smile breaking out on his face as he sat down.

'And well done too, Aogán,' said Salvadóir. 'It was a huge thing that you put into the pot about *Leabhar Mhic Cárthaigh Riabhaigh*. I have no doubt that it's the very book that Robert Boyle was referring to.'

'But isn't it terrible that this tale is destroyed forever?' said Peadar. 'I went through the list of other narratives in the book, but I don't believe that there's anything else that's relevant. He must have torn it out and burnt it.'

'But he inspired me to look at something else, and I believe that I've found another piece of the jigsaw puzzle,' Salvadóir said cheerfully. 'Do you remember that Jan said in his diary that when he was in Saumur he spoke English with a young man called William from London, a man whose father was an admiral in the British Navy and whose mother was from the Netherlands? He didn't give us much information about this in his account, and even though I found it interesting at the time, I didn't think about it much afterwards. Then when I found out about *Leabhar Mhic Cárthaigh Riabhaigh*, I looked at the life of Fínghin himself and his wife Caitríona, the daughter of Thomas Fitzgerald, eighth Earl of Desmond. There's a big house near Rosscarbery. It's called Castle Salem now in English, but it was known as Cnoc na Miodóg long ago and it's said that Caitríona had it built around 1470. Herself and Fínghin must have been living there and had the book with them at the time, because it was written in celebration of their wedding. For some reason, I found this house interesting, and when I looked at the history of it, a name came up: William Penn.'

'The William Penn who founded Pennsylvania in America?' I asked.

'The very man. But when he was young, he lived in Cork City and his father owned land in the county. When the Boyle family seized Macroom Castle for the King, the King gave it to William's father for a while. His father was an important person amongst the nobility, but William himself was a pious man who was unimpressed with battles, castles and lands. He was a Quaker and very friendly with William Morris, who owned that house in Rosscarbery at the time. There are records to say that he stayed there regularly in 1670.'

'But the book wasn't in the house then,' said Peadar. 'Robert Boyle's brother had stolen it by then.'

'He had, but look now. William Penn's mother was from the Netherlands, and his father was an admiral in the British Navy. He was even there on the ship that brought Charles II back to England.'

'Do you think so, that it's him who's mentioned in Jan's diary as the young man he speaks English with in Saumur?' I asked.

'I do! I'm almost a hundred percent certain of it. Jan was there between October 1663 and September 1664 as a guest of Tanneguy Le Fèvre, who was a professor at Saumur University. William Penn was in Saumur at the same time as a guest of Professor Moïse Amyraut at the same university. Penn has to be the same young man mentioned in his diary.'

'Do you think that Jan told him the story of the Firíní?' Peadar asked.

'He could have. It doesn't say that he did, but it doesn't say that he didn't either,' said Salvadóir, shrugging.

'So, you're proposing that they met in Saumur and that Jan told him the story,' I said, trying to tie the strings together, 'and then that he'd spent time in Fínghin Mhic Cárthaigh's house years later. Does this house relate to the matter? Did he find out information about the Firíní there? Maybe there was some other text there that referred to them.'

'There's more than that,' said Salvadóir. 'Penn was elected as a member of the Royal Society in 1681. The members of the Society are all men of science and no one knew why an unscientific, religious man – a Quaker no less – was allowed in at all. But there was another member of the Society who was very powerful in it, a person who helped in its foundation, a person who was even elected as president of the Society in 1680, although he didn't accept the honour: Robert Boyle.'

'So Boyle gave Penn membership of the Royal Society?' asked Aogán. 'Why, to shut him up?'

'I think so,' Salvadóir said firmly, 'And there's more than that.'

'Newton's letter!' said Peadar.

'Exactly,' said Salvadóir. 'What did he say again? *The conspirator Boyle may ensure the silence of others by installing them, despite their utter unsuitability, in the Royal Academy!*'

'This is incredible!' I said.

'It is,' said Salvadóir proudly. 'I understand that it's all circumstantial evidence, but everything is pointing in that direction. In that same year, the King gave Penn a charter to lands in America, 45,000 square miles, and he was established as the biggest non-royal landowner on earth.'

'Jesus!' I said. 'Isn't a piece of information a valuable thing?'

'It's circumstantial evidence alright, but it's hard not to see the hand of the Firíní in it,' said Peadar.

'But do you think that the King of England was part of this conspiracy too?' I asked him. 'Which king was in power in 1681?'

'Charles II was still there, and he was from Medici descent on his mother's side. Marie de' Medici was his grandmother, and she was the Queen of France and first cousin to Cosimo II, Grand Duke of Tuscany. That was the boy Galileo taught.'

'It's like a spider's web,' said Aogán morosely; 'or maybe a viper's nest.'

'It's hard to be certain what knowledge the King had about the Firíní. It's true as well that he wanted to get the Quakers out of England, and giving them land in America was an effective device.'

'No one knows what goes on behind the scenes in this world,' Peadar said.

We were all quiet for a little while, and then Salvadóir broke the silence. 'But what about yourselves anyway? What this new information that ye have?'

'I learned that I'm a fool,' I answered.

With that, Aogán burst out laughing: 'I could have told you that twenty years ago.'

'I thought that Saint Finbarr's church was in Guagán Barra, but it wasn't. It was half a kilometre from here, where Saint Finbarr's Cathedral is now. It was that thing about the *lake isle* that put me astray. The lake mentioned in the poem isn't in Guagán Barra at all. It's over there!' I said, pointing to the Lough before us. 'That's it! The bog in the Lough. That's the place mentioned in the poem at the back of the Bible. This is the *lake isle where Tondolus did dine on anguishe to the bone* and so, the place where the story of *Visio Tnugdali* happens.'

They all turned to the Lough and stared at it quietly. 'The gates of Hell ... are in the bog in the Lough!' said Aogán, an expression on his face halfway between confusion and impatience.

'If we're to believe the poem,' I answered. 'But we don't know exactly what information Robert Tighe had. What he says is that El, or God, banished Lucifer and Beelzebub to a lake island in a cold place. He says *Shem drove north oppresséd Hamm* as well. That relates to terms of banishment again, and I think that it's the direction that's interesting. He banished them north, maybe from the Middle East to Ireland.'

'You're telling me so,' said Aogán in bewilderment, 'that you believe that that's Hell! That God expelled Satan, Beelzebub and all the other devils … to the bog in the Lough! That ... bush there in the middle of the Lough is actually Hell?'

He clearly had some problems with this theory, but Salvadóir came to my aid. 'It's mentioned alright in *Visio Tungdali* that this man went to Hell,' he said. 'But maybe that story is based on something else that actually happened, something that related to the Firíní.

We don't have the original Irish version of the story. We're not proposing that it's the same hell that's spoken of in the Christian tradition, the hell where devils with horns and pitchforks are torturing the souls of the dead. But maybe the old story is based on some sliver of the truth.'

'I don't know,' said Aogán, shrugging. 'I don't know about anything anymore.'

'What news have you so, Peadar?' asked Salvadóir.

'The thing that I have to tell you, well …' he said cautiously. 'It's not a story or a discovery. It's really nothing but a hypothesis.'

'There's nothing wrong with that. Go on,' said Salvadóir.

Peadar was quiet for a while, and then he spoke softly: 'I was never a religious person, but I've been studying Bible stories lately, as well as stories from Canaanite mythology. I read unofficial texts as well, the Book of Enoch and such, to find something that would give us a glimmer of light, some insight into what's going on in this crazy story of ours. I understand the problems you have with this, Aogán. It's all insane. I have to find an answer or I'll become insane myself. As I said, I read those religious texts. "Watchers" are mentioned in the Book of Enoch and the Book of Daniel. These were a sort of angel who would look at us. And then I read one line that gave me an idea. It's a line from the Bible, Genesis 6:4: "There were giants in the earth in those days" '

'And who were those giants?' Salvadóir asked.

'Us,' said Peadar solemnly. 'We are the giants. We're giants to them. I'm not suggesting that the Bible can be read like a textbook on what happened. It's a mixture of every notion that those societies had long ago, political stories, heroic stories – things that relate only to the human race. But maybe there's a little spark of the truth there because that spark is not part of our story at all. It's their story – the story of the Firíní who came to us through whatever contact existed between us and them long ago. But the ancient Jews wrote it down as religion, as the story of God. What I'm trying to say is that maybe there was a *coup d'état* thousands of years ago in Firíní society. Maybe that *coup* failed and the rebels were banished. The human race found out about this story, or a little piece of it here and there, and put it together as religion. Milton was aware of the existence of the Firíní, yet he wrote about the fall of the Devil. I don't believe he told Robert Boyle everything that he had learned from Galileo or Barberini. Robert Tighe had the same story. What did he say again: *banish to colde and bitter climes usurper to the throne*. It's a political story, the political story of the Firíní themselves, and we're getting only the tiniest part of it through our religions and cultures.'

'There's a certain sense to it,' said Salvadóir. 'Especially in the context of the other things we've learned.'

'As I said, it's only a hypothesis,' said Peadar, and he lowered his head. We were all quiet for a while again. It was clear that relating this theory to us took something out of Peadar. He always had sense and reason and these kept him together as if they were metal strings. Then when he saw the Firíní, those strings turned to elastic bands. Those elastic bands were stretched with every turn of the story and now, I thought, they were ready to snap. 'I have something to tell you as well, and I believe that it relates to this situation of yours,' said Aogán. 'There's someone following me everywhere I go.'

Scene Six

Letter from Melchisédech Thévenot
to Nicolaus Steno
12th September 1667

My dear friend, Niels,

I was delighted to receive your letter and to read of your exploits in Florence. I understand, of course, that there are certain people in the Accademia del Cimento who are disposed to listen to their own voices from morning until night and who spend their energies looking for the most eloquent ways to speak of theories of which they have no understanding whatsoever, but I am certain that a man as intelligent and accomplished as yourself will be able to stand against any argument that is advanced. By the way, ask Vincenzo Viviani about Borelli and he will tell you some tales.

There is no need to thank me at all, my friend, because I am only a humble link between the centre of power and the heroes of intellect, between those with means without creativity and those with creativity without support. If there is any hope of progress for the poor human race in this world, full support must be given to wise men like yourself who are extending our understanding and our possibilities with the power of their intellect. I have spent a great deal of my life making connections and sustaining relations with powerful, renowned and wealthy people. I do not believe that there is any great worth to humanity in this political world except to the one in ten thousand who have access to that golden circle, but if there is any worth at all, it is that it opens doors to men who can do real service to humanity, men like yourself. I was very happy that I could make connections for you in Florence, and I hope that you take the advantages which you so well deserve. Of course, there is no golden circle on earth like that in which the Medici live. I have known the Grand Duke for many years and, as you know, he was always an ally to knowledge.

But, my friend, I have an important matter to discuss with you in this letter, a subject that relates very much with your patron, the Grand Duke, and with his family. It also relates to the conversation we had in Paris on the night of the comet when we took our dinner in Bourdelot's house: I am certain that you recall the discussion in regard to our good friend Jan Swammerdam's studies on the flies. I understand, of course, that you said at the time that this is not your field of study and that you did not wish to be a party to such an affair, but forgive me, my friend, I must write to you now about it because I need to warn you. It is extremely important that you understand the political aspects of this matter, particularly amongst people whom you know in Florence. These people would be very interested in Jan's discovery, and unfortunately, I believe that they are already aware of it. I do not know how they came by this knowledge, but I assure you that it was not from me.

I would thus recommend that you be extremely cautious with your own speech and alert to the speech of others around you. The questions will come from the court, and perhaps from the Grand Duke Ferdinando himself or someone who is very close to him. The Medici will be friendly and generous when they speak with you on this matter, but you will have to exercise the utmost caution with them because you may be certain, if they discuss this matter with you, that they already have knowledge of it and are looking only for confirmation from you that they are correct. The conversation will begin in a relaxed manner on the subject of insects and those who have studied them, and you will have to be honest and mention your friend Jan Swammerdam, but it will not take long before they make casual, indirect references to the heart of the matter: the little men themselves. The Medici can be very charming, but I would recommend that you pretend to have no knowledge at all on the matter, and even though they won't believe you, there is a chance that they will not press the matter unless they are certain that you are lying. If they ask you about Robert Hooke in England, tell them that he has published a wonderful book on the subject, but apart from that, say nothing.

This is very important, my friend, not just for the sake of Jan and Robert Hooke but for your own safety. They will want to speak to Jan then, and I believe that they will ask you to make the connection with him. Tell them that you would be very happy to do so, and give every praise to Jan as a learned man. It has been reported to me recently that someone from the court will come to Amsterdam to speak with him, and there is every possibility that they will make the connection through you. I will make certain that I am in the house with Jan on the day when they arrive and I will give him all the support and strength that is in me to give, no little thing after years spent in the diplomatic service in those same courts.

I remember once that someone showed me a serpent that he had brought back from the New World, a serpent with skin of a dazzling colour, so beautiful that you could not take your eyes off it. It was like a living jewel that glistened in the sunlight and it beguiled me with its slow, majestic movement. But the man told me that day that it was the most poisonous serpent in all the world. Then a few days later, I heard that it had killed him and escaped from the house, never to be seen again. I tell you this now so that you may understand what these people are, not only the Medici family but every family of their kind throughout Europe, people who live in the golden circles of that beautiful, elegant world, circles covered in jewels, circles that will beguile the eye and place you under a spell. But believe me, my friend, this world is nothing but a nest of vipers.

I well understand, Niels, that you have no desire to be part of this business, and I promise you that I will do my best to keep you out of it. As I said to you, you can put your complete trust in my old friend Vincenzo Viviani. He is an understanding and honest man who will help you in any way he can. I would recommend that you burn this letter as soon as you have read it. Farewell now, Niels, and be certain that I will always be here to give you help if you need it.

Your faithful friend,
Melchisédech Thévenot

Scene Seven

Jan's house, Amsterdam, the Netherlands
7th January 1668

It was a gloomy winter's day. The grey light struggled through the milky fog, a fog that still hung in the frozen air around him, even now in the early afternoon. The trees loomed through it like black carcasses before the white of the snow, ravens and crows settling in them as if they and the black twisted branches were carved from the same substance. They moved restlessly from claw to claw and looked hungrily down upon the hard ground like lost spirits.

They looked down at Thévenot as well, standing there in his great coat with his breath coming out in great gusts of vapour. He didn't wear a hat but his long black hair hung down to his chest. He wasn't dissimilar to those birds as he waited, almost as a ghost in the garden, moving slowly like a dark animal in the whiteness, waiting for that which was to come. His eyes were as black as the plumage of the birds and he looked about him as if he were in a graveyard amongst the headstones, as if he were the last man alive on earth. It was strange, yet still a kind of solace to imagine himself and the crows waiting together on the end of the world.

But it wasn't true. There were other crows coming now. They always knew that he was aware of their secret, but they accepted it because that knowledge was firmly settled in the world of politics, in the world of diplomacy. That world has its own truth and they need not be worried about an ambassador here and there who had heard some word on the wind. They lived in the world of money, and in that world there was only money. They ate it, they wore it, they married it. In a strange way, he felt sorry for them, living their lives like pieces on a board game, yet still believing themselves to be the most powerful people on Earth.

Thévenot was waiting now on Prince Cosimo de' Medici who was coming to Jan's house, supposedly, to view his collection of insects. This was the son of Ferdinando, the Grand Duke of Tuscany who had supported Galileo from the venom of the Barberini.

Thinking of it now, maybe Ferdinando was only playing his own part in that drama. Thévenot remembered this young Prince Cosimo when he was ten years old, a dull-witted lump of a boy. That's what he thought at the time anyway, but maybe this was an uncharitable impression of the child. He heard that when he was eighteen, he had married the granddaughter of King Henry IV of France and that she had his heart broken now. It was a marriage by proxy which had been organised by legal contract.

Thévenot wanted to meet Cosimo somewhere else and then bring him to Jan's house, but that didn't suit the young Prince, on his father's orders, most likely. They knew, of course, how it so happened that he was here in Amsterdam for this meeting. He knew Ferdinando well and was sure that they wouldn't want him interfering in their plans. But what were those plans? It was almost impossible to be certain of what they had in mind, but generally they would protect themselves, as any animal would. If you weren't a threat to them, you'd be alright. They were in no danger from Galileo in the end, even though he had given them quite a shock at first. They knew that he and Viviani had only ever second-hand information, but still they kept a close eye on them.

But what about Hodierna? That was Giovanni Battista Hodierna, who wrote *L'Occhio della Mosca*, a book describing his work with the microscope on the eye of the fly. Even though there was nothing in that book about the little men, it came to light bit by bit that he too had seen them. He dedicated his other book, *Ephemerides medicaeorum*, to Ferdinando in 1656, but apparently they had a falling out after that. Maybe Hodierna changed his mind and chose to bring the story to light. Thévenot did not know what had happened between them, but he was almost certain that Ferdinando had him killed.

But what about Jan? Had Ferdinando given this job to Cosimo to test him, to see if he could protect the family secret? Maybe Cosimo was coming to Jan's house today as a judge and they would decide to put Jan to death as well. Of course, they had that power, and no one, himself included, could stop them.

He turned and went back into the house. Jan was preparing things in his laboratory, and Thévenot had taken the chance to escape out to the garden at the back of the house for some air and to collect his thoughts. He was worried about this visit but didn't want to show it. When he walked back in, Jan was almost finished and had laid out a multitude of specimens neatly on the table. 'What do you think?' he asked, as if he had forgotten the real reason why Cosimo de' Medici was coming to visit.

'Wonderful!' Thévenot said with an enthusiastic smile. 'It's an incredible collection, Jan, and it shows your technique of preservation very well. It won't be long now, I'd say.'

With that, they heard the noise of a coach on the road outside, and Jan went out to it. The coach pulled up to the door and Prince Cosimo de' Medici got out. He was a young man, about twenty-five, but he was tall and bulky with plump jowls. The coach itself wasn't as elegant as it might have been, because the Prince was travelling incognito, but he wore an ornate coat of the most expensive material with flounced sleeves. Jan greeted him politely.

His first impression was that of a jaunty buffoon, a broad gleeful smile on his face and a simple and naive look in his eyes. He carried the bliss of youth in his features, and extended his hands as if he was the one welcoming Jan. 'Mr Swammerdam, is it you? It's marvellous to meet you at last! I've heard wonderful stories of your work and I'm exceedingly interested in it.'

'You are very welcome, Prince Cosimo,' Jan said as he directed him through the front door. 'Our dear friend Melchisédech Thévenot is inside waiting on your visit as well.'

Jan saw that a certain unease darted across the young Prince's face for a second before the expression of lazy decadence returned again. 'Oh, wonderful!' he said, pretending to be surprised and enthusiastic. 'I remember Mr Thévenot well.'

Thévenot gave him a grand welcome in the laboratory when they walked in but here, his years of experience in the diplomatic service could be clearly seen. He was respectful, yet there was no trace in his voice of the oily fawning of toadies that one could expect in the courts of the nobility. 'Prince Cosimo, it's a pleasure to see you again after so many years. I hope that you are enjoying your visit to these northern lands.'

'Apart from the cold, Mr Thévenot, I love this land. But I began in Austria when I visited my Aunt Anna and then I took a barge down the Rhine to Amsterdam. Isn't it a beautiful landscape, Mr Thévenot? Everything in the north appears to be of the old style, the buildings and so on. And the clothing of the people is very amusing indeed. I often feel as though I'm in a fairy-tale and that I shall meet an ogre or a witch.'

'Marvellous,' said Thévenot with a cold smile.

'But, of course, your friend from Denmark, Nicolaus Steno, is with us now in Florence. He is a noble and learned man. I have great respect for him. Have you heard that he has converted to Catholicism? I myself received the good tidings recently. I think it's glorious news that this finest of men is now in the Holy Mother Church of Rome.'

'We read of this in a letter he recently sent to Jan, Prince Cosimo,' Thévenot said. 'He's clearly very happy with his choice, and we're all happy about that.'

'I believe he's been thinking about this for some time. Maybe it's the best choice for him,' said Jan.

'Fine man!' Cosimo said bombastically.

'But now, Prince Cosimo, I hope that you shall enjoy my humble laboratory as well. I have a demonstration of my collection laid out here.' said Jan, directing him to the first specimen on the table.

'Oh, of course,' said Cosimo, remembering why he had come.

Jan first showed him the insects he had arranged on the table, but the Prince was surprised when he saw that there were a great many more in the open cupboards around the room. There were thousands of them: beetles, butterflies and caterpillars, moths, bees, ants, maggots, snails, spiders, flies and other insects besides. They were all organised precisely with the different species of every type filling the shelves.

'But will they not rot in the cases?' Cosimo asked.

'They won't. I have my own system to stop that. I inject wax into their bodies and I also use alcohol. They will never rot.'

'Very interesting,' said Cosimo, looking at a little frog in a bottle of alcohol. 'Would this work with people as well?'

'It would, certainly.'

'Excellent!' said Cosimo, a mischievous smile spreading across his face. 'I have the worst wife on the face of the Earth, and it would brighten my heart to see her in an exhibition such as this, frozen forever in a single posture. We could drag her out if there was a special occasion, yet keep her happily enough in some cupboard otherwise. She could no longer be arguing with me or disrespecting me. She wouldn't try to steal my family's wealth and send it back to France. I'm not lying to you, Mr Swammerdam: I have to put guards on her, or she'll steal some valuable item from the house and we'll never see it again. She brought her own cooks with her from France because she thinks that we'll poison her food. It's a terrible pity that she isn't as stupid as she is dishonest, or we could actually do that and there'd be an end to this dreadful situation.'

Jan didn't know how to answer that, but Thévenot came to his rescue. 'When you are a member of the noblest family in Europe, Prince Cosimo, it is often the case that love and marriage do not go together. But I am certain that the situation will be resolved sooner or later.'

'Love and marriage together? I wasn't even at the wedding, and neither was she. It was a marriage by proxy,' said Cosimo. 'But let's not allow that hag to interfere with our lovely day. We'll carry on with the demonstration, Mr Swammerdam.'

'Of course, Prince Cosimo,' said Jan. 'Have you ever looked through a microscope?'

A frozen expression came across Cosimo's face, a look of fear. Jan had not thought of flies or little men, however. He had only wanted to show him a caterpillar in the microscope, but he understood from this expression that Cosimo thought at that moment that he would show him little men, drowning in water. It was interesting to Jan that a member of the Medici family would be so frightened of those little men. It gave him courage and he spoke more boldly now. 'It is a special device that allows us to see another world, one not permitted to most people in *this* world. We are a special few to have such permission.'

'What shall we be looking at?' Cosimo asked awkwardly.

'A caterpillar. I have something interesting to show you.' Jan took a caterpillar from a glass of alcohol, cut a slice from its body and placed it under the microscope. He looked through it for a while to adjust it, and then stepped to one side to allow him step in. 'If you please, Prince Cosimo.'

There was apprehension on the young Prince's face and he clearly didn't want to approach the microscope.

'I promise that it shall be interesting,' said Jan, playing with Cosimo's fear. 'It's a wonderful world in which these little beings live. Look!'

Cosimo put his eye to the lens, slowly and cautiously. He looked through it for a few seconds and then raised his head with a look of relief on his face. 'It's the body of the caterpillar,' he said.

'Of course, Prince, but did you see anything interesting? Look again. You'll see that the wings of the butterfly are already in the body of the caterpillar. It is thought that the caterpillar is changed entirely through metamorphosis into the butterfly, but my study here shows that this is not true. The advantage of the microscope is that we are able to correct our errors. For example, there are many people who still believe in spontaneous generation – that life can sprout from inanimate matter. People see that flies spring from excrement and they believe that life will grow in places in which it had previously not been, but this is not true. Only God can do that, and we would be wise to always remember it.' It was clear that Jan had disconcerted the young Prince and he decided to carry on. He didn't care now about the power of the Medici. The microscope can perform a miracle in that it allows you to see everything in its correct size. Jan saw Cosimo de' Medici now as a little boy in the wrong place. It was a mistake to send the son in place of the father, and Cosimo himself knew it. 'Now,' Jan said directly. 'What can you tell us about little men in flies.'

The question even shocked Thévenot, who was always so assured and composed, but it was like a thunderbolt to Cosimo.

He looked directly in Jan's eyes before he spoke. 'I came here to ask you that question, Mr Swammerdam,' he said nervously.

'Well, ask it then! I am a scientist. I have no interest in the scheming of the political world. The wealth of your family is connected in some way with those little men, you and the Barberini. I don't care about that: it doesn't involve me. But I saw them with my own eyes, and you, I believe, see this as a threat.'

'Are we correct in that opinion?' said Cosimo, finding his voice again.

'Maybe. I don't have enough information to answer that question. What business do you have with them? How would it interfere with that business if I were to release to the world the knowledge of the little men's existence? I will leave those questions to you. I had planned to publish a book and tell my story, but I won't do it now, and not for fear that I'll suffer the wrath of the Medici. I will not write it because I do not believe that I would ever finish it. The little men themselves would kill me if I broke my promise to them not to start it again. And so the knowledge shall live in the darkness, behind an ugly, dirty curtain with pearls sewn through the threads.'

'You gave them a promise?' Cosimo asked in surprise. 'Did you actually speak to them?'

'I did. And now it's my turn. I asked you a question just now, and it's time for you to answer it. What knowledge do you have on them?

Cosimo stopped for a while and looked down at the floor. He was clearly thinking about the correct answer to this question. In the end, he raised his head. 'You have spoken directly and honestly to me, and I will do the same. In truth, I have very little knowledge. My ancestors received some advantage from them and our wealth is based upon that, but the connection between us is decreasing now with every generation that passes. My father did not tell me a great deal, maybe for fear that I would say too much to you, or because he himself did not know. Galileo saw them as well and that shocked us greatly, but my father believes that the Barberini went too far with it. They wanted to protect their share rather than to expand it. My father wanted to work with Galileo rather than silence him. The connection between the little men and our family is not what it was, and my father would have loved if Galileo had been able to strengthen that connection, but after the oppression that the Barberini played on him, and the blindness on top of that, there was no chance. My great-grandmother was of the same opinion as the Barberini, and that was no help either in convincing Galileo to cooperate with us. But let me say one thing to you: I am not here to threaten you. If you want to write a book on the little men, carry on. Maybe not many people would believe you, and maybe, as you said, the little men would kill you before you finished it, but we ourselves will not hinder you. But perhaps there is another way. Galileo was old, blind and bad-tempered, but you are young and clever. If you can work with us to strengthen the connection, you will find that the Medici family are more generous than you can imagine.'

'Work with you?' said Jan. 'It would be a waste of time. The little men will communicate with no one if they don't want to, and if they do, they certainly won't be shy about it. It would be nothing to you but a waste of money.'

'Let us worry about that.'

'They left me alive and I promised myself then that I would devote my remaining years to my own work. That's the work that's all around us here in this room. I will do it to glorify God, something more important than any political or economic relations between the beings of this world.'

'We can give you every assistance with that work.'

'Thank you for your generous offer, Prince Cosimo, but I must decline.'

Cosimo could see that it was a waste of time and bowed his head. 'Very well, Mr Swammerdam,' he said. 'But if you should change your mind, you know where we are. I will leave you to your work now.' He turned then to Thévenot. 'If there is one thing that I don't understand, Monsieur Thévenot, it is *your* part in all of this. But let it be, as it has always been. Goodbye now.' He left then without waiting for anyone to show him to the door, and they heard his carriage rumbling up the road.

'You've done very well, Jan,' Thévenot said to him. 'I came here to help you, but you had no need of my assistance. You were right to refuse his offer, but you may be sure that it's not the last time you'll receive it. He'll come back to you when he believes the time is right.'

'And he'll get the same answer,' said Jan indifferently. 'But it's clear that the Medici don't have much knowledge of the little men either. He wanted my help to strengthen their bond.'

'That's what he said anyway, but you can't believe a word from his mouth. I don't know, maybe it's true.'

'Perhaps we'll never know the truth,' said Jan, covering his eyes with the palms of his hands.

'I can see that you're tired, my friend. I will leave you now and come back tomorrow. We can talk then. You did very well, Jan. Goodbye now.'

'Thank you, Melchisédech, for everything.'

'Don't mention it,' he said, and left quickly.

Jan sat quietly on his own for a while and thought of Cosimo's visit as if it had been a dream. It was getting darker now outside. A moroseness overcame him when he looked around the room. Why was he engaged in this work at all? Was it for the glory of God or for his own glory that he did it? Was it the glory of God that brought one of the elites of Europe in through his door offering him the wealth of the world? Did God want him to bring the world of insects to light? Maybe the little men themselves were a warning from God – or from the Devil. He was tired. He would go to bed early tonight and hope that the sickness would not return now again.

Scene Eight

It's difficult for me to tell this part of the story. It was a terrible experience and if things had happened differently, I wouldn't be here to tell the story at all. Aogán was right that day at the Lough: someone was following him, and we all saw him over the next few days. We recognised the same blue car everywhere around the city as well. This person looked at us from dark corners on the street, always too far for us to see him properly, always gone if you'd go after him. It was a man with a big coat and a hood that he kept up all the time. We would see him outside the house and then again in the city centre. I was very unsettled with this unexpected turn of events, and I saw that Peadar's nerves were starting to fail. He ran into the house one day, out of breath and with a wildness in his eyes. He said that he'd seen the man again, but when he ran after him, he'd vanished as if the ground had swallowed him up. Salvadóir thought that it might be Kane – the person whose house we had broken into – but we were all thinking the other theory as well: that the agents of the Firíní were after us.

We decided it was vital to keep the books safe. They were hard evidence of the truth of our story. Without them, we would have nothing but our own account of what happened, and of course, there are many stories in this world today. We decided to never leave the books unguarded, and Peadar and I took the floorboards up in the living room in order to make a safe space to hide them in. Salvadóir wanted to put them in a safety deposit box in the city centre, and had even arranged this for the following day.

Everything happened on Halloween night, as if the universe had organised some grotesque pantomime for us. Some of the houses around us had been decorated with the gaudy figures of witches, ghosts and the like, and children had been going around with masks even in the afternoon. It was a bitterly cold day, much colder than is normal for this time of year, with an icy wind and hailstone showers. Salvadóir called on us at about half past four when it was just getting dark so he could leave the books with us for the night. He needed to go somewhere himself that night and we all believed it would be safer. We put the bundle under the floorboards and laid the carpet over it, so that nobody could find it if they didn't know that it was there.

Salvadóir sat down for a while and drank a cup of coffee with us. We had a good fire burning in the stove and I remember Salvadóir joking about it: 'Be sure now that ye keep that fire going. This is Halloween, the divide between this world and the next, between the living and the dead.'

'Don't say that to us now!' said Peadar, half-laughing as he stood up to put more coal on the fire. 'We have enough troubles already.'

We were all in good humour, and Salvadóir left after a little while. I said goodbye to him at the door and watched as he ran to his van under a heavy shower of hailstones. Peadar and I then settled in to watch television.

At around six o'clock, a knock came to the door. I remember we thought it might be Salvadóir coming back because he'd forgotten something, and Peadar went out to answer it. I heard him opening the door, and then nothing. I found this odd and waited on some sign as to what was going on in the hallway. Then the living room door opened and Peadar walked in slowly, a look of terror in his eyes. There was a man behind him wearing a long coat with a hood, the same man who had been following us, but now he had a gun in his hand and it was pointed at Peadar. When he saw me, he turned the gun in my direction and lowered his hood. I recognised him immediately. A slouching old man with long grey hair that straggled down to his shoulders, even though the top of his head itself was bald. His cheeks were drooping as if he was an old bloodhound. The man who had been eating chicken, the man who spoke to us on the street outside the art gallery on the night of the Jazz festival. I jumped up and the three of us stood looking at each other without a word.

An ugly smile came across the man's face then, and he spoke to us in English using a dramatic, exaggerated voice, like someone reciting Shakespeare: '*Oh, what wonder is the student life, to ponder and peruse!*'

I didn't know what sort of answer you should give to someone who comes into your living room with a gun saying a sentence like that. We did nothing anyway except to continue staring at him.

'*I do so miss my own student days you know,*' he began again. '*I also attended University College Cork, you know. A fine institution. But of course, in my day they didn't allow in the kind of people who break into other people's houses and steal their property.*'

We both knew on the spot who this man was: Kane. I didn't know what I should say to him, however. Should I deny that I had any knowledge of the situation? It was clear that he knew very well that it was us who had broken into his house. I decided to be bold with him.

'*Interesting hypothesis, Mr. Kane. Where do you get your information from? Did a little bird tell you?*'

A vile grimace ran across his face, and I understood that it was a sensitive subject for him. '*If I do have to shoot either of you with this gun, then first it will be in some painful spot, and only after that shall I permit you to die,*' he said coldly. He looked into the kitchen and saw that we had chairs with metal frames. '*Wonderful! Good strong chairs: just the thing. Could one of you please bring two of them in here before the fire,*' he said, looking at Peadar to let him know that it was he that should carry out this request. Peadar did so and then Kane pulled a handful of cable ties from his pocket. '*Now, if both of you will be so kind as to sit on these chairs, I will endeavour to make you as comfortable as possible.*'

We sat down and he tied our hands and feet to the frames of the chairs in such a way that we couldn't move an inch. '*Now, gentlemen. I'm quite sure you can see the predicament that you're in. I'm also sure that the books are here in this house, and if you tell me now where they are, then you will save yourself a great deal of pain and distress.*'

'*They're not here,*' said Peadar with a shake in his voice. '*Salvadóir took them with him.*'

'*I don't like liars,*' said Kane righteously, and with that he struck him across the face, knocking his glasses to the ground. '*But I will attempt to find the books first without resorting to ugliness. It's called common decency. I hope someday that you boys will learn what that means.*' He began ransacking the house then, the living room and kitchen first. He cut open the sofa, pulled out every drawer, and threw their contents onto the floor. Then he went upstairs and we heard him pulling everything apart as if there was a bull up there destroying the house.

'What'll we do?' said Peadar with fear in his voice.

'We can't give him the books, anyway,' I said as firmly as I could. 'It's evidence that we saw what we did that day. It was true. We both saw it. If he takes the books, we'll have lost all proof. The truth, our truth, will be lost forever.'

'I know … I know,' Peadar said quietly, like someone talking to himself.

After a while, a strange silence fell on the house, and we didn't know whether Kane was still there or if he'd gone.

'Maybe he left,' said Peadar.

'Christ, I hope so!' I said, my heart jumping in my chest.

'We can't give him the books,' said Peadar, 'whatever he does. We have to be strong. We'll regret it forever if we lose them tonight.'

'Those books belong to Salvadóir,' I said. 'It's our duty to keep them safe. Whatever happens.'

'Whatever happens?' asked the voice in the hall, speaking now in Irish. He had been there all the time listening to us, and came back in again now with a smug look on his face. 'Well, isn't it wonderful that you have the Irish language,' he said sarcastically. 'I myself speak fourteen languages – did you know that? I have the European languages, but I specialised in the ancient tongues: Latin, Greek, Hebrew, of course, as well as Hittite and Aramaic. I can read Egyptian hieroglyphics as well. I knew, of course, that you spoke Irish, but I pretended that I didn't, in the hope that I could discover the whereabouts of the books through eavesdropping. Oh, by the way, those books aren't Salvadóir's; they are mine. I bought them from Birdy's widow.'

'After you'd killed him, was it?' I said. 'Birdy wanted to give them to Salvadóir. He sent him a text.'

A look of confusion came over Kane's face for a moment, and when he spoke again, there was more humility in his voice. 'I can read Egyptian hieroglyphics and the cuneiform Hittite script but … I'm embarrassed to tell you that I've never actually understood that text.'

'*Comix bag*: it's an anagram for *magic box*, the term that Birdy had for the secret shelf in the cabinet.'

'Ah!' he exclaimed. 'Thank you very much, Seán. I am in your debt. That's been bothering me for years.'

'Well, you understand it now, and you understand that they're Salvadóir's by right.'

'Oh, Seán, it doesn't matter now anyway. They're mine because I want them, and I'm the man with the gun.'

'Is that part of the *common decency* you were talking about just now?'

'Aren't you a very clever boy,' he said with a laugh. 'Too clever, perhaps. But do you know, I do have regrets about poor Birdy. We were close friends for years. We worked together to bring the miracles of the ancient world to light. He was a very intelligent man indeed. It was he who discovered the existence of the little men. He could see things that ten thousand other people would be blind to. He could put different types of evidence together to find some secret truth in them. I remember the day when he first came to me with the story of the little men. I didn't believe it initially, of course, but after a while, I saw that he was right. Then he met Salvadóir's father, and was delighted that he could speak with someone who had actually seen them with his own eyes. But something changed then. Maybe it was me who changed. This wasn't the ancient history of the Phoenicians or the Jews. It wasn't the discovery of the century, or a subject suitable for academic study at all. We were trespassing in God's garden, trampling on his flowers. These little men are not beings like us: they're not like any being at all. I read the same texts that Birdy read, but where he saw earthly knowledge and historical facts, I saw the hand of God and heard the whispers of divinity. I knew that I would have to keep this knowledge a secret. It isn't a subject that's suitable for humanity.'

'Is that why you killed him?' I asked.

'Well, I didn't *want* to kill him. I wanted to torture him so he'd tell me where the books were, those books that you stole. But he was old at the time, and had a heart attack before he had the chance to tell me. In the end, I bought his library from his wife and, in the course of time, found the books anyway. I should have put them in the fire then, but I was always an old scholar and didn't have the courage to do it at the time. Anyway,

I'll do it tonight. You're both young and strong and I'm certain that neither of you has a weak heart.' With that, he opened the door of the stove, picked up the poker, and thrust it into the fire. 'It'll just take a little while to heat up, and we'll start then,' he said calmly.

I didn't know whether I could stand the pain or not. Maybe I'd tell him where the books were as soon as I felt the first touch of the poker.

I looked at Peadar. There was sweat on his forehead and terror in his eyes. He couldn't speak at first, but then the words came to him slowly. 'I'll be … ok … I'll be ok,' he said. I didn't know if he was speaking to me or to himself.

I would have to say something to stop this. Kane was intelligent. He could listen to reason. 'I believe that you're a good person, Mr Kane,' I began. 'You're not a sadistic person who would torture two young men for no reason. You believe that you have no choice but to destroy these books. I understand that. But allow me to give you another argument for a moment.'

'Carry on. We have to wait on the poker anyway.'

I knew very well that I couldn't change his steadfast opinions on the matter, but maybe I could delay him until something else happened. I didn't know what that could be, but at that moment I desperately needed to delay things, and I could see no other way to do it. I remembered what I was thinking about while in the church in Guagán Barra.

'When you mention God, who are you referring to?' I asked. 'Is it the god that Abraham worshipped, the god of the Jews? Are you referring to El himself?'

'I am indeed! Or maybe that isn't as fashionable as it used to be.'

'I was thinking about El the other day,' I said, as if we were discussing philosophical and religious matters over a few pints in the pub. 'I believe that he is nothing but the personification of the concept of absolute truth. This is the single unquestionable truth, the truth on which all other truths depend, a truth from which all other truths flow. I believe that this is an enticing concept for people because it gives them simplicity in this complicated world.'

'I agree with you,' he replied. 'The concept of a universal truth, or absolute truth, as you say, is in the religions of the East as well. But it's true that the Jews made a personification of it in the form of El, and it's true that this gives solace to people in this complicated world. But if you look at this point as proof that God doesn't exist, I myself look at it as proof that he does.'

'Explain that to me,' I said, in the hope that it might take him a while.

'God is the basis of all truth. It's as simple as that,' he said, destroying my hopes.

But I carried on anyway. 'You must know that the Jews created their religion from the religion of the Canaanites. They threw out all the other gods, but they kept one of them, this El, to create their monotheistic religion. El himself says in Exodus that he is a "jealous god", but if there *were* no other gods, who was he jealous of? You must understand through your study of the history of this religion that it was created by the hand of man, in order to elevate one tribe over another.'

'That's one way of looking at it. But I believe that it wasn't because of tribalism that the Jews decided to abandon the polytheism of the Canaanites, but because they had received information about the one single universal God through their contact with the little men. Maybe that was only an uncertain smattering of knowledge, and that's the reason why we cannot depend on the old texts, other than as guides, but still they understood the essence of that message and followed it. It was a message that told of a complete unity in God.'

'But how do you believe that?' Peadar asked. The terror was still in his eyes, but I could see that he understood what I was doing. 'If the ancient Jews had contact with the little men, why do you believe that their understanding of that contact was correct? At the end of the day, they were an undeveloped people in the Bronze Age. What view could they have of that contact except through the lens of their own religion. But you received a modern education at university, a place where knowledge is understood through a process of reason. You should understand, more than anyone, that every religion in the world is founded on a process of deference, through a process in which deference is given to the opinions of other people all the time. This is the complete opposite of reason.'

'But don't we all do that same thing, Peadar?' Kane asked. 'You are a scientist and you put your faith in the process of reason. But you accept things as well through the process of deference. Do you believe in the Big Bang?'

'I do.'

'And can you do the complex mathematics to prove that it's true?'

'I can't, but—'

'You believe it because you give deference to the people who can do that maths – exactly as peasants in the Middle Ages gave deference to the priest and the bishop when they said that God created the world in seven days. You believe that the universe began at one point and exploded out from that. I myself believe that the universe started with one God and stretched from Him. What's the difference? We know that dark matter exists, for example, but we have no idea what it is. Isn't it possible that God is in that dark matter? Seán here says that I believe in absolute truth, but doesn't every scientist believe in the same thing? They understand that they don't know everything, but they believe that universal knowledge exists, that absolute truth is there, if they could dig deep enough into the fabric of the universe to find it. What's that name that physicists working on quantum mechanics gave to a theory recently? 'The Theory of Everything'. That's a religious term if ever I heard one. But science will fail to give us absolute answers. The human mind is not strong enough to understand the complex truths of the universe. Sooner or later, we'll come to a brick wall that we cannot go over or through. There's a phrase for this: *you can teach a dog tricks, but you can't teach it trigonometry*. There is no way to the truth but through God. With all the understanding that the scientists of the world have, they haven't the slightest understanding of what human sentience is, the very ways in which the function of neurons and synapses in the brain turns to consciousness.'

I saw a painful strain on Peadar's face as he struggled with the different aspects of Kane's argument.

'The scientist and godly person both believe in absolute truth, but the scientist wants to find it on his own. He wants to make a god of himself, just as Lucifer did during his insurrection in Heaven.'

The poker was hot enough now, and I saw Kane look towards it again. I had to say something: 'But didn't you say that we can't depend on the old texts, old stories about the Devil and such? But maybe there's some truth in the Bible after all. When Adam and Eve ate from the tree of knowledge, they received the awareness that this absolute truth does not exist. Before that, they lived in God's paradise – or a system of belief that we create to tell ourselves that there's a structured, ordered place for us in the universe. After that, they were no longer able to believe in this comfortable dream, and they had to live out in the cold world of multiple truths – truths that fight with one another all the time. Maybe that's the story that the Jews got from the Firíní! And don't we all live now in the cold world of multiple truths? People can go back to Paradise anytime, of course. All they have to do is believe in that absolute truth. But it's difficult to maintain that state, because the world continually shows us that it's not true. That's why people cling to spirituality. It's a trick to keep our focus on this concept of absolute truth, a belief in the simplicity of the universe. But if this simplicity gives you solace, then believe it – if you can.'

I knew that I was being very brave here with a person who was ready to thrust a red-hot poker into my flesh, but I could see that I had to provoke him to keep his interest in the argument.

'You're right, Seán. This is a complex, entangled world, and that belief that there is an absolute truth behind everything gives solace and peace to people. But just because people like that belief, it doesn't mean that it isn't true. Your reason is failing you now, boy. You are confused because you're mixing up correlation with causation.'

Maybe there was some sense to his argument, but I couldn't stop now, because I knew what would happen if I did. I did my best to think of something to say, but he cut across me again:

'Our truths are based on choices,' he proclaimed, like a lawyer giving his closing argument in court, 'and we are all the same in this regard. Look at the solipsism in Descartes' *cogito ergo sum* – I think, therefore I am. This is the view that you cannot be certain of anything except that your own mind exists. Everything else could be in your imagination, everyone you've ever met, everything you've ever seen. What are the odds on that? Well, it's 50/50, because it must be either true or false. There is no third option. But we choose to believe that the world around us exists. In the same way, people chose to believe that God exists.

Don't you remember what I said to you on the street the other night, the line from *Ben-Hur?* "*Perfection is God; simplicity is perfection. The curse of curses is that men will not let truths like these alone.*" Absolute truth exists, Seán. You're right: it is simplicity, a beautiful simplicity.'

'But how would you recognise that truth if you saw it? If the sky brightened one day with the face of God proclaiming the end of the world and welcoming us all in through the gates of heaven, how would we know that there isn't another god above him, and another one above him again? I don't know whether absolute truth exists or not, but there's a good chance that we'll never find it.'

'Oh, ye of little faith,' he said simply. I could think of nothing else to say to him. We looked at each other, and I could see the ugly smile coming across his face again. 'As they say, it's all a matter of opinion. Have you nothing else to delay me except that old potato, Seán, the old argument between universalism and relativism? Well, it's getting late now anyway, and I'll have to take my books and go.' With that, he reached down and took the poker, which was white hot at this stage, from the fire. The fear ran through me as if it was a mad dog. I pulled at the cable ties and they cut into my wrists.

'Fuck you!' shouted Peadar with a venom in his voice that I'd never heard before. 'The books are ours. It's we who saw the Firíní and it's we who'll say what they are. Do you think you're so clever? Do you think that truth is something you can summon into being? You've learned nothing from your hieroglyphics or from your fourteen languages. Fuck you, and fuck you again!'

I looked at the vile grin stretching even further across Kane's face. He began to laugh. 'I'll start with you so, Peadar,' he said joyfully and he raised the poker up to his face. Peadar made every attempt to move his head left and right, but Kane grabbed him by the hair and moved the poker slowly towards his eye. He screamed fiercely but could do no more.

I screamed myself, in the hope that the neighbours would call the Guards, but I knew that they would take a while to arrive, and what damage could Kane do with the poker in that time. 'Let him go!' I shouted at him.

'Wait your turn, Seán,' Kane said laughing. 'I think I'll do a job on you even if Peadar tells me where the books are.'

It's a strange thing, but a sort of madness comes over you with that fear. I shouted again and again at him. I shouted every curse I knew.

Then a voice came from the living-room door. 'Stop!' it said loudly and firmly. Salvadóir was standing there, his huge frame making a powerful presence in the room.

When Kane saw him, he grabbed the gun that he'd put on the mantelpiece and pointed it at him. He tried to keep up his bravado, but it was clear that it disconcerted him a great deal that Salvadóir was there. 'Stay where you are now,' he said, a false authority in his voice.

'Let them go and put down the gun,' said Salvadóir. 'You have no chance of escaping from this now.'

'I have no chance?' Kane said with a weak laugh. 'Well, aren't you a big man now, Salvadóir! You were a big boy as well, I have to say. But there's a little piece of lead in this gun, and it doesn't care what size you are. You can be big and dead at the same time. Now, go to that corner and sit down.'

'Fuck you, ya old lunatic! What do you want?'

'Old lunatic! Do you think that you can call me that name, like your bastard of a father did? Do you think that you can—'

'My father was right about you from the start. But Birdy believed there was a little bit of goodness still in you. He believed it even when he saw that you were losing your mind. He kept that hope because he was always a true friend to you. He was a faithful and honourable man, but you let him down. You betrayed that friendship because that's the type of person you are. Now, I'll ask you again: What do you want?'

'I want my books! The books that you robbed from my house!' he screamed.

'Those books are mine. Birdy gave them to me, but I'll give them to you now.'

'Salvadóir, don't do it!' I shouted.

'We already have the information, Seán,' Salvadóir said. 'We don't have to prove anything to anyone. You saw the Firíní, but it was me who dragged you into such an awful situation with this maniac. I'm sorry about that. I can't permit this horror.' Salvadóir turned and walked to the corner. He raised the carpet and floorboards and took out the bundle with the books.

I saw the ugly smirk on Kane's face again when Salvadóir gave the bundle to him, and I wanted to punch that hateful pus. He took out the books and looked at them, his gun pointed all the while at Salvadóir. He picked up Newton's letter first and put it on the fire.

Then he saw the little poetry book that Peadar had found in the library, and it was clear that he recognised it. He went through it and stopped on one page, where the poem attributed to Catharina Questiers was. He read it and looked at us with a wry smile before tossing it into the fire as well. Jan's diary was the next thing he took up and he laid it neatly on the flames. I almost cried looking at those brown pages with their ancient penmanship burning in the fire. Kane then took up the Bible.

'I know that I don't have to burn all of this book, but I want to be done with this business in its entirety,' he said thoughtfully. With that, he laid the ancient book face down in the fire in a way that it was half-open so as the flames would creep between its dry, old pages.

He turned it with the poker until it was fragments of ash and the flames had subsided. That was the end of it, and I felt the loss deeply. We had evidence in our hands that proved what we had seen in the microscope that day, that even proved to ourselves that we weren't mad. Now, it was all gone.

'I should have done that years ago when I first found them in the cabinet. Now, it is finished,' he said.

'You have what you wanted. Go now and don't bother us again,' Salvadóir said firmly.

'Don't bother you? Have you forgotten that you broke into my house; that it was you who stole from me?'

'Those books were *mine*. Birdy sent me a text to tell me where they were.'

'Oh that text. Wonderful,' exclaimed Kane joyfully. 'The lads told me what it meant. I have to admit that I never understood it, that *comix bag*. But I remember when he sent it to you. I went to his house that day and we had an argument about the books. I told him that the little men were agents from the other world, that this was the corporeal form that the angels took … and the devils. I told him that he was thrusting the ugly hand of humanity into the unearthly realm, a realm forbidden to us. He didn't believe me. He said that there was a natural explanation for the existence of these beings. I hated his belief that the shabbiness of the normal world had a part in this miracle. I tried to explain this to him, but he didn't understand. Anyway, he understood that I was up to something, and he took his phone from his pocket, as if he'd heard a text, but what he did was to send that text to you. I grabbed it from his hand and read it, but I could make no sense of it, and he wouldn't explain it to me. I ordered him to give me the books so I could destroy them. He refused outright.

I beat him and threatened him with a knife, but he still refused. I pushed him down into the chair – he was a very small man, as you remember, and I put the poker in the fire, just as I did with the lads here tonight. I ordered him again. He refused again. I took the poker from the fire, red-hot, and put it before his face. But alas, his heart as weak, and that was the end of poor Birdy. He died on the chair, and I left him there.'

As Kane was telling this story, I saw the anger rise on Salvadóir's face. It was clear that the story hurt him deeply. Birdy was like a father to him, especially after his own father had died.

Kane recognised the anger and the hatred on his face. 'Oh poor Salvadóir,' he said, and he began to laugh mockingly again. 'But you must have had an inkling before this that I was behind his death. I was very disappointed that day that his weak heart had robbed me of my sport. But maybe I'll have another chance tonight.' With that, he turned his hideous smirk again on us who were tied to the chairs.

Salvadóir was a huge man, and maybe I hadn't imagined that he'd be able to move as fast as he did. He thrust his fist out, swung it towards Kane's head like a shot from a gun, and I heard the terrible thud when it struck. But unfortunately, I heard another sound half a second afterwards. Kane pulled the trigger at the same time and shot Salvadóir in the chest. They both fell back onto the ground, and I saw a red patch of blood growing on Salvadóir's chest beside his heart.

'He killed him!' screamed Peadar, and I saw his eyes fill with tears of sorrow and rage. But I couldn't speak myself at that moment. The big man lay before me on the ground like a dead whale on the beach. It was horrible. I couldn't move from the chair and I couldn't speak. I sat there. That was all.

But after a while, it was clear that our troubles were not over: Kane wasn't dead and he was slowly regaining consciousness. I knew that he wouldn't want to leave witnesses to his crime and that he'd kill us too. He woke up slowly, but when he realised where he was, he jumped forward. Salvadóir's fist had broken a few teeth from his mouth, and I think his jaw was broken as well. He looked at Salvadóir lying on the ground and then at us. '*Bwaistrd! Fackin darty bwastid!*' he screamed through his broken mouth at Salvadóir. He stood up and looked at us again, hatred and venom in his eyes. '*I'll sond ye to hell ta pway for your cwimes! Bwastrds!*' he screamed.

But at that moment, he perceived someone else in the room and turned towards the door. Aogán was standing there. I saw the ugly look on Kane's face again, but it was mixed with fear and confusion now. His eyes ran across the floor and found the gun where it had fallen. He dived at it suddenly and grabbed it, but hadn't time to point it at Aogán before receiving a heavy kick into the stomach, and the gun fell from his hand. He curled up in a ball on the ground and let out a horrible wail.

Aogán looked at us then and at Salvadóir on the ground. 'Are ye ok?' he said, but my head began to swim and I didn't have the strength to answer him. I remember him cutting the ties on my hands, and on the phone calling for an ambulance and for the Guards.

Scene Nine

Husum, Duchy of Schleswig
17th May 1675

Jan stood on board a ship making its way to the town of Husum. It was a fine day, and the sunlight glittered on the surface of the water as they entered the bay. One could imagine it to be a broad bay anyway, even though he knew that the land on their port side was a large island. It was called Nordstrand, and he looked at it now from time to time because this was where she had lived when she first came here. This country was very similar to the Netherlands in that the land spread out on both sides in a level plain to the horizon, the ground almost as flat as the sea. He had taken a schooner from Amsterdam four days earlier and it had been a pleasant voyage, even though they had to stop at different places on the way. But he was almost there now, and he saw Husum in a little cove before him.

He kept a book in his hand as he looked out at the sea and the land. He hadn't many books with him, but this was an important one. It was a book in English and he had read it many times since he'd received it four years earlier. He thought of the things that had happened to him over the last five or six years: the sickness, the poverty and, worse still, the spiritual distress that grieved him to the core and made him question everything, even those things he had thought to be essential to who he was. Everything except his faith in God, of course: that was the immovable rock.

He closed his eyes for a moment, and saw two men drowning in a drop of water. Maybe he would be better off if he'd had the sense at that time to turn from his mistakes – almost twelve years ago now – but it wasn't too late for him yet. Pride and vanity were the problems, even though he didn't see that at the time. He told himself that he did everything for the glory of God, but that was a lie. It was the vanity of his own heart that directed him to look at himself as a wise man, as a great scientist. But she had shown him the error of his ways, this new Eve, Antoinette Bourignon, and if he could go back to the start, he'd put everything right. He had written to her two years earlier and they had corresponded regularly since then. He had told her the whole story in his letters, and she understood immediately where the fault lay. He had looked into places that were not permitted to him, that were not permitted to the human race. This wasn't the first time he had thought that, of course, but it struck him forcefully when she said it, because she had access to a pure truth, something higher than that which was given to scientists and learned men. He could no longer deny it now, nor lie to himself that he was doing God's work. He had thought that nature was another of God's books, and he had done his best to read and understand that book, but he understood now that God wanted nothing from him except his simple love.

But Antoinette Bourignon wasn't the only person to tell him that truth. He looked down now at the book in his hands, a book almost battered with the many times he'd read it. It was a book by a person who had awareness of the truth long before he understood it himself, a person who wrote truths that he would have to understand now. He rubbed the tips of his fingers to the title on the cover and his lips moved to say those words, words that told of his own story: *Paradise Lost.* He opened it to a page that he had marked and read the words to himself as if it were a prayer:

Sollicit not thy thoughts with matters hid,
Leave them to God above, him serve and feare;
Of other Creatures, as him pleases best,
Wherever plac't, let him dispose: joy thou
In what he gives to thee, this Paradise
And thy faire Eve; Heav'n is for thee too high
To know what passes there; be lowlie wise:
Think onely what concernes thee and thy being;
Dream not of other Worlds, what Creatures there
Live, in what state, condition or degree,
Contented that thus farr hath been reveal'd
Not of Earth onely but of highest Heav'n.

Jan let the words run over him like waves on the shore, like balsam for his exhausted mind. They took him from where he was to another world, a world in which the light glistened more pleasantly on the water, in which the clouds above him were more gently blown. He liked the words *be lowlie wise* very much. That's what he would do from now on. He would find the wisdom to be humble. He would not search for the multitude of questions and answers that ran like rabbits through the world of knowledge, but instead he would give his energy entirely to God.

He remembered John Milton's name very well from that day in London when they received a letter from Robert Boyle that told of his visit to the house of that blind old man. He remembered Milton's own story, his visit to Italy and his conversations with Galileo and Barberini. He remembered Milton's warning then to avoid any contact with the little men. Unfortunately, he didn't have the sense then to heed it. Robert Hooke had sent him a copy of *Paradise Lost* when it was published, directing his attention to the last line and the anagram within it. This book had a huge effect on him when he read it, but still he carried on with his work. Gradually, however, with Antoinette Bourignon telling him the same thing, he understood what he had to do. He would finish his scientific studies entirely and turn to God. He alone would be a fitting subject for his work now.

Paradise Lost told the story of Adam and Eve, of the fall of man and the fall of Satan. Was it possible that this was a message that alluded to a link between these events and the story of the little men? Wasn't Beelzebub, Lord of the Flies, mentioned clearly at the start of the book? Wasn't it a book by someone who understood the story of Galileo, of the Barberini and the Medici very well? Jan could only imagine that everything was connected in some way, but yet he no longer wanted this knowledge. He was finished with all that, and wanted only an intuitive connection with God himself. He hoped that Antoinette Bourignon could show this to him.

Even though they had written letters to each other, Jan had never met this wise woman. Steno had met her once and had said that he was very impressed by her. That learned man Comenius had even invited her to be at his bedside as he died. She had a great gift, a gift beyond that which anyone else had. Other people would give you their opinions on 'God's will', but she received direct communication from the spirits of the other world and from God himself. God spoke through her and told her that the end was coming, that the human race was living in the last days, and that she would have to gather together the true Christians. Jan had spent his life looking for the truth, and now it was at hand.

She was originally from Lille, but had spent a good portion of her life in the Netherlands. He had heard that she had such devotion to God when she was young that she adamantly refused her father's orders to marry and escaped from the house, sleeping in coffins by night. She founded a circle of people who were willing to hear the truth, but she suffered oppression from the authorities everywhere she went. They didn't like the fact that a woman would instruct men and have authority over them, particularly over upper-class men, but Jan didn't care about that. If God had chosen her, then there would be nothing to question. Did he not create both men and women? But she suffered and was often expelled from places. Then one of her followers, a man called de Cort, left land to her in his will. That was the island of Nordstrand, and she moved with her followers to Schleswig. They lived on that island for a while, but alas, de Cort had left many debts in his will as well, and they had to leave and find a place in the town itself, Husum.

She invited Jan to come and live in that fellowship, and he accepted readily. It wasn't that he didn't have doubts about her: he certainly did, initially. He understood that there are many charlatans in this world, and he well remembered London during the time of the plague when people ran after them in the street. But when he read her book, it made a great impression on him and he felt that he was in contact with an intuition that existed deeply in his soul. Before that, his mind was organised in the Cartesian system, the system of reason on which the new sciences were built. But she taught him that this system was a lie, a chimera that blinded people to the truth of God. That was a truth that could not be found through logic or reason but through spiritual intuition. Antoinette Bourignon was in direct contact with the spirits and the angels. These eternal beings would speak with her and through her, and Jan was ready now to listen to them. With all of the strange things he had seen in his life, he was eager for a different path.

There was a scramble on the quay when the boat came in to Husum, and he imagined the simple lives of these people, lives based on God and on food. He had only one bag, and he thrust his copy of *Paradise Lost* into it before walking down the gangplank and on into the town itself. He saw the great tower of the church in the distance as the ship came in, and he strolled towards it now. People were coming and going in every direction, pushing carts before them and selling goods. He came to a tavern and went in for something to eat. It was a quiet place compared to the street. There was an old woman there who was quite deaf, but eventually, he was able to make her understand what he wanted.

He thought about Steno while he was eating, as he wasn't far now from his old home in Copenhagen. Jan had received a letter from him a few months earlier to say that he had become a Catholic priest. He had converted to Catholicism in 1667, and since then was moving in the direction of the priesthood all the time. He had asked Jan if he would become a Catholic as well, but he couldn't do it. Steno had done the same thing as Jan was doing now, however, and had completely given up his scientific studies. Maybe they were both walking on different sides of the same path, but in another way there wasn't the slightest similarity to their lives now.

Steno was under the patronage of the Medici in Florence. Young Cosimo was made Grand Duke of Tuscany when his father Ferdinando died, and who did he want as his own son's teacher but Steno. He agreed, of course, and was made an important member of the Catholic de' Medici court in Florence. Just as Thévenot had predicted, Cosimo came back to Jan with his offer when he thought the time was right, and if it was ever to be right, it was right then.

Jan's father never wanted him to spend his life studying insects and had warned him many times that he would stop his allowance if he didn't take up a position as a doctor, something that he didn't want to do. He published his book *Historia insectorum generalis* in 1669, and they fell out to such a degree that his father kept his promise and cut him off. Those were difficult days for

Jan because he couldn't cease his work with the insects. He knew that he didn't have much time as the illness recurred often and would finish him before long. He took up positions here and there, but continued with his own studies as often as he could.

Then Steno came to him in Amsterdam with a letter from Cosimo. He would buy his entire collection for an enormous price, all three thousand specimens, and put it in a grand demonstration, on condition that Jan himself would come to Tuscany to take charge of it. It was an enticing offer after years of suffering poverty and sickness, and he nearly accepted it, but in the end he couldn't. Antoinette Bourignon gave him every warning that his soul would be in peril if he took that offer, and even if she wasn't against it, he himself looked at it as a vile degradation, a corruption of everything that he believed. He refused Cosimo again and carried on with his work. He wrote a book on bees and it almost killed him. He composed an anagram that would be there as an indirect reference to the little men, but didn't have the courage to use it. He wrote that book through thousands of mental torments and the heavy weight of self-reproach. On the one hand, his intellect urged him to study the miracles of God, but on the other, he believed that it was God himself, as opposed to his little creatures, who was worthy of his attention. He suffered with this internal struggle the whole time that he was writing the book, and then he gave it away as soon as it was finished because it no longer meant anything to him. He wrote another book on the larva of the silkworm but he burnt it, again on the advice of Antoinette Bourignon. Everything was finished now. He would give up all dealings with the world and devote the time he had left to God.

Jan went out onto the busy street after his meal and walked about the town at his ease. He felt a peace in his heart for the first time in many years. Before long, he noticed that he had come out onto the quays again, and asked for directions to the house from a fisherman who was mending nets there. He was an old man with a rough beard on his chin, even though his upper lip was clean shaven, and he smiled roguishly to himself when Jan told him that he wanted to go to Antoinette Bourignon's fellowship. 'Another gentleman from the Netherlands looking for salvation! They're not on the island anymore. They had to leave it because of the trouble,' he said heartily.

'I know about that, my friend. Do you know where they are now?'

'Oh, yes! They have a house on the other side of the church. Wait a minute now,' and he stood up. 'Siegmund! Siegmund, come here, boy,' he shouted, and Jan saw a young boy running up the quay. When he reached the spot, the old man laid a hand on his shoulder. 'Siegmund, do you know which house the soldiers of Christ are living in now?'

'I do, Grandad,' said the boy.

'Bring this gentleman to the house so,' he said, turning back to his work.

Jan thanked him, and walked down the quay again with the boy. Within ten minutes, he was standing before a big house in the town. But if it was big, it was in no way elegant, with its rough, broken door and the plaster falling from the walls. He gave a coin to Siegmund, who was delighted with his profit, and knocked at the door. 'Thank you, sir!' shouted the boy to him as he ran back towards the quay.

He gave another knock, but again, nothing happened. Then he heard slow footsteps coming laboriously towards the door. It was opened by a middle-aged man with long cheeks and bags under his eyes. He wore a jacket that had once been elegant but now the age and use it had suffered could be seen on the collar. The two men stood looking at each other in silence.

'I am Jan Swammerdam,' he said. 'I wrote a letter to Mistress Bourignon. She invited me to come.'

'Come in,' the man said. He turned on his heels and went through the broad, dark hall, directing Jan to a little room directly on the left. 'Wait here,' he said cheerlessly.

There were two hard chairs and a table in the room. No picture or image hung on the walls and the paint was falling from them in places. There wasn't much light there either, except the weak rays that crept in through the curtains. Jan sat down quietly.

Within two minutes, he heard a rustling sound in the hall and suddenly she was in the room. Antoinette Bourignon was a small woman, but she had enormous presence when she blew in like a dark cloud in the sky. She was covered from head to toe in black cloth, a dress of rough fabric and a big black head-piece of the same material which made a rigid, five-sided frame around her face and was tied tightly just beneath her chin. Her clothes were like a suit of armour, or something carved from an enormous lump of coal. But the most remarkable thing was her face itself. It was a pointed, slender face with eyes like those of a serpent. Jan thought he saw poison in those eyes and they sent a shiver through his body. She had a long, slender nose and a sharp chin that stuck out beyond the thick knot of cloth that kept her head-piece in position. He perceived her like a great, dark force in the room, but when she spoke her voice was low and gentle, as if it was coming to him from the other side of the universe. 'Mr Swammerdam,' she said in measured tones, and he felt her voice dragging him into some other dark world, 'it is wonderful that you are here. You that looked upon the face of the Devil himself. But we still have time. Sit down again, and we will speak together.'

He sat down and she sat beside him. This was how he imagined confession among the Catholics, the quiet space in which your soul was bared before God. The room was dark and narrow and he felt that there was nothing else in this world now outside those walls. She looked directly into his eyes and held his consciousness with one swift, firm grip, her own eyes very close together, he thought. He felt everything else in the world slipping away from him. There was nothing left now but her eyes, her low voice, and a strange, dark contentment in her presence.

'You told me the story in your letters. Now I want to hear it in your own voice,' she said.

He started at the beginning: that day in Steno's garden, the two men drowning in a drop of water, the horrible swarm of flies. He mentioned everyone who was a party to the story: Steno, Thévenot, Bourdelot, Hooke, Boyle, Milton, Galileo, the Barberini and the Medici. He didn't leave out those he'd met on the streets of London either, or the sickness that came afterwards, or the fever dreams in which he met the little men: the whole story. He cleared it all out of his soul with one broad sweep. She listened to him carefully from start to finish without saying a word, her eyes fixed into him, her own dark form unmoving in the dim light of the room. In the end, there was nothing more to say and he stopped. He sat there quietly for a while until he perceived that she was about to speak again.

'You have come closer to the darkness than almost any other person, Jan,' she said. 'It is certain that it was the Devil and his soldiers you saw, as I have always told you. He has a hand in the highest courts of the world and in the most well-established churches. That is why I would have nothing to do with any of them. There is no church except the invisible church of God, that church without buildings, without chapels, without the adornment of power woven with golden threads that are forged in the furnaces of Hell. It was not a good thing that you gave a promise to the Devil not to write about that which you have seen, but the biggest mistake was made at the very beginning: that you desired to look into the secrets of God, that you wanted to understand the miracles that he created in every drop of rain. There are many who practise this new learning, but it is a defilement of God's law. Leave the secrets of God to God himself and take care of your eternal soul.'

'This is precisely what I shall do from now on,' Jan said firmly. 'It is finished.'

'The books on the mayfly and the bees, are they finished? Did you publish them?'

'They are in print, but I don't care about them now. It is finished.'

'And the other one, the one about the larva of the silkworm?' she asked more keenly now.

'I burnt it,' he said, and she nodded her head in agreement.

'I do not agree with this study of the miracles of God,' she said, 'but I understand that you did it out of a desire to glorify him. I know of other Christians with the same fault. One of them you mentioned in your tragedy: that Englishman Robert Boyle. He is a good Christian. He translated my own book into English and had it published over there. I gave him the same warning to direct all his strength to saving his soul. Does he still practise that craft?'

'He doesn't. I heard that he was struck down with a fit of apoplexy five years ago and that he remains quietly in his house now.'

'Maybe it will save his soul,' she said coldly, 'but he gave you good counsel to stay clear of this evil. What of this other person, Milton? You mentioned his book in your letters.'

Jan took up the bag and pulled out his copy of *Paradise Lost*. 'This is the book that he wrote. He heard of the little men thirty years before I saw them, but this book is based on the fall of man and the fall of Satan. Do you think that Milton had further information on these events, that my own story with the little men is connected with that story?'

'This is your inquisitive mind again!' she said sharply. 'Leave the care of those questions to God himself.'

'You are right,' he said. 'Forgive me. Milton says the same thing in this book when the Angel Raphael gives advice to Adam. He recommends that he not question the secrets of God.' He offered her the book, but she refused it.

'I do not read the language of the English, and even if I did, I would have no interest in it. I was never a learned woman. I receive my wisdom directly from God himself. All other wisdom comes between him and you. But I do have knowledge from this eternal source of the beginning of the world when the fall of man occurred.'

'Tell me of it, please,' said Jan excitedly.

She remained quiet for a while again and looked at him. It was difficult for him to read her face, and he was afraid that he had made a terrible mistake in asking this. He felt her sharp eyes cutting into him, but in the end she began speaking again, quietly and slowly. 'The first man was made of clay, but it was not ordinary clay. His body was purer and more transparent than the finest crystal. It was lit from within by streams of light that illuminated his internal vessels, vessels containing liquid of every type and colour. This shining creature was larger than humans are now. His dark hair was short and curly; a dark moustache adorned his upper lip. He did not have a penis. Where his genitals would have been, there was something with the shape of a face from which emerged delicious odours. There was a vessel in his abdomen that bore small eggs, and another vessel that contained a liquid capable of impregnating these eggs. When this man became inflamed with the love of God, a great desire would overwhelm him that there be other creatures to share in this adoration, a desire that would rise until the liquid would overflow, spreading itself over the eggs. One of them would be fertilised then and another perfect man would issue from it. So at least it was meant to be when God told the human race to be fruitful and multiply, but it happened this way only once. The man that was hatched then was the Messiah, who turned himself into a foetus and awaited the time to enter Mary's womb. All other humans were born in a different way when Adam and Eve were expelled from Paradise. Driven from the sacred land, their bodies coarsened and became like ours are now. They lost their crystalline transparency; their inward light dimmed and then went out. As for their inner vessels, they became the internal organs whose sight only repels us now. And in the place of that beautiful face that once emitted such marvellous perfumes, there are now only the ugly genitals that all humans cover in shame.'

Jan listened in wonder until she had finished. 'You received these truths from God?' he asked.

'God tells me these things. He speaks to me every day. He speaks to me in the depth of my soul. He gives me visions. I am often asked of the way in which I hear God and speak to him. I will tell you this now, as clearly as I can. God is spirit; the soul is spirit; they converse together in spirit. No words are used but a supernatural correspondence which is more understandable than the greatest eloquence in the world. God makes himself known to the soul, and the soul perceives him. As the soul loses its connection to the world, it is thus the way in which the connection with God is increased. But how can one recognise this connection? How can one recognise whether it comes from God, from nature or from the Devil? You need divine light for this task. The tricks of the Devil are all around us and he has a firm grip on the life of man. He can still speak of the Divine

Mysteries as well as when he was yet an angel. He lost none of his knowledge but kept it all with him in Hell. This was the predicament that befell you because you could not tell, even with all your education, whether the thing which you saw was from God, from nature or from the Devil. You needed divine light, but they do not teach that in college.'

'That's it precisely. That was the problem from the very start.'

'God gave me that light, and I will show you the error of your ways.'

'I am very grateful to you for your help,' Jan said.

But then he saw a dark expression come across her face and she lowered her voice even more. 'I will tell you something,' she said. 'It happened more than twenty years ago, when I was living in Mons. I received an inheritance and used it to establish an orphanage for girls in the town. I spent nine years there, and every day I received a communication from the spirits or from God himself, communication that I shared with the girls. But towards the end, I received a disturbing message from the spirits to say that the girls under my care had made a pact with the Devil himself. They all denied it, but I did my best to get the truth from them and save their souls. I locked them in the building and gave them no food, in order to expel the devils from them. I beat them until my limbs were exhausted, but still they were within them: so said the spirits. But I carried on as steadfastly as I could, without stop, even without sleep. In the end, one devil left the body of a girl. She was a girl of about eight years of age. Marie was her name. But alas, a short while afterwards she died, her body broken by the hard work I had to do to expel that devil. The next day, the town magistrate came to the orphanage because people had called him on account of the screams that the devils made when I was trying to expel them. This magistrate did not believe me and wanted to put me in prison. I had to escape to Ghent, and I don't know what happened to the poor girls after that. But let this story be a lesson to you about the power of darkness. You saw it yourself with your own eyes!'

Antoinette's story left Jan very disturbed and she saw this on his face.

'Do you know what Hell is?' she asked abruptly.

He was taken aback by the suddenness of the question and couldn't immediately answer.

'Come with me now,' she said, standing up, 'and I will show you something.'

He stood up and they both walked to the door. The confession was over. He followed her down the hall to another room on the ground floor. When she opened the door, the first thing he saw was a large device, made of wood and metal, standing in the middle of the room. It had a high rectangular frame and a horizontal board at the height of his waist that extended from it. There was a big metal vice at the point at which the board and the frame came together, and two men stood on either side of it, men in black coats with dour expressions on their faces. For a moment, a terrible panic ran through Jan. This was a torture chamber, the hell that was reserved for him.

But it lasted only a moment. He recognised the device as a printing press, and saw implements scattered around: paper, ink bottles, and the metal types laid out in boxes on the table.

'We create leaflets here to tell people of the communication that I receive from God. We hand them out at fairs and markets in order to save souls. These leaflets tell them about Hell, about the torments that await them all if they keep on the path they are on, if they carry on with the Lutheran, the Catholic or whatever long-established church it is that has lost its true connection with God. The end is coming, it will come soon now, and it is our duty to save as many souls as we can.'

Jan saw that there were two other men in the room. They were behind the door when he walked in: one of them was the man who had opened the door for him. The four of them had long beards and a worn expression on their faces. One man, who was standing beside the printing press, stepped forward and spoke to him, an intense look in his eyes. 'We are a collection of true Christians and we do our utmost to live according to the will of God. Mistress Bourignon gives us direction.'

'This is Mr Jan Swammerdam,' Antoinette said, raising her voice more than she had up to now. 'He is a writer of books, books that are steeped in the world of man. But now he can work with us on other writing, writing directed at the word of God to save the souls of true Christians. He can live here with us until the end, until God puts an end to this curséd world. And on that day we shall all go to Heaven and sit with Jesus Christ, our saviour, forever in that eternal land!'

'Amen,' said the four other men with one voice.

This choir gave Jan an eerie feeling. Had he made another mistake?

He swept the thought to one side: he hadn't. 'Amen,' he said.

Scene Ten

When Aogán set us free from the chairs, I went straight to Salvadóir on the ground. He was still breathing, but there was a lot of blood. The three of us were gathered around him, and I heard Peadar's voice telling Aogán about everything that had happened: the threat of the hot poker, Salvadóir's arrival, the burning of the books, the punch and the gunshot. My eyes were fixed on Salvadóir's face, but there was no movement from him. I knew that an ambulance was coming and hoped it would be quick. I heard a whining from Kane in the corner. Aogán had taken up the gun, but Kane was trying to get his hands on the poker again, even though it was now cold. Aogán ran to him and knocked it from his hand. He grabbed him firmly by the hair and said something into his ear. It was clear that Kane understood it. He retreated back to his corner and there wasn't a sound from him then until the Guards came.

We heard the sirens first when they were some distance away. This noise increased as if the end of the world was coming, getting louder with every second until they were blaring directly outside the house. Dancing multi-coloured lights broke in on us through the front door and down the hall. Within a minute, we heard an authoritative voice coming from outside: '*This is the Gardaí! If anyone in there is armed, you are to put down your weapon and come out immediately!*'

'*No one is armed!*' Aogán shouted out to them. '*The gun has been made safe. There is an injured man here. Be quick!*'

The Rapid Response Unit of the Guards were in upon us then in their black clothes, bullet-proof vests, helmets and automatic weapons. I have only a partial memory of what happened next because it was all like a crazed dream to me. The paramedics came in to help Salvadóir, but they turned to me and Peadar as well. I didn't understand why at the time because I wasn't hurt. The voices were all swirling around the room like spirits in the air, and I remember that I looked up to the ceiling to find them, those words disconnected from the real world. I thought again that I was in a film, that I'd fallen into the television at around six o'clock and that I was now living there amongst those voices. It was a crime drama of some sort apparently, a film that I'd seen before. I didn't understand a great deal. I think they believed at first that Aogán was the cause of everything. I heard his voice explaining the situation to them calmly. 'Him. It was him in the corner who did it'. Peadar's voice descended as well into this drama. 'He's the cause of it! He had a red-hot poker!' The intensity in his voice was increasing with every word, sentences stumbling over each other, cutting across one another.

The big face of a guard in my own face then. I became confused. The face of the paramedic. A calm, direct voice. Questions: *Is this your house?* An examination of my hands. There was pain there and in my ankles. I sat down and looked up at the swirl that was going on above my head. Down at Salvadóir. How many people would it take to carry him out? They didn't know.

Kane's voice in the corner speaking through his broken mouth, but still a voice that was conceited and pompous in its tone, explaining his part of the story. '*Of courshe, you musht understand I ... Indeed yesh ... Well, officer ... you shee –*'

A panic ran through me that they would believe him over us. 'He shot Salvadóir!' I exclaimed loudly, but it was strange how far away my own voice seemed compared to those of the others. '*He killed him! He fucking killed Salvadóir!*' I looked at that smug, ugly face in the corner and I wanted to kill him. Then I was face down on the ground with strong hands keeping me there. I don't remember to this day what happened between those two events. I must have tried to attack him.

They moved us out of the house then, out through the crowd that had come to look at the show. There were two ambulances, two squad cars and one van. The malevolent faces of pumpkins and ghosts looked at me from the gardens up the road as I was directed out. They put myself and Peadar into one ambulance. I remember his pale face shining in the bright light as he sat there. He looked at me with an empty expression on his face. 'This is the absolute truth now,' he said. I don't know if I understood him or not. I didn't answer anyway. We proceeded through the streets with the sirens wailing.

In the hospital, bright lights and green sterile walls, cheerless people waiting in hard chairs. They took me in and looked at my hands. I saw them now. There were angry, red lines around my wrists, deep cuts where the cable ties had been. I must have done it to myself, but I didn't remember. It would need a couple of stitches in places, it was that bad. There were cuts on my ankles as well. I became disorientated. I didn't even know where Aogán or Peadar were. Where was Salvadóir? Was he dead? I didn't like this film.

Peadar and Aogán were waiting for me outside when they let me out, and I saw that the same bandages were on Peadar's wrists. 'Where's Salvadóir?' I asked.

'He's here somewhere,' answered Aogán. 'The bullet is near his heart. That's what I understood from what the paramedics were saying. They'll have to operate. We can only wait for news.'

'And Kane?'

'I don't know. They arrested him anyway. I gave them an account in the house, but they want to speak to ye now as well.'

'Let's go quickly' said Peadar with a rattled expression on his face. 'I can't deal with questions now.'

So we went quickly out of the hospital and into the cold night. The wind had decreased a little, but there was still a biting cold in the air.

'We can't go home,' Peadar exclaimed suddenly. 'That's the scene of the crime. The Guards will still be there.'

'But you're the victims of that crime, Peadar,' said Aogán. 'Anyway, they'll be gone by now.'

Peadar said nothing in response, but shook his head firmly to let it be known that he wouldn't go.

'We'll get something to drink so,' I said to him. 'There's a pub across the road.' So we went across to that big suburban bar directly in front of the hospital. It's an elegant enough pub on the inside, serving hot food during the day, but it was quiet when we walked in. 'Ye sit down and I'll get the drinks,' said Aogán.

We went to the most remote corner of the place and sat down. I tried to speak to Peadar, but he had no desire to talk. His face was as white as snow, and I saw black circles rising under his eyes. The expression in those eyes was the worst thing though, a cold, distant expression that I didn't recognise. I didn't know what to say anyway. Salvadóir was badly injured. Maybe he was dead by now. The books were burnt: Jan's diary, Isaac Newton's letter, the Bible with Robert Tighe's poem, and even the little poetry book that Peadar had found in the library. Everything destroyed, except the horrible memory that was now burnt into my mind. Tied to a chair waiting to be tortured; carrying on a logical discussion with a lunatic to delay the moment. How could you make a conversation out of that?

Aogán came back and laid three pints and three whiskeys on the table. I myself took a big sip from the whiskey, but there was no sign from Peadar that he even noticed the drinks were there.

'Salvadóir is a big man and I'd say that it would take more than one little bullet to kill him,' Aogán said. 'Ye suffered a terrible experience tonight, but ye're not badly hurt and ye're still alive. It was always difficult for me to believe your story, but a blind man could see that there's something serious going on here and it's laying heavily on both of you. But ye'll come through it because ye're strong and clever.'

A cold laugh slid out of Peadar then, a laugh without the slightest hint of cheer in it but he still said nothing.

'The books are gone,' I said sorrowfully.

'Haven't you everything written down and translated into Irish anyway?' said Aogán. 'Yes, but those books were evidence.'

'You have the information. No one can burn that.'

'Today's world is full of information. There's nothing but information. Information of every type. But we had evidence in our hands, and he destroyed it. He destroyed it because he believed that the Firíní were angels or devils. He believed that we were trespassing in God's field with our investigation of them. I had to discuss the matter with him in order to delay him in the hope that something would happen, and it did. Salvadóir came back, and then you did. But it was difficult to make logical arguments with Kane. He's an intelligent man behind his madness.'

'I thought that things were becoming dangerous. That's the reason I came around to you tonight. It's a good thing that the front door was left open. You both did very well, whatever it was. You're brave. Many would have given up the books on the spot. And Salvadóir gave them to him then when he came in?'

'He did, unfortunately.'

'He was right, and a good man to do so. He was right to hit him as well and take the chance to stop him. Maybe he would have killed you, even after burning the books.'

'But what will he say to the Guards now?' I asked.

'I was thinking about that. He will say that we stole the books from him. The neighbours called the Guards that day, and they must have given a very good description of Salvadóir at least – perhaps, of us all. The Guards will come back to us tomorrow with questions about that, and it won't be easy to say we don't know Kane when there are eye-witnesses to tell them we were at his house.'

'Christ!' I said, and I felt the walls closing in on me. 'And of course, we can't tell them we saw little men in the head of a fly.'

'I wouldn't recommend saying that, anyway,' Aogán said. 'But we'll think of something. Drink your pint.'

Peadar had said nothing up to this point, but now he raised his head and looked at Aogán through glass eyes. 'Isn't it a strange thing that you're organising a plan for us when you've never believed even the tiniest bit of this story.'

'I recognise that you're in trouble, and I believe that. I'm only trying to help.'

'Oh, I see that, Aogán, and I'm very grateful to you,' Peadar said, as if he was speaking from another room. 'I'm only saying it's a strange thing.'

'Is there anything in this story that isn't strange?' Aogán said.

'There's not, but maybe you were right from the beginning,' he replied.

We didn't know what to read from that, and Peadar didn't speak again for a while, but I could see that he was suffering under a heavy load. I was suffering myself, of course. When I look back at that night, it's like a bad dream. But there was something else going on with Peadar, a different dark cloud that I didn't properly understand at the time.

'Maybe ye should go home now and take a rest,' said Aogán, but Peadar shook his head without saying a word.

'Somewhere else, so?' I asked him. With that, he got up from his chair and threw back what drink he had left.

There were no taxis to be had, and so we had to walk in the piercing cold towards the city centre. When we were going past Flannery's, the heavens opened again and we were lashed mercilessly with hailstones. We escaped into the pub for refuge, and seeing as we were there, we ordered three more pints. It was another roomy suburban bar, and I thought that the barman looked at us suspiciously when we stood at the counter, but he didn't refuse to serve us anyway. We got the drinks and sat into a quiet corner again.

Peadar still wouldn't speak to us, however, and when he got up to go to the toilet, Aogán turned to me with a worried look. 'His nerves are failing. They shouldn't have let him out of the hospital. We'll have to bring him back there, or else home if he won't go. After everything that happened tonight … Christ, after this whole story, it's no wonder that his nerves would fail. I don't know why we're not all up in the lunatic asylum.'

But Peadar wouldn't listen to us when he came back from the toilet. He just shook his head. To tell the truth, I was starting to feel the strain myself now. When I looked around, I saw the normal people of Glasheen speckled about the pub, drinking and talking, and I felt at that moment that nothing was real, that it was all just a fake image. I didn't believe that anything in the universe was real except that there were two Firíní in one-piece suits of pale blue in every fly in the room. And there were flies there as well now. I've mentioned it here before how I'd found it strange that I hadn't seen a lot of flies from the day when I saw the little men through the microscope. I stopped now and thought of the number of times that I'd seen them. They were in Noel Murphy's, and in the library a couple of days afterwards, but where else had I seen them? Were they hiding from us in the corner of every room? What exactly was going on with them? We were so tied up with Jan's story and that of his contemporaries that we'd forgotten about the Firíní of the present day. I saw two flies now flying around the bar and the sight of them cut deeply into my nerves.

The television in the bar drew my attention. The sound was turned down, but I could still see the images. I didn't understand the context, but it was a show about politics, with people waving flags. I felt uncomfortable with these images, as if I was under a tide of ugliness. The politicians on the screen were only personifications of concepts as well. They created a concept in the mind of the public and succeeded in identifying themselves with it. Nothing was real. They were all actors.

'We have to go!' I announced suddenly. Aogán looked at me and saw that my own nerves were failing. Peadar just nodded. We went out again into the cold and up the hill towards the city centre. There wouldn't be a pub again until we reached Bandon Road, and I hoped that the skies would have pity on us as we travelled.

They did, and when we reached it, we carried on to Barrack Street and Tom Barry's. It was busy enough, with people there more fashionable than those in the suburbs. We were on the edges of the city centre now, where traditional turns to retro. We got seats and I bought three pints from the bar, but Peadar went up again and came down with three double whiskeys. He took a big sip from his pint and then started on the whiskey.

Aogán made another attempt to talk to him. 'Something terrible happened to you tonight, Peadar,' he said. 'You're suffering from it. I'd be the same if it happened to me. But you stood your ground. You have courage. But you have to take it easy now and mind yourself. Go home after these drinks, or if you don't want to go back to your own house, you can stay with me tonight. Everything will be better by the morning.'

Peadar said nothing but looked straight ahead like some kind of robot, taking sups from the whiskey glass. His hair was clinging to his forehead with the dampness of the evening, and he hadn't gotten his glasses back when we left the house amid all the commotion. He had a look like iron in his eyes now, hot iron from the fire.

'It was an awful thing that happened tonight, Peadar,' I said to him, trying to break through that wall. 'Kane, Salvadóir, the books: it was all horrible! But we'd be better off talking about it rather than just drinking in silence. I'm worried about you now, my friend. Speak to me.'

'The books? What were the books at the end of the day?' he said scornfully. 'Information on Jan Swammerdam, on Thévenot, Galileo, Milton? Was there anything there about the Firíní themselves? Even the way in which we call them 'the Firíní'. What's their actual name? What do they call themselves? There was nothing about them in those books!'

I was happy that he was talking again, even though I didn't agree with him. I was about to say something else, but he cut across me.

'Why did I buy it?' he said. I didn't understand what he meant by this. He stopped and shook his head before taking a big slug from his whiskey glass. When he started to speak again, he was like someone talking to himself. 'Why did I buy that microscope at all? My own studies are in physics. No connection at all to biology. I bought it one day because, I don't know, the notion just took me, I suppose. That was a big mistake, wasn't it? But I've always had an interest in physics, in the mysteries of the universe, astrophysics, quantum mechanics, dark matter, dark energy, string theory, that kind of thing. I've always believed that those mysteries were there to be found.'

'And aren't they?' I asked.

'I saw a television programme one day on the subject of astrophysics. There was someone talking about black holes and the Big Bang, all the mysteries of the universe in one television programme. It's true that I couldn't do the complicated maths to prove the Big Bang, by the way. It's a pity I wasn't able tell Kane that I could, but that's the way it is now.

'Fuck Kane!' I said. 'You don't have to prove anything to him.'

'But there was a piece of music playing behind the commentary on this TV show: heavenly music, music in which you'd imagine the God of glory and all the angels there before you. I looked at the credits at the end of the programme. It was the third part of the Dante Symphony by Liszt: Paradiso. The commentator talked about the mysteries of the universe, the mysteries of science, with this choir of angels singing behind him. In a strange way tonight, I completely understood what Kane said to me.'

'Christ, Peadar!' I exclaimed. 'Don't let that bastard into your head. That was only a TV show. Scientists have no absolute truth outside of objective reality and there's nothing spiritual about the search for it. The world is not flat. That's an objective truth, and we found out about it through science.'

'Ok, but what is objective reality? Will we ever know? Certainly, science gives us an understanding of the world around us – the roundness of the earth, the knowledge to make vaccines and put men on the moon. But there has to be an absolute truth to the functioning of objective reality, a truth we don't understand now, and perhaps never will. These are the joyful mysteries of the universe, and I've always loved them. Maybe I'm more spiritual than I thought.' He let out a cold laugh and looked down into his glass. 'Wasn't it strange that you brought up that subject to delay him? There was one thing of importance in Jan Swammerdam's diary, right enough, the thing that woman said at the end. I didn't understand it when I read it, but you did.'

'I was trying to delay him. That was all. I don't understand anything. But I know that science always searches for a logical reality. Don't let that bollocks ruin science on you.'

'Even if we could do the maths to understand the darkest mysteries in the universe, if we could travel to parallel universes, even then, how would we ever know that we weren't just beginning on true understanding? We wouldn't know, and never will. But that belief in pure, perfect, absolute truth is always before us. Science has an imagined goal as well, even if it doesn't admit it. It's there because people believe in an absolute truth that keeps the universe moving. The same belief that's behind all religions – the same absolute truth. I always thought I was better than that, but maybe I was mistaken.'

'Don't let that bastard steal your love of science from you, Peadar,' Aogán said to him.

'As I said to you already, Aogán, maybe you were right from the start. It's a waste of time trying to find any truth.'

'I never said that.'

'Mysterious truths of the universe or the tiniest truth about the Firíní. We'll never be allowed to understand any of them,' he said.

But then I saw another light coming into Peadar's eyes and he looked about him in the pub. There were flies there as well, and I thought at first that he was looking at them. There were a few people around who were dressed up for Halloween – witches, vampires and the like – and I noticed that he was studying them. 'Maybe everything that I believe in is false,' he said, like someone in a trance, '… and everything false is true.' He raised his pint from the table, took a huge slug from it and laid it down again. 'What did Salvadóir say again about Samhain: the divide between this world and the next, wasn't it?' With that, he jumped up from the seat, took a dive for the front door, and was gone before we had a chance to say a word.

Aogán and I looked at each other in surprise for a while – for too long, perhaps – and then we ran out after him. We looked up and down the street, but there was no sign of him. There are lanes beside the pub and he could have gone into any of them. I called him on his phone but got no answer. I became worried when I thought of what could happen to him in the state he was in. 'Between this world and the next,' I said to Aogán. 'That's what Salvadóir said tonight. He was only joking, but he also said 'between the living and the dead'. You don't think that he jumped into the river?'

'I don't,' he said. 'But let's go down that way anyway.'

So we went down the hill to the city centre. There were a lot of people about the place, in spite of the bad weather, some of them dressed in gaudy clothes for the evening. There were young women shouting at one another from opposite sides of the South Mall, decorated with plastic devil forks and face paint. A shower of hailstones fell down on us again, and many of them ran into bars and shops. Myself and Aogán went to the riverbank and looked down at the river Lee as it ran forcefully through the ancient cut limestone of the quay walls. I imagined it swallowing Peadar into its icy waters. I put my coat over my head as a shelter from the battering hailstones that fell on us, but that let the cold air into my body. Luckily, the shower didn't last long.

'He's not here,' said Aogán after a while. 'Let's go around the streets.'

And that's what we did. We spent a good while searching through the streets of Cork, looking in corners, up narrow lanes. The drunken crowd increased around us, shouting and singing. The cold cut through me, and I imagined the pain of the hot poker in place of this cold. My hope faded with every empty lane, but we carried on. I don't know what I would have done without Aogán. We had no choice in the end but to go in somewhere for warmth.

We picked one pub, packed with people, and stood at the counter with glasses of hot whiskey in order to put heat back into our bones.

'Maybe he went back home,' I said, thinking out loud.

'I don't think he'd do that after what happened there tonight,' Aogán replied. We stood there quietly amid the revelry, under the din of the music that beat from every corner of the house and made one single sound with the exaggerated laughs and blissful yells. I felt the hot whiskey warming me inside, but after everything that had happened that night, there was nothing in me now but a cold, black hole.

Then I felt Aogán's hand on my shoulder. 'I know where he is,' he said with something like an epiphany in his eyes. 'He's at the Lough.'

This was like a stroke of lightning to me. Of course! The Lough. The site of *Visio Tnugdali*, the gates between this world and the next, between the living and the dead. Aogán was right. He had to be. Peadar was going to a place in which there had been contact long ago between people and the Firíní, a place that was mentioned in the poem as their sanctuary, or their prison. He was going to the gates of Hell.

We ran out of the pub and into the street. Luckily, there was a taxi outside. We jumped in quickly and rose up again out of the bowl of the city and on towards the Lough. We saw a split coming in the clouds and the face of the bright full moon looking down on us. The driver slid quickly through the streets. He was a gruff, unkempt old man with a rough beard, and he never spoke to us as he drove but just looked out at the road before him. When we reached the Lough, Aogán gave him a handful of coins and we walked out across the green towards the water.

A terrible dread struck me now when I looked at the great entangled mesh of bushes in the middle of the lake. It had a dark, terrifying appearance with its limbs rising like the arms of the damned, forever imploring to a cruel sky. I was born here and knew very well that it wasn't permitted to go there. I felt the fear in my guts, and the cold cut into me again. We walked around the circle so as to reach a place where the island would be closer to the bank, since we'd have to walk out through the icy water. There were bats here that slipped past our faces from time to time like devils guarding the gate.

'This will do,' said Aogán when we reached a dark point in the circle, and he walked into the Lough. I followed him and felt the icy cold water around my legs. It was only fifty metres to the island and I knew that we could walk out to it, but it was still an awful journey and I imagined devilish creatures under that water waiting to drag me down forever. The cold water rose to my crotch, up over my belly, and reached my chest before it started to recede.

We reached the entangled branches, but our feet were still in the water. We pushed through as if it was a jungle, and the thorns cut into my hands and legs.

But, in a while, we were standing on dry land again and could see a way through the branches. Unfortunately, the battery in Aogán's phone had died, but I turned on the torch in my own phone, which gave us a ghostly, white view of the surroundings. Nobody ever comes to this place, and there are no human paths through the twisted branches to guide you.

Suddenly, a fierce, white creature jumped out at us, crying out hoarsely, and we retreated from it. It was a big swan, and it didn't like that we were on its land. We struggled on with eyes watching us from every bush and every branch, but there was no sign at all of Peadar. We came out onto a piece of land that was almost free of vegetation, and I shone the light over the ground. There was nothing there but dark earth.

But then something happened that, to this day, I don't understand. Firstly, the phone fell from my hand. It must have fallen face down, because we couldn't even see the light, and so we were left in darkness. We searched with our hands on the ground, but it was no use.

The moonlight crept weakly through the thicket above us, but it was only a ghostly whiteness that didn't help us at all. Then we heard a loud noise, a deafening drone that came from everywhere around us. It lasted about ten seconds, and then it was gone.

I stood in the darkness for a while until I heard Aogán speaking. 'The phone. Find it!' he said, urgency in his voice.

We searched on the ground again but my hand hit against something this time and I saw the flash of white light again. I picked up the phone and shone it around the place to find the source of the sound. I didn't find it, but we saw something else. There was a body on the ground right in the centre of the space. It was Peadar.

We ran to him and turned him on his back. He was unconscious, but I saw that he opened his eyes for a second or two before losing consciousness again. We weren't able to wake him after that, but he was still alive anyway.

'Why didn't we see him earlier?' asked Aogán. 'He was right before us all the time!'

'That noise,' I said, 'it was like thousands and thousands of flies.'

'Were they covering him? Like a blanket?' he said, confusion in his voice.

'He's soaking wet and freezing,' I said, drawing attention to the urgency of the situation. 'We'll have to bring him back to the hospital!'

We carried Peadar through the sharp branches and the bushes until we reached the bank, and then walked back through the cold water, raising him so that his body would not go under. On the other side, we carried him to the road and I called an ambulance. I was afraid that he would die with the cold, but they came within five minutes, and for the second time in one day, Peadar got a ride in an ambulance. They wouldn't allow us to go with him, however, and we had to walk the two kilometres back to the hospital.

I looked at the ambulance as it drove away from us, and thought of everything that had happened that day. Salvadóir and Peadar were both in the hospital now. All the evidence we had collected was burnt, everything destroyed and lost. I looked down at my soaking wet clothes, and felt the sharp cold cutting into me. But I remembered the noise that we had heard on the island and I heard it again now in my mind as we started on the journey back to the hospital.

Scene Eleven

Copenhagen, Denmark
30th March 1676

Jan looked down at his shoes as he walked along the street. He was happy that they had lasted through the long winter, but now they were falling apart with the sole on the left shoe ready to go. His clothes hadn't fared much better through the long, cold months in that house in Husum, and he noticed the holes, the torn stitching and the missing buttons as he walked through this elegant part of Copenhagen. It wasn't unlike the district in Amsterdam in which he'd been raised; the same neat middle-class eye that arranged everything, and even some of the architecture was in the Dutch style. He hadn't paid too much attention to his clothes in Husum, except when his shoes let in the wet snow or when the cold north wind came through his coat. But on this middle-class street, he felt a sort of shame that he hadn't experienced in a while, and imagined the displeased look that would be on his father's face if he could see him. But his father was a long way from here, and besides, he would have other reasons for his disappointment in him.

Jan hoped that Steno's mother would not be too disturbed by his physical appearance, but if she was anything like her son, he was sure that she wouldn't. Anne Nielsdatter was her name, and even though he had never met her before, Steno had often spoken of her when they were students. However, this visit wasn't the reason he had come to Copenhagen. He was here on Antoinette Bourignon's business. But when he told Steno in a letter that he'd be coming, he wrote back asking him to visit her. In spite of the discomfort he felt in his torn clothes and broken shoes, Jan was very much looking forward to this meeting. After the year he'd spent in Husum in the company of those around Antoinette Bourignon, he had a desperate need for a normal conversation with someone.

But it was difficult for him to see how the society of true Christians that Antoinette had founded in Husum could survive, since the Lutheran clergy were resolved to expel her, and all her company, from the area. It was always an open place for different groups who wanted to practise their beliefs, but they'd had enough of Antoinette Bourignon now. They were people who spent their lives praising God, and Jan understood that it was difficult for them to accept her claim that God spoke through her when she proclaimed publicly that they and their flock were damned to Hell. Jan understood that she could be a difficult woman, a person unlike anyone he had ever met. She was determined and would stick to a plan as if her soul depended on it – and maybe it did. Yet she did everything with a strange bearing, as if she was disconnected from the world, with no natural affection or empathy for anyone else. For most of the time, she appeared to lack any emotion at all, but Jan had seen another side of Antoinette when a fierce temper would descend upon her. She would not shout at a person. It was worse than that. Her black eyes would seize the poor victim and burn into him like the fires of Hell, her cold, measured voice cutting through him mercilessly. It happened to Jan himself once, and it was a terrifying experience. She would stay in her room then for a few days after one of these outbursts.

Antoinette often believed that there was a great conspiracy going on against her. She saw plots everywhere, even in the house itself. She often called herself the New Eve (something else that exasperated the Lutheran clergy) and if Jan had thought initially that she was a humble woman, he saw a level of loftiness and grandeur in her now. It was always difficult for him to speak to her logically about anything, and it seemed that her mind would not function in this way. He told himself that she was so close to God that she was separated from the human race, but it became more difficult each day to believe this.

There were other problems in the house too. Jan suffered great deprivation during the winter, and even though all the other men came from wealthy backgrounds, none of them wanted to share what they had because they believed that poverty cleansed the soul. They were a dour and churlish group, and Jan never really understood them. There was only one woman there amongst five men, and all the other men believed that housework was not suitable for them. They saw it as woman's work, and of course, the New Eve couldn't do it either. That meant that everything fell to this one woman alone. She was from a wealthy family in the Netherlands and had no experience of housework. But yet, outside of Jan, who did his own share, she did everything for the other men without complaint because she believed it to be God's work. Jan could see now, however, that her patience had just about worn out and she was ready to go. When that happened, the men could not survive on their own.

Then news came from the authorities in Schleswig and in Holstein that it had been decided to expel Bourignon from the area. Jan accepted the commission that he and Hans de Smet, another man from the group, would go to Copenhagen and make a petition to the King of Denmark that they be given a sanctuary in that country. It was all in vain, however, and the petition was refused. They had already heard the name of the false prophetess, and said they wouldn't give her so much as a spoonful of land upon which to spread her heresies. They would listen to no argument, and that was the end of it.

So the following day, Jan left his lodgings and walked alone through the streets of Copenhagen to find the house in which Steno's mother lived. He liked this red city very much, and felt some recognition of it from Steno's stories. Many of the beautiful stone houses he saw were in the Dutch style, especially the more recently built ones, but there were many more houses constructed in the old style, with wooden frames and bricks. Almost every house had been coloured with red paint, even those that were made entirely from bricks of a natural red hue. Spring was in the air around this red city now, and it gave Jan courage and a lightness that he hadn't felt for a long time.

He followed Steno's directions, leaving the river with Copenhagen Castle at his back and walking towards the great tower, the Rundetårn. It was an astronomical observatory, and he was very impressed with the people of Denmark that they had such a thing here in the city.

It was an amazing sight, and he told himself that he would get permission to go up there before he left Copenhagen. He looked down at his shoes and his ragged clothes, and wasn't sure if the university authorities would believe that he was a learned man who had worked alongside the greatest minds in Europe.

It wasn't long before he came to the house of Anne Nielsdatter. It was a three-storey brick house situated in an agreeable, middle-class district. Steno told him that his father had been a goldsmith to the king and that after he died, his mother had married another goldsmith. He tried to imagine this woman now before he knocked on the door: a widow twice to meticulous men, a quiet and careful old woman perhaps. He knocked at the door and felt a strange excitement as he waited for it to be opened, as if he was a small boy before the parents of his friend. A young servant girl opened it.

'Could you inform the mistress of the house that Mr Jan Swammerdam from Amsterdam is calling on her? Tell her that I am a great friend of her son Niels, and that I was a student with him at Leiden,' he said with all the composure he had.

He saw that she looked at his clothes in doubt for a second, but it was clear that they were expecting his visit, and a smile spread across her face. 'Of course, Mr Swammerdam. The mistress is expecting you. Please come in,' she said, more at ease than a housemaid would normally be. She directed him to the parlour on the first floor and went to inform her mistress that he had arrived.

It was a beautiful room, coloured in red and white, with art on the wall and the finest furniture. He sat down carefully on a comfortable sofa, covered in luxurious fabric. There was a large mantelpiece over the fire, made of dark wood and carved with exquisite workmanship. Just one item stood upon it, a golden clock of the most exquisite design he had ever seen. He stood up to look at it, but just then heard a rustling in the hall and suddenly she was there: Anne Nielsdatter, Steno's mother.

'Mr Swammerdam! Niels wrote to say that you might visit. I am so very happy to meet you. Please sit down,' she said warmly. She was an elegant woman who carried herself with a noble, dignified bearing. She had a vibrant glint in her eyes when she spoke, but there was also a graciousness in her voice. He thought he recognised a keen insight on that face, and surmised that perhaps his friend's intellect had come to him from his mother. She was a woman in her early sixties, but still wore a fashionable dress of dark blue satin with white lace on the sleeves. She also wore golden jewellery, rings and a necklace of the finest workmanship. Of course, she was a woman who had married two goldsmiths in her life. Jan immediately noticed the necklace. It was a golden ouroboros wrapped around a turquoise stone, and he remembered that they were both symbols of eternity.

'I'm very happy to meet you too,' he said. For some reason, he was expecting a dry, matronly old lady, and was quite taken aback now in the company of this refined woman. But maybe it was just the time he'd spent in that dour house in Husum that had created this impression, that he was simply not used to fashionable company. He sat down, and she sat beside him on the sofa.

'I don't often see my son these days, but it's wonderful that I get to meet his old friend Jan at long last. He spoke to me many times of you and of your friendship. I don't believe that the move to the Netherlands was very easy for Niels at first, but you helped him a great deal. I am truly thankful to you for that.'

'Many people had great respect and affection for Niels in Leiden, and I was just one of his friends. But I'm happy that he mentioned me to you. He was always a great friend to me as well, in Leiden and in Paris afterwards.'

'And you are still in regular correspondence, he told me.'

'As often as we can, but he's very busy now, and I myself have been … occupied with something as well lately.'

'I have to say, if I had been told when I was young that I would one day be the mother of a Catholic priest, I wouldn't have believed it. But that's as it is. I have always believed that it's the heart of a person, rather than the colour of his prayer book, that opens the gates of heaven.'

'I agree with you entirely,' he said.

'But tell me about yourself. You spent some time in Schleswig recently, didn't you? How was it?'

'I was very busy there. Like Niels, I have given up my scientific studies entirely to focus on the glorification of God. Of course, I had always believed that the glorification of God was the main reason for those studies, but over the years I have changed my mind about this. I decided a year ago that I would go to Schleswig and live amongst a society that was guided by a wonderful woman, a woman through whom God himself speaks. Her name is Antoinette Bourignon, and the help that she has given me is immense. She has taught me that it's my devotion God wants, rather than my intellect – a simple love of God, as opposed to the complicated study of the world he has created. I have spent almost a year trying to understand and spread her message.'

'Have you been successful with that?'

'It was difficult, but I believe that we've done God's work. But now, unfortunately, I think that our fellowship is coming to an end. At first, the Lutheran church was open enough to us, but gradually they came to the opinion that she and her teachings were a threat to them, and now they have decided to expel her and all her followers. I took on the task, of my own free will, to come here and get permission from the King of Denmark, so she can practise her beliefs in this country.'

'And what answer did they give you?'

'They refused,' he said despondently. 'They believe that she's a dangerous woman who makes a leader of herself over people. But she's only trying to tell the truth as she understands it. People come to her because they want new answers and they are no longer satisfied to listen to the long-established churches. I had hoped that they would accept her here, but alas, it's clear that they won't. The authorities here are as much against her as those in Schleswig and in Holstein.'

'You say that she's trying to tell the truth as she understands it. Do you yourself have any doubts about that understanding of hers?'

She put the question to him quite naturally, but it still took him off guard. He did have doubts, even from the start, but he hadn't the chance to say that out loud until now. There was no one in the house in Husum with whom he could discuss a question like that. 'I think that she's a … good woman,' he said, thinking suddenly of young Marie in the orphanage. 'Niels was impressed with her as well when they met.'

'I'm not saying that she isn't. But let me tell you a story. There was a great scandal here in Copenhagen when I was a young girl. There was a wealthy man in this city who was acquainted with my father, and the story came out one day that the spirits and even God himself was speaking through him. He was always a very devout person, and many people believed him. He would often be seen in the street speaking to people, telling them that Hell awaited them. I saw him one day and he frightened the life out of me. But there's a tragic end to this story. This man was convinced that there was a great conspiracy going on around him and that a certain shoemaker in the town was behind it. This shoemaker was a simple old man with no badness in him at all, apparently, yet he still believed him to be a tool of the Devil.

The poor man was dragged before the court and accused of sorcery, on this man's word, and he was burned at the stake. But the following year his accuser himself was arrested. They said that he had burned down his own house with his wife and children inside it – again, because they were tools of the Devil. He was decapitated and his body parts put up on wheels and stakes.

'Forgive me for telling you this ugly story, Jan. I'm not saying that Antoinette Bourignon is dangerous in this way, but I believe that there are different reasons why people hear voices. Maybe they are the voices of the spirits, but it's possible as well that they have a sickness of the mind and it's their own voice they hear, except that they don't recognise it. When you practised your scientific studies, you followed the process of Descartes. In that process, one must accept every possibility and judge them, one against the other. I ask you now: are you certain that Antoinette Bourignon does not have a sickness such as this?'

It was difficult for him to deny this calm logic. Yet it wasn't as if he hadn't thought these same things while he was living in the house in Husum. He asked himself every day whether he was on the right path in being a follower of this New Eve. He controlled his doubts, but maybe what he needed was to hear those questions from someone else. The gates had been opened now, and the doubts were given free rein. He waited a while before speaking, and then looked at her.

'I'm not,' he said in a low voice. 'I'm not certain at all. Maybe God is speaking through her, or maybe she is sick, as you said. Maybe she's a lunatic. Maybe I just wanted answers so much that I accepted what she had to say. But I see now that she's more lost than I am. I came to her to find certainty. That was all I wanted. But maybe I'll never find it. 'Maybe': I think sometimes that this is the only word I've ever said. After the things I've seen in my life, I'd hoped that I would have deserved a little certainty.'

'Are you referring to the little men in the fly?' she asked.

This question was like a thunderbolt to Jan. 'Niels told you that?'

'I'm a lucky woman, Jan. My son talks to me. There are many mothers who can't say that.'

'It was a terrible thing,' he said now with a new openness. 'Believe me, I would love to find out that those little men were nothing but a representation of that sickness of the mind of which you spoke. But other people have seen them too. They will kill me in the end. All I wanted was some certainty before I died.'

'Did I steal that certainty from you with my questions, Jan?'

'No. It dispersed piece by piece in Schleswig.'

'I can't help you with the little men. But perhaps I can help you with that certainty you desire. You're searching for the truth, aren't you?'

'Yes.'

'What is God but truth? He is the absolute truth, a truth on which all other truths depend. But weren't you and Niels looking for the same thing with your studies in science? Whether it's astronomy or anatomy, all science has one goal. You look through facts in order to find the perfect understanding. Religion and science are both searching for the same Holy Grail: the universal absolute truth.'

Jan didn't speak but sat quietly with a lost expression on his face.

'Do you see that clock on the mantelpiece?' she asked.

He looked again at the golden clock sitting on the black wood of the mantelpiece, glittering in the sunlight. 'It's beautiful,' he said.

'Niels' father was a goldsmith, and he made that clock. He didn't make the mechanism itself, but the exterior part of it, the golden ornate frame and that beautiful face. I think that the clock is a wonderful device, isn't it? It's made of little wheels that turn on each other, all of them working perfectly together. Not one of them can be too small or too big. They all have to be in the perfect place or it won't work at all. There's a wonderful truth in that perfection, and it's possible to imagine the workings of God's creation like that – everything in the right place working with everything else. It's possible to imagine that there is one truth behind everything, a truth that explains all other truths.' She stood up from the sofa then and signalled him to follow her. 'Come with me, Jan, and I will show you something.'

They went out to an adjoining room. It was a parlour decorated with the same good judgement, and there was another clock hanging on the wall, one that was bigger than the first one and with a pendulum moving back and forth beneath it. Like the first clock, this one was also exquisitely decorated in gold, every detail of it expertly placed. They both looked at it for a while before she spoke again.

'Niels' father died when he was only six years old, and I married another man after a time, another goldsmith. It was he who created this clock. Again, he only created the exterior part of it, and Salomon Coster made the mechanism, based on a plan by Christiaan Huygens. This clock has a pendulum and it works much better than the other one. That other clock loses a quarter of an hour each day: this one loses a quarter of a minute. In a hundred years, they will make a clock that only loses a quarter second, and so on. But will they ever find perfection? Will there be a clock one day that tells the perfect time? I'm not a scientist, but I don't believe there will be. This search for the perfect truth is part of the human race. We see it both in religion and in science. You and my son searched for it in both those places, and I'm not telling you to give up on that search: it is in you, as it is in Niels. But don't be too hard on yourself when you cannot find that certainty, because you will never find it, and neither shall the human race. Do you remember the Allegory of the Cave by Plato, where people were tied up in a cave, unable to even move their heads? There was a fire behind them and it projected shadows of the things that went past it onto the wall before them. Because they had been put there when they were very young, they had never seen anything in their lives except those shadows, and they gave them names. That was the reality of the world for them as they understood it. That's exactly how we, the human race, live in this world. Except that no one has escaped to show us the world as it really is, as happens in Plato's story. If we really did see the world as it is, perhaps we wouldn't understand it. And even if we did, how could we know that this other world wasn't just another projection? All we can do here is to try and make sense of the shadows as we see them. That's not a bad thing. But if you are always searching for that absolute truth, you will fail. Go back to your studies, Jan. You don't have to make a choice between one way and the other, because neither of them will give you that perfection you desire, that absolute truth.'

He saw the golden ouroboros on her breast and smiled to himself for the first time in a long while. Her words had a greater effect on him than anything ever said by a preacher or professor. He felt that a heavy weight had been lifted from his shoulders, and he took in a deep breath before he spoke. 'Thank you,' he said.

Three days later, Jan boarded a ship and left on the tide back to Amsterdam. He gave a letter to Hans for Antoinette Bourignon, asking her forgiveness that he had failed to find sanctuary for her in the Kingdom of Denmark and to tell her that he was leaving the fellowship. He sincerely wished her the very best for the future. Steno's mother offered him her house for as long as he was in Copenhagen, but he said that he needed to settle his business on his own.

She pressed a box of old clothes belonging to Steno on him, however, arguing that he no longer needed them now that he wore a priest's habit, and he was unable to refute her reasoning. He did go up the Rundetårn tower before he left the city, and was surprised that there were no steps in it but a spiral incline so wide that you could drive a carriage up through it. He looked over that red city from Copenhagen Castle and Christiania to the Kastellet and back again to Rosenborg with its beautiful gardens. The words she had said went through his mind again, and he felt a freedom that he hadn't known in years. He would go back and finish his *Bible of Nature*. He would put his heart into it and, even though he would not find the truth – about the little men or anything else, he would find some truth, the truth that was best suited to his own heart, and he would leave it to God to decide. He didn't know how long he had left, but when the end came, he would be ready for it and he would be satisfied.

Scene Twelve

I woke up the following morning with the sun casting its rays in through the splits in the curtains of my room. There were things broken and thrown all over the place from the ransacking that Kane had done, but I still felt it to be a safe space. They took Peadar into the Emergency Department for the second time that night and told us that they would keep him there this time. They recognised me from my first visit to the hospital and wanted to examine me again, but I told them that there was nothing wrong with me. There wasn't really, outside of the fact that I was soaking wet, cold and tired. Peadar was still unconscious, and apparently hadn't woken again after he'd opened his eyes for that brief moment at the Lough.

There was nothing for us to do but stay in the waiting room, and watch the Halloween night revellers come in one by one. We wanted to go looking for information on Salvadóir, but we knew they wouldn't leave us in at that time of night. We stayed there for a while, shivering with the cold.

'Let's go home, Seán,' Aogán said. 'We can do nothing here now.'

I could only agree with him. So we left, but this time we got a taxi right outside the hospital and were back in Ballyphehane within ten minutes. I changed my clothes and gave some dry clothes to Aogán. We drank hot soup, and I could hardly keep my eyes open until it was finished. I told Aogán to take Peadar's room and I struggled up the stairs to my own.

That was the end of the day.

I felt a kind of peace in the sunlight that morning when I woke. It filled the room like a healing balm, flooding every corner with its orange warmth like an ancient memory of summer. But I remembered Salvadóir and Peadar in the hospital, I remembered back over everything that had happened since that day with the microscope when it all began. It was difficult for me to believe that it had been only a month and a half before. It would have been easy to believe that it was all a dream, except that I felt the pain in my wrists to tell me that it wasn't. I looked now at the bandages that were still wrapped around them. But I was fine physically outside of that.

I went down to the living room and Aogán was there before me drinking a cup of coffee. He poured me out a cup from the pot, and I sat down beside him. 'Drink that,' he said to me. 'How are ya this morning?'

'I'm not too bad. I don't know. Did all that really happen last night, Aogán?' I looked at him with the cup turning in his hands to give heat to his fingers. He was thinking. 'It was an awful thing that happened last night … to you, to Peadar and Salvadóir. I don't know who that bastard Kane is with the gun, but we're lucky that you're still alive.' He stopped here and looked down into his cup. 'I was never able to accept this story, but I can't deny that you're stuck in something very strange, something so big that that lunatic last night was willing to commit an atrocity for it. And the noise we heard just before we saw Peadar, it was like thousands of flies buzzing at the same time. I don't know anymore… about anything.'

'Me neither, Aogán. I didn't from the beginning, to tell ya the truth.'

We both ate something small and went out to the car. It was still cold, but the wind had eased off and there was a warmth in the sun. Again, I felt something in the air as if it was a spring day and it gave me a hope that wasn't there before. I noticed the birds as they darted from the telephone wires to the rooftops and to the branches of the trees, singing their songs as if the world was as it had always been. We jumped into the car and I drove back to the hospital, through that normal world of normal people living their lives. It was a beautiful day with the sunlight shining through the red leaves on the trees, and they all gathered before us like a guard of honour on our way up the Clashduv Road.

I parked and we walked the short distance to the door of the Emergency Department, but when we were directly in front of it, we saw Peadar walking out. A cheerful expression came on his face when he saw us, something I found strange after everything that had happened.

'Peadar! Are you ok?' I asked.

'I'm grand,' he said in a calm voice. 'I'm sorry for the fit of madness last night. It was ye that brought me here, wasn't it? Thanks for that. You saved my life, probably. Have you heard anything about Salvadóir?'

'We came to check on you first and then planned to go and see him,' said Aogán. 'You look better, anyway.'

It was true. I saw that the plight he was in the night before was gone and there was a new energy in his eyes. It was clear as well that he was eager to tell us something.

'Something happened last night after I left the pub. Can we sit down somewhere so I can tell ye about it properly?'

But I was worried whether Salvadóir was alive or dead, and I wanted and check on him.

'Of course, you're right,' Peadar said, steadying himself. 'Let's go to the reception. Maybe they'll be able to tell us something about him there.'

We walked around to the other side of the building and in through the main entrance, but when we reached the reception, they wouldn't tell us anything. We couldn't see Salvadóir outside of visiting hours, and they would give us no information about him anyway because we weren't related. But at least we learned that he was still alive. Peadar was still eager to tell us his story, and we said that we'd find a place to sit down. We went somewhere that was quiet enough and Peadar settled himself before speaking.

'I was in an awful condition last night when I ran out of that pub,' he began. 'I'm sorry about that, but I knew that I had to be on my own. I had to go to the Lough because I believed that I'd find answers there … I don't know … the gates between the worlds that are opened on Halloween night … and that thing about *Visio Tnugdali* as well. You were trying to take care of me, and thanks for that, but I was in a bad way.'

'It's no wonder after what had happened to you earlier, Peadar,' said Aogán. 'Of course, but I was worse than ye. Everything was falling apart for me. I was losing every certainty that I'd ever had. I ran as fast as I could towards the Lough and jumped in just at the point farthest from the island. It gets deep enough on that side as you're walking out, and I had to swim in the end. I was soaked to the skin when I reached the island, and my phone was wet as well, of course, and I had no light. I struggled through the bushes and the trees, calling on the Firíní to come to me and give me an answer. I remember cursing and swearing at them that they'd showed themselves to me at all, that they had given me that curse. I don't remember exactly what happened then. It was dark, cold and wet. I must have fallen and lost consciousness.'

'That's how we found you,' I said. 'We came to an open space but we didn't see you on the ground at first. The phone fell from my hand and we were in darkness for a while. Then we heard a great drone, a noise like there were thousands of flies there. When the noise stopped, we found the phone again and lit the light. It was then we saw you lying right in front of us. We thought the reason we hadn't seen you at first, perhaps, was because you'd been covered by the flies earlier, like a blanket.'

'You think that the flies covered me… like a blanket? That's interesting.'

'We don't know. We didn't see anything until we got the light back and then we just saw you lying there.'

'I remember the light. I remember ye standing over me. I woke for a second, but something had happened to me before that, between the time I lost consciousness and the time I saw you with the light. I had a vision!'

'A vision?' I asked.

'It wasn't a dream,' he said firmly. 'I'm certain of that. It was different from any other dream I've ever had. It happened! It was contact with them … with the Firíní!' Peadar stopped then for a while and settled himself again to begin his story:

'I opened my eyes, but it was no longer dark or cold. It was a lovely summer's day, and I was lying on a rocky height that looked down onto the bank of a broad lake. I stood up to look around me, and got the impression that I was standing on a huge boulder that was about a hundred metres wide. There was a dark forest behind me with thick trunks and entangled branches woven into one another, a sight that reminded me of the Amazon. I turned around and looked back at the beautiful day and out over the expansive waters of the lake. There were huge trees far away on the other side, so big that I thought they were like the Alps, but instead of the white snow caps there was a mass of green leaves that glittered in the soft breeze. I noticed something strange about the water itself. It was lapping slowly on the bank as if it was a lake of honey, more viscous than water usually is. I thought that I'd fallen down into a world like something in *Alice in Wonderland*.

'But then things became even stranger, and I heard a deafening sound above me. I looked up, but it was directly overhead and all I could see was a black mass before the bright blue of the sky. I thought at first it was a helicopter, but when it came closer to me, I saw the black legs sticking out from the body. It moved to one side to land and I could see it properly now. It was a gigantic fly hovering in the air like an enormous black vessel. I saw the hairs sticking out like sharp spikes all over its body, and I thought of some torture device from the Middle Ages, something that the Spanish Inquisition would have used. I saw the two bulging orbs of its eyes with thousands of points on them glittering in the light. I saw the transparent wings in a haze of movement so fast that they appeared to only swing slowly back and forth. This terrible machine hung in the air for a moment with its deafening noise, and then landed on the rock a good distance from me, and the noise suddenly stopped.

'It was terrifying to be in the presence of this fearsome creature. It stood there like it was staring at me, and I just froze. It lowered its head until its nose was on the ground, and then I heard another noise. It was a noise like wind in the trees, and the two eyes separated from one another to reveal a space on the fly's forehead, a space with a door, and I saw someone in a one-piece suit of pale blue walk out and down nimbly over the face of the fly as if there were steps there. This person reached the ground and then walked boldly in my direction.

'It was an attractive young woman, about my own age, I'd say, with blonde hair down to her shoulders. When she came closer to me, I saw her face, and she smiled at me as if she knew me. When I first saw the Firíní, I thought that those one-piece suits were like something you'd see in some science fiction show on television in the nineteen eighties, and when I saw that same suit up close now, that's exactly what it was like. She wore high white boots as well, and a thick, dark blue belt with things like holsters on both sides. She came up and looked at me for a moment before speaking. 'How are you, Peadar? It's nice to meet you. I'm Liliúirí,' she said in a gentle voice, and extended her arm out to shake hands with me. I remember thinking that she did this clumsily, as if it was her first time practising this custom. I shook hands with her, even more clumsily, but I had no idea what to say to her. I saw a little laugh spread across her face. 'I like the term that you use for us, you and the other lads … the Firíní, is it?' she said. 'I've never heard that before, but maybe then you weren't expecting to see a little *woman* here.'

'Maybe I wasn't … I'm sorry … I don't know why I wasn't,' I mumbled awkwardly.

'It doesn't matter, Peadar. You're here now anyway.'

'And where is … here?'

'You're in the same place that you wanted to be. You came here. You swam out. You are on the island in the Lough, and I am speaking to you now in your mind, and because of that I can make changes. I wanted to show you the place as it used to be. I was born at the end of the sixteenth century, as you count it, and this is the Lough as it was when I myself was a little girl. Look over there under the trees and you'll see a hut with smoke coming from it. There was a man living there for years and I used often fly around looking down at him. I like that you speak Irish, by the way. There were very few people outside the city walls who spoke English when I was young.

'So I'm the same size as you now, microscopic?'

'You are,' she said, laughing again. 'Isn't it nice?'

'But … what's going on?'

'I'm here to give you answers, Peadar. I'm not permitted to say everything to you, but I think you deserve it after all your work and everything that you've suffered. What information do you want?'

'I thought for a little while about this. After all the information we'd gathered, it was difficult to say in one question what I wanted to find out. 'Who are you?'

'I am Liliúirí, daughter of Dreacalóbus and granddaughter of Beelzebub,' she said casually.

'You're the granddaughter of Beelzebub – Beelzebub the devil?' I asked, with a mixture of surprise and fear.

'But she smiled pleasantly again to put me at my ease. 'I'm the granddaughter of Beelzebub alright, and this is Hell as well, if you want to use that term, but you won't find the eternal torment here that people imagine. The human race has a little bit of the story, pieces of information that you've picked up over the years, but it's quite skewed and full of elements of your own composition. Would you like to hear how things actually happened?'

'I would!' I said eagerly.

'Ok. Let's sit down here so,' she said, pointing to a bit of the rock that was raised a little. We sat down and she began the story. 'I'll tell you about our history, about El, Lucifer and Beelzebub. But you have to understand now that I'm using names that the human race has to refer to these people. They have different names in our own language. Anyway, there was a centralised government in our society long ago and different people would contend with one another for control of it. Gradually, El came to the fore as a loud voice amongst the crowd. He began to argue that he could rebuild our society as it had been in the Golden Age. He created the impression that this age was a perfect time and said he would bring those days back. He gathered a group around him who were loyal, but there were many more who hated him. They thought he was a crook who would destroy the world with lies and misguided notions. But he took power and started glorifying himself above everyone else, saying that his word was unquestionable, proclaiming as an undeniable truth that he was the essence of truth itself. He imagined himself as one of the great leaders, the ancient leaders whose memory lives forever in our history, but it was clear to many that this was only bravado. His boasts became more absurd every day, each proclamation more unreasonable than the one before it, until people couldn't tell the sun from the moon. El said then that there had never been a leader except him, that the world began with his word. Many people couldn't accept this, and they rose against him. It separated people into different camps, those who were in favour of El and those who were against him. Lucifer came forward then as leader of the rebels, and my grandad Beelzebub was his general. The rising was terrible.

'People fought ferociously and many died. In my opinion, Lucifer himself wasn't much better than El. He, too, wanted to glorify himself over everyone, but don't tell my grandad that I said that. It was a long, hard war, more than three hundred years, but El won in the end and took his absolute power. He expelled everyone who was against him from the Golden Circle: that's a great city situated in a place that you call the Middle East now. I don't know: I wasn't born then and I've never been there myself. He expelled them all to *this* place, this little island in a lake in a cold, wet, windy land far from the Golden Circle. But I don't care. I was born here and I like it! I might be the devil's granddaughter, but I'm still an Irish girl.

'Anyway, our society was split in two halves from then on. But things changed bit by bit as well. The will of El was to always keep absolute power for himself and he would share it with no one. But because of that, now that he's old and weak, there's no one to take the throne. He has sons, but they can do nothing except fight amongst themselves. The days of centralised power are over, and there are a lot of independent regions now.'

'But who did Jan Swammerdam see then, or Hooke or Galileo? Who were they aligned with?' I asked.

'There were generally independent groups by then in northern Europe, the Netherlands, England and so on. In the south, the Medici and the Barberini were aligned with two different sons of El. I heard that it was very fashionable at the time to go about in bees, and the youngest son was very taken with this trend. It was him, of course, that was in contact with the Barberini. These two young princes are as stupid as they are petulant, apparently. But their age is coming to an end now. El is very old and will die sooner or later. Most of that old generation is almost dead. My grandad is still alive, and long may he last, but Lucifer died about sixty years ago.'

'Lucifer died!' I said in amazement. 'You've no idea how much joy it would give people around the world to hear that!'

'I remember him as a cranky old man who was always complaining that he lost his place amongst the nobles and moaning that he had to spend his life in this cold country. He was descended from nobility, and would never be happy with anything but that life. My grandad isn't like that. He really likes this country, but he was only ever an old soldier.'

'I looked at her as she spoke, and it was amazing to me that I was sitting down talking to the granddaughter of Beelzebub. Smoke was coming out of the hut across the lake and I saw a man standing outside it now. He was like a giant to me, a giant that was a couple of kilometres away but I could still see his thick beard and his rough tan shirt. I saw him as if I had gone back in time. 'How can I be sure that this isn't a dream?' I asked her.

'How can I be sure that you're not a dream?' she answered with a laugh. 'How does anyone know that this whole world isn't a dream or a hallucination? We can only make a decision to either accept it or not. This isn't a dream, Peadar. It's a vision!'

'A smile must have come on my face then, and she noticed it. 'I'm sorry, Liliúirí, but I'm thinking of those old poems by Aogán Ó Rathaille and people like that, in which someone would have a vision of a sky woman who would be the personification of Ireland.'

'Well, aren't I a sky woman?' she said. 'Did I not just descend from the air in an enormous fly?'

'You're right! It never occurred to me to take that phrase literally.'

'And the personification of Ireland,' she said. 'I like that.'

'She had a beautiful, warm way about her as she sat there next to me, and to be honest, I felt like someone from one of those old poems. I wanted to sing her a verse of 'Táimse im' Chodladh' to please her and to see that gentle smile. But then I saw a worried look on her face.

'You know, Peadar, that you must go now,' she said sadly. 'It's a cold night, and it's not safe for you here. I'm worried about you.' I had forgotten that the world was still there, that I had run through the streets in showers of hailstones, that I had come to the Lough and swam out to the island. She stood up to go.

'Will I see you again?' I asked her.

'No,' she said. 'It's very seldom that there's any contact between our species. But I really enjoyed meeting you, Peadar. Goodbye.' She turned and walked back to the fly.

'Before she ascended the steps, she turned again and looked at me. I felt a terrible cold in my body then. A weakness came over me as if I was falling. It was then that I saw you standing over me, and the light of your phone in my face. I was only conscious for a second, and I remember nothing then until I woke up here this morning. I would have died if ye hadn't been there, and I'll be forever grateful to ye for that. And you, Aogán, it was the second time in one night that you saved my life. That's my story, anyway. I don't know. Maybe you think that it was just a dream, but I believe in what I saw. I believe that it was all real. I believe she was real.'

Myself and Aogán listened to him as he told his story. His eyes lit up and I saw an energy in him as he spoke. I was very happy that he wasn't still as he had been the night before. Peadar was always a reasonable person and he didn't believe in things easily, but he believed in this vision one hundred percent. It was a big story, so big that I didn't know at first what I should say about it.

'That's amazing!' I began, but I didn't have the chance to say any more than that because my phone rang at that moment. I was surprised when I looked at it. 'Christ! It's Salvadóir!' I shouted. I answered it and heard his cheerful voice on the other end of the line asking me how we were. 'How are we? You were shot in the chest, Salvadóir! How are *you*? We're fine. We have news for you, as it happens. We're not far from you! We're in the hospital now.' I listened again to his deep voice lapping over the airwaves like the tide. The other two were eager to hear the news. 'Ok! We're coming now. A couple of minutes,' I said and hung up the phone. 'He's … alright, I think,' I told them and I saw the relief on their faces. 'He had an operation last night and they took out the bullet. We can go up to him now. He told me which ward he's in.'

We went up in the lift and found him sitting up in bed. A smile broke across his face when he saw us come in and his gold tooth reflected the bright sunlight in the room. He wore a hospital gown, but it was clear that they didn't have his size, so they'd sewed two of them together somehow. 'Come in!' he said cheerfully. I heard the normal levity in his voice, but it was mixed now with a certain worry about us and our state of mind after the horror of the night before. 'Are ye ok? You're not hurt?' he asked.

'We're fine, Salvadóir. Better than you'd expect,' Peadar replied.

'He was always a twisted bastard,' he said with a flash of anger in his eyes now thinking about Kane.

'Tell us about yourself, Salvadóir,' Aogán asked. 'They were able to take the bullet out?'

'They were. It was next to my heart apparently, but they went in and pulled it out. Look,' he said, picking up a pill box from the locker beside him and shaking it to rattle the little piece of metal inside. 'They gave me a souvenir of the occasion. Isn't it lovely?'

'Aren't you embarrassed, a man as big as you to be knocked by something so small,' Aogán said to him jokingly.

'Do ya know, Aogán, it's the little things that make all the trouble in this world!'

'Well, maybe you're right about that!'

'Were any of ye speaking to the Guards yet? Did ye hear about Kane?' he asked us now.

'We didn't,' I said.

'They came to me this morning. They were very soft-spoken with me as the victim of the crime, but they wanted some information, maybe in fear that I'd die before they got the chance. They asked me about everything, but I found it strange that they started speaking then about Birdy. Kane admitted shooting me and doing that atrocity with ye, but apparently, he started telling stories as well about little men in flies, about the devil and about his old friend Birdy that he tried the poker trick with as well, only that he had died from a heart attack before he had the chance. He told them that we stole the books from his house, but I completely denied it, even though I admitted that we were at the house that day. I said that it was he who asked us to come but that we left when he began raving. The guard told me that they'll charge him with attempted murder, but he believes that he'll be found not guilty by reason of insanity: in other words, that he'll be put in a mental asylum, and maybe that's the best place for him.'

'There's some justice, anyway,' I said. 'But he still succeeded in destroying the books.'

'We have our translation of Jan Swammerdam's book and all the information that was in it. That's the most important thing,' he said.

'Maybe you're right, Salvadóir,' said Peadar, 'but we have more information now. Something happened last night after the event in the house.'

Peadar began then to retell the story of the second part of the night. He told the part about his nervous breakdown in the pub honestly, I thought, and then he told him of the vision he'd had at the Lough. He went through everything precisely as he had done with us. Salvadóir listened carefully to every word until the end, and when Peadar was finished, he closed his eyes. When he opened them again, there was a big smile on his face. 'It makes me very happy to hear this, Peadar,' he said. 'I think that you're right. I believe that this was a vision rather than a dream. With everything that's happened to us, there's a certain sense to it. Not only that, but I believe Birdy was coming around to the same opinion regarding the Firíní and their history before he died. It gives me peace of mind that I followed on with Birdy and my father's work until there were answers, answers to the questions that have bothered me all my life. Whatever I have done, I did it with the help of the three of you, and I'm very grateful to ye for that. We have achieved an enormous feat in getting a small glimpse of that world in which the Firíní live. It's something that hasn't happened often in the history of the human race.'

'But what can we do with this knowledge?' Peadar asked.

'I don't know,' Salvadóir said. 'The books are burnt, and even if they weren't, perhaps not many people would have believed it anyway. But still, we've seen that world, we got a glimpse of it, and that's an important thing in itself, even if we can never convince anyone else of it. As for me, I'd love to see that island, with the trees like mountains and the bushes like the forests of the Amazon, with flies like gigantic flying machines and a princess of the line of Beelzebub coming to me like a sky woman. One day perhaps.'

EPILOGUE

There's nothing left for me to do now but finish the story. As for the historical parts of it, all the information is available in books and on the internet (and I would recommend that you look for it) but I'll give you a summary here anyway on the things that happened to these people after the point at which I left them.

Jan Swammerdam came directly back to Amsterdam from Copenhagen after his conversation with Steno's mother. He worked tirelessly then for four years to finish the *Bybel der Natuure*, his life's work and the dream that drove him on. He made certain that the anagram he had composed years before was in the book now. When it was finished, he left the manuscript to his friend Melchisédech Thévenot in the hope it would be published, and he died on the 17th February 1680. He was only forty-three years old. Thévenot did his best to fulfil his friend's last wishes, but it was a project beset with difficulties, and he had to fight a long court case for years to get the manuscript back from a translator. He succeeded in doing this in the end, but he himself died in 1692 before he could publish it. The manuscript was passed from hand to hand then until it was bought by a man called Herman Boerhaave from someone who was trying to pass it off as his own work, and Boerhaave eventually published it in 1737. Jan Swammerdam's name lives on now as a pioneer who gave a new understanding to humanity on the mysterious, invisible world that is beside us always.

Steno was ordained a bishop in 1678 and went to Hanover and then on to Hamburg as an important figure of the Counter-Reformation. It was said that he led an austere life at this time, living only on bread and beer, that he sold the ring and cross he had received on becoming a bishop so as to give the money to the poor, that he always wore an old cloak and drove in an open carriage, even in the wind and the snow. He suffered physically from this style of life and died in 1686 when he was only forty-eight. But if the end of his life was hard, he still received a grand burial. On the orders of Cosimo III de' Medici, his body was brought back to Florence and buried in the Basilica of San Lorenzo. Pope John Paul II declared him to be *beatus* in 1988, the third of four steps in becoming a saint.

As Jan had predicted, Antoinette Bourignon's fellowship in Husum failed when the only woman there put an end to her household duties. Her printing press was confiscated then and she was accused of sorcery. She travelled from place to place after that, losing her followers all the time, until she herself died on her way back to Amsterdam in October 1680, eight months after Jan had died.

Robert Hooke lived until 1703, and received great respect for the work he did in rebuilding London after the great fire of 1666. He was a renowned person among scientific circles in England, but his name did not live on in the history books as well as it should have done – maybe because of the new star that shone over the public, Isaac Newton, and perhaps, too, because of the poisonous rancour that existed between the two men.

If the scientific community had great respect for Robert Boyle until his death, he himself did very little work in that regard after the stroke he had in 1670. He and his sister Katherine were always close: he lived with her until she died in 1691, and he himself died the following week. By the way, I heard that *Leabhar Mhic Cárthaigh Riabhaigh*, the book from which he had torn the pages, was given back to Ireland recently and is kept now at University College Cork.

Cosimo III de' Medici lived until 1723, and was the Grand Duke of Tuscany for fifty-three years. During his reign, the economy of the country failed terribly, and he imposed many laws to suppress the freedom of the people. He had three children of his own but none of them gave him a grandchild, and the Medici family lost the Grand Duchy of Tuscany in 1737.

These people lived through an important time in the history of Europe and the world. Not only did these scientists create new discoveries and foster progress that had never been seen before, but a new perspective was also created: an awareness that the human race could cut out its own space in this world rather than wait on the will of God. Humanism came to the fore when people understood that they could make their own examination of the mysteries of the world, find their own answers, and choose their own destiny from that.

And what about ourselves then, myself and the lads? Salvadóir recovered quickly after the operation. If I had thought him a cheerful person before that, I saw that he was becoming even more cheerful and light-hearted now with each day, as if a weight had been lifted from his shoulders. He called me a couple of weeks ago to tell me that he was getting married and he invited us all to the wedding. I called Aogán straight away in Morocco to tell him, and he was delighted when he heard the news. He went back a couple of months after life returned to normal again, but he told me on the phone that he'd definitely be there for the wedding. Peadar finished his degree and started a postgraduate course on particle physics in college. He moved out to West Cork a while ago, but he comes back a couple of times a week and I meet him for a coffee or a pint from time to time. He mentioned Kane the last day when we were talking. He's in the mental asylum now, just as the guard had predicted.

That's how it all happened, anyway. We've written down everything that was in Jan's diary in Dutch and in Irish if anyone wants to read it, and Peadar took pictures of those pages as well. As regards my own account here, I promise you that I was as precise and honest with the facts of the story as I could be. I've told this story in the form of a novel so as to put it out publicly, but it was never my intention that it be read as a novel. As I told you from the start, I recommend that you do your own research on the historical characters in this text, and I promise you that you'll see the truth in it. I'll be satisfied that I told the story and, after everything that's happened, I could do nothing else anyway. I study literature, and I thought that if I saw it written down on paper, I could make some sense of it for myself. I told the other lads that I wanted to write this book, and they gave it their blessing.

But what can I say, now that I've written it? What do I know about the whole thing at the end of the day? Do I believe that Peadar was really in contact with the Firíní on the island in the Lough? I don't know: maybe. Salvadóir really likes Peadar's vision, and I can understand why. He spent his life with the awareness that the Firíní were there, and he wants a conclusion to this story: he wants to believe that he has fulfilled his duty to his father and to Birdy. I think he deserves his peace. Peadar wants that peace as well. When I met him for a cup of coffee the other day, he referred again to that last piece in Jan's diary when he's speaking to Steno's mother, Anne Nielsdatter. That was the piece that got me thinking in the church in Guagán Barra, and it was the basis of the argument I had with Kane. I could see that those questions were still in his mind now.

'As regards the concept of absolute truth,' he said to me. 'Maybe that belief has always been at the heart of human society, but I think it's more under siege now in the age of the internet with all the other truths we have, all the voices that echo off each other around the world. That's the reason, perhaps, that other people cling to it so devotedly. But the more truth is seen as an abstract concept, the harder it becomes to believe in absolutes. Maybe the struggle of our age is that between this single, universal truth and the pluralism of truths – the billions of them that swarm about us today like flies.'

We said goodbye to each other that day and he went back to West Cork. I thought of Liliúirí, the sky woman on the island in the Lough. Was she there at all, or was she just another part of the mythology from which this world is made? I don't know. But I'm happy that I was able to tell you this story. If I ever manage to get this book published, I think I'll use a pseudonym. I like the name Thaddeus because Saint Thaddeus is the patron saint of hopeless causes, and that's exactly the chance there is that anyone is going to believe me, even though it's a true story from beginning to end. Anyway, I'll finish up now.

All the best,
Seán

www.ingramcontent.com/pod-product-compliance
Lightning Source LLC
LaVergne TN
LVHW040825090826
845145LV00001BA/206

* 9 7 8 1 7 8 1 1 7 9 5 3 6 *